"You know too [barcode: ID896302]

"A lover would what you saw in me, what made you take me under your wing. Mayhap he would have even heard of my attraction for women and be doubly jealous. Therefore, I'll have to assume there is no lover . . . " Liam shrugged. "You're not the sort."

"And pray, in your wise estimation, what sort am I?"

"You're the marrying sort," he murmured.

Her gaze remained on his for a fraction of an instant, then flitted downward. "So I am told repeatedly."

Then tension that had just eased in his gut knotted up a hundredfold. The image of her in another man's arms appeared again. "By whom?" he asked, forcing the question.

"The man I'm going to marry," she said.

~⚬⚬~

"A charming and magical tale."
Tami Hoag on *Highland Scoundrel*

Other **AVON ROMANCES**

THE FORBIDDEN LORD *by Sabrina Jeffries*
MY LORD STRANGER *by Eve Byron*
THE PRICE OF INNOCENCE *by Susan Sizemore*
THE RENEGADES: COLE *by Genell Dellin*
A SCOUNDREL'S KISS *by Margaret Moore*
TAMING RAFE *by Suzanne Enoch*
UNTAMED HEART *by Maureen McKade*

Coming Soon

LOVING LINSEY *by Rachelle Morgan*
THE MEN OF PRIDE COUNTY: THE PRETENDER
by Rosalyn West

And Don't Miss These
ROMANTIC TREASURES
from Avon Books

HOW TO MARRY A MARQUIS *by Julia Quinn*
SCANDAL'S BRIDE *by Stephanie Laurens*
THE WEDDING NIGHT *by Linda Needham*

Avon Books are available at special quantity discounts for bulk purchases for sales promotions, premiums, fund raising or educational use. Special books, or book excerpts, can also be created to fit specific needs.

For details write or telephone the office of the Director of Special Markets, Avon Books, Inc., Dept. FP, 1350 Avenue of the Americas, New York, New York 10019, 1-800-238-0658.

LOIS GREIMAN

Highland Brides
HIGHLAND ENCHANTMENT

AVON BOOKS  NEW YORK

To Justin,
who has given me nothing but happiness
since the day he was born

This is a work of fiction. Names, characters, places, and incidents either are products of the author's imagination or are used fictitiously. Any resemblance to actual events, locales, organizations, or persons, living or dead, is entire coincidental and beyond the intent of either the author or the publisher.

AVON BOOKS, INC.
1350 Avenue of the Americas
New York, New York 10019

Copyright © 1999 by Lois Greiman
Inside cover author photo by Barbara Ridenous
Published by arrangement with the author
Library of Congress Catalog Card Number: 98-94811
ISBN: 0-380-80366-6
www.avonbooks.com/romance

All rights reserved, which includes the right to reproduce this book or portions thereof in any form whatsoever except as provided by the U.S. Copyright Law. For information address Avon Books, Inc.

First Avon Books Printing: April 1999

AVON TRADEMARK REG. U.S. PAT. OFF. AND IN OTHER COUNTRIES, MARCA REGISTRADA, HECHO EN U.S.A.

Printed in the U.S.A.

WCD 10 9 8 7 6 5 4 3 2 1

If you purchased this book without a cover, you should be aware that this book is stolen property. It was reported as "unsold and destroyed" to the publisher, and neither the author nor the publisher has received any payment for this "stripped book."

Prologue

Burn Creag Castle
The Year of our Lord 1509

Lightning forked across the inky sky, slamming white light through the tower's arrow slits. Fire winked in the dragon's ruby heart.

"The dragon brooch!" Shona crooned. "You stole it from—"

Thunder crashed like a giant's wicked fist against the tower, shaking the stones around them and startling the three girls who crouched on the floor in the wavering candlelight. The noise rolled slowly away, leaving the air taut in its aftermath.

"You stole it from Liam?" Shona finished breathlessly. She was the youngest of the three, barely nine years old and trembling in her voluminous, white nightgown.

"Aye." Rachel's face was pale, her sassy lips sober this night. "I took it whilst he slept."

"'Tis magic," Shona whispered, seeming transfixed by the silver dragon that looked docile but indomitable against her cousin's palm.

"It cannot be magic," Sara corrected, still holding Shona's small hand in her own.

"But Liam said twas," Shona argued.

"Tis the very reason I doubted," Rachel whispered. "But even Liam must tell the truth sometimes, I suppose. And twas the truth he said when he told me of our great grandmother."

"*Our* great grandmother?" Sara asked. "But how does *he* know about our ancestry?"

"I cannot say how he knows," Rachel admitted. "But this is the story he spewed. Long ago there lived a lass in this very castle. Her name was Ula. Small she was, like me, with Shona's fiery hair and Sara's kindness. Her mother died when she was but a babe, and she was scared to be left alone at night. Sometimes she would cry out."

"And her father would come and tell her outlandish stories to make her laugh?" Shona suggested.

"Aye." Rachel smiled. "Aye, he would tell her stories. But still she was afraid. So he called on the best mason in the land to craft a magical stone dragon near her room to protect her."

"He must have loved her so," said Sara, her voice small and wistful.

"They built the dragon out on the roof to overlook the land about," Rachel said. "Now the lass felt safe in the comfort of her quarters. But her father worried that something might happen to him and Glen Creag would fall into the hands of the evil sorcerer. Then wee Ula would be left alone. He knew if such was the case she would be forced to leave her home, and he wished for her to be bold enough to make the journey. So he had a silver amulet crafted. A magical brooch, it was, graced with a blood red gem taken from the enchanted waters of Loch Ness."

"Where Nessie lives?"

"Aye. That amulet would protect Ula wherever she went."

"And this is that very amulet?"

"Aye."

"But Rachel," Sara said, "though I do not understand it, you never believe a thing Liam says. Why do you trust him in this?"

Rachel closed her fingers over the dragon. "Come here," she whispered, and stepped toward the window. The three clustered together, tilting their heads close. Auburn hair sparked against flaxen and sable. "Look out there."

"Where?"

"'Tis dark," Shona said, but suddenly a fork of lightning slashed across the sky, soaking the night in silvery light.

"There!"

"A dragon!" Sara gasped. "How did it get there?"

Rachel drew the amulet closer to her chest. "It must have been there for many long years, but you cannot see it from most points, only from here and from that room beside it."

"Ula's room," whispered Shona

"'Tis truly magic, then," breathed Sara.

"Aye," said Rachel, "and tonight we will bend its magic to our will."

"We will?" asked Shona.

"Aye. Tomorrow Sara will return to her home. And shortly after, you will go back to Dun Ard. 'Tis impossible to know when we shall be together again."

The tower room fell silent.

"I will miss you," Sara whispered.

"And I you," Rachel said, reaching out to take

her cousin's hand in her own. "You are the sisters of my heart."

"We will see you soon," Shona said. "When the weather warms . . ."

"One of us will surely be betrothed soon. In fact, Laird MacMurt asked for my hand—" Rachel stopped abruptly, glancing quickly at the barrels stacked along the curved wall. "What was that noise?"

Every girl held her breath and listened.

Behind the barrels Liam did the same, careful to make no sound, though frustration screamed through his soul. Surely the girls could not be promised at such tender ages—bartered off like so many wooly sheep. Not his wee little lassies. Of course, they could take Rachel. He cared little if she married someone as old as a rock and half as handsome. After all, Rachel Forbes was vain and aloof and when she smiled it made his heart . . .

She was nothing but a silly girl, he reminded himself. She'd believed his ridiculous stories about magic. She'd actually thought him asleep when she'd snatched his amulet! God's balls, she was a terrible thief! Still, he shouldn't have duped the other two bonny lasses.

"It must have been a mouse," Sara said, then turned her gaze back to Rachel. "Promise you'll not move far from us."

"I'm not going to move away," said Shona fiercely. "I will marry Liam and live forever at Dun Ard."

"Liam!" Rachel said. "Not that wild rogue. You will marry a great laird as will we all."

Liam tightened his fists with a quiet snarl.

"The mice are certainly restless," Shona murmured, glancing nervously toward the wall.

"Please do not leave us," Sara whispered again.

"That's why I asked you to come to the tower," Rachel said. "If the dragon is truly magical it can grant us our fondest desires and bind us together. We will each touch the amulet and make a vow to take care of the others."

"But if we're far apart, how will we know when we're needed?" Sara asked.

"The dragon will know," Rachel murmured, her voice a whisper of drama in the stillness.

Liam rolled his eyes.

"The dragon will make certain we are safe or he will send help," she continued.

Sara nodded. Her expression was somber, but even from Liam's vantage point, he could see that she shivered as they formed a circle. "We shall all touch it together."

They did so now. Piling their small hands atop the thing with careful timidity, they closed their eyes in unison.

"My fondest desire is to be a great healer like my mother," Rachel began.

Thunder boomed again. Shona jumped.

"I wish to be bold!" she chirped. "Like Father and the Flame."

"I but wish for my own family to care for," Sara said softly. "My own babes, by my own hearth. Nothing more."

Silence fell upon the room.

"Now we must make a solemn vow," Rachel said.

Shona giggled, then fell silent.

"Forever and always we shall be friends. Neither time nor distance shall separate us. When one of us is in need another shall come and assist her, for we that are gathered in this room are bound together for eternity."

The world seemed suddenly utterly still.

"Now we must swear to it," whispered Sara.

"I swear," they vowed.

Thunder crashed. The candle was snuffed out, pitching the tower into blackness. Wild energy crackled through the room.

The girls shrieked in unison.

The portal slammed open. Bare feet pattered down the stairs. The room fell silent. Behind the barrels, Liam lay sprawled against the wall, limp as a doll of rags.

Mother of God, what had just happened? It must have been the storm, of course. Just an errant stroke of lightning let loose in the tower, and those silly girls had surely dropped his amulet in their fright.

He should go find it—shift through the rushes and retrieve it—but his limbs felt weak and his mind strangely boggled.

He'd best leave this place. Now! he decided, and launching himself from the floor, fled down the stairs after the girls.

Silence ruled the world. A crescent moon crept from behind a tattered cloud to smile on the earth below. And deep in the rushes, the dragon waited.

Chapter 1

The Year of our Lord 1520

Liam grabbed his balls and let the knife fall. It sliced through the air, skimmed past his chest, and sank, reverberating, into the pungent earth between his feet. The crowd stared in dumbstruck silence for an astonished moment, then lifted their collective gaze from the quivering handle and burst into applause.

"My thanks," Liam said. Bowing, he tossed his wooden juggling balls over his back. He knew without looking that they landed easily, one atop the other in a bag that hung on an oaken branch behind him. "You are too kind. But now I would ask a favor."

He paused as he snatched the long knife from the earth. Twas one of his favorites, a well-crafted steel he'd taken from a too loud Welshman some years back. The Welshman had had a daughter, the daughter had had a roving eye. Enough said. He wasn't the type to kiss and tell. Kiss and lie, yes. Kiss and run. Definitely.

"I would ask for some assistance," he called, striding along the edge of the crowd. His stage was nothing more than a grassy knoll, but the slope of the hill gave him a slight height advantage over the mob below him. Long ago, he had learned to take his advantages where he could.

"After all," he continued, "a man can only amuse himself with his balls for so long." A few snickers sounded from the crowd. He tossed the knife straight up into the air. It spun wildly end over end, only to land safely in his grip moments later.

He liked the feel of a knife in his hand. It was far preferable to a knife in someone else's hand, for that scenario often boded ill for his continued survival. Perhaps other men were jealous of him, he mused.

True, he was not a particularly brawny fellow, and merry old England had seen more elegant men, but he had certain traits women seemed to find appealing.

Even now a bonny lass smiled at him from the center of the crowd. He smiled back. Evening was fast approaching on market day in the village of Rainich. A fair-sized crowd had gathered to watch him perform, but it was the smiling woman that drew his attention. She was a plump maid, showing dimples and enough cleavage to make a man start cataloging his own attributes in the hopes of gaining some attention. If he wasn't mistaken, she'd been flirting with him for the better part of his act. And if there was one thing he was never wrong about, it was the fine art of flirting.

Liam flipped the knife over his shoulder and caught it casually behind his back. "A man cannot do everything with his own two hands. Eventually he needs a partner," he said, allowing a shadow of a grin and making certain his gaze didn't dwell too long where it shouldn't. Just because the maid was a flirt, did not mean she was attending his performance without an escort. He'd learned that lesson the painful way. "Is there anyone present willing to assist me?"

There were murmurs among the crowd.

"Oh, come now. Surely you are not afraid to consort with the likes of me, even if I am an Irishman." He burred the words as he paced side to side, his back perfectly straight. With each step, his large, horsehide sporran swung, his cape swirled, and his plaid swished against his bare thighs. The advantages to wearing a plaid in England were twofold. One, it drew attention to himself. And as a performer, that was imperative. Two, it fascinated women, and he was not one to disallow further education, even if it involved nothing more than the age-old question of undergarments.

Two adolescent boys had been robustly jostling each other throughout his entire routine, and were now working up their courage to volunteer, but they were not quite the sort of assistant Liam had in mind. "I assure you, tis quite safe," he said. "My assistants are never wounded. Well, not badly. . . . At the least, they've never lost any *noticeable* body parts." The boys' mouths fell open, and they stepped back in rapid unison.

Liam grinned and let his gaze rest momentarily on the woman with the dimples. She shrugged. The amount of bosom forced into sight made the blood rush from his head.

"I could help you," she called out.

Liam's grin expanded. "Come forth," he said, and she did, sashaying through the crowd with a wiggle and a bounce. Snapping his hand over his shoulder, Liam sent the knife *thwapping* into the tree behind him. Then, reaching out, he took her hand to help her ascend the hill. "And what be your name, lass?"

"Mairi," she said, tilting her head at him.

"A bonny name." He bowed over her hand. "Almost as bonny as its mistress. And do you live here in the village?"

"Nay, I've come today to sell pigs with my husband and his brothers."

"Ahh." Liam straightened, one hand behind his back, his expression disappointed. "You have a . . . pig."

The crowd laughed. He shrugged, nonplussed.

"You must have made a goodly sum selling your swine."

She gave him a quizzical look, and he drew his hand from hers to display the coin she apparently had given him.

"Still," he said. "I cannot accept this."

Her eyes widened in surprise.

"Here, I insist. You must take it back." Pressing the coin firmly into her palm, he folded her plump fingers over it, then let his jaw drop and proceeded to pull the same coin from her ear.

He set it back into her hand. It came out her nose, from behind her neck, out the bottom of her sleeve. He could barely move fast enough to keep up with the rain of money, and now the crowd was howling.

Finally, he placed the coin decisively back into her hand, then turned to the crowd to bow. But just as he was about to do so, he did a double take. Pivoting back toward the maid, he stared in astonishment, for the large copper was pressed warm and firm between her bounteous breasts.

Her gaze followed his own, but instead of

shocked dismay, she grinned lasciviously as she spied the coin.

Liam cleared his throat and dramatically wiped his brow. "Mayhap you'd best retrieve that one yourself, lass," he said.

But she canted her head at him, her expression sly. "And why is that, Sir? I thought surely you had the . . . balls for it."

Far be it from him to pass up such an opportunity, if the lass was willing. Shrugging, he reached forward.

A bellow of outrage interrupted Liam's intent. He spun toward the noise, but he was already too late. A fist slammed into his ear. He careened sideways and hit the ground like a pounded stake, but Liam the Irishman was no babe in the woods. With the lithe fluidity of one who had angered husbands before, he rolled sideways, leapt to his feet, and bolted for cover. But an arm reached out from nowhere.

"You'll not mess with *my* brother's wife!" someone yelled.

Colors exploded in Liam's head, and from there on things only got worse.

There were shrieks and screams and fists like battering rams.

Bodies as big as small fortresses loomed over him, swinging wildly as he crouched, trying to protect himself. He grunted in pain and glanced up just long enough to see the drink-reddened faces of four angry brothers.

"I meant no offence," he rasped.

But the four were far beyond listening.

Bending his arm, Liam shielded his face. A fist glanced off his elbow, shooting his own hand toward the man's belt. He had only a moment to take advantage of that position before the next blow caught him in the belly, spilling him onto the grass. Darting his hand beneath his cape, he hid away the purloined pouch, then curled into a ball to protect his vitals . . . and his privates. After all, a man had to preserve his best qualities.

A booted foot caught him in the back. He grunted in agony and fought for lucidness, but darkness was descending. From somewhere in another dimension he heard a woman ordering them to halt. So plump Mairi cared for him a little, he thought hazily and slid toward oblivion. But in that instant, oblivion drew back a hair. He lay still and realized with dim relief that no new pains were being vented on his body.

Instead, a gentle hand touched his shoulder. A soothing voice reached his ears.

He concentrated on the softness of it, on the wonderful cessation of violence.

"Are you all right?" A woman's voice, melodious and sweet. So the lovely Mairi had finally gained control of her husband.

"Aye. I am well." His own voice sounded *less* than melodious, rather resembling the scrunch of metal wheels on gravel, while every inch of him ached with screaming intensity. It seemed as good a reason as any to come up with a likely insult. "They hit like babes."

"A babe am I?" someone roared. From the edge of his swimming eyesight, Liam saw a mountain of a man lunge forward.

But in an instant a fellow in a blue doublet intercepted him. The husband crumpled like a pile of dry chaff. A woman screamed then launched from the crowd to crouch by the fallen man. It was Mairi.

If Liam weren't quite so battered, he might wonder how she could be in two places at once. But as it was, he only accepted the situation.

"What have you done?" Mairi shrieked, her expression tortured as she turned toward Liam.

"Get them out of here." Twas the woman who crouched beside him that gave the order. The woman whose voice, Liam noticed, was not as high-pitched, nor as coarse as that of the bonny Mairi. A voice that spoke with authority and confidence. A voice that tugged at some distant memories that he could not quite . . .

No! It couldn't be. Not here. Not hundreds of miles from her homeland, logic insisted.

Still, logic seemed a dim thing, whereas her presence seemed very real.

He turned to her slowly, but there was really no need for him to see her face. He already knew it was she. Knew it by the feel of the air around him, knew by the electrical jolt he could now distinguish from his other pains.

Still, he couldn't very well simply lie there and pretend she hadn't just saved his life. Twould be rather like refusing to accept the end of the world. So he twisted about slightly, gazed at her through the blood and hair that smeared his vision and said, "I wasn't expecting you this far to the south, Rachel. Is someone ill?"

He watched her eyes widen in surprise. They were fascinating eyes. Otherworldly eyes. And if he felt like being fair, he could understand why, long ago, she had been dubbed the Lady Saint.

Liam was silent as he waited with a certain amount of desperation for the saintly expression to fade. He was not disappointed. Saintliness fled; disapproval set in. He could tell by the slight stiffening of her back, the narrowing of her eyes.

"I would ask what you're doing here, Liam, but the truth seems quite apparent," she said.

"I'll kill 'im! I'll kill 'im!" the husband bellowed.

"I am but spreading peace and goodwill as is my wont," Liam said. He attempted, for one mind-spinning second, to sit up, then decided he was quite comfortable where he was.

"Spreading your seed like dust in the wind more like," she countered.

He tried a grin and found to his everlasting gratification and not unwarranted surprise, that his face didn't split in two with the effort. "We cannot all be saints, Rachel," he said.

She snorted. The sound wasn't quite as ladylike as her dress and demeanor suggested and prompted a thousand hot memories in Liam's battered head.

"Do you think you could at least try for *sanity*?" she asked.

"Are you suggesting I'm insane?"

"I'll tear his heart from his chest!" came a distant roar.

"Tell me, Liam, couldn't you have found a smaller man whose wife you might proposition? Or one with fewer brothers, at the least."

"I didn't proposition her." Not yet, he thought.

"Not yet," she said.

He scowled at her. Twas said that Rachel Forbes had a nasty habit of mucking about in people's brains. He'd never believed a word of it. Still, she did at times give him an eerie feeling. It was one of the many things he'd never liked about her. Dabbing at his lip with the back of his hand, he managed to sit up.

"She wasn't my type," he said.

"Truly?" She gave him a look of surprise, the raising of ebon brows beneath her immaculate white coif. "It looked as if she was breathing to me. And not grotesquely fat."

He tried another grin. It hurt like hell. "Not fat at all," he corrected and rose valiantly to his feet. Unfortunately, the world tilted strangely with the movement, and the earth pitched beneath him like a recalcitrant steed. His knees buckled without warning.

Rachel reached out with instinctual speed, and suddenly her arms were around him.

"Liam!" Her voice was raspy in his ear as she struggled to keep him upright, and in that moment he made the dreadful mistake of glancing at her lips. Damn it all. She may have the eyes of a saint and the skin of a princess, but her lips were the devil's own.

A hundred unwanted feelings washed through him, feelings of need and desire so painful it all but stopped his heart. But reality came quickly, so he pressed more firmly into her and said, "Why, Rachel, I didn't think you cared."

"You've always been wiser than you look," she said, her mouth hardening. "Davin." Her tone was chill as she pulled away her support and turned to a huge blue-garbed fellow who hovered nearby. "Take the Irishman to an inn. See that he has a decent meal and a room for the night."

"I'll rip his balls off!" The threat was distant, but still quite impressive.

"I think the woman's husband may be holding a grudge," Davin said. Liam watched his face for some sign of sarcasm, but his Scandinavian features were no more expressive than a mason's trowel.

"What are you suggesting?" Rachel asked.

"You wish the Irishman to survive the night?"

She remained silent for a moment, her devil's mouth pursed. "My family is rather fond of him."

"Then we'd best see him beyond the husband's reach," Davin suggested.

Rachel scowled, first at her guard then at Liam.

"Very well." Her concession was grudging. "Help him gather his things and see him mounted. But do not let him tarry. We've no time to squander on the likes of him."

Evening lay about them in a dense sheet of gray. Night prodded the gloaming aside, but night could not come soon enough for Liam, for he felt as if he'd been pounded with a battering ram, then tumbled down the road in a wine barrel.

He'd insisted that he would be fine if left in Rainich, but Rachel had been determined to torture him with this ride. And Davin, it seemed, was not the sort to listen to an Irishman's arguments when his mistress' mind was made up.

Beneath him, his gelding stumbled for the fifth time.

"God's balls, horse," Liam gritted. "I don't care if I did pay five times your value. Once more and I'll trade your hide for a poor pair of boots."

Bocan stumbled again. Liam stifled a groan.

"There's a place just ahead, Lady," Davin reported, riding back to Rachel's side. The company of twelve or so blue-clad soldiers stopped to listen. "Water and forage for the horses. Twill be easily guarded."

"Very well. Set up camp."

Dropping his head, Bocan spread his legs and shook himself violently.

Liam grabbed for the pommel and tried to remain lucid as spasms of pain rolled over him. The gelding straightened, bobbed his elegant head, and snorted. Liam considered passing out.

"But first," Rachel said, never turning her gaze from Davin, "you'd best help the Irishman from his steed."

"You're too kind," Liam mumbled.

"Tis a well-known fact," Rachel agreed.

Davin dismounted and crossed the distance that separated them. Liam dragged one leg over the cantle of his saddle, determined to show some fortitude, but just as he was about to step off, the Norseman grabbed him by the back of the tunic and hauled him down. Pain pounded like running hooves across Liam's trammeled body, but he refused to faint.

Davin, seemingly oblivious to Liam's gallant battle, dragged him across the grass.

Pain kicked up in earnest.

"Will this do, my lady?" asked the huge Norseman.

"That will be fine."

With a nod, Davin loosened his grip and tumbled his cargo to the earth.

"Holy bones!" Liam gasped, grasping for consciousness as pain slammed through him. "Why not just have him take a club to me?"

"I considered it," Rachel said. She stood only a few yards away and turned her mare over to one of her men. "But I thought this might be more satisfying."

Liam groaned as he shifted to a sitting position. "Prefer a slow death, do you, Rachel?"

"I doubt you're going to die."

"You might be surprised."

"I rarely am," she said, stepping toward him.

He snorted and forced his gaze away.

"Where does it hurt?"

Liam jerked his attention back to her with a start. "Nay! You'll not use your witchy potions on me."

"Where do you hurt?" she asked again.

She had the perfect diction afforded her by a fine education. Maybe it was that education that made her so difficult, Liam thought. But no, she'd been a pain in the ass since the day he'd met her over a decade earlier. Even now he could remember how she had looked—with her dark hair bound up in scarlet ribbons, and her face so . . .

Well, she'd always had that damned angelic face, he thought, jerking his musings to a halt. It was that face that fooled men every time. Even the post-headed Davin probably considered himself her conquering hero, when the truth was, the lady needed no hero at all. She could slice an adversary to shreds with nothing more than the sharp edge of her tongue, and he had the scars to prove it.

"Does your head hurt?" she asked, crouching down beside him.

He scowled at her. "I've been trounced by four drunken brothers, jostled down the road, and tumbled onto the grass like a sack of moldy meal. Do you think my head might hurt?"

"I think if you cannot bear the pain, you shouldn't do the deed," she said.

"They deserved it," he countered, thinking of the coins he'd stolen from the brother's pouch and hidden in his own oversized sporran.

"Deserved what?"

He realized suddenly that he'd spoken too quickly and shrugged, trying to look nonchalant. "They deserve whatever they get."

"What did you do, Liam?" she asked, her tone suspicious and more than a little weary, as if she were his long-suffering mother.

"Me?" He gestured toward his chest, hoping he looked affronted. "Lest you forget, I am the one injured here. I did nothing but perform a wee bit of simple sleight of hand for their entertainment."

Her expression didn't change a whit.

"I am the one wounded," Liam insisted, and wondered if it were too late for him to make a name for himself on the stage. Surely he had the talent. "How could you of all people think I would do something dishonest?"

She stared at him with tired boredom.

"I no longer steal," he said, then grinned. "Unless someone wrongs me . . . or someone I know . . . or I someone—"

"Lie back," she interrupted irritably. "I'll fetch my things."

He watched her go and told himself that he didn't want her to fetch her things. He didn't want her tending him, he didn't want her near him. Through the trunks of the surrounding trees, he could see the flicker of a fire and the bustle of men as they erected tents and saw to the horses.

"You'll need to move."

Liam jerked around at the sound of her voice. The moon had come out. It shone on her face, highlighting the heavenly brilliance of her eyes, shadowing the delicate lawn of her cheeks like the loving stroke of an artist's brush.

"What?" he asked, and slammed a lid on those foolish poetic words that reared their ugly heads in his mind. The blows to his noggin must have rattled his thinking. He was hardly the poetic type.

"You'll have to move to the fire if I am to tend your wounds."

"You've no need to bother," he said. "I am quite whole."

He could predict her scowl even before it began, even before her brows lowered and her ungodly lips puckered into sassy disapproval. Lifting the lavender skirt of her gown, she knelt down beside him. "Mayhap you think I have dragged you out here for the pleasure of your company. But I assure you, Liam, I have not. I've no time to waste on your foolishness. So let us see this done."

"In a hurry to get somewhere, Rachel?" he asked.

"Aye. I am," she said, offering no more as she touched his brow. "Does that hurt?"

"Of course it hurts," he snapped. "Where are you going in such a rush?"

"Do you feel dizzy? Disoriented?" She moved her fingers upward, skimming them through his hair. A thousand unacceptable feelings shivered through him. He stifled a moan and kept his eyes wide open lest she realize the ecstacy of her touch.

"Shouldn't you have worried about me before?" he asked, managing a grimace.

She scowled, and for a moment he wondered if he saw the edge of guilt in her expression. That mystery aided in his attempt to shove away the raw emotions caused by the touch of her fingertips. She pulled her hand away. He remembered to breathe.

It was clear by her expression that she thought she should have seen to his wounds earlier, but something had made her push on until nightfall. That wasn't like the Rachel he'd known since adolescence She was a healer first and foremost. All else was secondary.

"Why the rush?" he asked. "Is there a babe somewhere that refuses to be birthed without your assistance?"

"Is your vision impaired?"

"Nay," he answered. "Tis not your cousin's babe that waits to be born is it? Shona's? Sara's?"

"My cousins are fine." Her hand neared again. He caught his breath, and then she was touching him again, skimming her fingers light as moondust along the edge of his jaw and downward. Poetry danced like wicked sirens in his mind. "You're lucky. Your face is mostly unscathed. No broken bones there."

"I'm an entertainer." It was difficult to speech, more difficult still to act nonchalant. "I must protect my best assets. At least my best *visible* assets." He forced a grin. "Else how will I entice those buxom young maids to perform with me? Ouch! God's balls, Rachel!" he scolded, covering his chest with his hand. "Are you trying to kill me?"

"There's blood seeping through your tunic."

"I noticed," he said irritably.

"I thought perhaps you hadn't. There *was* a buxom maid involved," she said, settling back on her heels.

"I but hope it didn't break her heart that I left so abruptly."

"Last I saw of her, she was hanging on her husband's arm, admiring him for the manly way he trounced you."

"More than probably she's scared of him."

"And you're more than probably a fool!" she countered. They glared at each other for a moment, then she exhaled deeply and glanced away. "You'll have to remove your tunic."

"I—" he began, but Rachel interrupted.

"Is my water boiling, Davin?"

"Aye, my lady."

Liam refused to contemplate how she knew the huge soldier was approaching from behind her.

"Help me get the Irishman to the fire," she said. "Then you may find your pallet."

"But . . ."

She glanced up at the huge warrior. "Liam has long been a friend of my clan. I assure you, I am quite safe."

With a brief nod, Davin bent over Liam. His hands closed like meat hooks around his burden's arms and Liam was wrenched to his feet. The distance to the fire was short. It only *seemed* as grueling as a journey to the Holy Land. But eventually he was dropped in front of the fire like so much ruined millet.

"You are certain—" Davin began.

"I will be safe," Rachel assured him. "And I need you rested. Go. Find your bed."

Liam watched the huge guard turn, watched his blond head duck as he disappeared into a nearby tent.

"So what hole did this Davin crawl from?" he asked.

"You needn't concern yourself," Rachel said, and wrapping her hand in a scrap of woolen cloth, lifted a pot from the fire. "It seems you have enough to worry on."

"Has some fat earl taken ill? Is Davin *his* man?"

She poured the water into a pewter mug, then dipped her hand into a huge leather satchel and brought out a doeskin bag. Pulling out a few crispy leaves, she dropped them into the cup, swirled the contents about and set it aside.

"Has Lord Haldane relapsed?" Liam asked, watching her closely.

"When I left the duke he was on the mend," she said, and poured half the remaining water into a wooden bowl. Adding a dram of oil from a tiny jar, she dunked a folded cloth into the bowl and lifted it toward his face.

So she *had* traveled to London to tend the duke. He had wondered why she was so far from home. "On the mend?" He narrowed his eyes at her. "You traveled all the way to London to see the duke healed, then left before he was completely recovered?"

She said nothing.

"Tis not like you."

She touched the cloth to his lip. It stung, but not unbearably.

"I believe myself far beyond the point where I've a need to explain my actions to you, Liam," she said.

So she was hiding something. But why? In truth, the Lady Saint's actions were rarely anything but saintly, except where he was concerned. Why now would she be keeping secrets? he wondered. But there seemed little point in asking her outright, for it had been a long while since she felt inclined to grant *him* any favors.

"Ahh." He watched her eyes closely in the hopes of intercepting some unspoken thought as he goaded her. "So you go to meet a lover? A private tryst?"

She dunked the cloth into the water, wrung it out, then returned it to his face, where she wiped at the dried blood on his chin.

"Does your father know?" he asked.

Smoothing the rag over his cheek once, she returned it to the bowl.

"Remove your tunic, Liam," she ordered dryly.

He gave her his best shocked expression. "What would your beloved say?"

She lifted her peeved expression to him in an instant. "He would say, I should have left you to the fat-chested slut's husband and his mutton-headed brothers."

Liam stared at her for a moment then laughed with almost painful relief, for she was obviously just as naive as ever. The horrid images of her in another man's arms faded slowly. "You still know little of men, Rachel. That's not what a lover would say atall. He would be jealous. He would ask what you saw in the Irishman that made you take him under your wing. Mayhap he would have even heard of my attraction for women and be doubly jealous. Therefore I'll have to assume there is no lover. And too . . ."—he shrugged—"you're not the sort."

Removing several rolls of bandages from her bag, she set them beside her before returning her gaze to his. "And pray, Liam, in your wise estimation, what sort am I?"

Her face, ivory pale and princess perfect, seemed little changed from the moment he had first met her in her father's castle.

"You're the marrying sort," he murmured.

Her gaze, sharp as cut amethyst, remained on his for a fraction of an instant, then flitted downward as her fingers mixed some evil concoction. "So I am told repeatedly."

The tension that had just eased in his gut, knotted up a hundredfold The image of her naked appeared again. Naked and ecstatic, writhing in another man's arms, her wicked lips parted as she crooned an unknown name. "By whom?" he asked, forcing the question.

"The man I am to marry," she said.

Chapter 2

"**Y**ou are promised to be wed?" Liam asked. His tone, he was happy to note, was casual, but his gut had twisted into something akin to a cruel sailor's knot.

She said nothing, her expression unreadable, her fingers quick.

"Rachel," he said, forcing out the word a little too sharply.

"I am no blushing maid." She glanced quickly up. "I am five and twenty years old. Tis well past time I am wed."

Liam clenched his teeth and considered trying a smile, but he was a man who well knew his limitations, and a smile was, just now, far beyond those boundaries. The knot tightened.

"Who?" he asked, his voice quiet.

"Tis none of your affair."

Nay. It was not. It was *not*. But . . . God's balls! His gut hurt. He jerked to his feet, and reveled momentarily in the bracing pain.

"Someone I know?" he asked.

"Tis difficult to say."

"So that is where you go in such haste," he said,

. watching her face. "And the hulk? This Davin. He is your . . . betrothed's man?"

She raised her chin. "I suppose you would not believe me if I said Davin is the one I am to wed."

She had always had a biting sense of humor when the mood suited her. But making him believe she would settle for someone whose station was little above his own was cruel beyond words. Though he hoped with all his misguided soul that she did not know it.

"I always imagined you with someone different," he said with forced civility.

"Oh?"

"Aye. Someone who could breathe and talk at the same time," he said.

"And this from a thief who would wear a plaid in Rainich."

"And why should I not?" he asked.

"Because twill give them only one more reason to trounce you, and you very well know it," she snapped.

Ah, yes. Maybe that was the third reason to wear a plaid in England. But there were decided advantages to remembering one's place in life. He pulled his gaze from her face.

"And that sporran," she added, scowling at the pouch strapped to his waist. Made of fine hide and decorated with long tassels of black horsehair, it was an ostentatious Gaelic display that hung nearly to his knees. "Must you always make a spectacle of yourself, Liam? Must you always wear the brightest plaid, the biggest sporran? Have you stolen so much coin that you need more space to tote it about?"

"You being Scots yourself and you don't know the true purpose of the sporran? Tis not the wealth it is there to hide, tis the wick." She had the tendency to bring out the devil in him, though her cousin, Shona, had always said it was not necessarily a difficult task. "And hence . . ."—he swept his hand downward to display his sporran's unusual proportions and grinned—"its ponderous size."

She stared at him, her eyes expressionless. "Take off your tunic," she ordered.

Wasn't she even shocked by his language? She was a lady! Naive, soft, delicate. And experienced? The possibility sent tiny shards of pain ripping through him. "I know you are tempted, lass," he said, scowling at her. "But I assure you, I do not need . . ." he began.

She stepped forward, her lips pursed, her movements quick as they touched the strip of leather that laced up his tunic at the neck. Her fingers brushed his throat. Liam gritted his teeth against the slash of feelings that sliced him from neck to groin. "I'll do it," he said and swept her hands aside.

She stepped slowly back. Forcing his fingers to do his bidding, Liam unfastened his pewter brooch and pulled the ends of the shirt from beneath his plaid. Shards of pain splintering off in every direction.

"Lift your arms." It was an order, given from a lady to a subject.

If he had the wits of a turnip, he would refuse, but she was too close for him to muster any manly fortitude.

He lifted his arms with an effort. Grasping the hem of his tunic, she eased it upward. Her knuckles skimmed his ribs, his chest, then paused. Her gaze, bright as liquid fire, caught his. Memories of forbidden dreams leapt in Liam's mind. Dreams of creamy skin, shivery caresses, the sigh of his name from her sweet lips.

But reality was only a moment behind. Crossing his arms against his chest, he knocked her hands aside, grabbed the tunic and tore it over his head, then yanked his arms down to a crashing cord of satisfying pain.

She had already moved away to crouch by the fire.

Silence settled in. His gut loosened enough to allow him to breathe.

"Surely your ..." For a moment he could find no acceptable words to call the man she apparently intended to marry, but he reprimanded himself as a thousand kinds of fool and continued. "Surely your lover would take offense if he knew of this."

"Of what?"

"Of ..." Liam gestured breathlessly toward his own naked chest, but she shrugged after the briefest glance, as if there was nothing there of even the mildest interest. But it had not always been such. God, no. He could remember a time ... He shut off the thoughts in wild panic. "Take offense to this," he said hoarsely. "You and I."

"My laird knows I am called to heal. He doesn't resent that."

"Truly?" He snorted. "How gallant of him."

"Aye."

"Tis not like the English to be so noble."

"I did not say he was English. Sit down."

He remained as he was. "A lowlander then. I wouldn't have thought your father would allow it."

"Sit," she said again. "I've no wish to see you faint standing up."

"Don't you?"

She glanced up finally, her expression peeved. "You mistake me for the lass I once was," she said, and lifted a mug toward him. "Drink this."

He ignored her order. "So you have changed since you last covered my pallet in nettles?"

She laughed. The sound was short and quick. But did he imagine a singing note of tension. "Twas over a decade ago that I visited such revenge on you, Liam. I had all but forgotten."

"I have not. And though you may think me a dolt, I am hardly such a fool as to trust your evil concoction."

"Then I shall have Davin hold you still while I pour it down your throat."

He snorted. "As charming as ever, I see," he said, and sat down, for if the truth be told, he just might faint. And *that* the saintly Rachel would never forget. "Does the good earl know of your true temperament?"

"I did not say he was an earl," she said, and prodded the mug into his hand. "Drink it all at once."

Liam gazed into the potion. "A bit of powdered bat wing?"

"Saliva from a black adder's tongue."

He glanced up warily, but she merely put a finger beneath the bottom, pressing it firmly toward his lips. "Tis naught but a bit of white willow and meadowsweet. Truly, Liam, I've never known you to be so gullible."

He scowled. The brew smelled distasteful at best. "And what of your marquess? I suppose he is never fooled by your wit?"

"I know no marquess," she said, and tipped the contents of the mug onto his lips.

Liam shivered as it coursed past his taste buds

and down his throat. Finally, the mug empty, he said, "You must not have tried to mend his wounds yet, if he still plans to marry you."

"He's not been so foolish as to be injured," she said, and touched her cloth to the wound on his chest.

His muscles recoiled as she washed away the blood.

"A reopened wound?" she asked.

"Aye." It was all he could manage for a moment. But she soon dropped the rag back into the water, letting him breathe again.

"So your beloved is no great fighter," he deduced after a moment.

The woods were silent for a moment, then, "Why do you want to know, Liam?" she asked softly.

"Simple curiosity." He managed a shrug. "Naught else."

"If I tell you of him will you cease your badgering?"

He nodded.

"Laird Dunlock resides some leagues north of here. He is not a young man, nor is he particularly wealthy. But he is a fine man—kind and wise. It has been some years since he asked for my hand." She touched his chest to smooth ointment carefully onto his wound.

"And you agreed?" Liam could not quite manage to raise his voice above a whisper.

"Why should I not?"

Her fingers were feather-soft against his skin, tantalizing him, reminding him of a thousand moments spent in her company.

"No reason," he said.

She nodded as she reached for a bandage. Placing the end over his wound, she leaned forward to wind it about his chest. The scent of her filled his head, conjuring a host of vintage images of her, laughing with her cousins as they practiced their silly feats of horsemanship, somber as she held an ailing babe against her breast.

Her fingers brushed his shoulder, his arm, the tensed muscles of his chest. Shivers coursed through him. He willed himself to remain still beneath her touch.

"No reason you should not marry," he repeated.

She glanced up, their faces inches apart. "Tis so good to know I have your approval, Liam," she said. Settling back, she took hold of his arm. There was a scratch along his biceps, but it was not deep. "I would stitch this, but I won't be here to remove the sutures, and I cannot trust you to see to it properly."

"So I am not invited to your betroth's holdings?"

"Nay." She didn't glance up as she worked. "You're not."

"Tis not like you to be so selfish, Rachel."

She tied off the bandage.

Their gazes met. A thousand truths raced through his mind. A thousand pleas. A thousand apologies. But regardless of everything, she was still the haughty daughter of a Highland laird, and he was still a bastard.

"Is there anything else I should see to?" Her voice was throaty, as it would sound in the throes of passion, with her clever hands pressed against the heat of his flesh, and her . . .

"Aye, there is," he rasped, grappling to get a grip on his emotions, to gain some modicum of control. "But your betrothed might well be offended if I showed you."

She rose swiftly and turned away. Liam

squeezed his eyes shut and tried to remain where he was, but there was little hope of that.

He was on his feet in a moment, following her, moving away from the shifting firelight.

At the edge of the river that rushed by them, she knelt to wash her hands, then remained there for a moment before she rose and looked across the wide burn.

"I'll not delay you if you feel the need to leave us this night," she said, not turning toward him.

"I thought it was your duty as a healer to insist that I rest and mend. Why the hurry to see me gone?"

She turned now, her face shadowed and limned by the moonlight. "As you said, my laird might well be jealous. I'd hate to see him challenge you simply because you had the poor sense to proposition a pig-farmer's wife and get yourself wounded."

"Dare I hope you're worried for me?" he asked, hoping his tone evidenced some sarcasm.

"Though I don't understand it, my mother is rather fond of you. Twould be an onerous task to tell her that you've been sliced into a thousand ribbons by my own betrothed."

"So he is an accomplished swordsman?"

"Not particularly," she said. "But I've seen your talents in that arena."

"Some men's wit is sharper than any blade," he said.

"Aye, I saw how cleverly you fought off the husband and his brothers."

He managed a shrug. "I cannot help it if maids throw themselves at me."

"And I cannot help it if you get yourself killed because of your own wandering eye," she snapped, and turned away to walk along the shore.

Liam told himself a thousand times that he should go back to camp, collect his haughty gelding, and leave.

In a moment he had caught up to her.

"So this Dunlock," he began. "He has been wed before?"

"'Tis none of your concern."

"I just wonder."

She opened her mouth as if to berate him but finally nodded. "Aye, he was widowed some years ago."

"A short mourning," he said.

"What?"

"He asked for your hand some years ago," he said. "'Tis unseemly that he should not have spent some time to mourn his wife."

"'Tis hardly your place to judge others' morals, Liam," she said, turning on him.

"I simply worry for your well being and—"

"You don't worry for me atall," she countered hotly. "You simply torment me. And why, I wonder. Why do you insist on bedeviling me?"

Because she made him spout miserable poetry in his mind, made him sleepless and hot and discontented. Made him think of a hundred places he would like to kiss, to caress. But he was not such a fool as to tell her. So he opened his mouth to lie, but in that moment a flash of something caught his eye.

He turned toward it, thinking for a moment that it was nothing but the gleam of errant moonlight on the waves. But in an instant he caught his breath.

"God's balls," he whispered.

"What is it?"

Liam wrenched his gaze from the shore. "Tis nothing."

She scowled at him, then turned her attention slowly back toward the swollen river. "What . . ." she began, but her words stopped and she gasped softly as she stared at the silver glimmer beneath the hustling waves.

"Tis nothing," Liam rasped again, but she was already pacing toward it. He dashed after her and grabbed her arm just at the water's edge. "Rachel!"

"What?" They were inches apart, face to face.

Fear gripped him, fear as hard and sharp as a Scotsman's claymore. "Don't touch it."

She stared at him, her eyes wide, her mouth rounded as she turned back toward the river. "Do not touch what? What is it?"

"Tis—tis a bad omen," he stuttered.

She stared at him, at the glimmer beneath the waves, at him, and then she laughed and snatched her arm from his grasp.

"Truly, Liam? A bad omen?" she said, and pulling up her sleeve, reached into the water.

The waves seemed to turn to liquid silver for a moment, and then the glimmer was resting in her hand. Even in the darkness, even the first moment he saw it, he knew what it was. Knew in his heart. In his gut. In his soul, if he still had one.

"Dragonheart!" Rachel whispered.

Liam squeezed his eyes closed. Fear turned to terror.

"Liam, tis Dragonheart," she said, amazement in her voice. "But . . ." She shook her head and skimmed a finger over the dragon's ruby breast. "It cannot be. Many months ago James lost it in Beith Burn. However would it come here?"

He said nothing. The knot in his gut had been

stretched tight, as if pulled hard by battling warriors.

Rachel turned toward him. "Mayhap it washed downriver. It could be that the Beith connects with this burn somewhere," she said and scowled. "Are you not surprised to see it?"

He wished he could be. Wished with everything in him. But he knew too much for that, had spent too many years learning the truth.

"Liam," she said, canting her head at him. "Are you not happy to see it? There was a time you would not be parted from it."

"Twas a long time ago," he intoned.

"It seems to have returned to you," she said, and lifted the amulet toward him.

"Tis not for me!" he snapped and jerked back a pace.

She stared at him, her eyes as eerie as the dragon's inexplicable presence. "You're not afraid of a wee bit of metal and stone. Are you, Liam?"

"Nay," he said, but he failed to pull his gaze from it.

"Could it be you've come to believe your own wild tales?"

Wild tales! If only they were. In fact, he had once thought the stories he spewed were just that. There were, it turned out, few things more frightening than learning one's lies were nothing more than misbegotten truths.

"Its presence here is strange. But I'm certain there's an explanation. Still, if it bothers you I can surely return it to the water," she said, and drew her hand back as if to toss it into the river.

"Nay!" he rasped, and leapt forward. But she had already stopped the movement of her arm and was staring at him. "Nay," he repeated, and cleared his throat, feeling foolish.

True, the dragon amulet had been crafted long ago by a man known for his mystical powers, and true, strange things happened when it was near. But telling Rachel that he was certain it had come to them under its own power was somehow beyond his ability.

"I don't think it would be wise to be rid of it," he said instead.

"And why might that be?" There was something in her voice. Was it laughter? he wondered, and said nothing.

"Why shouldn't I be rid of it?" she asked.

He gritted his teeth and remained silent. She already thought him a fool, why prove her point?

Finally, with a shrug, she drew her hand back again as if to toss it.

"It has come for you!" he blurted.

Even in the darkness he could see the surprise on her face. Whatever she had expected him to say, it hadn't been that.

"And it knew I would be passing by this way? It knew and thus made certain it was in my path?"

No. He had learned too much to believe there was luck involved in this. Dragonheart had called Rachel to him. But he was hardly prepared to tell her that. "Mayhap," he said instead.

For a moment she seemed shocked beyond words, then, "Mayhap it knew *you* would be passing this way. Mayhap it was you it wanted to be with."

"Nay. It prefers the lassies."

She laughed aloud. "If I did not know you so well, I would almost think you believe it, Liam."

He would give a king's ransom *not* to believe it,

but there was no hope of that. Rachel's cousin, Sara, had possessed the amulet for a while. She had lost it, and some months later it had been found by Shona, far from the place where it had disappeared. And during the time that the women held it, there had been nothing but tribulation. Nothing but hardships, terror, death.

Liam shivered at the thought and said nothing.

"If it is clever enough to find me, it must also be clever enough to know I have no time for this," Rachel said. "I must be on my way with the first light tomorrow, and you . . ." She paused. "You shall return to propositioning other men's—"

"Nay!" He spoke without thinking, the denial torn from his lips.

"What?"

"I will not be leaving," he said. "I'll be traveling with you."

Chapter 3

~~~~~~ ∽◯◯∼ ~~~~~~

Rachel closed her fingers over the warm weight of the dragon amulet and stared at Liam. The moon was hiding again, but the darkness did nothing to diminish the intensity of his eyes. It was his eyes that had pulled at her soul from the first moment she'd met him. Indeed, it was his eyes that had made her act the fool time and again. But no more.

"You think to join me on my journey?" she asked. Haughtiness was her right by birth. She had honed it at King James's court and was not above using it like a well-sharpened dagger when the situation warranted. The situation warranted now.

He stared at her, not speaking for a moment, then, "There be safety in numbers."

Not if he were one of the number.

"So you are suddenly worried about your safety?" she queried, making certain her tone was cool. "After spending the better part of two decades traveling alone?"

His eyes again, as intense as midnight. "Mayhap I'm concerned for *you*," he said.

"Me?" She couldn't help but laugh, for she had learned long ago that Liam the Irishman cared about no one but himself. "You're concerned about me? When I am surrounded by Hawk's best guards?"

"Hawk!"

Rachel swore in silence. There was little point in attempting to weave a fine lie if she were only going to ruin the warp moments later. Aye, Liam may be as self-centered as a stone, but he was not as dense as one. Wit, sleight of hand, and a decided lack of morals had ascertained his survival these many years since his mother's death. She would have to watch her tongue or bear the circumstances.

"Davin is the Hawk's man?" Liam asked, taking a step toward her. "I thought he was Dunlock's guard."

"I fear you misunderstood." Actually, she wasn't certain what she'd said, for she was a hideously poor liar. Her cousin Shona had tried to help her in that regard, and for a time Rachel had even tried to gain a bit of knowledge from Liam, the master of lies. But she had been born hopelessly honest. Even her mother, Lady Fiona, who had spent some years in a convent, had a certain flare for creating misconceptions. Rachel had always felt rather cheated that she'd inherited her father's rigid sense of honor.

"So Hawk sent the guards?" Liam asked, holding to the subject like a hound to a bone.

"Aye." It was too short an answer. She knew enough about lying to realize one had to embellish a little while making certain she didn't go too far. She'd just never figured out how to achieve that perfect blend of dishonesty. The truth was so pitifully alluring to her. She wished now she'd never started down this path of dishonesty, but Liam's smug assurance that she had no lover had stirred childish resentments she'd long ago put to rest.

"Why?" Liam asked. "I would have thought your betrothed would have come himself to fetch his bride, or at least sent his own escort. And what of your father? Did he not—"

"Busy." The single word sped from her lips as if it were poison. Haughty she could managed. But dear God, she was pathetic at being devious.

"What?"

"Father is busy."

"Too busy to see to his only daughter's safety?" Liam canted his head at her as if he could read the truth in her eyes. But that was *her* role, and she resented an amateur like him trying to muddle about in her mind. "That doesn't sound like the Laird Leith I've known. Couldn't he have sent Harlow? What of the Rogue? Your uncle Roderic has coddled you since the day of your birth. Didn't he send a single man? Bullock or—"

"Hear me, Liam," she interrupted frantically. "Mayhap you have nothing better to do than stand about and discuss the deeds of my family. But that luxury is not mine. If you do not want the dragon amulet I'll simply . . ." She opened her fingers to distract him by tossing it back into the water, but the dragon's ruby heart was incomparably bright in the moonlight. "I'll just . . . wear it for a time," she said, and slipped it without a moment's thought around her neck.

The weight felt comfortably right there.

"Against your breast."

"What?" She glanced up, drawn from the dragon's crimson light.

He cleared his throat. "Wear it under your gown. Against your . . . skin."

She meant to scoff at him, but found she was already slipping the amulet beneath her bodice.

Drawing her hand away with an effort, she turned back to him. "There now," she said, trying to sound casual. "Are you happy, Liam, now that foolishness is finished? Will you be on your way?"

He seemed tense, as if he were fighting a private battle. "I'll go where you go."

"You will not." Frustration spurred through her like a hot lance. It was bad enough that he showed up at all, disturbing her peace, conjuring up a thousand memories best left forgot. But to insist on following her was too much to accept. He would ruin everything. Would . . . Well, he'd at least find out what a really poor liar she was if he accompanied her. "You are not invited, Liam," she said, steadying her tone. "And I've no idea why you would wish to come."

For a moment he almost seemed to struggle, then he grinned, the roguish expression a slash of memories in her mind. "Mayhap I've a wish to see who the Lady Saint has consented to marry—this time."

It was true that she'd been betrothed more than once. But each time something had stopped her, an impending birth, a sick child. Her healing skills were much in demand. It was those skills that gave her both honor and respect in the wild hills of her homeland. They also gave her certain responsibilities that she couldn't ignore simply to be wed. "I'll not accept your company."

"And I'll not have you risking your life."

"Why?"

He straightened as if slapped. "I owe your parents a good deal."

"Then go steal them some priceless gift."

"And allow you to risk your skin to save

some . . ."—he gestured angrily as he searched for words—"nobleman you have not even met."

She opened her mouth to retort but realized his implications suddenly. "I am not going to save anyone," she said. "I go to be with my . . . beloved."

He remained in silent tension for a moment, then, "Aye. Of course you do," Liam said, and stepped forward. She felt his tension like a rush of tide. "He must be quite the saint himself if you are in such a hurry to see him."

"Aye." She forced out the word. "He is that."

"Then surely you will not mind if I meet him."

"On the contrary. I do mind."

"Why?"

"Because . . ." Because there was no beloved, and just now she'd rather be pelted with rotten fruit than admit the truth to him. "Because I know you, Liam. You'll do naught but cause trouble."

He stepped closer still. "What kind of trouble?"

"You'll distract . . . my guards."

"If they're so easily distracted, I suggest you could use another to keep you safe during your travels."

"And ask you to neglect your *duties* just to see to my safety? I couldn't."

"I insist."

"I refuse."

"Then I'll follow along behind. But think of it. I will be at risk, for surely I would be safer in your midst."

Damn him and his shifty Irish ways. "And you think I care, Liam?"

His eyes were as eerie as a cat's in the darkness. "Aye, I do, Rachel. I think you cannot help but care. Even about me."

"You're wrong."

"Then why did you not let the brothers four pummel me?"

"I . . ." The memory made her feel somewhat sick. The sound of their fists against his flesh. "I didn't realize it was you."

"Now you do," he said. "And now I owe you a kindness. I insist on paying my debt."

She opened her mouth to argue, but he had already turned away and disappeared into the darkness.

Sometime during the night, it began to rain. By morning, the campground was a bog, the men irritable, and the horses testy. The river, already high, was reaching toward them in slate gray waves.

Rachel broke the fast on cold oatcakes inside Davin's tent.

"Time is of the essence," she said, tucking her hands into her oversized sleeves. "You know that as well as I, Davin."

"The river is swollen."

"Swollen!" Liam, never one to be absent simply because he was uninvited, stepped inside the tent and straightened somewhat. "The river is suicide. Surely you're not thinking of crossing here, are you Rachel?" he asked.

"Twould be fastest," she said. She noticed, without meaning to, that he moved with just a little less than his usual catlike grace, that slight stiffness a concession to the beating he had taken the day before. It was said of some that they landed on their feet. But of Liam twas said that he could walk through the rain without getting wet. Luck was his closest companion.

"Fastest. Twould be the fastest way to your death mayhap," Liam countered. "But not the fastest way to reach your destination. By the by," he said, turning toward Davin. "Where does this Laird Dunlock reside?"

"North of here," Rachel answered quickly, though Davin seemed in no hurry to either answer the Irishman or negate her story. "But I fear there is nothing to be done but hasten east and hope for a better crossing."

"There's a ferry some leagues from here, I believe," Liam said.

"Can we reach it by nightfall?"

"Tell me, Rachel, is this rush to be reunited with your betrothed your idea or is it your beloved who is so impatient?"

Rachel felt Davin's dispassionate gaze turn toward her. She stood abruptly. "Tell the men to prepare to ride as soon as possible. We'll travel to the ferry and hope to camp this night on the farside."

By noon Rachel decided that Liam had lied. There probably wasn't a single ferry between them and the Holy Land. Three hours later she didn't care. All she wanted was to curl up somewhere dry and sleep for eternity.

She'd spent the previous night haunted by doubts and nagged by worries. Now she rode hunched miserably over her mare's neck, exhausted, wet, and chafed from the woolen cape that rubbed her raw at her wrists and neck.

Liam, wrapped in a dark cloak, suggested they find shelter and stop until the weather improved, but Rachel was in no mood for a delay. After a quick and miserable meal, they pushed on.

Some hours before dusk, they came to a place

where the river narrowed in its twisting course. Perhaps it would have been a good crossing point at other times, but the wind had begun to rise, keeling from the northwest and causing the river to slap, gray and rough, against the shore.

Davin's dry statement that "twould be as good a way to die as any" was discouraging enough for her to decide to continue on.

They wrapped their cloaks more closely about themselves and hurried eastward. By the time they reached the ferry crossing, the wind was blowing the night upon them. Through the fading light, Rachel saw a humble vessel tied in a shallow port. For a moment she feared that in such weather the ferry driver would have abandoned his post, but he sat, huddled and hooded under a tarp that sagged above a small portion of his vessel.

It was a simple craft with a low, uncertain railing and a rectangular form. Made of a rough-slatted floor and little else, it was attached to a rope that slapped across the turbulent river to the farside, some ninety yards across.

Liam pushed his gelding closer to Rachel's mount. "Mayhap you think twould be better to die than to wed your fat laird," he said. "But for myself, I've things to live for."

Wet, cold, and in no mood for his dubious sense of humor, Rachel turned to him. "Are you trying to tell me something, Liam?"

"Mayhap we should wait till the wind dies down before we attempt to cross," he said, but just at that moment the gale diminished a mite, lulled as if some fractious giant had ceased his blowing.

"Feel free to stay here if you like," she said, and pushed her mare up to Davin.

"Pay the man his fee," she ordered, nodding toward the ferry. "If we hurry we'll still have some daylight left to travel on."

It only took Davin a few moments to conduct business with the hooded man and return. "If you've no wish to swim in these waters, I would suggest we hurry you across whilst the wind is somewhat quiet. There is room for us, a couple others, and the supplies."

She nodded, eager to see the opposite shore.

In only a few minutes their provisions were packed onto the restless vessel. The Norseman helped her onto the ferry. It rocked erratically beneath her feet, and Liam, apparently not caring that he was not invited, hopped on behind her.

Davin, his hood drooping across his forehead, nodded for them to set out. The ferry driver lurched across the deck and untied the vessel.

They launched immediately into the tide. Rachel huddled deeper between two canvas bags and prepared to be seasick. But in moments the wind dropped away completely. The water smoothed, lapping softly against the ferry. Shifting her attention over the bags, she let the sound of the waves soothe her. All would be well. Despite everything, she had made good time; and now that the weather was letting up she would improve upon that. Soon she would reach her destination.

"Eerie," Liam said, standing close beside her.

"What?" She glanced up. His brow was furrowed and his eyes turned sideways toward the approaching shore.

"Don't you feel it?" he hissed.

"Feel what?"

"That—" He stopped as if fighting for words. "Breathlessness?"

"Whatever are you talking about?" she asked,

but suddenly the world did not seem so peaceful. Instead, it felt as if they were perched on the edge of a precipice.

"Do you feel it, Davin?" Liam asked, not taking his gaze from the shore.

No answer.

"Davin?" Liam said.

The Norseman turned toward him, his face shadowed by his hood as he reached a hand inside his cape.

Liam hissed, then, like a racing steed, he lunged forward, slamming his shoulder into the other. Knocked off balance, Davin crashed against the railing. It shattered under his immense weight. For a moment, he teetered on the edge, then toppled, flailing, over the side.

"Liam!" Rachel gasped, but the Irishman was already lunging past her. She swiveled frantically about, only to see Liam barrel toward the ferry driver.

Just swinging his pole from the water, the driver shrieked as Liam crashed into his side. He staggered, dropped his pole, and toppled through the opening in the rail.

Liam skidded to a halt, barely keeping himself from the water.

"Liam!" Rachel yelled, but he was already racing toward the front of the ferry, and suddenly, in a wild rush, the wind blasted them again.

With the suddenness of death, waves lapped angrily against the ferry, washing it side to side. Bereft of the benefit of the ferry driver's pole, it tore at its rope.

Shocked and terrified, Rachel clung to a bag of supplies. "What have you done?" she shrieked.

"Didn't you . . ." Liam turned back to her, his

legs braced wide against the rock of the raft. "Didn't you feel it?"

"What?"

He gestured wildly toward the waves that tore at their flimsy vessel. "The evil! He meant you harm."

"What?" He was making no sense. The wind tore at her as she staggered to her feet and searched the water. "What are you talking about? Twas Hawk's man you've . . ."

"He's found us," Liam rasped. The truth struck him with terrifying force, slamming with white-hot intensity into his brain. "He is here!"

Rachel jerked toward him.

"What? Who?" she gasped, but he could no longer pull his gaze from the shore.

A handful of men stood near the galloping waves. Just some unidentified men, nothing more horrible than that, and yet Liam could feel the moment the terror crept over her, could feel her fear as clearly as he could feel her fingers curl into his sleeve.

"Who is it?" she whispered.

"He's found us," he whispered. "But he'll not have you."

"Who?"

"Not while I've breath in my body!" he rasped, and ripping through the bonds of his terror, he dropped onto the deck of the ferry and pulled out his knife.

"Liam! Nay!" Rachel screamed, but she was already too late.

The rope snapped beneath his blade. The ferry tilted wildly sideways, torn from its path by the ravenous waves.

Rachel fell, grasping a bag that rolled at her feet.

"Hold on!" Liam yelled. He crawled toward her, fighting against the rolling movement to her side. "Don't let go!"

"Liam!" she shrieked, and slid a few inches toward the yawning waves. He grabbed her arm, frantically pulling her closer.

"He'll not follow. Not fast enough," he yelled into the wind.

A towering wave torpedoed over the side, drenching them with frigid water and sliding them toward the edge of the raft. Rachel gasped for breath. Two bags swirled madly, slipped overboard and out of sight. Beneath them, the ferry bucked like a crazed steed. She grabbed a railing post.

"Who'll not follow? Who?" she rasped.

Waves leapt over them. The wind howled about them. They were tossed and tortured and dizzied, and yet, suddenly all seemed quiet except one thought in Liam's mind. "He is too late."

"Who?"

"Too late."

"Liam. What . . ." she began, but the ferry bucked again. Beneath them, timber creaked.

"Hold on!" he yelled. "It's coming!"

The dull roaring rushed louder.

"What's coming?" she shouted, her fingers like talons on his arm. "What?"

Liam rose to his knees. His cape whipped behind him. His hair, torn loose from its mooring, slapped across his cheek.

"What's coming?" she screamed.

"The waterfalls!"

"Waterfalls? Liam! Nay!"

"Twill not be so bad. Not so high. Hang on, Rachel. You can do this! Hang on."

A wave, big as a fortified castle, swept down on them. The raft swamped, guttered, and was tossed high.

Rachel screamed. Liam yelled.

The edge of the ferry dipped then bucked toward the sky. Their bodies were swept off the floor. Hung from their aching arms, they dangled in mid-air.

For an instant, for one fractured, horrified second before he was slammed to the floor boards again, Liam saw the falls, saw the foam, saw the crashing water, and a thousand lifetimes below, saw the river swirl away into peace.

"Dear God!" he rasped. Twas far bigger than he remembered. They'd never survive. Never!

"How—" Another wave swamped them, washing the words from her mouth. "How far? How far a drop?" she gasped.

"Hold on!"

The ferry moved faster now, but smoother—the paved road to hell.

He found her hand and pulled it between them. Her eyes, wide with terror, turned up to him. So beautiful. The eyes of a saint.

"Rachel." He breathed her name and brushed his lips across her knuckles. "I'm sorry . . ." His voice broke. Water crashed over them. He should shut up, prepare for the worst, but there was no hope. All they had was this one sparkling moment. Twas a moment for truth. Lies were swept away like hapless flotsam.

"You are all that is good, Rachel," he whispered. "It has always been so and I have always known it. No matter what I have said."

The ferry tilted, swept along more and more swiftly. Their gazes met.

"Liam . . ." Her heavenly lips parted, but there was no need for her to speak, for he knew what she would say, knew the truth as he knew his own name.

"I will love you forever, for eternity and beyond," he said, and then they fell, thrust over the cliff like flightless sparrows.

Chapter 4

The ferry broke apart like a ship of matches and flew into a thousand tiny splinters. Liam saw Rachel scream. Saw her mouth open, felt the vibration of her terror, but the sound was lost in a roar of water. They fell into the frothing spray like dolls of rag, their feet scrambling, their hair billowing, but even now he could not let her go, could not risk eternity without her.

They struck the water together. The surface was as hard as glass, jarring him like the blow of a hammer. He tried to hold on to her hand, tried with all his might to keep her near him, but the shock of the landing drove them apart.

"Rachel!" He screamed her name, but she was already gone, ripped beneath the waves. He yelled again. The current swirled, taking him too.

It dragged him under. His leg struck something hard and sharp, numbing him with the force. But in that instant, he realized his opportunity. Kicking wildly, he sought purchase on the very thing that had wounded him. His feet struck something firm. His body pistoned through the frothing water, but whether he was going up or down, he had no way of knowing. An object rushed past him. He

53

grabbed for it and missed. He was rolled and tumbled. His head struck something solid. Blackness rushed in, but there, in the back of his mind, he saw Rachel, drowning, falling.

"Nay!" he shrieked. Water filled his mouth and screamed into his lungs.

Gagging and fighting, he searched for the surface, and just when he thought his lungs would burst, his head broke above the waves.

Air seared his chest with sweet pain. He gasped, dragging in mouthfuls until he was sucked under again. He spun and rolled, froth all around him. Something brushed his arm. He grabbed for it. His fingers seemed to close on nothing, but when he rolled again, he realized he was dragging it with him. Desperate, he held on tight, his fingers paralyzed with the hope that it would pull him back up.

Air again, like a flash of heaven before he was tossed back under. But in an instant, he surfaced. He was on his back, being dragged along through the night. He filled his lungs, gasping for breath. It came more easily now. Terror dulled a mite. The roar in his head quieted. He was leaving the falls behind. Or was he losing consciousness. But no. The frantic rush of the waves was slower, the water almost clear. Lowering his feet, he kicked frantically for the bottom, and suddenly his entire torso was free of the water and he was crouched on the shore, his legs curled under him and his right arm twisted behind him as he stubbornly clung to whatever had dragged him to safety.

Fighting to draw in air, he rasped in a few painful breaths. His stomach churned, his lungs ached. But he had no time to choke or vomit or pass out.

"Rachel!" He croaked her name, already searching.

It was then that he heard the coughing.

Turning weakly he saw that his fingers had not caught a branch at all. But Rachel's sleeve.

She coughed again, facedown in the water.

He managed to draw her into his arms, to pull her against his chest, to hold her as life returned to his body and hope to his heart.

She sucked great draughts of air raggedly into her lungs.

She was alive. He laughed, because he could manage nothing else.

Their eyes met, their souls melded. It was true what people said about near-death experiences; it made everything clear. He could see the truth in her eyes. She loved him, always had.

She moved closer, her lips slightly parted. He bent forward, awaiting her words. Her lips moved again, and then she bent double and vomited in his lap.

Liam waited until her spasms passed, then pushed her hair back and stared into her pale face.

"Dammit it, Liam, what have you done!" she croaked.

He recoiled as if struck. "I saved your life."

"Saved my life. You nearly killed me!"

"Nay." He shook his head. "You were in mortal danger. Davin—he was going to kill you."

"Kill me! Are you daft? He was my guard."

He was baffled. Stunned. "So you did not feel the evil?"

"Evil! I was safe and protected until you—"

"You were not safe," he argued, but now that the trauma was past, things seemed less clear, like the memory of nightmares fading in the morning's light.

"You think me safe down here?" she asked.

She had a point there. "We'd best find somewhere to spend the night," he said.

"I had somewhere to spend the night. I had a tent and food and guards. Davin—"

"Davin!" The name all but stuck in his throat. Uncertain emotions smoked in his head. "Why would you trust him so after all we've been through?" he asked, and fought to stand up. Once on his feet, he found that his leg burned only slightly more than the fires of hell.

"You're mad," she said, and stumbled to her feet.

Liam took a single step, felt the strength drain from his injured leg, and tumbled toward the water like a stringless marionette. But he had no wish to look like a weak-kneed fool, so he grappled wildly, searching for something to hold on to.

Her skirt was the only thing available. He snagged his fingers in it as he fell.

With a small shriek, she toppled down beside him.

They sat in the water face-to-face, panting, half-drowned. Nevertheless, Liam could not help but notice certain things. Firstly, her cape had disappeared. Secondly, her cap was gone, spilling her hair in wild disarray. Thirdly, and most importantly, her gown had been ripped down the front, exposing one shoulder and the high, pale rise of her right breast.

"Is this the sort of view that kept Davin so close to your side?" he asked.

"What are you . . ." she began, but in a moment she realized where his attention lay. "Sweet Mary!"

she rasped, and lifting a hand, tried to scrape up enough fabric to cover herself. It was pretty much a hopeless endeavor.

And despite everything, the pain in his leg, their present state of hopelessness, her wrath, he couldn't help but chuckle.

"Get on your feet," she growled.

To his mild surprise, he managed to do just that. His leg throbbed and his head spun, but one glance at her haughty expression cranked up the devil in him. "Hell of a ride, wasn't it?" he asked.

Lightning streaked through an ebony sky, and a half-mile away the falls roared. "We'd best find some kind of shelter or the night won't be so pleasant as the journey."

"Mayhap you've a bonny house close to hand."

"Certainly," he said. Pain was crashing through his leg. Unconsciousness seemed a pleasant diversion, if somewhat cowardly. "But I thought you might prefer my castle. The solar is quite lovely in the—"

"Shut up," she said. "And let me . . ." Her words stopped midsentence.

"What?" Liam braced himself and jerked his attention to the right, then the left, ready to do battle, to brave the dragons and face the foes. But no foes caught his attention. He realized quite suddenly that she was staring directly into his face. He stared back. "What is it?" he asked warily.

He watched her lips move. But finally she shook her head. "'Tis nothing," she said.

"Nothing?"

"I remember . . ." she whispered, then paused as if confused. "Something."

He canted his head at her. She was watching him with a strange expression, as if she were seeing things that weren't really there, as if . . .

Back on the ferry! He'd said he loved her. Had gasped out that foolish declaration as if it were truth. But that's when he'd been lulled into thinking they would both die and she'd have no chance to bludgeon him to death with his own idiotic words.

How was he to know he'd be unlucky enough to live through such an experience? What kind of God would allow that?

"Rachel," he said, drawing back a scant few inches and preparing to deny everything, to conjure up his best lies and stand behind them until death. "You were scared out of your wits back there. I doubt if you remember much."

"There's a shelter not far from here," she murmured.

He wouldn't have been more surprised if she'd said she'd left her winged mount tied to the sun. "What?"

She shook her head. "I . . . remember it."

"You've been here before?" he asked dubiously.

"Nay." Her tone was wrought with uncertainty.

Reality dawned on him. He scoffed softly. "If you're about to conjure up a castle, you'd best have at it. Otherwise, you can save your witchy act for the peasants."

She snapped from her trance, exhaled shakily, and managed a glare all in one quick motion.

"Were I able to conjure up anything, I'd design a gag," she said, and turning away from him, strode quickly into the woods.

In less than a heartbeat she was out of sight.

Taking a deep breath, Liam limped after her.

The wind howled around them like spirits, cutting wickedly through the trees and driving the cold straight to Liam's bones. Rain slanted through the leaves and stung his face with biting intensity.

It seemed like they walked through hell and back, though Liam knew the farther they got from the water the safer they'd be. The ground became steep and rocky. The trees thinned out, granting them even less shelter. Liam's leg throbbed like the beat of a drum, but he'd be damned before he asked her to stop.

He was nearly ready to reverse that decision, when he bumped into her back.

"There." She breathed the word like a prayer.

"What?" he asked, but she didn't answer. Instead, she bent beneath a dripping branch and moved toward a wall of stone that was directly in front of them.

Liam glanced behind him. He was not such a fool to believe that the darkness, their heart-stopping rush down the falls, or their retreat would hide them from the powers that hunted them. Despite what Rachel believed or refused to believe, her life had been in dire peril. He knew that. Felt it in his soul. Of course, their present situation wasn't exactly a day at the fair, either.

"Find that castle?" he asked, facing forward. But he realized suddenly that she was gone, nowhere to be seen, with the black face of the rock stretching off in both directions. "Rachel?" Despite every jaded instinct in him, he couldn't arrest the panic that flashed through him. Plunging forward, he reached out toward the cliff.

His hand met nothing but air. He stumbled forward over jagged rocks, jarring his wounded leg and nearly falling flat on his face in the absolute darkness.

"Rachel!" he said, staggering to a halt.

"A cave," she whispered.

That much was apparent. But he wanted to know how she'd found it. No he didn't, he told himself sternly. He'd made a vow long ago not to fall into her spider's trap. Still, the idea that they'd walked for more than an hour through the darkness only to come to this place in the heart of the stone was a bit too eerie to disregard without some effort.

"Someone told you of this place?" he asked hopefully.

"N-Nay," she stuttered slightly, and he wondered suddenly if it was from the cold or if she felt the same eerie sensations he did. Perhaps it was absolute luck that had brought them safely out of the elements and she was just as surprised as he.

"I think we can chance a fire here," he said, turning his mind aside.

"Have you a flint and steel?"

"Nay, my sporran is gone."

"That wee bonny thing?"

"It served its purpose," he said distractedly. His leg throbbed and his head was beginning to pound. But just at that moment his fingers brushed against something beneath his cape.

A glimmer of hope surged through him.

"What is it?" Her voice came from close beside him.

"The husband's purse," he said, feeling a splash of satisfaction as he drew it forward on his belt.

"You stole it."

It was really quite amazing, he thought, how, despite everything, she managed to sound offended.

"Aye, I did," he said, "and quite artfully."

His fingers were stiff and numb, but he finally managed to untie the knot. Even then, it took him a moment to wrench the thing open. Kneeling on

the unyielding floor of the cave, he spilled the contents noisily onto the rock and tried to distinguish
the contents by feel alone.

"Is there a steel?"

"Nay. Just money." Under other circumstances,
his dismissive statement about something as wondrous as money may well have been amusing. It
was somehow disconcerting to think he might be
losing his sense of humor, or his sense of values.

"Mayhap we could find a s-stone," she stuttered,
"and strike it against a coin."

She'd always been clever. He rose rustily to his
feet and grabbed her arm to turn her in an arbitrary
direction. "You look over there. I'll try the opposite
side."

They moved apart, walking slowly, for it was impossible to tell when they would run into a wall,
or a wildcat, or anything else that might be here in
the dark interior of this musty place.

"And kindling," she said.

"Aye," he agreed.

She cried out suddenly. He spun toward her, the
movement nearly spilling him to the rocky floor.

"What is it?"

"My toes found a rock."

He chuckled. Ahh. So his sense of humor was
restored. Twas good to know. Or mayhap fatigue
and hypothermia were contriving against his better
sense. "You always had smart feet."

She stumbled toward him, handed him the stone,
then turned away in search of kindling. He did the
same, but in a few minutes she returned to shakily
deposit a small pile of indistinguishable something
on the floor in front of him.

Squatting, he gripped a coin in ungainly fingers
and struck it against the stone. It felt rather like

trying to remove a sliver with a pair of turnips.

Nevertheless, Rachel hurried away, searching again. Liam struck, hit his fingers on the rock, swore, and tried again. A spark streaked from the stone, but extinguished before it hit their precious pile of kindling.

Time moved on, punctuated by the keeling of the wind outside and their own chattering teeth.

Something cracked behind him. Liam jumped, nearly dropping his stone. "Rachel!"

"Tis me," she rasped, breathing hard.

"What the devil are you doing?"

"Scaring you witless, apparently."

"What have you got?"

"Start the fire and you'll find out."

Something cracked near at hand, and he could only assume she'd found a tree limb.

He set to striking again, rhythmically now, forcing his fingers to do his bidding again and again until finally another spark flashed from the stone. It lit precariously onto the tinder. Liam leaned forward, blowing frantically . . . and blew the tiny flame into nothingness.

"Sweet Mary," Rachel rasped, and for a moment Liam wondered if he heard tears in her voice. She hunkered down beside him. Their arms brushed. He felt her shiver against him. "You strike, I'll nurture the flame. Hurry."

Liam fell stiffly to his job again. An eternity later another spark streaked in the darkness. The fragile flame soared into the kindling.

Liam held his breath. Rachel leaned over the spark and blew.

"Carefully! Carefully!" Liam chattered, but she didn't respond.

Hands cupped around the tiny pile of twigs and

feathers, she blew again. The tiny spark flared. Dropping his tools, Liam snatched up a dry stalk of something and fed it to the infant flame. It ate into the chaff.

"More! More kindling!" Rachel rasped.

Liam jolted to his feet and rushed away to search the walls, the floor, the ceiling only a few inches above his head.

"Here!" A short time later he knelt before her, bearing gifts.

"Bless you," she breathed, and snatching up a dried bird's nest, carefully fed it to the flame.

It crackled greedily, the size of his fist now, and Liam was nearly overpowered by an aching desire to bend over it, to absorb its timid heat. But by its glow, he could see Rachel's face. It was as pale as death, and her lips were nearly the color of her eyes, an eerie mixture of blue and purple.

Straightening with a jolt, he hurried off to scour the cave again.

It took an eternity to conjure up a real fire, but finally after breathless care and muscle-numbing worry, they nursed it into the world, feeding it scraps and twigs until it was ready for small branches.

"We did it!" Rachel stared into the flame, her narrow hands spread to catch its warmth.

"Aye." He was crouched on the opposite side. "'Tis a good thing you have such clever feet."

She glanced up.

"They found the rock," he explained.

Her face had gained a tiny bit of color, he noticed, and the corners of her lips twitched ever so slightly. They had regained some of their usual raspberry hue, but not nearly enough.

"And 'tis a good thing you're immoral," she said.

"Or we would have no coins with which to strike a fire."

Her lips tilted up more dramatically. She was near exhaustion, he told himself. Near exhaustion and flirting with hysteria, but still, her expression conjured up memories of a time when there had been peace between them. A time when she had been young and trusting. Before . . . Well, before many things, and he wasn't going to think about it. There were more important matters to consider. Survival, for instance.

"We'd best get out of these clothes." He knew better than to look at her when he said it, but he couldn't help himself.

Her eyes looked only slightly larger than their precious fire when she glanced up, her body as stiff as death.

"God's balls, Rachel, I'm not about to throw myself upon you. But I wouldn't care to explain your demise to your laird and father when you die of the ague. After all, you—

"What are you doing?" he asked, jerking to his feet when her fingers brushed his neck.

"Removing your clothes," she said, rising with him.

"What?"

She reached for the ties that bound his tattered cape to his neck.

He moved his lips, trying to speak.

"We were safe enough whilst we kept walking," she said. "The movement kept us warm. But we cannot walk forever." The ties gave way beneath her icy fingers. The cape fell heavily to the floor. "There's no time to waste now, for our fire may not last long."

Panic would have well described his state of

mind. A panic that nearly dulled the emotions he had felt during the fall down the river. "Shouldn't we . . ."

"We must hurry. We'll hang your clothes over the tree limb near the fire, then search for other wood."

He moved his lips wordlessly again, but her fingers were already on the laces of his tunic. One sleeve had been ripped off and the other severed at the cuff.

"I can . . ." he began, but she brusquely pushed his hands away.

The ties came open in a moment. She reached for the hem, tugged it upward, and pulled it over his head. Goosebumps followed its exit. Liam stared at her.

"The bandage is doing you no good," she said.

Looking down, he saw that her handiwork of yesterday was little more than shreds hanging from his shoulder.

She removed it quickly.

"Here. Move closer to the fire. Rub your hands together." She took them between her own and rubbed brusquely. "It'll help you . . ."

Her gaze snagged on his. Their breath stopped in unison. So she had finally realized the erotica of this moment, he thought. She'd finally seen that the bodice of her gown had been mangled and that her breasts, pale and magical as moonlight, swelled into view like ripe, forbidden fruit.

So she would finally find her good sense and draw away.

He forced his gaze to her face and watched her lips move. Although he knew she spoke words of caution, he could not quite distinguish them.

"What?" he rasped finally.

"You must remove your plaid," she said quickly.

Liam's jaw dropped. If he had had to guess what she was about to say, that would have been at the bottom of the list, although in his dreams . . . He dashed the thoughts aside with the hard image of her father's claymore. It was a huge weapon, longer than Liam was tall and wielded by a man who was notably attached to his only daughter.

"I'm really quite warm now," he managed pitifully.

But she shook her head. "We've no time to waste, Liam," she said, and skimmed her gaze down his body as if he were no more interesting than an overcooked onion. Less actually, since an onion was, at least, edible. "You'll dry more quickly without your clothes. And it'll give me a chance to see to your wounds."

And to see other stuff, stuff that, despite everything—her haughty demeanor, their mutual dislike for each other, these horrible circumstances—refused to stay were he had put it. Stuff, that, ever since he'd met her years ago, had ached at the sight of her, the scent of her, the mention of her.

"I'm fine," he said.

She reached for the belt that held his plaid in place. "You must not—"

"Rachel!" He caught her arms in a hard grip. "I'm fine."

Their gazes caught again. She blinked, her amethyst eyes as wide as a promise.

"I need you, Liam," she whispered.

He was dreaming again, had slipped into unconsciousness, he thought. But in a moment, she continued.

"I have no time to waste. On the morrow I must be traveling. I must not fail! No matter if we cannot find my guards or our horses or our supplies. Somehow I must see my way through. But I cannot do it alone. I need your help."

He blinked, trying to catch up to her thoughts and lose his foolish dreams. "With what?" he rasped.

"Please," she pleaded. "I need you healthy and hale. I must see to your wounds. Let me take off your clothes."

There were probably any number of things a man could say in this position, Liam thought. He could refuse to comply unless she told him why she was so desperate to get to her fiancé. He could insist that she take off her clothes first. He could refuse to take them off at all unless she gave herself to him.

That last one was particularly interesting, but made his heart do funny, twisty things in his chest.

Still, Liam did none of those things. Instead, he swallowed once and nodded.

She exhaled softly as if she'd been holding her breath, and then her hands moved again. He found he couldn't look. Instead, he stood like a statue, staring straight ahead, his hands balled into fists at his sides.

The belt proved to be tricky, the leather thick and difficult. She worked at it for a moment, then dropped to her knees.

Liam tightened his jaw and concentrated on thoughts of her father. He was a big man. Big! And powerful—not just physically but politically. Twould be no great feat for him to see Liam eviscerated, decapitated, and emasculated.

Rachel leaned slightly closer. He felt her breath against the tense planes of his abdomen, felt her fingers brush his skin. That single, simple touch struck a fire where no fire should be lit. He opened his hand to reach for her.

Her mother! Lady Fiona's face flashed into Liam's mind. He yanked his hand back. Fiona was a healer, gentle, loving. Never for a moment had she dismissed him as a thieving bastard. Never for a moment had she treated him as less than an equal. Surely he owed her something for that.

He felt his belt ease open. Despite his certainty that it could not happen, sweat popped out on his forehead. Rachel's hands were gentle as she unwrapped his plaid. His breathing escalated. His hands shook.

He forced the thought of Shona in his mind. Shona, Rachel's cousin. Shona would never forgive him if he took advantage of this moment. She trusted him, maybe even loved him.

He calmed his breathing with an effort and tightened his hands into fists.

Rachel reached around him, her cheek nearly touching his crotch as she unwrapped the great length of his sodden plaid.

Liam held his breath, waiting and trying to pretend he was a eunuch. It didn't work. Because eunuchs didn't get erections. Erections that ached and throbbed and longed for the one haughty, witchy woman who had tormented him for—

Sara! Rachel's other cousin. He loved Sara like a sister. She was as sweet as a lambkin, as gentle as a kitten, and she'd never, never understand if he lost his battle to lust and . . .

Rachel tugged again. The last layer of plaid slipped downward. His penis, thick and eager and turgid, sprang upward like a floating log.

For a moment, he felt her pause, but he dared not glance down. An eternity inched along, and finally he felt her move again. He tried to remember to breathe, and managed to step out when he felt his plaid brush his feet.

Silence filled the cave. Liam stared straight forward, his jaw set, his will as hard as other parts.

The fire crackled. Eternity stretched before them. He felt her hands on his thigh near his wound. Her touch sparked off a million deadly desires, making his desire tighten so that it moved of its own accord.

He tried to think, to hold steady, to pretend she was old and ugly, or at least fat and crotchety. Gripping his hands harder at his sides, he sent off a prayer to a God who must surely be surprised at this correspondence at such a late date.

Liam cleared his throat, clenched his jaw, and tried for normalcy. She was a healer, a healer, nothing more. "How does it look?" he asked, his tone raspy.

Silence filled the cave. Moments slipped away, then, "It . . . it looks good," she murmured.

Chapter 5

"Well, it hurts like hell!" Liam blurted.

It hurt? Rachel stared at it. True, she was a healer, and therefore, no stranger to the human body. But *his* body! Despite the imaginings of her youth, she'd never thought Liam would be so . . . Well, to be frank, he reminded her of Aunt Flanna's prized stallions. The thought made her face burn, and yet she found she lacked the decency to turn away. In fact, she longed to touch it, to skim her finger along the length of it, to feel it dance beneath her fingers. What made it move so and why did it hurt?

"I hit it on a rock in the river." His tone was tense. "Will it have to be stitched?"

"Stitched?" she murmured, horrified. "Oh!" Reality dawned on her in a rush of embarrassment. "Your leg!"

He jerked his gaze down just as she lifted hers up.

"What the devil did you think I was talking about?"

"Your . . ." What were the chances that the floor would swallow her up? Probably not good. Dear God! "Your leg," she said, but her tone was too high-pitched. She cleared her throat. "Of course."

"God's balls!" he murmured through clenched teeth.

"I was not!" She snapped to her feet as fluttery as a nesting wren. "They are not, I wasn't staring, it won't need to be stitched," she sputtered, her words jumbled.

They gaped at each other. She snapped her mouth shut and twisted her hands together. "I . . ." What? Lusted after him despite everything? Had for over a decade, like some hare-brained wench who refused to learn. "I have no needle."

"Oh." He breathed out the word, but he didn't seem to be thinking about his wounded leg at all. His eyes were intense. His hair had come loose of its queue and spread dark as midnight across his shoulders. They were the shoulders of a juggler, sculpted, strong, with muscles that danced just beneath the tan satin surface of his skin.

"It should heal well on its own," she managed.

"Oh."

"If I had my potions, I'd rub some on it so "— she blinked, cleared her mind of a thousand suffocating thoughts and tried again—"twould reduce the swelling."

"I have my doubts."

"What?"

He squeezed his eyes closed. She watched a muscle dance in his jaw. "I'll get you back to your guards. You'll replenish your supplies."

The fire crackled.

"That's not what you said," she murmured.

"Forget what I said. Don't listen to what I say." He popped his eyes open. "Why do you still have your clothes on?"

"I—" She clutched her bodice together, though

in truth it was quite late to act modest. After all, she'd just been staring at the more outstanding parts of his anatomy from quite close proximity. Certain details were, in fact, indelibly etched in her memory. Hot blood flushed her face. "I'm warm now."

His laugh could definitely be called maniacal. "Take your damn clothes off!" he growled.

"Really, I—"

"Take them off," he ordered, and stepped forward.

"Very well." She retreated a rapid pace. He was right, of course. She was on a mission. She couldn't afford the luxury of modesty. "Just . . . turn your back."

He raised his brows. The corners of his satyr's mouth twitched slightly. "I think not."

She scowled. Funny little tongues of flame were licking her insides, sending tingling tendrils of heat curling down from the pit of her stomach to places best left unstimulated. "Fine then," she said and twisting her arms behind her, unfastened the tiny wooden buttons that held her tattered gown in place. He was just a man, she told herself. She'd seen a hundred just like him, had healed a hundred just like him. So what if she had lusted after him since girlhood. Lust was a simple thing, easily thwarted.

The slick wooden buttons gave way slowly. She slipped the gown off her shoulders and lowered by cautious degrees. Dragonheart felt heavy and warm between her breasts, and though she tried, she couldn't quite take her gaze from Liam's.

His eyes shone dark as fire-lit ebony in the dancing light of the flame, and not for a moment did they waver.

She slipped the dress lower. Her nipples, puckered, hard, and aching, scraped out of bondage.

Liam muttered something indistinguishable. But before she could ask what he'd said, he'd jerked away. She stared befuddled at his back, the solid, bunched muscles of his arms, the mounded hillocks of his buttocks, the sculpted strength of his thighs. He was a marvel, really, tightly packed muscle, dusky skin, magic fingers. With some effort, she remembered to breathe.

Muttering again.

"What?" she asked, yanking her gaze upward.

"Are you staring at me?" he asked, not turning toward her.

"Nay!" Too squeaky. "Nay." And for some reason unknown to her, she giggled.

He swung jerkily about. "What are you laughing at?"

"Laughing? I wasn't . . . I didn't . . ." Truly, she wasn't the giggling type. Normally. But she felt as if her insides had been possessed by a demon. A funny little demon with a fiendish sense of humor.

"This is not amusing," he said, every lean muscle tight as a drum and sparks flying from his eyes.

She tried not to grin, but . . .

"This is *not* amusing!" he repeated and strode toward her.

She shook her head and tried to retreat, but he was already upon her, curling his hand behind her neck and jerking her to him. His lips crashed against hers, his kiss as fierce as the storm outside.

Rachel's fingers managed to hold on to her gown for a fraction of a second, and then they gave way. Her clothing fell in a wet heap. Her arms wound about him of their own accord, and she answered his passion with a flaring, long-suppressed heat of her own, pressing up against him with all her might.

His tongue probed her lips, and she opened for him. His palm pressed down her back. She moaned and arched closer as he squeezed her buttocks.

Against her belly, his erection pulsed with turgid life. She pressed against it, feeling its heat, its intensity, its longing.

His kisses burned lower, searing her throat, her shoulder, the upper portions of her breasts, and suddenly they were on the ground. He was between her thighs and pulsing with passion. And it all felt right, like a feast too long delayed.

She arched against him, living a hundred steamy dreams all at once, feeling the straining muscles of his back against her palm, the hard slope of his chest against her nipples. "Liam," she whispered.

But suddenly he went still.

She opened her eyes. Their gazes met only inches apart, his eyes dark and wild.

"Rachel!" he rasped. His tone registered surprise, as if he were shocked that it was she. As if *mortified* that it was she.

And then he was scrambling raggedly to his feet.

"Rachel! I . . ." He was breathing hard, as was she. She raised herself to her elbows and stared at him. "I'm sorry," he rasped.

"Are you?"

"Aye. Aye." His hand was shaking when he dragged it through his wet hair. "'Tis the beast in me."

She lowered her gaze for a fraction of a second. The beast was pulsing against the rippled expanse of his abdomen. "Is that what you call it?"

"Rachel!" His jaw dropped. He stood absolutely still, scandalized to immobility.

She tried to be ashamed, but found she couldn't quite manage it, for it had felt right. As if she had seen it all in a dream. And indeed, in a way she had, for only hours before, standing at the river's edge, she had seen this very cave in her mind, had seen them naked in the firelight, their bodies fused and their minds melded.

"What has come over you?" he asked.

She rose slowly to her feet, not shifting her gaze from his. "Mayhap tis the beastie in *me*."

He shook his head, his eyes wild, his body tense. "There is no beast in you. There is none."

"How would you know what is in me, Liam?" she asked. Trying to understand his tortured tone, she reached for him.

"What would your father say? What would—" He sputtered to a halt and stepped back out of her reach. She noticed, although with some embarrassment, that his penis, hard and erect and surprisingly large, was pressed up tight against his belly. "What are you thinking?"

"What are *you* thinking?" she murmured, mesmerized.

"Me? Me! I'm a—a bastard!" he sputtered. "Born in the underbelly of Firthport with a sire who . . ." he stopped abruptly, still breathing hard. "But still I . . ." He stared at her, seeming to realize suddenly that her gaze was trained considerably below his eye level. He gasped, and ripped his cape from the ground to cover his nudity.

She managed to raise her gaze to his. "Why did you kiss me, Liam?" she asked softly.

"Me?" He glanced about as if hoping to see someone else languidly residing there, someone to take the blame for his errant display of passion. "I . . ." He licked his lips, then glared at her as if the answer were oh so obvious. "I was but trying to warm you up."

"Truly?"

"Aye." He gave her a short nod. "Your parents have been kind to me. I've no wish to see you . . ." He motioned roughly toward her, then groaned. "Christ!" He seemed to find it hard to breathe for a moment. "I've no wish to see you die of the ague."

"So . . ." She took a slim step nearer as she held his gaze with her own.

He retreated, the cape wrapped sloppily about his waist. The slanted gap in the side revealed one lean hip and a length of leg honed hard by years of travel and performances. "I didn't expect you to—to . . . Good Christmas! Had I known you were so desperate for a man, I would have warned your father long ago to see you married off."

Rachel stopped her advance. Her body cooled. Anger settled into her mind. This was the Liam she had known for so long, the Liam she had vowed to forget. "So you kissed me for naught but my own good?" she asked, pleased that despite everything she could sound quite normal, calm even.

"Aye. Aye, I did," he said.

"Oh." She took one more step forward. Then, heart pounding, she touched his chest. Beneath her fingertips, his muscles jumped to attention. Twas that simple movement that sent shivers of emotion up her arm and into her body. She withstood the sensation. Indeed, she did her best to ignore it, concentrating instead on him, on how his eyelids dropped closed for an instant, how his jaw tightened, making a small knot of muscle dance near his ear. "How very selfless of you, Liam. How wonderfully kind of you to forego your own wants, your own desires for naught but my welfare."

"Aye." The single word was little more than a growl.

"And here I thought..." Reversing her hand, she slid the pads of her nails up the undulated expanse of his abdomen. "I thought mayhap twas your undying devotion for me that made you do it."

His eyes snapped open. "What?"

She smiled at him in cold, aching fury. "Just before the ferry broke apart, you admitted your love for me."

He jerked back a pace. "I did no such thing."

"Oh, aye. You did."

"Twas the roar of the water that confused you."

"I assure you..." She stepped close to him again. "I heard you quite clearly." In fact, it had seemed that his heart had spoken directly to hers and hadn't involved her ears at all, as if the emotion had hummed straight into her soul. But that was when she was certain she was about to die. Minutes later, when the terror dulled, she knew she'd imagined the words. How pathetic that even during such a horrific situation she had been so needy. Would she never learn?

But just now it didn't matter. For she had found a way to torment him.

"So all of these years you have loved me from afar," she said on a breathy whisper. "All these years you have kept yourself from the Highlands because you knew you could not bear to be near me and not have me."

"You're..."—a muscle clenched in his jaw again—"daft. Twas you who acted the randy hound. Mayhap tis you who is enamored with *me*."

She smiled—the pitying expression of the gen-

erous noblewoman—she hoped. "Tis so romantic.
So chivalrous. The poor wandering performer loving a lady from afar." She sighed. Her gut clenched
with anger. "When I marry this shall make the perfect ballad. Bards shall—"

"Marry! Marry! How can you speak of marriage
when you . . ." He motioned wildly toward the
ground upon which they had rolled only minutes
before. "When you feel for me what you do?"

She smiled at him with the careful benevolence
of an angel. The Lady Saint. Twas a nomenclature
that had kept her apart from the general populace
for years. "When I feel what *I* do. Twas *you* who
said you loved *me*, Liam."

"Any bloody bastard could tell you that. It hardly means you should—"

"So you admit it, then?"

"What?"

"You admit that you said you love me?"

He tried to form a word. It didn't come. She
forced a laugh and hoped it sounded frivolous.

"You are right, I suppose. I should not succumb
to every lad who whispers sweet nothings."

"Every . . ."

"But they always seem so earnest and so besot-
ted."

"Always?"

"And I will be wed soon." She shrugged. "Tis
my last chance to sample the fare."

"Sample the fare!" He grabbed her arms, his
hands like talons. "Are you saying others have
seen you like this? That you have given yourself
to—" He sputtered to a halt, breathing hard.
"Nay." His eyes narrowed as he stared at her.
"You are not that sort."

"Not what sort?" she whispered innocently.

He stared at her. A tremor passed through him, shaking her with its violence. "Bloody hell, Rachel! Cover yourself," he ordered. But there was nothing to cover herself with. So he whipped the cape from about his own hips and swirled it around her back.

The frigid wind from the garment caused goose bumps to rise on her arms and her nipples to pucker like budding roses. But she paid them no mind.

Liam, however, seemed momentarily transfixed, before he plucked the cape together, hiding her nipples and her breasts and Dragonheart all in one fell swoop.

"What sort of woman am I not?" she asked again. "The sort like the woman in the village?"

He remained silent for a moment, watching her face from inches away.

"That's right," he said. "You're not that sort atall."

Nay. Not the sort who would truly attract him. Oh, yes, he had lost his head for a moment. Maybe it was the horror of being so close to death that had made him think that even *she* would be preferable to being alone. He had changed his mind quickly enough.

Twas not so for her. Never had she felt her own needs with such consuming ferocity. Always, in the past, she had worried for the needs of others, her clan, her family, her country. Twas how she was raised to be.

But there was no one here to judge her actions, to weigh her against her mother's perfection or her cousins' beauty or her father's courage. To judge her as they had judged her from birth. She had only her own life to care for now.

There was a certain freedom in that. Enough

freedom so that she could let the cape fall open as she stepped toward the fire. A glimpse of leg showed, a curve of breast. She reached her hands toward the warmth of the flame.

"I think it's time you explained why you attacked my guard, Liam."

He had snatched his tunic from the floor and wrapped it about his bare hips. "I did not attack your guards," he said, and offered no more for a moment.

"Truly? He certainly looked like Davin to me."

Liam turned his dark gaze on her and snorted. "And there are those who say you have the gift."

"I know my guards, Liam. They saw me safely from London, and they saw me safely aboard the ferry."

"You're thinking with your head, Rachel."

"Some of us do," she said, skimming her gaze to his nether regions and back.

He gritted his teeth, "Think with your soul!" he growled. "Did you not feel the evil?"

Goose bumps again, spreading beneath the cape. But they were not goose bumps from the cold now, but from the emotions his words conjured up. For a moment, she almost believed him. But the truth was, he had told a thousand wild stories in the past. And in the past she had believed him and regretted it.

"So tell me, Liam, whose angry husband is after you this time?"

She watched his jaw clench. "Tis no angry husband."

"Truly? Who then?"

He stared at her for one taut moment, then finally shrugged. Mayhap he tried to make the expression look casual, but she could see the tension in the set of his bare shoulders. "Tis no one to concern yourself with, your ladyship. Just a crazed wizard who lusts for immortality and my head on a spit."

She laughed, though the goose bumps were so crisp now that they hurt. "A wizard?"

"Not just *a* wizard." His gaze was level and deadly serious. "*The* wizard."

The night went silent.

Rachel longed to believe she didn't know who he meant. But there was no hope of that. Fear crept with chilly fingers up her spine. "Warwick is dead," she whispered.

Liam's jaw clenched. "Not dead enough," he countered.

Chapter 6

⌒◯⌒

Liam sat in silent thought, watching Rachel. Despite everything, the still damp clothes she'd insisted on wearing, the terror of their position, the rock-hard floor of the cave, she slept.

As for himself, he sat awake and stared at her.

Ragged uncertainties chased around and around in his head. Maybe he was wrong. Maybe he was insane. After all, what Rachel said was true; Warwick was dead.

Warwick, the ancient wizard who had nearly destroyed Sara in his quest to take Dragonheart from her. Warwick, who had almost killed Shona when she had worn the amulet. Warwick, who had plunged into a blazing inferno in an attempt to retrieve the dragon.

Liam himself had seen the wizard disappear into the fire. Liam himself had made certain Warwick had not come out.

And yet . . .

He couldn't have been mistaken about the feelings that had overwhelmed him on the ferry. He'd felt the dark wizard's evil aura enough times to distinguish it. Those past experiences had felt just as it had on the river.

All had seemed well. But suddenly it had been as if a dark cloud was blown from his mind, and he had recognized the evil, just as he had recognized the source. It had emanated from Davin—one of Warwick's men.

Terror had caught Liam in a grip of steel. For one terrified instant, he had wanted nothing more than to throw himself from the ferry and die rather than fall into Warwick's hands. But then he had glanced at Rachel . . .

Liam scooped his fingers through his hair in aching frustration. Maybe he *should* have leapt from the boat. He was no warrior. Hardly that. He was a thief, a magician, an acrobat. Not someone to impress the likes of her.

A fat lot of good he'd done her thus far. She'd nearly been killed. Indeed, twas beyond miraculous that they'd survived the falls.

And now she thought him insane. Glancing at her sleeping form, he snorted.

He wasn't the one who was insane. She was. What the hell had she been thinking—kissing him like that? She was . . .

His hands began to sweat. He curled them into fists and tried to breathe normally. She was not for him. She was not, and she knew it.

True, long ago in her innocence, she hadn't understood the ways of the world, had not known that a wealthy laird's beloved daughter could never belong to a bastard.

Liam remembered that now. Remembered how she had come to him in naught but her night rail, her gossamer hair loose, her eyes uncertain. Aye, he remembered it all, her scent, her shyness, her mind-numbing declaration of love.

But he had never been afforded the luxury of

naivete. He knew then the consequences of touching a laird's daughter just as he did now. Still, even knowing the consequences, only a bastard or a hero could have turned her away, and he was no hero.

Aye. She had been innocent and sweet once. But no more. Now she was . . .

What? What was she? She'd all but begged him to take her. Rachel, the Lady Saint! Why would she do that unless she cared for him. Maybe—

But no. He was acting the fool. She'd implied that she'd offered herself to others. Indeed, she'd implied more than that.

Liam tightened his fists and struggled for control. But it was no use. He was exhausted. Exhausted from terror, and travel, and years without her.

God yes, he wanted her in his bed. Had always wanted that. And why would he not? She was everything he could never have—breeding, refinement, goodness. But he had controlled himself. And why? Certainly not because she deserved someone better.

Nay, twas not that at all. Twas simply because he had no wish to die at the hands of her outraged father. True, Laird Leith had been kind to him in the past, but there was a great chasm of difference between the flicker of pity he felt for a homeless bastard and the enduring love he felt for his only daughter. If Leith thought an Irish bastard had compromised his lass in any way, the laird would have that Irishman leisurely dismembered and fed to the crows. Of that much Liam was certain.

Still, she had seemed, for a moment, to want him.

But apparently she had wanted others. Had taken them to her bed. Had let them touch her satin skin and . . . The thoughts stormed through Liam's system like potent wine. He jerked himself to his feet, prepared to shake her awake, to interrogate her. But once he squatted beside her, he stopped all movement.

She was lying on her side, facing the door of the cave. Dawn was just breaking in the world outside, and the first glimmer of morn shone on her.

Her gown was torn and filthy. Her hair, usually pulled up and hidden beneath some ornate coif, lay dark as silt, tangled and twisted behind her. Her feet were bare and the back of one hand had been scraped raw. The great lady brought low, he told himself. But even as he thought it, his gaze skimmed her alabaster skin, her downy lashes, her devilish raspberry lips, slightly parted as she breathed between them. And suddenly he knew that nothing would bring her to his level.

No matter what she had done, no matter if she had lain with a hundred men, she was still not for the likes of him.

Scowling, he prepared to rise, but in that moment, she awoke.

"Where..." She propped herself on an elbow without a second's notice, her eyes as wide and eerie as Loch Ness. Then she drew a shuddering breath and let her gaze skim the narrow walls of their shelter. "I remember."

He watched her, watched the fear, the fortitude, and suddenly he was tempted almost beyond control to take her into his arms and promise her all would be well.

He squelched those foolish emotions with tight resolve and rose to his feet. He would not play the fool for her again. He would be clever, reserved, just as she was.

"There'll be no breakfast in bed this morn, lass."

She rose slowly to her feet. "You mean to say you've failed to secure me a meal?"

It was that haughty tone that always made the hair on the back of his neck rise. Never mind that the curve of her sulky bottom lip drew him in like a trout on a hook. "I'm not your manservant," he reminded her.

"I've noticed," she said, and turned away.

"Not everyone can be as well-endowed as I."

There was absolute silence for a moment. So he had shocked her. Good.

"Actually," she said, her tone cool as morning dew, "my manservant is hung like a horse. But he's not so rude."

"You've seen him naked?" Liam rasped.

She didn't turn toward him.

He strode across the cave, seized her arm, and swung her toward him. "You've seen him?" he growled. But he realized suddenly that her face was flushed with a color that had nothing to do with the rising sun. Flushed with the embarrassment of innocence.

He calmed himself with an effort.

"You've not been with a man," he said softly.

She didn't respond.

"Admit it, Rachel."

"'Tis not true," she said, but her face was even brighter.

He made no effort to stop his laughter.

She raised her chin in that way he remembered from a hundred times before. "I would condemn you for your rudeness, Liam," she said stiffly. "But I suppose 'tis caused by naught but your unrequited love for me."

He prepared to snarl back a rejoinder, but she was already sweeping past him, the hem of her gown caught in one hand as if she were a princess on her way to an audience with the king.

"Come along," she said. "I've no time to wait for you." But when she stepped into the rain-drenched woods, she stopped. He watched her turn in the direction of the river.

Liam tightened his fists, ready to beg her not to return to her guards, but in a moment, she turned and strode off along the face of the cliff.

"Stop," Liam said, and reached for Rachel's arm.

"What is it?" She turned toward him. Her face was taut with fatigue and a pink line marred her cheek where a thorn had scratched her, but her expression looked no less haughty than it had three hours before.

"You cannot walk forever like this. Sit down."

"I've no time to spare."

"Sit down," he repeated. "I'll fashion you some shoes."

"I've been barefoot before," she said, but he'd had too many hours to think of her with other men to leave him with any patience. Thumping her on the shoulder, he knocked her onto the log behind her.

She sat with a muffled groan, and he wondered if she were, perhaps, as achy and tired as he. Where the hell was she going in such a hurry?

But asking her would do little good. He knew her well enough to realize that.

"So you finally believe me," he said, kneeling down to lift one narrow foot onto his knee. It was small and fragile, the arch as delicate as a sparrow's wing.

"I do not believe you," she countered, glaring at his hands.

"You don't even know what I'm talking about." He tried to work up some righteous anger. After all, he had saved her life. But even her ankle distracted him. It was gently curved and impossibly narrow, sweeping up to the devilishly soft curve of her calf.

"It matters little," she said. "I disbelieve *everything* you say."

He wrenched his gaze from her mesmerizing leg. "You believe it was the wizard who was waiting at the shore. Else you would be heading back to the river instead of traveling north."

"I've no time to attempt to find my guards," she said, and tried to wrench her foot away.

He snatched it back onto his knee and managed to rip a strip of cloth from her underskirt at the same time.

"What do you think you are doing?" she rasped, realizing a moment too late where his hands had been.

He grinned as he began to wrap the rag about her heel. "You must be eager indeed to see your betrothed, if you cannot even wait for me to bandage your feet."

"What can I say?" she asked flippantly. "The thought of him sets my heart aflutter. I cannot bear to be away from him a moment longer."

"So he is such an exceptional lover?"

She sighed.

Anger ground through Liam, but he stifled it. "Huh!" he spat, dropping her bandaged foot to the ground only to retrieve the other one. "There is no betrothed."

"What are you talking about?" She almost managed to wrench her foot from his grasp.

"You haven't been so frivolous since . . ." He paused. In his mind he remembered once again when she had come to him as a young girl. But even to humiliate her, he had never found the strength to besmirch those memories. "You're not the frivolous sort, Rachel. And so I wonder, where do you rush off to in such a hurry?"

His question was accented by the rending of cloth again. She jumped at the sound, glared at him, but kept her foot on his knee.

"It may be I don't think of the sanctity of marriage as a frivolous thing, Liam," she said. "Indeed, I *am* to be married. And I go to him even now."

"Maybe. If he's dying."

"What does that mean?"

"Not since you were old enough to tend a wound did you rush about like this for any reason other than someone's failing health."

"Little you know, Liam," she said. "It so happens I've long wanted babes of mine own. And despite my . . . well . . ." She paused and somehow managed to give him a prim look despite her disheveled appearance. "Despite my vast experience with men, I've decided to marry before creating a child."

"How moral of you."

"Aye. Laird Dunlock thought so."

"I've no doubt." He dropped her foot to the ground.

She tipped her ankle with a scowl. "Where did you learn to do that?"

"I was born a bastard," he reminded her. "Shoes don't come with the title. Now tell me where you're bound?"

"I already said." She tried to rise to her feet, but he still held her ankle. Tilting her slightly off balance, he spilled her back onto the log.

"Hear me well, Rachel. We've some rather nasty

men after us. And I, for one, would like to know why."

"What men?" she snapped, waving her arm to the side. "I see none."

"They come," he assured.

"They?"

"You know who?"

"Warwick?" she scoffed.

"Don't say his name!" Liam hissed, panic filling him.

She laughed. Actually laughed. "So you really do believe he's still alive."

"Did you think I was jesting?"

"Liam! Tis madness. He cannot possibly have survived the fire at Kirkwood Castle. But if he did—why would he wish me harm? He's a nobleman. A—"

"Aye! He was once a nobleman!" Liam said. "Indeed, he was once wealthy, an advisor of kings. And thus you would trust him I suppose? Because he is one of your own?"

"He is dead."

"He is not. He is after you, and I wish to know why. Why this hurry, Rachel? Where are you bound?"

Her expression was solemn. "Do you suppose..." Her hand crept to Dragonheart. "Are they after the amulet."

Terror smote Liam. Twas the answer he'd considered a hundred times since she'd saved his hide. The only answer that seemed logical. But that was impossible. He shook his head. "He couldn't already know you have it. He couldn't. Could he?"

Their gazes met in silent fear.

But Rachel finally laughed, breaking the spell as she jerked to her feet. "You've been telling wild tales so long that you finally believe them yourself, Liam. I am bound to see my betrothed. Nothing else."

"Aye," he said, rising beside her. "And I am the King of Kalmar."

It was nearly dark when Rachel stopped abruptly ahead of Liam.

"What is it?" he hissed.

"Did you hear something?"

He shook his head but remained silent for a time, listening. Then, "Hoofbeats."

Her nod was quick, her expression hopeful, but he dared not be so optimistic. Instead he held up a hand for silence, then quick as his aching body could manage, he slipped through the woods toward the sound of the horses.

It wasn't long before they came to a road.

She turned to him, her expression shocked. "There's been a road here all the while?"

"I can only assume it hasn't moved on your account."

"Then why the devil did you not tell me—"

He shushed her. "Let me do the talking."

"What?"

He nodded toward the distance. Nearly a quarter mile away a white cob was pulling a covered dray toward them. Behind the wagon, two men rode on horseback. "You stay hidden."

"Why?" Despite everything, the wearing miles, the mud that sucked at their feet, the torn bodice she'd covered with a scrap from her hem, she managed to sound haughty.

He bristled. "Maybe with your new-found low morals, you think yourself quite presentable, but I beg to differ."

"I suppose you believe yourself—"

"Just—" He held up a hand in grinding frustration. "Just let me do the talking," he hissed, and she finally acquiesced and settled into the brush.

Liam immediately stepped onto the road and held up a hand in friendly greeting. There was little point in waiting until the dray was upon him and scaring the poor driver to death.

"Whoa, Siegmund," called the man who held the reins. Twas obvious by both his voice and his garb that he was Italian, a narrow fellow of middle age dressed in dark hose and a red, slashed doublet. Beside him sat an older man with a gray, short-cropped beard. He had one hand thrust rather suspiciously beneath his doublet.

Liam didn't spare a glance for the riders behind, for it was clear by both their bearing and their garb that they were guards of sorts, and therefore beneath the dignity of the character he was just now assuming. Gathering his energy, Liam tried his best smile. But just now even his best smile was a little strained and the men looked wary.

"Is something amiss, lad?" asked the older fellow. His tone was friendly enough, but his hand didn't appear from beneath his jacket.

"Aye," Liam said, assessing the two quickly. They were men of business, these two merchants. The younger fellow had a touch of arrogance about him—a lady's man perhaps. The older chap was no stranger to wealth.

It was an easy enough task to cover his Irish brogue with an English accent, and simpler still to hold his body just so, like a man of means—not too cocky, but not too lowly either. "I've had a spot of trouble and hoped you could help me."

"Trouble?"

"Aye. I am Archibald of Horsham. I was on my

way to Coventry to meet with Lord Windsley when I fell on hard luck."

"Brigands?" asked the man who held the reins.

"Nay. I fear twas my own impatience." He managed a sheepish grin. "Tis said that women and haste most oft make fools of men."

"I suspect twas not a woman this time."

"If it were I would not look so forlorn," Liam said, "for tis far better to be made a fool by a woman than to be made a prince by a man, aye? As it was, I fear I made a fool of myself. I knew the river was too high to cross, but I was in a rush to meet with Windsley. My mount lost his footing on the way across, damned near drowned me."

The older fellow eyed Liam's plaid with narrowed eyes. "You do not speak like a Scot."

"Indeed, I am not. But my hose were torn asunder during my wild ride in the river. Twas purest luck that let me find this bit of woolen. I fear the Scot what lost it may not have been as lucky as I."

"Indeed."

"I suppose I should be glad that I am still alive, and that I've not lost everything. But I do hate to approach Lord Windsley in such shabby attire," Liam said, and reaching under his tattered tunic, pulled out the purloined purse. "Thus, I thought you might be able to help me."

Chapter 7

"**D**amned Italians," Liam said and reached around his bundle of new purchases to hand Rachel half a loaf of round bread.

"Blessed Italians," she corrected, immediately tearing into the dark loaf. "Had they seen my guards on the road?"

"I didn't ask. They charged me a king's ransom for what I have here. I dared not think what they would ask for information." In truth, he *had* been afraid to ask, lest he arouse suspicions. After the eerie incident on the ferry, he vowed to trust no one.

"Had they seen any trouble?"

"Nay. Eat this," he said, handing her a slab of cheese as he took a swig from a bottle of wine. "There's a village ahead."

"Village?"

"Aye. Five or so leagues down the road, they said."

"Then let's make haste," she ordered, but he shook his head.

"Not in those clothes."

"You bought me clothing?"

"Aye," he said, and pulled an array of garments from beneath his arm. "Put these on."

"They had garb for *me*?"

He shrugged. "Call me Liam the lucky. I thought you were in a rush."

She turned away and hustled deeper into the woods.

Liam waited to don his own newly purchased clothing, for he could easily predict the second she would reappear. She didn't disappointment him. He controlled his grin with an effort admirable even for an Irishman.

"I fear your humor is sadly lacking," she said.

"Oh?" Still, he didn't allow himself to grin.

"These are men's clothing. As you are very well aware."

"Oh, that. Aye, I knew."

She stared at him. A lesser man might have called it a glare.

"Why?" It was a single word pronounced with neat diction.

"Think on it, Rachel," he said, taking another swig of wine and finishing off his own half a loaf. "Your life is endangered by a crazed—"

"I've no time to listen to your wild tales."

He raised the bottle, silencing her with the movement. "If you choose not to believe tis the wizard who follows you, tis your right. But you cannot deny there was evil. You have the gift. You must have sensed it."

She looked as if she would like to, but she did not.

"Someone is after you, Rachel," he said, wishing he could afford that grin he had denied before, but finding the mood sadly lacking as he remembered the terror on the ferry. "Someone wishes you ill.

They know who you are. They know how you look. And they know where you are hiding." He let his words fester in silence for a moment. "And you are in a great rush to be away on a mission of your own. A secret mission." He watched her eyes carefully, waiting for her denial. But she said nothing. "You cannot afford to be caught, whether it be the wizard who follows you or some other. Tis your decision, of course, but the daughter Lady Fiona raised would not endanger another because of her own vanity. Fiona's daughter would don the clothes, assume the disguise, and pray for safe-keeping."

Rachel raised her chin slightly and remained silent for a moment, then, "I'll give you this, Liam, you are more manipulative even than I knew."

His grin surfaced now and he gave a shallow bow, holding the bottle upright so that it wouldn't spill. "My thanks."

"I meant every word," she added graciously, and he laughed as she turned back into the woods.

Liam donned his own garments quickly. It was simple clothing, dark hose, a rust-colored belted tunic, and shoes that almost fit. Unexciting, except for the cape. It was a lovely piece, made of forest green cloth that seemed to shift hues when it moved, casting it from green into an indescribable gray. Around the wide hem, pewter spangles had been hooked into the fabric.

Liam swirled the cape around his shoulders, admired the way it flared and settled, tied the dark cord around his neck, and waited.

But apparently, Rachel was not so familiar with men's clothing, for it took her awhile to reappear. Liam couldn't help but smile at the implications of the delay, but when she finally stepped into his line of vision, things didn't seem so amusing.

Her devilish lips were puckered and her brow the same. "Tell me again, Liam, what did you hope to accomplish with this costume?" she asked. But in an instant, her brows rose. "And what, pray tell, are *you* wearing?"

"Tis my new garb," Liam said and skimmed her form. The red doublet with the black tunic that showed through the slashed sleeves had looked quite different on the narrow man who drove the dray. True, it had seemed a bit ostentatious with its tightly cinched waist and ridiculously wide shoulders. And true, he had not seen the black hose that accompanied the garment, but somehow he'd never thought it would make her look like . . . this.

He swallowed hard, skimmed the incredible length of her slim legs and tried not to imagine what soft, delectable treasures the ridiculously large codpiece hid.

"Tis so the villains will not . . . notice you," he said.

She nodded primly, like a lady at a fine ball. But somehow he could not help but imagine how she would have looked moments before with the black tunic barely covering the pale moon of her buttocks, caressing the slim tops of her thighs. It would have been so simple to slip his hand beneath the hem, to feel her satin-soft skin, the bristle of her most private hair. To . . .

"And? Will it work?"

He snapped his wayward thoughts to a shuddering halt and tried to ignore the ache of hard desire in parts no longer hidden by his oversized sporran. "What?" he asked, a bit more breathlessly than he had planned.

"Will the disguise keep me from being noticed?"

Was he drooling? he wondered hopelessly, then, "Of course not!" he said, and threw his arms out in wide relief. "You've not put on the hat yet."

"Oh! There's a hat!"

"Aye," he said, and stepped forward to plop the plumed, wide-rimmed beauty onto her head.

She gritted a smile at him. "Well?"

He shrugged dramatically and wished he were very, very drunk. But he'd already consumed half the bottle and Rachel would need her share. "Did I not know better I myself would think you nothing more than a traveling..."—he searched for words—"entertainer," he ended weakly.

"You truly think so?'

"Aye."

"Then you're a dolt!" she snapped, her long hat feather bobbing. "I couldn't fool a goat in these garments."

"Surely a goat," he said, and despite his own hopeless situation, couldn't help but grin.

Her mouth puckered again. "I'm not wearing them."

"Please." He grabbed her arm, but the contact was too great a temptation, so he dropped his arm and backed away a careful pace. "Please, Rachel. You cannot be seen in that gown you just removed. Tis too dangerous, for you'll surely be noticed."

"And you think I won't be noticed in *this*? I look like a...a..." She gestured a bit frantically toward her own body. "There is no word for what I look like."

Actually there was. But he had no wish to tell her she was beautiful, that she'd be beautiful even if she dressed in rags and shaved her head with a plow shear.

"Well, of course you look strange now. You're not acting the part."

"What part?"

"The part of my assistant."

Her expression didn't change a whit. That wasn't necessarily a good thing.

"Listen, Rachel, I know you're not telling me the truth of your destination. Nevertheless, I am willing to help you reach it. But I cannot magically make you appear there. We need horses, food, and shelter. But most of all we need to be unrecognizable. And we cannot have any of those things without money. Somehow we'll have to obtain some coin. More, much more, than what is in my purse."

She was still staring at him, which was better than a few options he could name.

"I could steal it—"

"I'll not have you compromising my soul," she interrupted.

He tightened his jaw. "If you have any talents worth a bit of coin, now might be the time to share them then, my *lady*." He drawled out the last word as he skimmed her unlikely garb.

"Well, normally I would sell my body," she said, her tone stiff. "But I fear you've taken that option from me with these outlandish garments."

"On the contrary. You might be surprised how many men would be interested in the diversions they'd expect you to offer. Unfortunately, you might not enjoy their attentions as much as you have your lord Dunlock's."

She shrugged. "Who can compare?"

"Why don't you admit that you—"

"As much as I enjoy your yammering at me, I don't have time to waste on it," she interrupted tersely. "Have you a plan or don't you?"

For a moment he was tempted to shake her until she admitted the truth, but he controlled himself.

"Here," he said, snatching a small pouch from the ground. "I've procured a needle and a bit of thread. Do something with those shoes, so they don't fall off your feet."

"I'm no seamstress," she said, taking the pouch.

"You're no lad either," he countered. "But you'd damned well better learn to pretend if you want to see your Lord Dunlock in your present virginal condition."

"I told you—"

"Spare me," he interrupted. "You've fooled half of Scotland into believing you're a living saint, I'm certain you can convince a few peasants you're a lad."

For a moment he thought she would argue, but instead she settled onto a log, kicked off an oversized, cloth slipper, and set a needle to its back. "What do I have to do?' she asked, her tone sullen.

"Twill be simple enough," he said, and began to explain.

Darkness settled in as they trudged down the road again. Finally, aching with fatigue, they turned into the woods to search for a relatively dry place to spend the night.

Some hundred rods into the trees, Rachel spotted a stand of comfrey. Tearing off a few stalks, she hiked on.

Finally, hidden away in a copse of hawthorn trees, they shared the last of the cheese and made themselves as comfortable as possible.

But sleep wouldn't come immediately. Nagged by a thousand problems, Rachel busied her fingers by tearing strips of cloth from her shattered gown and weaving them into a drawstring pouch. Finally, finding that that simple process had calmed her a little, she hung the comfrey to dry beside the pouch in a tree and searched blindly for sleep.

By morning, they were damp and cramped and ravenous. They saw to their morning business, finished off the wine and bread, and hurried on.

The morning stretched out forever. Once, just past noon, they came to a boggy spot in the road. Venturing into the forest, they found a patch of wild berries, gathered what they could and hurried on. A few hours later, they heard the sound of galloping hooves behind them.

"Into the woods. Quickly!" Liam ordered.

They scrambled off the road. Just as they settled into cover, five horses thundered past. Rachel held her breath until they were well out of sight, then turned her gaze to Liam.

"They were in a rush."

He nodded.

"Do you think . . ." She trailed off, finding she couldn't quite finish the thought.

"I don't know," he said, but for several hours after they trudged through the forest instead of down the road. And even after that, they were more cautious.

The sun was about to set and dark storm clouds crowded the sky when they finally reached the fair-sized village of Kilderry. A sturdy maid swung her half-filled milk bucket beside her as she flirted with a fisherman. Two young girls with bare feet and gap-toothed grins herded a gaggle of geese into a stone enclosure. A dog barked sharply off to their right, and the smell of fresh-baked bread and onion permeated the air, causing Rachel's stomach to whine.

Just down the cobbled way from a wattle-and-daub building that boasted a sign with a bottle and loaf, a small group of men stood around a hot forge arguing about various methods of shoeing. One of them was obviously a man of some means, while the others were working sorts, their square hands showing the wear of their various trades.

Near a candle shop a middle-aged woman bartered eggs for a bit of thread.

Rachel turned toward Liam, her stomach tight with hunger and nerves. "Mayhap we should simply appeal to that gentleman for help?"

Liam didn't even turn toward the man of which she spoke. Instead, he grasped her elbow lightly and kept her walking brusquely beside him. "Do you know him?"

"Of course not."

"But you knew Davin didn't you?"

"What—"

"You could not trust him. Do you think you can trust this man?"

"Your reasoning—"

He stopped her abruptly, his gaze intent. "We are dealing with more than you know here. Please, for your mother's sake, do as I ask."

She took a deep breath, allowed herself a moment of panic, and raised her voice. "Nay!"

"What?" Liam took his cue without a moment's hesitation, pitching his voice into a whisper that somehow managed to reach the tannery. "What do you mean, nay?" He tightened his grip on her elbow, glanced furtively about at the faces that were already turning their way, and inched closer to her. "What good will we do the king if we never arrive in London?"

Rachel swallowed hard, tried to force herself to

glance nervously about at the faces that watched them, and found she could not. Still, she managed to force out her next line. "You know we are to save our act for His Majesty alone."

"The act will be seriously lacking if we starve to death before we reach the palace."

"We would be nearing the palace now if you had not wagered away our horses."

He raised his brows at her, and she wondered momentarily if that was a sign of approval. Though they had rehearsed a fair bit, this much was improvised.

"Twas you who allowed our goods to be stolen. I must do something to replenish our fortunes," he hissed. "So while you stand about whining, I will find us a way to the king."

"You'll have to work alone if—"

"What's this about the king?" asked the gentleman, striding up.

"Oh, good sir," Liam gasped, as if embarrassed that he'd drawn the man's attention. "I am called Martin." He spread his hands and shrugged in a self-deprecating fashion. "Martin the Magnificent by some."

"Magnificent indeed!" Rachel muttered.

Liam gave her a slanted glare, then, "I fear I and my associate have fallen on hard times."

The gentleman narrowed his eyes. "What is this about the king?" he asked, seeming unconcerned by their personal woes.

"Twould be best to keep your voice down," Liam said. "Tis, well . . . tis not widely known that His Majesty has hired us to perform for him."

"Perform?"

"Aye. Just . . ." He shrugged as if modest. It was all Rachel could do not to snort. Modesty was not his forte. "Just a touch of magic and a wee bit of juggling."

"It must be more than a wee bit if it be good enough for the king."

Liam all but blushed. "Some say I have a gift."

"Well, let us be the judge," said the gentleman, sweeping a hand toward the onlookers.

"Nay," Rachel managed to say, but Liam scowled her down.

"I fear my assistant is unwilling to allow me to show our tricks to any but the king."

"Then show us other tricks."

A small crowd had gathered now. The faces were bright with curiosity. A few nodded.

"My assistant . . ."—he glared at Rachel again—"has lost our props as I've said. But mayhap I could improvise."

"Aye."

"Do."

The crowd was pressing in, making Rachel feel a bit breathless. But Liam smiled and spread his arms. "Very well, then. I'll need a few things. Let's see . . . a rope, strung between those two trees."

"I've one inside," said the blacksmith.

"Then fetch it if you will," Liam said. "And I need something to toss about, balls, stones . . ." He shrugged and glanced around him. His gaze snagged on a group of folk gathered outside a pottery shop where an old woman leaned from inside to dicker with the tanner. "Mugs," he said. "Jamie, be a good lad and ask the potter if we might borrow a few mugs. Assure him all will be well."

Rachel thought she should probably feign an argument. Indeed, she opened her mouth to try to force out a few words, but Liam hushed her before she had a chance.

"Go now. Let us not keep these good people waiting."

The potter turned out to be the woman who leaned out of the shop, an old, gnarled-faced crone with clay-covered hands and a sullen expression. Still, for the promise of recompense, she loaned out the mugs and made her crotchety way to the place where a rope had been strung tightly between two trees.

Rachel set three mugs into Liam's hands, and noticed, with growing stomach butterflies, that the crowd had more than doubled.

"Gather round then. For unless you will be at the king's feast, you'll not see the like of my performance again," Liam called, and tossed a trio of mugs into the air.

The elderly potter gasped, but Liam laughed as they spun one after another around in his hands.

"Not to worry," he said. "This is child's play." He backed up a step or two. "But this . . ." He paused for a moment and tossed the mugs high into the air. The crowd lifted their gazes to watch the pottery, and in that instant, Liam reached for the rope above his head.

When he snatched the mugs out of the air the next time, he was balanced atop the tightrope.

"This is more difficult," he said.

The crowd stared at him, stunned and silenced.

Liam smiled, nodded, teetered on his perch, then laughed at the oohs from below. "Worry not," he called. "I am not about to splatter on the ground like a squashed melon. Not when my very meal depends on my performance. And neither am I about to disappoint you, for you already know that this be an act fit for a king.

"Jamie, lad, toss me another mug."

Rachel forced her mouth closed. Liam had always been swift of hand and light of foot, but it had been many years since she'd seen him perform.

He grinned at her, seeming to read her thoughts. "Come now. Even the king will understand that we must eat. Toss it toward my chest."

Sweet Mary, she thought, she had no way of paying for something so simple as a mug should she break one. Still, there was nothing she could do but comply. Nervousness made her throw tilt off center. It wobbled toward his shoulder.

Nevertheless, he caught it easily and spun it off into orbit with the others.

"A fine throw, Jamie," he said, and rolled his eyes for the crowd's amusement. "Let's try that again. But this time throw it toward my other chest."

Rachel gritted a smile at him but picked up another mug and tossed on cue. It was centered better this time. He lobbed it into orbit, seemingly without effort.

After that, a number of clever tricks followed. Mugs circling behind his back, between his legs, over the branch of the tree. Until finally the crowd was all but mesmerized.

"I thank you for your attention," Liam called. "And I will thank you even more for your generosity. So if I have added some pleasure to your day, please put a bit of something into Jamie's . . ." He was going to say hat, Rachel knew. But he caught himself before the word was out, for he had no wish to give the crowd a chance to see her face. "Hand. And thank you again." He began catching the mugs, one after the other, but they were bulky and large and the fifth one slipped past his fingers.

He gasped. It careened toward the ground, but instead of a crash, there was a muffled whoosh, and when the crowd stared at it, they found it was not a mug at all, but a small rag pouch stuffed with comfrey.

Oohs of appreciation filled the place, and then the crowd began to babble.

Liam grinned as he jumped from the rope and handed four mugs to their owner.

"What about the other one?" the old potter croaked.

"Never fear," Liam said, and seemed to whisk the fifth from out of thin air. Inside the vessel was a bright bouquet of wildflowers. He bowed gallantly as he presented them to the old crone. "With my thanks," he said.

She gave him a crotchety glare, but he was undaunted.

"To be dulled only by your beauty and your generosity."

"Hogswaggle!" She gave him a glare, paused, then, "Here. You might as well keep the mug . . . since you've soiled it anyway."

Liam bowed again, swept the flowers from the mug, and handed them to her. "Tis oft said that a heart of gold is found with hands of clay."

"And tis just as oft said that clever hands are the hands of a rogue."

"It is indeed," Liam agreed with a laugh. Turning to the crowd at large, he saw that a goodly number were pressing gifts into Rachel's hands.

"I've little enough to give you," said the blacksmith, and sent a quick glance to the sky. "But you're welcome to the loft above my smithy if you've a mind to find shelter before the weather worsens."

Remembering the group of horsemen that had rushed by, Liam considered refusing. But one glance at the fatigue in Rachel's face changed his mind.

"Twould be greatly appreciated," he said instead.

Fat raindrops slanted in from the north. The crowd began to disperse. The old potter shuffled away, the bouquet of wildflowers clutched in a gnarled hand near her heart.

"My son will show you to the loft," said the blacksmith, and left to see to his own affairs.

Rachel and Liam gathered up their possessions, mostly newly acquired, and hurried after the lad to the smithy's shop. It was a large stone building with a huge opening in the front and a hearth in the middle.

The ladder up which they climbed was rickety, but the chaff at the top was deep and clean. Only at the far end had it begun to mold.

In no mood to complain about the accommodations, Rachel sighed as she settled onto the straw, then spread what was left of her gown in front of her. They placed their meal upon it—the mug, newly filled with milk still warm from the cow, a handful of roasted pecans, a loaf of onion bread, and two small, dried fishes.

"Nothing to spit at," Liam said, all but salivating at the fare they'd gained.

"Tis a feast," Rachel countered, her eyes bright beneath the broad brim of her plumed hat.

He glanced at her, wondering for a moment if she were being facetious. After all, she was a laird's daughter, accustomed to the fat of the land. But he saw neither sarcasm nor disdain in her expression.

"You did well," he said, though he thought he

would be wise to shove the food into his mouth and not speak at all.

"I stood at the side and stared with mouth agape," she argued as she tore off a bit of bread. "Nothing more."

What he truly didn't need was her modesty. He would be far better off to remember her hauteur and forget the rest. "Had you not made the ploy believable we would not have gained their attention. Tis all in perception. Had I simply begun to perform, they would have convinced themselves that every passing lad has the same talent as I. Even if I had the benefit of my black powder to add to the show, we would have been lucky to get an empty nutshell."

She took a bite of bread, but didn't turn her eyes away. "I think, mayhap . . ." She paused for a moment. "Could it be you think too little of yourself, Liam?"

Her angel eyes were entrancing while her devil's mouth was quirking. He was caught in the middle, between heaven and hell, unable to turn away.

The evening stretched into silence. The tiny trace of her smile diminished to solemn earnestness.

"Liam." Her voice was small, like a young lassie's. Like a slip of a girl dressed in voluminous white, with her sable hair unbound and her amethyst eyes full of softness and adoration. "I—"

"Eat." He said the word abruptly, for the truth was, he couldn't bear to hear her talk, to watch her lips move, to know that at this moment she felt some tenderness for him. He could not do that and resist her. Instead, he dropped his gaze away and snatched up a fish. "You'd best eat and get some sleep. The morrow will be upon us soon."

It took a moment, but he finally felt her gaze

drop away. "The men that galloped by us on the road ... Do you think they are in the village?"

He shrugged, trying to dispense with the heavy emotion caused by her nearness. "Don't fret about it. I'm certain no one recognized you as a woman." Although how they could fail to, he could not imagine. None of the folk present had seemed entirely daft.

They finished their meal in silence. Finally Liam undid his belt and set it aside. Rachel moved the mug to a safe location, hung her woven pouch over a nearby beam, and removed her hat. Then she pulled the ragged remains of her gown over her legs. But in a moment a tiny frown wrinkled her brow. "I could share," she said softly, lifting the sorry garment.

It was, suddenly, rather difficult to breathe, harder yet to respond. But he forced himself to remain calm. She wasn't offering herself naked and wet and needy, he reminded himself. She was merely sharing a tattered bit of cloth. Still, it was no mean task to force out a refusal. "Nay," he managed. "I've slept with less."

"As have I," she said. "But not until two nights ago."

Beneath them in the quiet stable, a horse sighed contentedly.

"I'm not unaccustomed to the cold," he assured her.

"But you're not used to walking day after day with a leg wound and too little food," she said. Their gazes caught. He wrenched his away.

"My leg feels—"

"Liam." Her voice drew his attention back to her face. "I need you well."

In his mind, he understood her words; she

needed help to reach her destination. And yet, in his *soul*, it sounded like she needed *him*. Needed *his* strength and *his* talents, and *his* person. Needed his hands against the warmth of her skin, needed his kisses, needed him deep inside, throbbing and . . .

God! He was a weak-willed bastard and he knew it, but suddenly he couldn't help himself. He was across the distance before he could formulate a decent excuse. But he was not foolish enough to touch her. They sat in silence for a moment, staring at each other.

"Sleep well, Rachel," he said finally, and turning his back, lay down on his side to stare into the darkness.

"Aye." She barely breathed the word. "You too," she said and spreading the tattered remains of the gown over both of them, turned in the opposite direction and went to sleep.

Chapter 8

It was the same old dream come to haunt him. The dream that Liam had, long ago, condemned as utter foolishness.

Even if he could have Rachel Forbes, even if he were some snot-nosed noble lord, he would not want her. She was haughty and cool and better than thou.

But it was damned difficult to remember that when the dream swelled up around him like a warm mist, when his heart was racing like a wild steed's and his every nerve ending was buzzing with delight.

Dear God, it was so real. He could feel her hand, satin soft against his flesh as she caressed his chest. He moaned and bent his leg, snuggling it between the warm embrace of hers. Her head, soft as a swallow, was cupped against the warmth of his heart. He drew her closer.

She sighed, her ungodly lips so soft, so close that there was nothing he could do but kiss her.

They awoke at the same moment, inches apart, their eyes wide.

"Liam!"

He jerked as if slapped, hoping to God that all

the talk had been wrong, that Rachel could not see inside his mind, because if she could read his thoughts this time she would never let him forget it.

But he realized slowly that her voice was breathless and that her hand lay beneath his tunic against the warmth of his flesh.

She yanked it out as if burned. Her devil's lips were slightly parted, but for a moment she said nothing, then, "I must have been..." She was breathing rather hard, and her cheeks were the color of a summer sunrise, but she didn't move back any farther. "I was dreaming."

Her words stopped his breath.

"Dreaming?"

She said nothing.

He tried to swallow, to think, to breathe. It was hopeless. "About what?"

"Maybe we should leave."

"Aye," he agreed, but she hadn't moved, and she was so close, and her eyes were just as wide and enchanting as they always were in his dreams, and her hair was all tousled, and... Dear God, what could he do when her hair was tousled. He had to kiss her!

His lips closed over hers.

"Da said to—"

Rachel shrieked. Liam jerked away, flashing his gaze toward the ladder.

The blacksmith's son stood as if suspended in midair, his head and shoulders just visible above the loft's floor, his jaw all but falling from his face as his eyes bugged at them.

"You was kissing him!" he gasped.

"Nay I—" Liam began.

But the boy was already scrambling down the

rungs. His feet missed a few in his haste. He fell the last two and landed on his rump on the hard-packed earth. But in a moment he was up and galloping away, already exercising his lungs. "Da, Da!"

"Bloody hell!" Liam rasped, lurching to his feet.

"Sweet Mary!" Rachel prayed. Snatching up her few possessions, she shoved them into her pouch.

"Hurry," Liam urged.

"What'll they do to us?"

"If they think you're a lad and I was kissing you, or if they find out you're a woman and I lied to them?"

The options seemed to be enough to silence her. She lurched for the ladder and all but slid down it. Liam was inches behind as she spurted for the wide front door.

"I saw them! With my own eyes, I saw them!" rasped the boy from just outside the door.

Rachel skidded to a halt. Liam snatched her arm, yanking her back toward the far wall.

They glanced desperately about. But no avenue of escape threw itself in their path.

"Up the ladder!" Liam rasped.

She didn't ask why, but scampered up the listing rungs like a harried squirrel.

Liam reached the top, raced past her, and slid onto the rotting straw that lay near the rear. True to his raging hopes, a small hole shone in the stonework. Bracing himself, he kicked at the wall with all his might. The rock teetered a bit.

"Come down from there, Master Martin," a voice called from below.

Liam kicked again. The stone let loose. The mortar gave way. Twas a small hole, but judging by the expression on Rachel's face, she was willing to squeeze.

He motioned raggedly toward her. She slid through feet first, grasped the rock with clawed fingers, and let herself down.

Liam followed as quickly as he could.

From inside, they heard feet on the ladder. It did nothing but hasten their retreat. Still two yards above the ground, Liam jumped to the earth. Grabbing Rachel's hand, he pulled her away from the smithy.

Quiet and quick as the dawn, they raced down a back alley, through a small herb garden, and across a narrow courtyard.

From around a corner, they heard the sound of whistling. Liam snatched Rachel down to a walk. In a second, the tanner was upon them, his broad face florid.

"Good morning to you, Martin. And young Jamie. Will you be performing for us again today?"

"Nay, I fear not," Liam said. "We must away."

"Ahh, tis a pity."

"Aye," Liam said, and pressing his hand to Rachel's back, hurried her out of the village and onto the road.

Sometime after noon, hunger drove them into the woods in search of food. But there was little to be found.

Finally, thirsty and fatigued, they wandered to the stream they'd been following. Once there, they scooped water into their hands, slaked their thirst, and considered options.

"My guards will be searching for me," Rachel said, not turning toward Liam as she watched the silvery waves roll by.

"Aye," he agreed. "But they'll be searching for your corpse along the river."

"Maybe not. Twill surely occur to them that I may have survived," she said, but the roaring memory of the falls made her doubt her own words. Even she couldn't say how she had survived. Still . . . "Maybe we should have stayed in the village. Eventually, they may arrive there."

"Stay as man and lad or man and woman?" Liam asked.

Neither of them had spoken a word about their time in the loft. Their gazes met now for a fraction of an instant, then hurried apart.

"There are those who frown on that particular form of perversion," Liam warned her.

"We might have told them the truth."

"Some would consider disguising a woman as a man an even more hideous crime. There be laws against it, you ken."

"Then why am I dressed as—"

"Because I cannot risk you!" The words shot from his mouth. "Because long ago and far away I vowed to protect you."

"What?"

"In the tower," he explained.

"What tower?"

"When you so clumsily stole my amulet and met your cousins to invoke a charm."

"You were there?" She all but whispered the words.

"Aye."

"Then twas you I heard behind the barrels."

"Aye."

"I thought it was a rat. It appears now that I was right," she said, and chuckled.

Liam turned irritably toward her. "Tis no laughing matter, Rachel."

"Aye, it is," she said. "Twas naught but a silly child's game."

Liam jerked to his feet. "Did you learn nothing from your cousins' misfortunes?"

"Misfortunes?"

"Sara—lost in the wilds of England. Alone but for a babe that was not her own. Not a bite to eat with brigands on her trail. How do you think she and the babe survived?"

"Sara is as sharp as the cut of a whip, and as caring as the Madonna," she said. "She would survive for the child. And too, I think mayhap Sir Boden had something to do with their good fortune."

"You give no credit to the dragon? None atall?"

"Nay," she said. "I do not."

"And what of Shona's adventures? She destroyed a plot against the crown and saved the boy king by her own hand. Not a scratch did she receive. Does that not seem amazing to you?"

"Shona is all but a warrior in her own right," Rachel said, but she found now that she had jerked to her feet without being aware of the movement and that Dragonheart was clasped tightly in her right hand.

"For one who is supposed to be gifted, you show a surprising lack of gifts," Liam said.

She lifted her chin. "Just because I do not believe in your toy, Liam?"

"Tis not mine, and tis not a toy. Do not underestimate it or its mission."

"Its mission?" she scoffed, but the amulet felt strangely warm in her palm. Almost as if it pulsed inside her fist.

"It has been sent to protect you." He paused. "As have I."

"Sent! By whom?"

He shrugged, but his eyes were intense. "God?"

"God!"

"You do believe in God, do you not, Rachel?"

"Of course I—"

"Then you think He is not capable of imbuing this thing with power?"

"He is capable of anything."

"Then might He not have sent it to protect you? Might He not have sent me?"

Rachel shook her head. It was all foolishness. Of that much she was certain. Liam had had no way of knowing she would pass through the village of Rainich at precisely the time he was being pummeled by an angry husband. And if *he* had no way of knowing, a piece of metal and stone certainly did not.

And yet . . .

"I do not care if you believe," Liam said. "but I will not have you risk yourself. I will take you where you wish to go, but not as the Lady of the Forbes. For I've no wish to see her die, no matter how she bedevils me."

She watched him for a moment, trying to sort things out in her mind. But there was no hope. So she turned toward the stream, her thoughts churning as quickly as the waves. Beneath the surface, a small fish streaked downstream.

"So you've been sent to protect me?" she asked.

"Maybe." His tone was wary and sounded more like the Liam of old.

"Then you'd best fetch me something to eat."

"Perhaps you think I can conjure up a feast from thin air?"

She turned back. "Maybe I should ask Dragon-heart."

He snorted. "Laugh if you like."

"I am not laughing. Surely if the amulet is so powerful, you and it together could gather us a meal. Here." She slipped it from her neck and handed it toward him. "Prove its powers," she said.

But Liam backed jerkily away. "Nay."

"Why ever not?" she asked, frustration rolling through her. "Why do you fear it if is naught but good?"

"Tis not mine. Tis yers. For now," he insisted, but she laughed.

"Since when has ownership mattered to Liam the Irishman? Take it," she said, and stepped toward him.

"Nay!" he barked.

She jumped at his anger.

"Put it away. Wear it against your skin."

"What is wrong with you?" Rachel whispered.

"Tis naught wrong with me. The dragon was not meant for me. That is all."

"Not meant for you? What do you mean by that? How do you know?"

"I know," he said and brushed past her. "Now you'd best start a fire. I've a lady's meal to fetch."

They dined on trout and stream water. Lacking a pot to boil it in, they skewered the three fishes and roasted them over the small fire Rachel had nurtured into life.

Not sated but no longer ravenous, Liam returned his spangle to his cape for future use as a fishhook.

"And you cast aspersions on my purchase," he said, standing up and turning quickly to let the garment wrap dramatically about his legs.

"You look like the devil in a bad festival play," she said, snuffing out their cooking fire.

"The devil indeed. I am Martin the Magnificent, and you'd be wise not to forget it."

Rising, she began to gather their small store of supplies. Every item was precious. "You are as magnificent as I am a lad," she said.

"Truly? And me, I thought your disguise less than spectacular."

"'Tis what I meant."

"With a bit of effort I believe you could make me a decent assistant," he said, leading the way through the forest. "But you'll have to learn to act the part of a man."

"I can be obnoxious, overbearing, and philandering?"

"Nay. I said you'd have to *act*."

She made a face, but he didn't turn around to appreciate it.

For the remainder of the afternoon, they traveled north by northeast, walking down the road when all seemed safe, hurrying into the woods on the few occasions when noises worried them. And all the time Liam made suggestions on how to act the lad.

By dusk, Rachel was too tired to care and too hungry to think. They'd found nothing to eat for many hours, and the streams they'd crossed had given up no more trout.

"We'd best stop for the night," Liam suggested. "I'll try fishing again."

Rachel nodded, but just when she was about to step into the woods, she stopped. "Did you hear something?"

"Nay, I . . . Wait." He held up one hand. "Horses. Coming from behind."

She nodded, still listening to the quick clop of approaching hoofbeats.

Liam put his hand to her back, but she delayed, her attention pinned on the road behind.

"I've no time to lose, Liam. Maybe these travelers could help us."

"Is that what you think?" His tone was tight.

"What?"

"Do you think they are folk of good heart?"

"How could I know?"

"You do not know. You just *feel*," he said. "Concentrate on the sound of the hooves."

She stared at him, but his eyes were turned down the road behind them.

"Do you feel evil?" he asked.

"Nay, I don't—"

"Neither do I." He exhaled softly. "'Tis not the sorcerer, I think. So what to do, risk the encounter or risk starvation."

She didn't understand his gibberish about the evil, but if the truth be told she didn't want to. She only wanted to be safely at her journey's end, to complete her mission, to know all was well.

"I say we greet them," she said.

Liam delayed a moment, glanced down the road, and then nodded.

In only a short while, the riders topped the hill behind them and came on. Finally, the front man held up his hand and slowed his mount to a walk.

"Ho," he called cautiously through the dimming light. "Who goes there?"

Through the distance and the gathering darkness, they could see little enough. But Liam absorbed as much as he could. They were eight men, all wearing plaids that showed broad knees and powerful thighs. They rode white horses and upon each man's head was a conical helmet of sorts.

"Tis naught but two lads in need of some assistance," Liam called back, making certain his Scottish burr was heavy.

The front man said something to his fellows, who spread out slightly to peer into the woods. "You are alone?"

"Aye. Alone with no weapons and no food."

The group came on, but slowly now, until finally they were only a short distance away. Rachel studied them in the dimming light. They did the same.

"You are English?" the nearest man asked, scanning their attire.

"Nay," Liam said, "We be a pair of Scots. We were but traveling back to our homeland when we were set upon by brigands."

"They left your fancy clothes, I see."

"Nay, they left us with naught but our lives. We had to labor for the garments we wear."

"Labor? What kind of labor do you?"

"We be entertainers."

The stout Scotsman shifted in his saddle, glanced pointedly at Rachel, then shifted his gaze back to Liam. "And what do you do?"

Liam canted his head and spread his hands. "Give us a meal and a place safe by your fire and we'll show you."

"But after the meal, twill be too late to refuse payment if we don't like your entertaining."

Liam shrugged. "I didn't think a Munro would fret over a little gamble."

The Scot straightened slightly, studying Liam more closely. "How do you know I'm a Munro?"

"You look to be the sort that eats his meat raw."

Silence filled the place. Rachel turned wide eyes on Liam, ready to bolt for the woods. But Munro threw back his head and guffawed his mirth to the heavens.

"You got balls, lad. I'll say that for you," he said, and flicked his gaze over Rachel. "We planned on riding on till we reach the monastery. But my appetite is piqued now. We'll have our meal here. Come along, we've plenty of raw meat to spare."

To Rachel's relief, they didn't actually eat their meat raw. In fact, they honed a good hot fire, dragged a few stout logs around it, and set to roasting small pieces of venison on spits placed over the flame. As the meat cooked, the men introduced themselves. But the intoxicating aromas made it difficult to concentrate on names.

Rachel sat on the thin end of a log and tried to be patient until the meat was cooked and her hunger slaked. Finally, the meal was ready and she was given her share. The meat was stringy and tough, but she was far past caring. Still, it was soon clear that her appetite did not compare to that of the Munros. Sated and sleepy, she had time to consider these strangers. Stashed away as she was on the end of a log with Liam between her and the man who called himself Calum Munro, she had time to think.

Oh, yes. She'd heard of the Munros. Though she hadn't recognized them on sight, she knew their reputation. They were Scotsmen from the far north. Mercenaries hired out to the highest bidder when their own laird had no use for them. She wondered what brought them this far south, and if they'd go to the bother of killing two traveling entertainers if they didn't like the show.

"Well," said Calum. "I think tis time for that entertainment. What is it you lads do?"

"Come, Jamie," Liam said, standing up. "Tis time to impress our good hosts."

Rachel prepared to stand up, but just as she did so, Calum rose to his feet. The log, held down by his great weight, teetered, tossing her off balance. She careened toward the fire, but Munro snagged her arm just in time and drew her back with a chuckle.

"Whoa there, Jamie lad. Maybe you'd best do this job alone, Martin. I fear you've been starving your young assistant too long. Why not let the boy sit on that soft moss over yonder for a spell?"

Rachel glanced at Liam. He nodded to her, and she gratefully pulled from Calum's ham-fisted grip to find the spot indicated, off to the side and just out of the firelight's glow.

"I'll need something to throw," Liam said. "Something . . . ahh, there it be," he sighed, and stepping toward the fire, snatched three burning branches from the flame. In an instant he had them spinning in the air. Flame arched through the night sky like a continuous circle of fire. The men, already mesmerized, watched in slack-jawed wonder.

Rachel settled back. Overjoyed to have the Munros' attention firmly entrenched somewhere else, she allowed herself to relax a mite.

"God's teeth," one of the men rasped. "Tis a wonder he has not burnt off his hands long ago."

"Not atall," Liam said with a laugh. "Tis no great feat. I'll bet you a copper I can do the same with four."

"Nay."

"Aye," he insisted. "Toss another in."

One of the Munros strode up to the fire and

tugged at a branch. The log it was attached to moved perceptibly..

"Not that big lugger," Liam objected. "There, that piece there."

Another stick was wrenched from the fire. One end aflame, it flared in the night, lighting the warrior's face.

"Toss it toward me chest."

He did so with no warning, but somehow Liam managed to catch it. It spun into orbit with the others. The men grunted their approval.

"Not bad."

Rachel jumped at the sound of Calum's voice at her elbow. When she turned, he was already settling down beside her, his dark eyes aglow, and his bearded face shadowed.

"I didn't mean to startle you."

"Nay," she said, but dared not utter more, for although her voice was low for a woman's, she had no wish to test her masculinity with this bullish Munro.

"A copper says I can handle another," Liam called.

The Munros rumbled among themselves, then one stood up to tug an additional branch from the fire. He intentionally tried to make Liam miss this time, but the Irishman dipped, snatched it out of the air, and sent it flying.

The men hooted and laughed, appreciative of his talent and quickness.

Calum chuckled. "This Martin may indeed be magnificent."

Rachel said nothing, but tilted her head to give him a better view of the brim of her broad hat. His closeness made her nervous, and she hoped he could not get too clear a look at her face—or any other part of her anatomy that might give him a clue to her gender.

"Do you not think so?"

She realized abruptly that he'd asked her a question. She cleared her throat and pitched her voice low. "What?"

"Do you find him magnificent?'

What kind of question was that? Rachel wondered.

"Tis not so great of feat," Liam said to his appreciative audience. "Had I me knives here, I'd show you a real trick."

"I've a knife," one of the warriors said.

"Nay." Liam chuckled. The sound was nervous. "I would not ask you for it."

"You said you could use it," one of the others argued.

"That's with my own knives," Liam murmured, his tone hesitant. It was that note of uncertainty that drew Rachel's attention, for Liam only acted unsure when he was not—when he was certain of whatever devious deed he was planning, such as putting frogs in her pallets or stealing her hair ribbons.

The thought of stealing hair ribbons from the Munros, however, didn't seem such a good idea to her. But still, if he were planning something, she'd best cooperate.

She told herself to match his performance, to try to look nervous, then realized she hardly had to worry on that account, for the hairs on the back of her neck were standing up like the bristles on a boar's back. "There be times he thinks too highly of himself," she said, remembering Munro's question and making certain her voice was gruff, her gaze pinned nervously on Liam as though she feared he might fail.

"But do you think him magnificent?" Calum asked again.

Rachel shifted her gaze warily to him. "Aye," she began, but suddenly Calum was atop her, crushing her to the earth, one hand slapped across her mouth, the other kneading her breast through the weight of her doublet.

"And I find *you* magnificent!" he rasped. "The most magnificent 'lad' I've ever seen."

Chapter 9

"**G**od's balls," Liam said, "that's not a knife. That's a damned claymore."

"Tis a knife, lad," argued the Munro warrior. "And you said you could toss the thing about."

"Nay, I did not," Liam countered, making certain his tone evidenced a good deal of nervousness. There was nothing like a bit of obvious reluctance to make an audience eager.

"Aye, you did. But I see now that you're too scared to try it, even for say . . . three coppers?"

"Three coppers?" Liam let his voice get hopeful, then shook his head while still spinning the flaming branches into the air. "Nay. Tis not worth the risk."

"Four coppers?"

"Come now, lad," another coaxed, and pulled out his knife. "The blades are not even on fire."

"Nay," Liam countered. "They are not aflame. Thus they'll do naught but slice off my ear."

"Your *ear*?" One of the men chuckled as a burning stick dipped a bit lower than planned, flaming dangerously near Liam's oversized codpiece. "Were I you, I'd be worrying about other parts of meself. Parts likely to give you more pleasure in the future."

Liam grinned. "Tis why I kept my own five blades rather dull."

"Well, mine be not dull," said one of the men, "but you do not have to play with five then. Say . . . three . . . for twice that number of coppers."

"Six coins?" Liam questioned as if doubtful, but if the truth be known, he could juggle three knives in his sleep, while standing on his head in a rainstorm with a ragtag bunch of children bombarding him with rotten fruit and a gaggle of geese feeding off the remains.

"Nay," Liam said after a moment's pause. "Tis a poor idea."

"Tis a grand idea," someone argued, and standing abruptly, tossed the knife directly at him.

Liam caught it without thinking. In a heartbeat it was spinning into orbit, replacing one of the sticks he let fall harmlessly to the grass.

Another knife spun toward him. He caught that with as much ease, but the truth was, there were eight men here, and even a master like himself might have a wee bit of trouble with eight . . .

Eight! He skimmed the men in front of him, counting as he did so. Seven! There were only seven men present! Where was Rachel?

He almost screamed her name, but managed to keep silent as he frantically searched the lightened area before grilling the darkness beyond.

It was then that he thought he heard something— a whimper? A muffled shriek?

"Jamie?" he called, careful not to alarm any of the big men who held big knives in big hands. "Jamie?" he repeated, but his heart was pounding now like a panicked steed's.

"Liam!"

His name was shrieked off and cut short.

"Rachel!" he yelled, and jerked about just in time to see her lunge out of the darkness.

But in a moment, she was snatched to the ground.

He yelled her name again. The flaming sticks fell to the earth. The knives fell into his hands. He let them fly without a second's thought.

There was a grunt of pain from the darkness. Calum dropped Rachel's arm and jerked about, clawing at the knife that pierced the back of his arm.

Yanking the blade from his flesh, he roared and staggered forward.

"Bloody hell! Run!" Liam yelled, but Rachel was already on her feet and bolting into the darkness of the woods.

He had only himself to worry about. Himself, a wounded warrior, and seven big men with knives. Shit!

"Now, lads," he said, holding his empty hands out in front of him. I want no trouble here."

"Get the woman," Calum growled, still coming on.

"Woman?" one of the men asked.

"Get the woman!" yelled their leader.

Three men spurted into the woods. The rest formed a semicircle around Liam, their swords gleaming in the fire's glow. Their eyes no less bright.

"Tis naught but a misunderstanding," Liam soothed, and wished to hell he had his black powder, or his knife, or . . . Damn! He'd be happy if he had a sharp stick right now. Just then he remembered the flaming brands he'd just dropped.

Bending, he snatched one off the ground.

"Stay back," he warned. "Stay back or you'll regret it." The threat was rather like a mouse roaring at a pack of wolves.

The closest man grinned. "A woman?" he asked. "Tell me, lad, might you be playing us for fools?"

"Fools? You?" Liam asked, backing away, his brand held in front of him. "Nay." It sounded a bit more sarcastic than he'd intended. He swallowed hard. "Stay back now, lad. I've no wish to hurt you?"

"Hurt me?" asked the closest man, and lunged.

Liam swung frantically. The branch cracked against the other's shoulder, thrusting the man sideways and breaking in half in the process.

Liam stared in horrified shock.

Calum roared as he charged.

Death screamed its war cry. Liam raised his arms to cover his face, but in that instant hoofbeats thundered behind him.

"Liam!" Rachel screamed.

He pivoted about. The horse reared nearly atop him. Liam stumbled backward. Something scraped across his cape. Panic spurred him forward. He leapt, grabbing for the steed. The horse was already spinning away, his mane flaring out.

Liam snatched the ends and was whipped forward. His feet hit the ground a second later. The horse thundered from camp. Liam's legs pistoned, trying to keep up, to prevent getting trampled. A hoof scraped his leg. Something clawed his back, and then he was on, one foot hooked over the stallion's back, one bent up against the animal's heaving ribs.

"Hold on!" Rachel shrieked.

Liam gritted his teeth and wondered what the options were.

Behind them men yelled and swore and ranted as they dashed toward their mounts. Liam clung to the stallion's side like a drowning tick. He tried to shimmy up, but his fingers were giving out. He felt himself slipping and tried not to scream.

But in that instant, Rachel hauled on the reins. The horse planted his haunches and slid. Liam dropped his feet to the ground, jolted at the impact, then lunged into action, running along beside as he gathered his strength.

"Get on!" Rachel rasped. "Before they catch their horses."

Clever girl. She'd turned their mounts loose. Panting for breath, Liam swung aboard, nearly pulling Rachel off as the stallion leapt back into a gallop.

Hanging on for dear life, Liam glanced back. Dark shapes materialized behind them. "They're after us!"

Rachel leaned over the stallion's crest and yelled something indistinguishable in his flattened ears. The horse lowered his head, gathered his strength, and flew through the woods.

Branches whipped them, thorns ripped at them. All the world was a blur of darkness as they careened into the night. But their mount was carrying a double load and the yells of their pursuers were growing louder.

Liam twisted about again.

Two shadows tore through the woods behind them. Only two, but they were gaining ground. Muscles taut, heart pounding, he leaned over Rachel's bent back.

"Keep going. No matter what, as long as you hear horses behind you, keep riding."

"What?" She tried to peer into his face.

"Keep going," he hissed.

Releasing Rachel's waist, Liam propped his feet beneath him on the horse's straining back and, perched there like a stymied monkey, glanced behind. The riders were almost upon them. Almost. But for a moment they were hidden from view.

Straightening his legs, he balanced for one precarious moment and reached for a branch.

His fingers snagged the limb an instant before it struck his chest. Air whooshed from his lungs, but he had no time to breathe anyway. Yanking his knees up under the branch, he glanced below him.

Horse and rider appeared in an instant, racing after them.

No time to think. Not a moment to spare. Coiling into himself, Liam swung his legs backward with all his might. Pain shot up his thigh as he struck the man's chest.

There was a grunt and wild grappling, but the rider was already falling, slipping toward the ground as his mount rushed on.

The next rider burst into view. Liam recoiled and swung his legs again, but his aim was off. Swinging wide, the warrior snagged Liam about the knees and dragged him from the branch. Beneath them, the horse reared. The world tilted, and then they were falling, tumbling over the animal's rump.

The earth struck Liam's head, but the blow of the man's fist was harder. Grappling for his wits, he opened his eyes and tried to think, but the fist was coming again. He rolled aside at the last second and scrambled to his feet.

The warrior pivoted toward him. Liam froze, his

back to a tree, his mind momentarily numbed, his muscles frozen with terror. And in that second, the Munro charged.

His battle cry ripped through the night. Liam tried to shriek back, to cow his opponent with his courage, but his mouth wouldn't open, his muscles wouldn't move, until finally, at the last second, he whipped his body into submission and leapt sideways.

The warrior, muscle-bound and enraged, tried to turn with him, but it was too late. He crashed head first into a tree and fell with a muffled grunt.

Liam remained as he was, half-bent and breathing hard as he realized with aching clarity that the horses he'd hoped to catch were gone.

It was the sound of hoofbeats that made him prepare to leap into the surrounding woods. But at the last instant, he realized they were coming from behind him.

A horse burst into view and skidded to a halt.

"Liam?"

His heart bumped against his backbone at the sound of her voice.

"Rachel. You weren't supposed to come back."

"You weren't supposed to fall off."

"Fall off!"

"Hurry. We've no time to lose."

He was nearly too weak to mount, but he managed somehow, though his legs shook.

"Hang on. I may not be able to save you if you fall off again."

He tried to mouth an objection, but their mount lunged beneath them, shoving the words down his throat as they galloped into the night.

*   *   *

"How bad?" Liam asked.

Rachel stroked the stallion's right foreleg and rose stiffly to her feet. "He needs naught but rest. But he needs that badly."

Liam ground his teeth. They had ridden through the night, but they would ride no more, for the horse was spent. Still, there was no time to rest.

"We'd best get walking, then," he said, and turned away.

It took him a moment to realize she wasn't following.

"What be you doing?"

"Removing his gear."

"We've no time."

"What do you suggest, Liam? That we leave him here to be caught in the brush and starved after he saved our lives?"

Liam considered reminding her that *he* too had saved her life, that *his* leg hurt and his stomach was empty. But there seemed little point for she had already turned back to the horse with a crooned word. Twas just like her to care more for a steed than a man.

It took only a few moments for her to finish her task. During that time, Liam gazed off in every direction, and prayed to God that they hadn't been followed, not by the Munros and not by worse.

"What are you waiting for?" Rachel asked, and turning away, trudged through the woods.

Fatigue rode Liam like a spurred horseman. Hunger clawed at his belly. But he would drop dead in his tracks before he'd admit as much, especially after she'd inferred that he'd *fallen* off the horse. Him! Liam the Irishman! He didn't fall off anything.

They walked for an eternity until they found the road, then continued doggedly on.

It was sometime after noon when Liam thought he heard a noise. He stopped abruptly, tension tightening like a hard knot in his belly. "Do you feel something?"

She didn't answer, and he didn't ask again, for suddenly it seemed as if the very breath had been sucked from his body.

"Into the woods," he hissed.

But Rachel was frozen in place.

"Hurry!" he ordered, and pushed her into the trees.

Once there, she stopped to turn back, but his heart was racing now and his mind working in synch. Grabbing her hand, he leapt deeper into the woods, dragging her behind as they stumbled into anonymity.

But finally Rachel's foot snagged on something, and she fell. Liam froze, still holding her hand. "Get up," he hissed.

"Nay." She shrunk into herself, pulling up her arm to cover her face. "He's coming! We can't— Nay!" she gasped.

"You must come," he said, but her answer was only a whimper.

Fresh terror spurred up, driving him to his knees. He reached for her, pulling her against him. Dragonheart pressed into his chest.

"Liam . . ." Her voice was raspy, her body tense with terror.

"Do not think about it."

"I feel—"

"Do not let him in. Close your mind."

"I can't."

He caught her gaze and shook her. "You shall!"

he ordered. "You shall. Think of your home."

"Liam . . ."

He tightened his grip. Fear roiled in his mind. Sweat dotted his forehead. "Think of your mother. Glen Creag when you were a lass."

She shivered. He squeezed his eyes closed and pulled her closer still, fighting to hold his mind from the evil that knocked at it.

"Remember when Shona fell in the moat."

Terror! Pain so real, he could taste it like blood in his mouth.

"Mid . . ." Rachel's whisper broke away, but she struggled on. "Midsummer's eve."

Warwick would not have her. Never. Rachel would be safe. Liam tightened his arms, his resolve. "She had vowed to scale the wall without being seen."

They were close. So close. His arms trembled. His voice lowered of its own accord, as if cowering in the sorcerer's dark shadow.

"Her father asked how she had become wet," he continued. Terror gripped them in steely talons, barely allowing him to breathe. "And all the while the Rogue knew the truth, for he'd tried the same feat himself." He rambled on, though he no longer knew what he said.

Fear loosened a bit, then a bit more until finally only the bitter aftermath lay on them. Exhausted and spent, they didn't try to move, but fell asleep, cowering in the shadowy woods with Liam's cape spread over them like a forest green shroud.

They awoke some hours later and lay in silence.

The air felt normal, devoid of the horrid crushing terror that had overcome them.

"I've no more time to waste," Rachel said softly. "At the next opportunity I will go to the laird of the nearest estate and plead for help."

"A laird," Liam said. Fear was like a bitter taste in his mouth. Death had been so close. His death. *Her* death.

"Aye. I'll explain my plight and beg for assistance."

"And because he is wealthy, you think he will be willing to help you?"

.She didn't answer.

Anger spurred through him. "Warwick was wealthy!" he rasped. "A favored advisor to kings. But maybe you don't believe that. You think that because a man be born in a castle instead of a hovel, he is trustworthy? Trustworthy enough to tell him the truth, while you spew your lies to me?"

"I did not lie to you!"

"Truly? Then your betrothed must be a phenomenal lover to put you in such a rush to reach him."

"Forgive me if I'm in a hurry to reach safety."

"Just because a man has wealth and power does not mean he will give you safety."

"Dressing as a lad has been less than successful!" she snapped.

Liam exhaled sharply, relieving his tension by slow increments. "I'll not ask you to pretend to be a lad again."

"Truly?" He watched her close her eyes, watched her slowly relax. There was nothing he wanted more at that moment than to pull her into his arms. To promise all would be well. But he was not so foolish.

"Truly," he said. "You made a pathetically poor lad. I've a better plan in mind."

Chapter 10

❧ ⟳⟲ ❧

Rachel rose abruptly to her feet. The woods were quiet. Too quiet, and her time there alone too long. Where was Liam? She held her breath, trying to see through the foliage, but night was coming on.

She'd busied herself by building a fire and gathering a few herbs. She'd even come across a patch of wild leeks, but even if she had an appropriate pot, she'd not dare put them on to cook. Their aromatic scent might well draw unwanted attention, and despite her revulsion at the knowledge, she realized she felt horribly vulnerable since Liam's exit some hours earlier.

A twig snapped. She spun toward the noise, her heart beating overtime and her breath coming hard.

"Did you miss me?"

She squawked like a snared peahen, jumping and twisting about at the same time as she tried to see behind her.

Liam laughed out loud. "You weren't scared were you?"

"Nay," she said, but her voice shook. "And where the devil have you been so long."

He grinned. "Fetching our supper."

"Supper?" She tried not to sound too wistful. But her stomach was cramped with hunger and just the sight of the bag he held in his hand made her mouth water. Still, she had some pride and lifted her chin to stare at him. "Where'd you get it?"

"Tis the duty of every good monk to feed the hungry."

"You stole it," she surmised.

He stared at her, his expression shocked. "I am much offended."

"You stole it," she repeated.

"I did not," he denied. "And more's the pity." Jiggling the empty pouch he'd stolen from the enraged husband, he frowned. "I used the last coin in our possession."

"You actually paid for it?" she asked, reaching for the bag.

He handed it over with a scowl. "You could, at least, pretend you're not shocked."

They reached the next village sometime on the following day. It was a fair-sized town. Bustling with activity, it was much livelier than Liam felt. They hadn't eaten since supper the night before, and his stomach complained vociferously.

He'd finally convinced Rachel to wear the garments he'd purchased. He was certain no one who knew her either by sight or reputation would easily recognize her in the gown. It was a bold garment, garish red with slashed sleeves, and a low, laced bodice. Not the sort of thing one would think to find at a monastery. But the bulky man's tunic Rachel had insisted on donning beneath the gown made it quite modest. Ugly, but modest. And the limp, drooping coif did nothing to improve the ensemble.

"How do you plan to obtain food?" she asked as they passed an inn. Crafted of slate gray stone, it boasted a listing sign and a single drunk who reeled out onto the street.

"Tis a lively town," Liam said, skimming a nearby crowd hopefully. "I'm certain to get some interest with me juggling, if I but—"

"Don't be shy!" someone yelled. "Tis plenty of room for you to see. Come along, squeeze in closer. See Catriona, the king's favorite entertainer."

Liam growled and stepping onto a nearby stone fence, gazed over the heads of the crowds. "The gypsies have stolen my line."

Rachel joined him. On the far side of the crowd, a young woman, graceful as a bending willow, leapt onto a cart and raised her hands to the crowd.

"Welcome one and all," she cried. Her elfin face beamed down at the gathering near her feet. Her costume, Liam had to admit, showed all her finest qualities.

Her arms were bare but for a tiny sleeve that capped her golden shoulders. Her bodice, though not low, was taut across her bosom, and her waist was cinched to impossible proportions.

"As I said, how do you plan to buy food?" Rachel repeated dryly.

"She may have prettier . . ." Liam paused for a moment, still staring. "Everything, than I do. Still, I'm certain I'm a better entertainer than . . ."

But just at that moment, the girl launched forward, tucked into a ball and spun over the side of the cart.

Liam's jaw dropped as, just at the last second, she stretched out her leonine body, only to be caught in the arms of a bare-chested man who stood by apparently just for that purpose.

"You were saying?" Rachel asked.

"I'm a hell of a pickpocket," Liam murmured, starring at the couple who grinned broadly out at their audience.

She raised her brows at him. He could barely see them beneath the sagging folds of her soiled coif. God, it was a homely thing.

He cleared his throat. "Stay here."

"Where are you going?"

"To take a look around."

"In people's pouches?"

"So jaded," he said, feigned disappointment rife in his voice as he stepped down from the fence. If theft was what was required, he certainly was not above such an approach.

Rachel lowered herself to sit on the rough stone. If he wanted to get himself killed it was fine by her. She was not his keeper. Indeed, she was not even his friend. All he did was bedevil her at every turn. Had it not been for him she probably would still be safely with her guards. She was a fool to listen to his ravings. Warwick was dead.

For a moment the memory of the terror in the woods gripped her but she shoved it aside. Fatigue and Liam's wild tales would frighten anyone, she told herself.

Surely she would be entirely better off without . . .

Just at that instant a flash of pain sliced through her mind, numbing her for a moment. But it was not her pain.

"Liam." She whispered his name, her heart thudding wildly in her chest. And then, in her mind's eye she saw him crumpled on the ground, his face bloody. A bear of a man loomed over him, his bald head shining, his shoulders hunched. "Liam," she whimpered again, and glanced wildly about, but she could see him only in her thoughts.

Panic spurred through her. She lunged into the depths of the crowd.

"Liam," she called, but her voice was lost in the melee.

She pressed on, fear and premonition driving her. And then, above the heads of the crowd, she saw a huge man with a shiny pate and a wolf-skin vest.

"Nay!" she rasped, and without thought, without hesitation, threw herself forward.

People parted reluctantly before her as she shoved them aside. Panic galloped in her chest.

A man stepped to the side and suddenly she saw Liam, saw his hand streak out and draw back, saw the huge man scowl and turn.

"Nay," Rachel cried, and throwing herself forward, collided with the huge man. She ricocheted off his chest like a sparrow on a windowpane. Her bottom struck the earth and her coif torpedoed from her head. Hair tumbled wildly across her face.

"What the devil are y' doing?" asked the big man. But in an instant, his eyes narrowed and the muscles in his bare arms bunched like striking snakes. Bending over, he snatched a pouch from the ground. "You were stealing my purse."

Rachel froze, her eyes popping and a denial frozen in her throat.

"A little thief," he said.

Panic seared through her. She tried to scramble backward on her hands and feet, but his arms went on forever. He reached out, grabbed her gown and tunic in one huge hand and yanked her to her feet.

Rachel sagged from his fist, every nerve atremble and her breasts rising and falling like windy bellows beneath his knuckles.

His gaze, dark as hell, skimmed her.

"You be a devil of a poor thief. But maybe you have other talents, aye?"

"I'm not a thief!" Her voice was no more than a whisper. "I simply . . . ran into you in my rush. Your purse must have popped out when I struck you."

He tightened his grip on her bodice and his mouth twisted as if she had made some poor attempt at a jest.

"And where were you off to in such a rush, wench?"

She tried to find her voice, but it was long gone. The crowd had moved aside. Faces turned toward her. She could feel their expectant gazes burn into her.

"Or were you in a hurry to see me?"

"I—I . . ."

"Aye?" He grinned into her face, happy with his cleverness. "Well, I'm eager to oblige you," he said, and began pulling her through the crowd.

"Nay!" she shrieked.

"Then you'd best tell me where you were bound in such a rush, or I'll be finding my own destination for you," he said, turning back.

"I was . . ." It was impossible to breathe. She skimmed her eyes sideways, searching for help and finding nothing but the Gypsy's small elfin face. "I was about to perform."

The huge man reared back slightly, his mouth still twisted. "You're with *them*?"

She stared at him, terrified and paralyzed. "Aye," she said, and managed a stilted nod.

He glanced up and down at her mismatched garments, noting how her black, mannish tunic bunched messily beneath the laces of the garish red gown. "In that garb?"

She raised her chin and tried to look haughty. But there was little hope of that.

"And what do you do then, lass?" he asked, stepping closer still. She could smell him, the melded odor of old sweat and cheap ale.

"I . . ." What? A dozen possibilities snapped through her mind. Juggling, magic, acrobatics! Dear God, she couldn't even sing. "Dance!" she gasped.

"What?" The gargantuan man canted his head and narrowed obsidian eyes.

"I dance."

There was a moment of absolute silence, before, "Let's see it, then," he said.

Her feet were frozen to the earth, the breath stuck in her throat. She'd be lucky if she could walk.

"You cannot expect her to dance without music."

Liam!

She snapped her gaze to him as he stepped to the perimeter of the crowd. He turned his eyes to hers for a fraction of an instant, then back to her tormentor's.

"Who are you?"

"I'm her brother."

"I think you lie, little man. You look nothing like her."

"And you look nothing like a human, yet I'm not calling you a liar," Liam said.

The huge fellow growled low in his throat, dropped his hold on Rachel, and turned ominously toward Liam.

"Nay!" Rachel screamed, but the word was drowned in the reedy trill of a pipe.

The huge man swiveled toward the sound.

Rachel held her breath, then turned too.

Standing at the edge of the crowd an old woman stood with a pipe to her wrinkled lips. Above the instrument, her eyes were as sharp and wily as those of a red fox. Rachel caught her gaze, and for a moment the world stood still. There was nothing suddenly, except this old woman and her entrancing eyes.

"So dance!" the huge man demanded.

Rachel pulled her gaze from the old woman's. She was breathing hard and her heart was pumping like a running horse in her chest, but she forced herself to take a few tentative steps.

The music played faster.

Rachel grasped her clumsy skirt in one hand and turned. The gown, heavy with muddy water, slapped between and around her legs, nearly tripping her up. She straightened with an effort.

All eyes were on her now. She could feel the attention like the heat of a flame, but it was too late to turn back, so she twirled again, trying to find the rhythm.

Faster and faster she moved. One shoe flew off. She stumbled, but terror drove her on until finally the music fell into ear-shattering silence.

Rachel careened to a halt, her head still spinning.

Her huge tormentor clenched his fists and took a step toward her.

"Tis enough of a free show for now, girl," said the old woman. Her voice creaked in the sudden stillness.

Rachel turned silently toward her.

"Get yourself to the wagon and stay out of trouble." The ancient eyes shifted to Liam. "You too, boy."

But Liam still stared at the huge man before him, every muscle taut as the other watched Rachel.

"Start another fight, laddie, and I'll whip you myself," snapped the old woman. "You're becoming more trouble than you're worth to me."

Liam turned his gaze to the matron, stared at her for a moment, then, stepping forward, pulled Rachel toward the wagon.

There was a few moments of silence, then, "What the devil did you think you were doing?" Liam hissed in her ear.

"Saving your hide." Every nerve was still jumping as he towed her away from the crowd.

"If you'd saved me any more, you'd a been raped and I'd a been dead!"

"Children!" snapped the old woman from close behind. "Shut your mouths and get inside the wagon before you get us all killed."

The wagon was narrow, high-sided, and covered with a painted tarp. A cage of sticks contained two tiny yellow finches near the small door through which Liam pushed Rachel.

The interior was dim and cool, crowded with the things necessary for life on the road—pans, trunks, clothes hung on pegs on the wall, blankets rolled up in the corners.

Liam ducked inside, taking in every detail.

"'Tis your decision, laddie," said the old woman, her gnarled face framed like a dried apple in the doorway, "but if you hope to see the lady safely to her destination, twould be wise to keep yourself alive."

"Who—" Liam began, but she cut off his question.

"Stay inside," she said, and closed the door. Darkness settled in.

Beside him, Rachel's breaths still came in hard, fast rasps.

"What the devil were you thinking?" he asked, not daring to turn toward her lest his emotions show in his face.

For a moment she said nothing, then, "I was thinking I'd just as soon not see you dead until I've completed my miss—" She stopped suddenly and pursed her lips.

Liam turned. The terror of seeing her in the huge man's grasp faded slowly. He narrowed his eyes. "Until you've completed what?" he asked.

"Until I've completed my journey to my laird Dunlock."

Silence settled in. Liam's mind raced.

"Until you've completed your mission. Twas what you were about to say."

"You're wrong," she said, but she didn't look at him.

"I'm right, and I know it."

"You know nothing!" Her words were rasped, and now she jerked her gaze to his. Her eyes sparked with anger. "Not even that I need—" She stopped again, breathing hard.

"What?" He all but croaked the word.

"I need you alive," she said, and raised her chin slightly. "If you're bent on theft, at least you could choose a more likely victim."

"More likely?" He made certain his expression was cocky, though his heart was racing overtime, and his mind too, wondering what she had meant to say. "There was none more likely than he."

"None more likely! He was the biggest man in the crowd. Nay!" She swept a hand angrily before her as if to encompass the universe. "The biggest in the world."

Liam stared at her, his gut clenched like a fist at the thought of her in danger. "Just so," he said, and turning his back to her, refused to speak again.

Chapter 11

Liam awoke with a start. It took a moment to remember where he was, an instant longer to realize Rachel slept beside him.

Evening had settled in. Though it had been dim before, it was darker now. Beneath him, the wagon shifted again, and he realized by the jangling noises and the rumbling voices outside that it was being hitched to a horse.

What now? Should he wake Rachel and insist that they leave this band? he wondered, but one glance at her slumbering features decided him.

She lay on her side, her lips slightly parted and one narrow hand nestled beneath her cheek. Her otherworldly eyes were closed, and beneath the silky lengths of her lashes, the skin was cast with purple shadows of fatigue.

His heart wrenched.

She was right. He shouldn't have chosen that particular man to steal from. But old habits die hard. Why choose an easy mark when you could endanger your life instead? Why take the well-trod path when he could assuage his guilt and quell her hunger all in one fell swoop?

Up front, the wagon seat creaked. The driver clicked, and they lurched forward.

Rachel moaned, shifted slightly, but didn't awaken. Liam settled in, watching her face as she fell back into oblivion.

Some hours later Liam sat staring across the fire at the ancient Gypsy woman who had piped the music for Rachel's dance—pathetic as it was.

They'd stopped only a short time before. He'd lain quietly for a while, watching Rachel awake at the cessation of movement, watching her eyes open, watching awareness come to her.

It had taken her a few moments to realize where they were, a few more to sit up and voice the obvious questions.

The old woman had eventually knocked at the narrow door, and now Rachel occupied the log beside him in the midst of a sheltered glen.

Across the bright fire, the old woman's eyes dulled the light of the flame. Taking her smoking pipe from her mouth, she squinted at him. "Tis your business, lad," she said. "But the next time you filch a purse, I'd suggest you choose someone more your own size."

"Filch a purse?" Liam lifted a hand innocently to his chest and gave her a practiced smile. Who was this woman who had initiated the dance that had saved Rachel? And why had she done it? Though these questions went unanswered, something told him his act was wasted on her. Still, he had to try, for he could afford to trust no one. "I fear you're mistaken, Grandmother."

She stared at him in silent speculation. Beside him, Rachel shifted slightly. She'd said no more than a dozen words since awakening, and he longed to glance at her, to assure himself that she was well. But there was little point. For he knew how she would look if he turned toward her—tattered and worn but with a frayed sort of elegance that was all her own.

Damn! Maybe he had been a fool. Perhaps his actions had been misguided from the start. Perhaps the hulking Davin was nothing but loyal, and Liam should have returned her into his protection. But Warwick—Damn Warwick! Liam's mind reeled. Maybe Rachel was right. Maybe Warwick was dead and it was nothing more than Liam's continuing terror that made him think otherwise. Or maybe . . .

For a moment, he refused to finish the thought, but just because one was an excellent liar did not give him free rein to lie to himself, so he forced the thought through to its finish.

Maybe he had wanted to believe it was Warwick on the opposite shore. Maybe he had wanted to believe in a fate so horrible that would give him an opportunity to play the hero. Maybe the risk of death in the rapids was worth having Rachel to himself, if only for a little while.

God's balls! He was a dolt. If he were going to pretend to be the man he was not, at least he could see her decently clothed and fed instead of allowing her to traipse about half-dressed and starving.

At least he could have snatched the giant man's purse with his usual aplomb. It wasn't like him to botch up a job. But suddenly Rachel had appeared, and the sight of her involved in his black deeds—

"Tis not like you to botch up a job so," said the old woman.

"What?" Liam nearly dropped the bowl some nameless man had handed him moments before.

The old woman chuckled. "But I suppose your lady distracted you."

"Me lady! Nay, she is my—" Liam began.

"Do not say she's your sister, lad," warned the crone quietly, the corner of a smirk on her dried-apple face. "If I were foolish enough to believe such tripe, twould make your feelings for her suspect indeed. We shall say she is your wife."

Liam stared agog. He was absolutely *not* going to pretend Rachel was his wife. For he knew his limitations, and such a pretense would put him hell and gone past them. He opened his mouth to argue, but before he could form appropriate words, the old woman spoke again.

"And what of you, lass? No permanent damage done, I see."

"I am well," Rachel said, her carefully schooled voice quiet in the darkness, her gaze not flickering from the old matriarch's. "You have my thanks, Grandmother."

"You may call me Marta," she said, and paused. "But not in that voice."

Liam tensed, knowing the old woman had recognized nobility. But when he glanced at Rachel, he saw no alarm, only a hint of humor, and maybe the flash of respect in her otherworldly eyes.

"You have me thanks, Marta," she corrected, her tone heavy with a Highland brogue.

The old woman's obsidian eyes sparkled. "So you think better than you dance. I hoped twas true. In fact, I would have wagered on it."

A young lad panted up, snaring their attention. Dressed in breeches and a tunic three times too large for his narrow body, he looked to be no more than eight years of age.

"Rory said you filched a purse," he spouted,

breathless as he stared wide-eyed at Liam. "Will you teach me how?"

"I did not—" Liam began, but suddenly a growl rumbled in his ear.

He lurched to his feet. A black beast reared from the darkness. Frantically, Liam searched for a weapon, but he had none. Quick as a snake, the beast snatched the boy up by the back of his tunic. The lad squawked and thrashed, but it did no good.

Liam yanked a branch from the fire, ready to do battle.

But a woman's voice stopped him. "Take him down to the river, Bear. And do not bring him back till you've washed such filthy notions from his mind."

Liam turned toward the voice. The slim Gypsy girl stood at the edge of the fire's light, her arms akimbo and her bright eyes perturbed.

"That was a . . . that was a bear!" Liam said. He tried to make his tone casual, but . . . the boy had just been snatched up by a bear. Surely that warranted some excitement.

"Aye." The girl turned her scowl from the darkness to Liam. "I but hope Lachlan does not corrupt him before their return."

Liam tried to formulate questions, but none found their way into words.

"My granddaughter, Catriona," the old woman introduced.

The girl stepped into the firelight. Shadows danced off exotic features—straight nose, high cheekbones, eyes slightly almond in shape and indescribable in color. Built like a restless reed was this small bundle of energy.

The outlandish costume she'd worn during her

performance was gone. Now she was dressed in a simple gown of nondescript hue. But if this was a simple woman, Liam was a saint.

Stepping up to the fire, she scooped a bit of soup into a wooden bowl and turned to Rachel. "Who taught you to dance?"

For a moment the woods were silent, then, "No one," Rachel said dryly.

"Good," Catriona said. "Then there is no one to blame."

A young man, just over twenty years of age, stepped into the fire's light. His black eyes skimmed to Rachel, settled there for a fraction of a second, then shifted aside. But a second was too long to Liam's way of thinking.

"This be Rory," Marta said.

Liam recognized him as the fellow who had caught Catriona during her high-flying performance, and guessed that, judging by how close he was standing to the girl, he claimed her for his own, at least in his own mind.

"What be your name?" he asked, skimming his attention from Liam to Rachel again.

"I am Hugh, and this be me wife, Flora." God, he was going to burn in hell for all eternity. He could feel the flames licking him even now. But he couldn't have Rory thinking . . . whatever he was thinking.

"And where are you heading?" asked Marta.

"North," said Liam succinctly. These nomads would expect no more explanations from other wanderers.

"Then you may as well travel with us for a time," Marta said. "For we go in the same direction, and tis less likely you'll be found if you travel with our familia, aye?"

"Found by whom?" Liam asked innocently, but Rachel spoke up, surprising him.

"We've no wish to endanger you or yours," she said, her gaze steady on the old woman's, her brogue still heavy.

For a moment Marta said nothing, then, "But you have deeds that must be done. And mayhaps your efforts will only aid our own." She paused, then nodded as if seeing things in Rachel's eyes. "Aye. You will travel with us for a spell, and we shall see what we can do with you."

Liam watched the old woman nervously, but her gaze didn't flicker from Rachel's.

"The eyes of a saint and the skin of a lady. But what of your soul?" she murmured.

Liam opened his mouth to object, but Marta raised a hand for silence.

"We shall eat now," she said.

The campground fell silent. There seemed nothing to do but follow her instructions. Liam noticed now that his stomach knotted with hunger as he tasted the soup again.

The boy called Lachlan hustled back to the campsite, the back of his tunic wet and his expression peeved as he glanced over his shoulder at the bear that lumbered along behind him. Liam warily watched the huge beast, but the bear seemed to have no appetite for Irishmen. Dropping to his haunches, he folded his legs beneath him, snored a note of contentment, and settled down with a freshly caught trout.

Quiet murmuring began up again as if this were an everyday occurrence. Bread was passed around and a bottle of wine was brought forth.

Further introductions were made. Hertha was a woman of middling years. She had a belly round with child, and two daughters who had a tendency to stare at Liam and giggle behind their hands. Their father's name was John and *his* father, a man with a limp who called Marta, Mother, was named Fane.

As far as Liam could tell, Rory was the only one without direct ties to the old woman.

Supper ended finally. Marta pushed herself stiffly to her feet, using a gnarled staff, its end worn smooth with wear.

"Rory, you and the boy shall give up your wagon this night," she pronounced.

"Can we sleep in the trees?" Lachlan asked.

"'Tis likely to rain," Rory said, his dark gaze flitting to Rachel. "Best to sleep beneath the wagon."

For a moment the old woman's eyes sparkled. "Methinks you would get more sleep in the trees," she said, and chuckling softly, disappeared inside the first wagon in the row of three.

Liam made a concerted effort not to clear his throat, not to fidget, not to burst into spontaneous flame. But he was expected to spend the night with Rachel! And he had neither the advantage of being freezing cold or ravenously hungry to save himself from her. What the hell were they thinking?

But when he glanced frantically about him, he realized with numbing surprise that no one seemed to realize the enormity of his problem. Lachlan was busy fighting off the advances of Bear, who had plopped a gargantuan paw on the boy's shoulder as he begged for treats. Catriona was braiding one of the girls' hair, and Hertha was already toting the bowls off to the river.

Only Rory was watching him.

"Well . . ." Liam rose to his feet. "Our thanks for

your beds," he said, nodding to the dark-eyed man.

The other made no response.

Liam extended a hand to Rachel, who rose with only a moment of hesitation.

The journey to the wagon seemed inordinately long. Inside, it was darker than ever. Liam closed the door behind them and turned toward Rachel. The world went quiet.

And now Liam did clear his throat, did fidget. He waited to burst into spontaneous flame. It didn't happen. Not immediately anyway, and that was some comfort. "Tis not as if this was my idea," he began.

"You could have argued."

"As could you," he said. "You could have insisted that you could not sleep with me. That you are my sister. How could they know different? It is not as if I am drooling over you." He snorted his derision, but here she was dressed in the world's homeliest costume, without having gone so far as to remove her damned shoes. "It's not as if I'm . . ." He searched momentarily for a good lie. "It's not as if I'm hopelessly tempted." As lies went, that was an impressive one.

For a moment she didn't speak, then, "Indeed, Liam, I think I can trust you," she said coolly. "After all, Rory is camped just beneath the wagon."

"Rory!" He knew he should remain silent, should quit while he was ahead, but anger and frustration were building to a fine boil within him. "You think you can trust him, but you don't trust me?"

Even in the darkness he could tell she shrugged.

Her casual attitude did nothing to improve his mood. "You think that I'll . . . what? Throw myself upon you? You think I'll be so overcome by your beauty, your charm, your . . . allure . . ." This last word was almost choked. "That I'll lose all control?"

She sighed dramatically as she sat down and slipped a blanket over her legs. "The truth is, Liam, I know you too well."

"You do not know me atall."

"You are mistaken."

"Oh? And what do you know of me, Rachel? What, but that I'm a bastard and a peasant?"

He could feel her gaze on him suddenly, chilly and steady. "I know that you laid with Elisa when you were but five and ten."

He felt the air leave his lungs in a hard whoosh. "You know about that?"

"Aye." Her voice was deep in the darkness. "All of Glen Creag knew. I doubt there was a soul she neglected to tell. It seems she was quite thrilled. But then she was a simple lass. It didn't take much to excite her."

Liam loosened his fists and silently vowed to neither throttle her nor kiss her. "Maybe wee Elisa was a connoisseur in the ways of love, and was only thrilled by the most thrilling of men."

She snorted. Liam tightened his fists again.

"In truth, I was surprised she settled on you. Tis said old Rendel showed some interest in her."

"Rendel cleaned the garderobes! He reeked of dung."

She shrugged again.

Her casualness made him grind his teeth. "Have you ever considered that maybe she begged me?" In actuality, she had.

"Nay," she said, "I haven't."

"Well, maybe you should."

"And maybe you have the morals of a snake," she hissed suddenly.

"Me? And what of yourself?" Anger and building frustration made him move closer. "Tis you who said you'll have little chance for . . . adventure once you're wed. Indeed, tis that very reason you gave for . . ." His mind steamed as he remembered their time together in the cave. Her kisses, hot as summer; her hands, quick and soft and heavenly as they skimmed his body. "For losing control in the cave."

"I did not lose control."

"Truly? Then, why?"

"I told you, I merely . . ." Her words failed for a moment. "I merely wished to take a bit of pleasure. Surely a man of your ilk can understand that."

"A man of my ilk?" He leaned closer still.

She leaned back, but they were still close enough so that he could feel her breath on his cheek. "A man who takes his pleasures wherever he wishes."

"Wherever I wish! Is that what you think of me?"

"Aye. I do."

"Well, you are sadly mistaken, lady!" he growled, "for if such was the truth I would—"

"What?" The question was soft, as if no more than a thought carried on a whisper of wind.

Liam watched her lips move, watched them form the word, watched them remain slightly parted as she breathed between them, and suddenly there was no hope for him. He could not resist. His hand raised without his command. His fingertip touched the ridge of her plump lower lip and smoothed feather soft along the curve. It was as soft as satin, as smooth as glass. He should draw back. He *must* draw back! But in that instant, he felt her tremble.

The movement shivered through his finger and up his arm, smiting his heart.

For a moment he struggled. For an instant eternity he tried to obey his conscience, but it was so dim and unfamiliar, while she was so clear and as familiar as a thousand dreams. His knuckles skimmed onto the silky lawn of her cheek. Any minute she would strike his hand away. Any second! He knew it. But instead, her eyes fell closed. She was breathing faster now, and she tilted her head ever so slightly against his fingers.

It was too much! Far too much. He was just a nameless bastard from Firthport. He had no morals. He couldn't be expected to resist her. He couldn't be expected to . . .

"Rachel!" he rasped, and slipping his hand behind her neck, he kissed her.

Pleasure seized him. He pressed closer, and she opened her mouth. Lightning exploded inside him, petrifying his muscles, galvanizing his desire. It pulsed against her thigh. He wrapped an arm about her waist, pulling her closer as he kissed the bewitching corner of her mouth, her cheek, the thrumming dell between her collarbones. Her skin was so soft there, so fantastically sweet. But lower still . . . Lower!

"Liam!"

He barely heard her. Indeed, it took several seconds before he realized she had a palm pressed against his chest, longer still to absorb the fact that he had already loosened the laces of the garish gown.

He dropped his arm from about her waist and stared in bewildered fascination at the dangling laces.

"What . . ." He lifted his gaze to her face for a

moment, trying to get his bearing. "What were we talking about?"

She was breathing through her mouth, her dusky lips parted. Liam tightened his hands into fists and refused to move closer.

"You were about to tell me what you would do if you took pleasure wherever you wished."

He tried not to wince. "As you can see you needn't worry," he said, and turned hopelessly toward the wall. "I'm perfectly in control."

Chapter 12

Rachel rose with the dawn, but the others were already awake and going about their morning chores. John and Hertha were working over the fire while their daughters, two nearly identical girls who reminded her of half-grown goslings, carried wooden buckets full of water from the nearby stream.

Some distance from camp, Rachel saw Catriona lift a white palfrey's front leg. Curious, Rachel wandered in that direction.

Catriona straightened when she neared.

"Was she injured?" Rachel asked.

"Just a bruise to the sole. She's healing well now. A beauty is she not?"

"Indeed." Rachel ran a hand down the elegant ivory neck. "Even the Flame would think . . ." She stopped herself abruptly, realizing belatedly that it would be unwise to reveal the fact that her aunt was the notorious lady of the MacGowans. "Anyone would think her a bonny lass," she finished, lamely finding her brogue.

She turned away, but still she could feel the girl's catlike gaze on her. Running her hand down the mare's sturdy back, she endeavored to turn attention away from her blunder. "Where did you find such a mount?"

"She was injured, starving, and skittish as a lark when I first saw her. Her master was happy enough to make a trade."

"Skittish? She seems a friendly sort."

"Aye, but high-strung." The girl shrugged and glanced for a moment at the bear just rising from the water, his freshly caught breakfast still flapping between his jaws. "Tis said by some that I have a way with the animals."

"Aye," Rory said, approaching from the woods and putting a hand to the small of the girl's back. "I was as wild as the winds when I first met Cat."

Catriona managed to look wry and peeved all at once. "I have more control over some animals than others."

Rory laughed. Rachel forced a smile, but turned rapidly away. Control seemed to be something she was sadly lacking, at least where Liam was concerned, for though her mind refused to admit it, her heart knew that if he had not drawn immediately away the previous night, she would have offered him all.

Just after breakfast it began to rain. The wandering band packed their belongings into their wagons and headed north. The horses plodded resolutely through the mud. They stopped twice that day, but Rachel barely noticed, for fatigue still wore at her and she slept when she could in the cozy warmth of the wagon.

That night she was again confined to that same small space with Liam, but she turned quickly away. She may be a fool, but she knew her limitations.

By morning the fog was as thick as bedbugs. Breakfast was damp and quiet.

The horses were harnessed again, and everyone made ready to travel. Marta motioned Rachel onto her own wagon. With some misgivings, Rachel did as requested.

Catriona snapped the lines over the horses' broad backs. They moved out with a jingle of harness. Lachlan rode behind on his silver-dappled pony. Marta said nothing. She sat hunched on the hard wooden seat, her shawl drawn up over her head.

But just when Rachel was certain the old woman had fallen asleep, she spoke. "We'll have our nooning in the sunshine."

"What?"

"The sun will shine when next we eat."

Though the fog lay around them as heavy and gray as a woolen blanket, Rachel didn't argue. Neither did she see the significance of Marta's statement. The trio fell into silence for several minutes before Marta spoke again.

"I'll have you pick dewberries," she said.

"What?" Rachel asked. She was beginning to feel foolish. It could be the old woman was simply toying with her, for in the past she'd sensed a restless sort of humor in the ancient Gypsy's eyes.

"We shall stop in a wee glen. On the hill behind a stand of hawthorns, there'll be a thicket of berries. You shall go alone to pick them—and to touch the sun."

What? seemed a silly thing to say again. Still, Rachel could think of nothing more intelligent. But before she could ask, Marta continued.

"I'll not see my familia endangered because of your fair skin."

The truth dawned on Rachel finally. She even

remembered her brogue. "You want me to darken my face."

Silence for several moments, then, "Do you not think the men will wonder if your shoulders are pale as goat's milk and your face dark like a hazelnut?"

Rachel shook her head. "I've no intention of allowing men to see me shoulders."

The old woman stared at her. "What we intend and what we do be two roads that seldom meet."

"'Tis not that I don't appreciate your help," Rachel said. "But I have no time to—"

"You'll do the lad little good if you die before you reach him," Marta interrupted.

"What lad?" Rachel hissed, her heart pounding in her chest.

But the old woman only shrugged. "If you do not want the evil to take you, you will do as I say," she insisted, and closing her eyes, she fell asleep.

They stopped their small caravan just past noon. Moments later, the sun burst out from behind the clouds.

Climbing down from the brightly colored wagon, Rachel stared up at the azure sky with some misgivings.

"Is something amiss?" Liam asked, striding up to her.

"Nay." She knew that her cousins sometimes thought her eerie. But there was nothing eerie about her. There were just times when she knew things other people didn't. Twas simple enough. But Marta—

"What did the old woman want?" Liam asked, his voice low.

"I didn't want to eat her alive if that's what you're

thinking," Marta said. For a person as old as the earth, she could approach with amazing silence. They jerked toward her. She gave them a toothless grin and handed Rachel a basket made of reeds. "Tis time," she said. "I shall fetch you when the meal is ready. Unless . . ." She shifted her sly old eyes. "Unless you'd rather have your husband fetch you."

"Nay," Rachel said, snatching the basket to her chest. "Tis certain you have other tasks for . . . Hugh."

The old woman grinned. "Aye, I've jobs to keep everyone busy. As for you, lad, you can help Catriona chain up the bear lest your love has to fight him for the berries."

Liam scowled, first at Marta, then at Rachel. "Maybe I had best help Flora . . ."

Marta laughed out loud now, and taking Liam's arm, steered him away. "Methinks you are the first lad to ever object to helping me granddaughter with anything."

Rachel could see him scowl over his shoulder at her. "But—"

"Your lady will be well," Marta interrupted. "I will make certain of that."

Rachel lifted her garish skirt and turned to climb the hill to the woods beyond. Up ahead, a tree pipit sang, and the sun felt lovely on her face.

Past a copse of hawthorn trees, just where Marta had said to look, Rachel found a patch of rambling dewberries hidden in the midst of the woods.

Setting her basket on the ground, she began to pick the dark berries, but even in the depths of the trees the sun found her. After the rainy morning, it felt warm and friendly, and even though it seemed she'd done nothing but sleep for the better part of two days, she felt drowsy again.

Finally, able to deny her fatigue no longer, she wandered to a kindly spot where the sun slanted down through the bright spring leaves. Setting her basket aside, she sat down on a bed of moss and removed her homely coif. The sun touched her face with tender fingers.

"The evil." Rachel remembered the old woman's words with some misgiving. "If you don't want the evil to take you, you will do as I say," she'd said.

Twas ridiculous, of course. Just an old woman's means of getting her way, Rachel thought. But Liam, too, had referred to "the evil." As if it were a tangible, finite thing.

Rachel scoffed at the idea, but if the truth be told, she had felt the bite of the ragged evil, had felt it in her heart like a poisoned spear. There was no explanation, no understanding. Yet she couldn't deny it.

Someone wished her ill. Though she couldn't say why, she knew that much was true. And if it was true, it certainly wasn't too much to believe that that someone knew how she looked. Thus, she'd have to be extremely careful. She couldn't afford to fail. She must get to Blackburn Castle, and she must get there soon. So, yes, maybe it would be wise to take some steps to change her appearance.

They traveled on again that afternoon, but stopped early.

Hertha made a sweet sauce with the dewberries Rachel had picked and saved the water they'd cooked in, though God knew what for.

They were a strange lot, these Roms, and Liam would just as soon have departed from them. But the trail ahead would be difficult, and if they were being followed, he and Rachel would not easily be found amongst them, for twas a well-known fact that the Roms did not easily accept outsiders.

Yet this Rory seemed to be accepting Rachel well enough. Liam glanced over to where they sat by the fire. Rory leaned close to murmur something and Rachel laughed aloud.

The sound did strange things to his belly, as did the sight of her face in the firelight. It had become pink in the sun today, and he couldn't help but wonder about Marta's reasons for sending Rachel alone into the woods.

Though Liam couldn't explain it, the old woman seemed to care about Rachel's safety. So maybe she simply hoped to change Rachel's appearance in an attempt to keep her safe. But Liam had grown up in the underbelly of Firthport. Tutored by a master of theft and disguise known only as the Shadow, he'd learned much of deception. Thus, to his way of thinking, a wee bit of the sun's color seemed a pathetic guise. So perhaps Marta had plans he knew nothing about. Whatever the case, he had best keep a close eye on things.

The night passed slowly. In the morning, they headed north again. Their pace seemed pathetically slow, but at least they could rest and eat during the journey, so Liam tried to be content. He passed the time by teaching Lachlan a few simple tricks and making a poor attempt to ignore Rachel's too close presence.

Being locked in with her at night was nearly more than his flagging self-control could bear, listening to the sound of her breath, imagining the softness of her skin. But the daylight hours were worse, for then she was out of his sight, leaving her fate to his imagination. Often Rachel would ride with one of the women, and each day Marta would find some reason to send Rachel off alone.

Finally, in a peaceful valley where the hills stretched up and away, they stopped to make a meal.

The clan fell to their usual chores, and Marta clumped up to Rachel with an earthenware jar.

Liam tried to hear what was said, but he was too far away, and in a moment Rachel was heading off alone.

He hurried after her and caught up before she reached the woods.

"Where are you bound?" he asked.

For a moment, he thought she looked embarrassed, but he couldn't be certain. "Marta said I could find motherwort growing just inside the woods. I think it best that I replenish my supply of remedies."

He nodded. Twas like Rachel to worry over her concoctions or the lack thereof. "I'll go with you." But just then Marta called him over. "Wait for me," he said, and turned away to speak to the old matron.

"We've a need for firewood, lad," she said.

"I'll be happy enough to fetch it after I accompany Flora to the woods."

The old woman's eyes sparkled. "Your Flora is already in the woods. And not likely to be out of them anytime soon, so if you've a hope of besting the dark one, you'll watch your step."

"What dark one?" Liam hissed.

"Don't play games with me, lad," Marta rasped. "You're sure to lose. Now fetch the wood, and when you're finished I have other chores for you."

It didn't seem possible that there could be so many tasks for such a small caravan of folk, Liam thought, but all seemed busy.

Lachlan and the girls gathered extra kindling, for the weather had been dry of late. John set to replacing a shoe on one of the cart horses. The women talked among themselves as they prepared the evening meal, and Rory set off toward the river with a willow switch and hook.

As for Liam, he was kept busy with a number of small jobs, carrying water, feeding the horses, sharpening Hertha's scaling knife.

The last was a pleasant task, for he could sit in the sun, letting the brightness of the day and the lush scent of grass fill his senses. The regular hiss of the blade against the whetting stone lulled him, and a gentle breeze whispered in time.

It was the cold slap of reality that made him realize finally that Rory had been gone for some time and had not yet returned with a single fish to show for his efforts.

The sun stroked Rachel with a bold caress. Maybe she should be ashamed of herself, she thought, but since the first time in the woods behind the dewberry plants, she'd found herself less and less reluctant to shed her clothes.

In truth, the feel of the sunlight against her bare skin was a sensual delight she'd never before imagined. But today she'd given herself a special treat. Feeling an aching need to bathe, she'd made certain there was no one in sight, then slipped out of her clothing and hurried into the water.

The soap Marta had given her smelled of lye and grease, and the dewberry water Hertha had saved still held the scent of the fruit when she poured it through her hair, but she did as ordered and finally emerged clean and chilled from the burn.

Maybe she should have dressed immediately,

but she had committed herself to this simple disguise Marta had thought up. Or so she told herself. In actually, twas the kind warmth of the sunlight that kept her naked, for it felt like a lover's gentle touch against her skin.

As Rachel sank onto a mossy bed, she scoffed at herself for that thought, for indeed, she knew little of lovers' touches. Even Liam, notorious womanizer that he was, did nothing but turn away and find sleep in the confinement of their wagon.

But with the sun caressing her bare skin, and her hair cascading about her shoulders in wet rivulets, she felt primitive and untamed. Twas not a feeling she had entertained before, for she had always been nothing more or less than Lady Rachel of the Forbes.

It wasn't that she thought herself unattractive to men. Men had always sought her out—poor men who wished for an advantageous match. Old men who needed a healer. Widowed men who knew she would be an asset to their households. She had, in fact, agreed to marry on several occasions. But twas certainly duty and not love, mutual or otherwise that made her agree.

Now, here in this quiet Eden, she wondered why she'd never been offered more. What of passion and heat? What of strong arms and whispered words of adoration? Her cousins had surely found that.

Why not she? She wasn't hideous to look at. She had all her teeth and her disposition wasn't beyond repair—regardless of Liam's opinion to the contrary.

The thought of the Irishman sent a spasm of emotion through her. True, he was like a nettle in her backside, but try as she might, she couldn't forget his kiss, the way he had scooped his hand behind her neck, how his body had felt tight and hard against hers.

Upon her chest, Dragonheart seemed to thrum to life. Reaching up, she touched its ruby heart, then slipped her fingers slowly down her body, between her breasts, shivering at the thrill of her naughtiness. Never had she been aught but the epitome of good breeding. Yet here she was, unclothed in the open air, kissed by the sun's gentle beams. Like a wild thing she was, a creature of the woods, lush, lovely, seductive, and suddenly she didn't care who saw—

What was that?

Sitting up quickly, she snatched her gown from the branch where she'd hung it to dry. Pulling it over her body, she couldn't help but see the humor in the situation. She'd felt quite decadent for a moment, but she was still herself. No enchanting seductress, just Rachel of the Forbes, healer, nurturer, lady. Twas a good thing Marta's approach brought her back to reality before she did something truly idiotic, or she'd find herself in trouble aplenty.

She grinned at her own foolishness, but just then a voice broke the silence.

"So there you be," Rory said, and stepped into view.

Chapter 13

Rachel stifled a gasp and scrunched her legs back another few inches, covering as much of her naked anatomy as possible with the full red skirt.

"I've been hoping to see you. Although I admit . . ." Rory grinned at her from no more than five yards away. His teeth were very white against his dark complexion, his black eyes intense. "I dared not hope I'd see so much of you."

Glancing sideways, Rachel wondered frantically what to do now. Decadence, it seemed, did not suit her.

"Marta . . ." Her voice sounded uncharacteristically high-pitched. She tried again. "Marta will be here in a moment to fetch me."

"Ahh. So twas Grandmother's idea." Crossing his arms against his chest, Rory leaned his shoulder on the knobby trunk of a poplar. "I must remember to thank her."

If she screamed, they would possibly hear her back at camp. But she didn't truly wish to cause a problem for these people who had protected her thus far. Not if she could avoid it. And it was all together possible that Rory meant no real harm.

"Thank her?" Rachel asked, eager to keep him talking.

His eyes were steady as the sun on her. "I have to think there could only be two reasons she would send you here. Either to darken your skin . . . or to wait for me."

Rachel kept her expression impassive. But her heart was beating overtime and her mind was spinning, searching frantically for the best way out of this mess.

"And since your skin surpassed lovely when it was pale . . ." He shifted his weight from the tree and straightened. "I can only assume she sent you here for the other purpose."

He took a step forward.

Rachel launched to her feet. True, it was impossible to keep all her parts covered with the dress that flopped over her arm, but if he came closer, she would be ready to run.

Sweet Mary, mother of God, please don't make her run buck naked through these woods, she prayed.

The Rom advanced another step, his lithe body moving with supple grace.

"Listen, Rory," she said, trying to remember to do all the necessary things at once—keep all her more scandalous body parts covered, speak with a brogue, and most importantly, figure out a way to keep the Rom at bay. "I appreciate all your familia has done for me, but—I be a married woman."

He stopped and shrugged as though wounded. "And so we cannot even talk."

She licked her lips and checked her exit route. She'd be heading downhill where her lighter weight would give her no advantage, so she'd better make her escape good if it came to that. "You just want to talk?" she asked, biding her time.

"Of course." He laughed. Let it never be said that he was an unattractive man. "What did *you* have in mind, bonny Flora."

Rachel swallowed hard and wondered if she should feel stupid for her misunderstanding. But reality sliced quickly through her. Regardless of her lack of sexual experience, she had *some* knowledge of men, and if all he wanted was to talk, she was a hare-brained bunny. Cotton tail and all. Still, verbiage seemed her best ally, for eventually, Marta *would* come.

"What is it you wished to speak of?" she asked, splaying her fingers over her chest.

"Your marriage," he said, not hesitating a moment. "Sometimes I sense that you are not wholly content with your husband."

She forced a laugh. "Of course I'm content." Her mind churned for her supposed spouse's supposed name for a moment, then, "Hugh is a good man."

Rory shrugged. "I don't argue with good. I only wondered . . ." His eyes skimmed down her body. She felt the heat of his intentions like a lurid caress. "I've slept beneath your bed for several days now. Not once has my rest been disturbed. Not once have I heard your moans of pleasure." He took a step toward her, moving like a hunting cat.

"Catriona!" The name burst from Rachel's lips as the girl's image popped into her mind.

"What of her?" Rory asked, immediately tense.

"I think I heard her calling."

He glanced quickly about them, then settled his sly gaze back on Rachel. "I think tis your imagination," he said, stepping closer still. "When I left camp she was well occupied with the—"

"Nay," Rachel rasped, retreating warily. "I'm certain I heard—"

"And I'm certain you did not. Now let us—"

But just then Rachel heard a low chuckle issue from the woods to her right. "Catriona," someone said. "You surprise me." It took her a moment to realize the voice was Liam's.

There was a whisper of indistinguishable, feminine words, then Liam laughed again, the sound a deep, seductive chuckle. "Nay! Right here?"

"Damn them!" Rory swore, and lurched off in the direction of the voices.

Rachel yanked her gown over her head with shaky hands. Still damp, it became bound up on her chest and refused to go lower. Popping her head through the neck hole, she scanned the woods as she struggled with the recalcitrant fabric.

"Need some help?" asked a voice from behind her.

Rachel squawked as she spun about. "Liam!"

He stood unmoving, his expression absolutely sober, his gaze burning into hers.

Heart pumping, Rachel finally managed to yank the gown into place. "What are you doing here?"

A muscle jumped in his jaw. "I wondered the same about you."

She licked her lips. Heat flooded her face. But suddenly she remembered his voice in the woods. Anger bubbled through her, broiling her embarrassment. "Where's Catriona?"

He didn't even blink. "In camp I suspect, where you should be."

Confusion rolled up with the anger and the embarrassment and the fading remnants of fear. "But I thought—"

"What?" he prompted. "That I was planning to

take advantage of the woods for a private tryst just as you were?"

She said nothing as she fought to make sense of things.

"Tis none of my affair, of course, to judge someone such as yourself—the Lady Saint," he said, his voice deep. "But were I you, I would be more discriminating about who I take as a lover. Rory does not seem the type—"

"If you were me!" she snarled, a medley of raw emotions melting together in a confusing mass in her gut. "In truth, Liam, I have seen your lovers. Tis not as though you choose them for their wit or the good they do their fellow—"

"We cannot all be saints!" he rasped. "But at least I can be fairly certain they are not going to ravage me body and slit me throat before leaving me to—"

A noise made him turn abruptly to the side. The cords in his neck stood out sharp as a well-honed blade above his tunic. But finally he turned back. His body was somewhat less tense, but his eyes had not lost their anger.

"I would suggest we return to camp, *Lady* Rachel," he murmured. "Unless you're still in the mood to entertain the Rom."

Rachel bit off a sharp retort. Lifting her skirt in one shaky hand, she retrieved her shoes from where she'd left them, and hurried from the woods.

The wagon was as silent as death that night. Rachel lay in the quiet, staring at the dark wall and wishing she couldn't feel Liam's gaze on her. Wishing she couldn't imagine his fingers against her skin.

"I'll need your assistance when we reach the next village."

His words broke the silence like the crack of an egg, but she didn't turn toward him.

"Assistance with what?"

"I spoke to Marta. They've agreed to lend me a few things. The old woman even has a bit of black powder for me. The explosion adds a certain element to my act. I shall be performing with the Roms."

She sat up. His face was barely visible in the darkness. "Do you think tis safe?"

"Would you rather I turned to thievery?"

She said nothing.

"If I'm not mistaken, you'll want to eat every day until you reach the king, Rachel."

Her stomach pitched. "I'm not going to the king."

He laughed, the sound low in the darkness. "Tis strange that after all these years you are still such a poor liar. You told me some days hence that you had to reach Blackburn Castle."

"I did no such thing."

"Aye you did," he countered. "It slipped out when you were not thinking. Maybe for a moment, you forgot who I was. Forgot that you cannot trust me."

"I'm going to Dunlock."

He snorted. "Truly, Rachel? To marry? And thus your tryst with the Rom? Because it may be your last fling?"

She considered telling him the truth. That she'd had no intention of meeting Rory there. But she'd learned long ago that pride was all she had where Liam was concerned, and little enough of that.

"You're right," she said. "A lass must take her

pleasure where she may, and Rory seemed as good a choice as any."

"If you're looking for naught but the feel of a lover's lance between your thighs, why not choose me?"

His crass words were like a sharp slap across her heart. For a moment she was breathless. But she struggled for control, trying to think, to be smart, but he had always brought out the worst in her. When he was near, it seemed she lost all she had been taught and was reduced to a mass of raw emotions. Even her precious pride was shattered. "If you remember correctly, Liam, you turned me down some years past. I thought maybe Rory would not be so particular."

"Damn it, Rachel! You'll stay away from him!" Liam stormed, leaning closer.

She stiffened her back. "I'll do as I like, Liam. And you've nothing to say about it."

"You'll do as I say!" he growled. "Do not touch the Rom."

"I fear I left my chastity belt at Glen Creag, hence—"

"Damn you!" he swore, and reaching out, grabbed her arm, and pulled her close.

Face-to-face, they stared at each other, their breath rasping, their bodies taut with sizzling emotion.

"You'll vow to leave the Rom be!" he gritted.

"Or what, Liam?" she asked, her voice barely audible to her own ears.

"Or I'll . . . truss you up like a wayward lamb. Not until I see you married with me own eyes will I set you free."

She lifted her chin, her chest aching with the hard beat of her heart.

"Then you'd best get a long tether, Liam. For you'll not be the one dictating my actions," she said, and yanking her arm from his grasp, turned shakily away.

The village of York was humming with life. Even so, the Rom's colorful wagons drew more than a few glances as they rolled through a towering gate and down a rutted street. They came to the marketplace, noted the size of the crowds, then found a courtyard of sorts where they unhitched their horses and began preparing for their show.

Rory led the sleek white mare forward. Catriona had hung a scarlet cloth over her back and coiled up her mane and tail in matching ribbons.

Light as the wind, she leapt to the horse's back. With her reins firmly attached to a surcingle beneath the cloth, the mare stood perfectly still, her elegant neck arched and dark eyes watchful as she champed her bit.

Straddling the steed for a moment, Catriona leaned forward to whisper a few words, then pushed herself easily to her feet. For the briefest moment she searched for her balance on the mare's crimson cloth, then she lifted her bare, slender arms above her head and clapped.

She'd donned the same costume she'd worn the first time they'd seen her, a sapphire gown of sorts. But instead of a free-flowing skirt, it had broad pant legs that were cuffed at the ankle. Her feet were bare and her waist was cinched as tight as a trussed goose.

"Lords and ladies, maids and masters, come hither and see the finest show in all of Britain, a show fit for the king himself. Bring your wee ones, bring your old ones. Bring your purses." She smiled, and even Rachel, who was helping Liam see to a few details, couldn't help but be captured by her charisma. Catriona was entrancing. Twas little wonder Liam had no interest in a woman called the Lady Saint.

A crowd had already begun to gather. Rachel looked out over the mass of people and felt her stomach churn. True, she was no hermit. Indeed, she had spent most of her life tending the needy with her mother. But never had she been looked at as they were looking at the Rom lass.

The mare shifted her feet, stepping restlessly in place. Catriona's body swayed with the easy movement, her hips undulating gently. More folk gathered around, as attracted by her perfect balance and bold demeanor as by her exotic beauty.

"Come hither," she called again, "and witness the magic of the Rom. Hear Marta's music." As if from nowhere, a bittersweet tune lifted into the air. "Learn Hertha's secrets for your future. Marvel at Hugh's clever hands." Liam stepped forward, bowed, then spun a trio of potatoes twirling into the air. "And see feats of balance and strength as you have never seen before." Leaping lightly from the mare's back, Catriona somersaulted into the air. The crowd gasped, but just before she struck the ground, Rory stepped out of nowhere. She landed in his arms, still smiling.

"You remember what we practiced?" Liam asked, drawing Rachel's attention back to him.

"Tis not so difficult," Rachel said. Not like somersaulting from a horse's back into a man's waiting arms. She felt just a bit more appealing than the potatoes he'd just finished tossing. She pulled her homely coif lower over her face, shifted her gaze to Catriona, then nervously to the crowd.

"Liam . . ." She didn't want to say the words, but she wasn't meant to be an entertainer. Twas not in her character. "I do not think I can—"

"Tis too bad you are not so demure with the Rom." His eyes were still sharp with anger. "The woman in the woods . . . the naked woman, would have had no trouble performing for a crowd."

Rachel drew herself up. "And me, I thought twas you who was supposed to draw the crowd."

"Of course. Tis far beneath her ladyship to be put on public display," he said.

"So it is a display you want?" she snapped.

"Huh! As if you could do such a thing! Nay. Your appeal is of a more personal nature."

"You are right. And not for the likes of you," she snarled, and turning on her heel, sped back to their wagon.

Pulling the door closed behind her, Rachel closed her eyes and tried to calm her breathing. But anger was sparking through her like lightning down a tree limb.

Damn the Irishman for everything he was. So he could draw a crowd and she could not. Twas certainly not a talent she wished to acquire. Her mother had raised her better. She had no wish to flaunt herself, to strut across a stage as Liam did.

But the fact that he thought she couldn't do it irritated her no end. She clenched her fists and snarled at the unoffending walls.

Damn the Irishman! she thought again, and glancing down at the homely, oversized tunic beneath her gown, made a decision.

Outside, Liam paced across his makeshift stage. Far be it from him to beg the haughty Lady Saint for her assistance. He certainly didn't need her. Nay. He'd been performing alone for more than a decade. He'd only insisted that she help him so that he might keep her close at hand, keep her out of trouble.

He'd never before thought of her as a foolish lass. Haughty, unbending, and self-important, yes. But not foolish. The day in the woods had proved him wrong, for no clever woman would be so careless with her innocence. And she was an innocent. That he knew. Didn't he? Of course he did. But Rory would change that if he had half an opportunity. And she was idiotic enough to give him that.

God's balls, he had to get her to Blackburn before she tempted the wrong man. True, she dressed like a nun, but it made no difference. No man could get a glimpse of her red-hued, sassy lips and not feel the sharp draw of her allure. In truth, he was glad she was gone, out of sight. Safe.

Catriona's performance wound down. With a wave and a swoop, she handed the crowd over to him.

It was nice to lose himself in the performance, to toss a knobby potato into the air, to catch it in the opposite hand, to toss up another and see the awed spectators turn expectantly toward him.

"Good day, me fine folk," he said. "'Tis good of you to stop by. Maybe you have need of a tasty tattie?" He spun another tuber into the air. "Or maybe—"

But suddenly his words snapped to a halt. He felt his jaw drop and his eyes pop open as Lady Rachel Forbes sauntered into view.

Damn her to bloody hell. She'd removed her tunic.

Chapter 14

⁓◦◦⁓

Rachel couldn't breathe. The laces on her bodice were too tight. Or maybe . . . She kept walking, forcing one leg in front of the other.

Maybe it was the people's stares that made her chest ache and her legs wooden. Maybe it was the little boy who was pointing at her or the miller whose eyes looked as if they might pop from his head like a pair of cooked turnips.

Or maybe it was Liam.

He stood immobile, a trio of potatoes in his hands, his eyes sparking black flame and his body stiff. She couldn't judge his expression, couldn't tell if he were angry or outraged or shocked.

But he was looking. That much she knew. But who would not? She was all but naked.

Her hands shook. She forced her feet to keep moving, forced her mind to reverse its line of thought. She was not almost naked. All she'd done was remove her tunic . . . and her shoes . . . and her coif . . . and tighten the laces of her bodice.

Sweet Mary! Her breasts were bare nearly to the nipples and tucked up under her chin like overzealous bread dough. Dragonheart purred between them.

Liam dropped one of his potatoes, but didn't seem to notice, and now Rachel stood only inches from him.

The crowd waited in expectant silence. Rachel's knees threatened to spill her face first onto the grass, but she clamped her muscles and refused to buckle. Instead, she cleared her throat. The noise did nothing to bring Liam around.

There were a few titters of amusement from the crowd. "Hugh," she said, but the word came out as no more than a whisper.

"I guess his hands aren't so clever just now," someone called.

"Maybe they're not where they wish to be."

There were guffaws of laughter.

"Woman, what have you done!" Liam finally hissed, his shocked gaze never leaving her bosom.

Rachel stiffened her back, every defensive instinct coming to the fore. Damn him for forcing her into this. But she wouldn't back down. He'd challenged her and she would win. "What is it?" she asked. "Did you not know I had . . ."—she forced herself to lift her skirt and take another step forward. Her bare toes peeked into view—"feet?" she asked.

The crowd chuckled.

"Maybe he didn't know they were so large," someone shouted.

"You'd best toss up them tatties, boy," a man called, "or we'll have to find another to amuse us."

Liam's gaze snapped to the man who had just spoken.

Rachel bent shakily to retrieve the fallen potato and press it into Liam's hand. "Do your tricks," she murmured desperately, her voice low and husky with fear.

A nearby man chuckled. "Drag your eyeballs out of her cleavage and do something, lad."

"Very well then," Liam said and tossed the tubers into the air with an obvious effort. For several seconds they did nothing but fly into orbit, caught and replaced by his hands. Finally he exhaled heavily and increased the speed. He shook his head, and though Rachel knew his grin was forced, maybe the crowd could not tell. Maybe they thought it was nothing more than a clever act. "Let it not be said that Hugh the great cannot work under pressure."

The potatoes swirled faster and faster, spinning finally into a continuous arc of brown. But suddenly the drab color was replaced by a flash of yellow.

"Oh, look," Liam exclaimed, and caught the spinning color with a flourish. Lifting his hand high, he revealed a long yellow scarf. "The fates have sent a bit of something to cover your immodesty." Stepping forward, he prepared to drape the bright cloth across Rachel's chest. But just as he did so, their gazes caught. Feelings as sharp as daggers sliced through Rachel.

The air seemed suddenly taut, as if lightning had just crackled through the sky. He reached forward. His fingers brushed her shoulder, feather soft. She shivered beneath his touch.

"Don't forget you've an audience," someone called.

Liam snapped his hand away as if burned, leaving the scarf behind. But suddenly it was gone, replaced by a tiny yellow finch that perched on her shoulder.

The crowd gasped.

"Bird's got the best view in the village," someone called.

Liam pulled himself back to his act. "Tis more than she's offered me," he retorted dryly.

Damn him, Rachel thought. So he was playing the rogue. But two could toss that die.

"And more than you'll ever get," she countered as she set the bird back in its cage.

Liam snorted as he retrieved a trio of knives from the earth and began to toss them into the air.

"Do you think you can throw me another one without anything falling from your gown?" Liam asked.

Embarrassment flooded through Rachel. She couldn't stop the color that seeped down her face toward her bosom, but neither could she change her course of action, for pride pressed her on. Tossing back her hair, she pushed out her chest. "We shall see," she said, and slowly bent to pick up the knife.

Not a man in the area breathed. Indeed, it seemed that not a breeze stirred in all of Christendom.

"Good God, throw it here before the fellow in the front faints," Liam snapped.

She did so, but her hands were shaking, and her aim was off. The knife wobbled low.

Liam snatched it up just before it struck his crotch. "Holy Christmas!" he swore, spinning it into space. "Watch where you throw it, lass. There may be something down there you will take a liking to some day."

"Not in this lifetime, laddie," she scoffed, and the crowd roared. The sound speared through Rachel, drowning her in a rush of adrenaline, and the show was on.

Tension rippled between them. Laughter and oohs and gasps sounded across the courtyard. And finally, with a flourish and a wave, Liam bowed.

The crowd applauded.

Rachel bowed.

The crowd exploded.

Liam scowled, grabbed Rachel's arm, and snatched her to his side, where they bowed together amidst whistles and laughter and ribald exchanges.

Lachlan, riding backward on his dappled pony and accompanied by a dancing bear, wove his way through the crowds with his cap extended. The spectators, intoxicated by the steamy performance, were generous.

Rachel straightened. Liam did the same. Their arms brushed. The air crackled between them. His hand felt warm and strong against her arm, and his eyes still snapped with a passion she could not quite name.

"Rachel . . ." he rasped.

Emotion curled through her stomach.

"Aye?"

He seemed to lean toward her, but in an instant, he drew sharply away. "What the hell be you thinking?" he growled.

Disappointment swamped her like bitter ale, but she raised her chin and squared her shoulders. "I was thinking I might manage to draw a wee bit of attention if I but tried."

"By flaunting yerself like a—"

"Flora," Rory said, approaching from behind.

Rachel turned brokenly toward him.

"Tis impressed I am," he murmured, letting his eyes roam for a moment. "And me I was thinking you might be a mite shy to perform. But you surprised me." He shifted his gaze momentarily to Liam.

"You didn't tell us your wife was so much the entertainer, Hugh," he said.

"She is a constant surprise."

"Aye. I can see that. The show did well," he said, jiggling a pouch of coins and shifting his dark eyes quickly back to Rachel. "Marta needs a few supplies and I wondered if you might like to accompany me to the marketplace."

"What of Catriona?" Liam asked.

The men's gazes clashed for a moment, then the corner of Rory's mouth lifted in a disarming grin. "She is busy," he said. "And I have no talent for bartering for a woman's needs. But Flora is your wife, and I would not dream of doing anything to cause trouble between the two of you."

A muscle jumped in Liam's jaw, but he shrugged as if unconcerned. "Well, if you do not even *dream* . . ." He laughed. The sound was rusty. "You must go of course, Flora. You deserve the distraction."

"You don't mind?" she asked, playing her part with care and precision, yet trying to see through the lies to his true thoughts. There were times when she felt she could guess people's minds. But Liam had never been one of those people.

"Of course not," he said. "I know you too well to think you'd do anything unseemly."

Anger spurred through her. "Do you now?" she murmured.

"Aye." His dark eyes flashed. "I do indeed."

"Then I shall go with Rory," she said, and placing her hand on the Rom's arm, turned toward the market.

*   *   *

They stayed all that day in York for Marta thought it wise to perform again that evening when others would have arrived and the previous spectators might well be lubricated into generosity by too much ale.

Ale, it seemed, was a performer's best ally.

As for Rachel, she lay curled up inside her wagon. Feigning a headache, she'd left Rory's company only minutes after they'd reached the marketplace. But though she'd returned to their small encampment shortly afterward, she had not seen Liam or Catriona since their performance.

Not that she cared what the two of them were doing. Long ago she had learned that caring for Liam was a fool's course. Ever since he'd turned her aside only to be found in Elisa's arms.

Rachel sat up abruptly. The wagon suddenly seemed too small. She needed air. Swinging the door open, she prepared to step outside.

Liam raised his head just as she glanced toward the fire. Their gazes flashed and fused. Rachel's heart yanked to life in her chest. Her breath rushed like a sharp wind, and then, shaken and uncertain, she ducked back inside.

"Bloody hell!' Liam murmured.

A chuckle sounded behind him. He turned with a scowl, spearing Marta with his gaze.

"I fear I fail to see the humor," he said.

She cackled as she took a seat on a log and placed a bundle between her feet. "Tis because you cannot see your own face, lad."

He snorted and sent a sour gaze toward the wagon. "I've seen more than I wished to for one day."

"That I doubt," she said. He turned to her and

she laughed again. "I'm thinking you've seen far less than you want to, laddie."

"I've no idea what you're speaking of."

"And I'm the Princess of Wales." She chuckled again. "The truth is, you're so hot for her you cannot think for the wanting."

"The truth is I'd just as soon throttle her as look at her."

"Aye. That too," she intoned with a sigh.

Rory sauntered past. Liam watched him and felt his body go tense and his nostrils flare.

"He has the Rom allure for women, does he not?"

Rory disappeared from sight. Liam shifted his scowl back to the matron. "Are you simply looking for new ways to flay me, or do you have a point, old woman?"

She cackled. "I am saying you cannot fight fire with damp chaff."

"What—"

"You!" she said, stabbing a gnarled finger at him. "You are damp chaff. Sodden and uncertain and of little use to the fire she burns for you."

Something lurched in Liam's gut, but he ignored it. Rachel carried no flame for him. That much he knew. Maybe long ago when she was still too naive to see the infinite chasm between a nameless bastard and a laird's daughter, she had felt something for him, but he'd made certain to change that. Since then he'd had nothing from her but barbed words and bitter feelings.

"Have you nothing to say, laddie?" Marta asked.

He scowled. "You didn't seem daft when first I met you."

"Aye. I am daft. But I see things you do not. And

if you had the balls, you might ask for me own advice."

He wasn't going to ask. She was an opinionated old woman with a penchant for meddling, he told himself, and Rachel Forbes didn't care for him. She was a lady, perfect, polished, preening. And he was *not* going to ask.

"What advice?" he asked.

Marta grinned toothlessly, then, reaching down, retrieved her dark bundle and tossed it at him. "Fan the flame, lad," she said.

The sun had set by the time Catriona called for an audience that evening. Five torches had been lit and thrust into the dirt in a half circle. The light illuminated her face, making her exotic beauty more impossible, her feats more spectacular.

Rachel watched her from a dark area near the wagon and wished to God she were a hundred miles away, that she'd never met Liam, that she had a boatload of cloth to hide her flushed face and mounded chest. She'd made a fool of herself once already today when sparring with Liam and she had no wish to do so again. But pride is a hard mistress and insisted that she not back down, that she stand up to Liam's challenge and prove herself capable of doing whatever he could do.

Finally Catriona performed her last twirling feat. Liam ducked out from another wagon. He was dressed in his usual hose and tunic, but over the simple linen shirt, he wore a vest of dark leather. It was laced part way up his chest and made his wide, white sleeves seem even more voluminous.

Their gazes met and fused.

"Tis not too late to find some decency," he said.

Rachel lifted her chin and stepped forward as Catriona introduced them to the crowds.

In a moment, Liam was tossing the potatoes into the air. His rhythm was perfect, his concentration undisturbed. So already her attire did nothing to distract him, Rachel thought, and swore she would not care. Instead, she would concentrate on the act, garner as many coins as possible, and hasten to Blackburn as quickly as possible.

Twas urgent that she get there soon, she told herself, but found to her chagrin, that despite everything, the edge to her need was gone. Before she had felt driven to reach the king, but now other things distracted her. Things that . . .

There was a gasp from the crowd. Gone were Liam's potatoes. The yellow scarf swished through the air, but instead of swirling about her shoulders, it hissed across his own. And then, with a flick of his wrist, the scarf was removed.

The crowd gasped again. Rachel gave a practiced smile, then snapped her gaze back to Liam. Her jaw fell slightly, for with the removal of the scarf, his tunic had also disappeared. Only the vest remained.

She stared in abject amazement. True, she had no idea where the shirt had disappeared to, but twas himself that made her gape. Beneath the laced leather of the vest, his chest gleamed in the firelight and his biceps danced as he twirled the scarf again. It swished around her shoulders and drooped away, but in a moment, he caught the opposite end.

It was then that Rachel realized that music was coming from somewhere. And suddenly they were turning in unison. The silk glided across her back, sensuous as a caress. His gaze caught her, hot and sharp and lurid in the flaring torches.

He tugged her closer with the silken bond. Their bodies nearly touched, but not quite. She felt his breath against her cheek, felt the warmth of his flesh even from inches away, saw the corded strength of his broad throat. His eyes mesmerized her. His hand touched hers. She stopped, made breathless by the emotion in his eyes, but he continued to circle her, and suddenly she realized her arms were behind her and bound by the silken scarf. Her back was to the audience. Their gasps alerted her, and suddenly her arms were released and she was clutching something clasped in her fingers.

Without a cue, curiosity made her pull her hands forward into her view.

Flowers. She stared at the yellow blossoms. But Liam was in front of her now. With a single touch, he urged her to turn toward the audience again. Then, tugging one bright bloom from the bouquet, he brushed it across his lips.

Something made her shiver at the sight. Soft as a sigh, he swiped it across her mouth. The shiver deepened.

The crowd was silent. Or perhaps she'd simply forgotten they were there. Liam leaned closer. His presence filled her. Her heart pounded and her lungs refused to breathe. He brushed the petals across her cheek, then down her neck, then flipped his hands away.

The spell was broken. The flower was planted firmly in a slit in her sleeve. He tugged the bouquet from her hands, and turning, tossed them into the crowd. But even before the last blossom had fallen, he had snatched up a trio of sticks. Having already been dipped in pitch, they flared as he set them to a nearby flame. First one end and then the other.

They flashed upward as Liam tossed them toward the sky, glowing in a golden arc of flame. But now he was moving, striding around her. She stood perfectly still, only shifting her eyes. He stepped behind her. She felt the heat of the slim torches on her shoulders, but suddenly they flashed in front of her face.

Gasping, she stepped back, but there was no room, for Liam was directly behind her. His chest felt hard and smooth as granite against her shoulders. His hands were beneath her arms, moving, always moving, catching and tossing the whirling flames.

Frightened and nervous, Rachel turned to the side. Liam's face was inches away, his black eyes intense as they stared into hers. His chest flexed against her back, his arms brushed her sides.

Her face felt hot, but whether it was from the flames or his proximity, she couldn't tell. She felt him turn, and there was nothing she could do but turn with him.

It felt like a slow, exotic dance. Skin brushed skin. Music throbbed from nowhere, and against her cheek, Liam breathed, "trust me."

It took a moment for her to find her voice, then, "With what?" she whispered.

His lips parted and nearly touched hers. She waited breathlessly for him to answer, but suddenly she realized the torches had ceased their flight and burned like a bonfire before their faces. And just as suddenly the crowd was cheering and they were bowing.

The music dwindled.

"It's a bear!" someone yelled, and the crowds

spilled away to watch Lachlan's huge beast dance.

Liam doused his torches in a nearby bucket without even turning away.

"Rachel." He breathed her name, but she was unable to respond, for his lips were so close to hers.

His skin gleamed in the firelight and his eyes were intense.

"Rachel," he whispered again, and a muscle danced in his jaw.

"Aye," she managed, though hoarsely.

"Tis not meant to be."

She was breathing hard and fast and refused to understand him. "What is not?"

"This," he rasped.

But just then their fingers inadvertently brushed. The fire just doused was renewed.

Liam clenched his jaw, and, seeming unable to help himself, he snatched her hand and moved toward the wagon. She could do nothing but follow him. *Wanted* to do nothing but follow him, to feel him pressed against her, to hear her name on his lips.

The door of the wagon creaked open. He urged her inside, and she went, crouching to enter, then swiveling around.

Liam stood in the doorway, his body rigid. Their gazes met and fused, and then, like a marionette on taut strings, Liam shut the door and turned away.

Chapter 15

~~~~◯◯~~~~

They traveled all the next day. Rachel kept to herself. Where Liam had spent the night, she didn't know. Neither did she care, she told herself. But her gaze kept straying to Catriona, who drove her own wagon. As for Liam, he walked most of the day, keeping silent and distant.

Sometime after noon they stopped in a clearing by a small lochan. John and Fane managed to catch several perch which Hertha happily cooked into a pot of cullen skink.

Lachlan played with Bear in the water as the sharp smell of onions and fish filled the air.

Finding she had nothing to occupy her hands, and nothing *useful* to fill her mind, Rachel wandered into the woods in search of herbs. In a stand of elm trees, she found mother of thyme creeping along a rocky outcropping. Once brewed into tea, the leaves would make a tonic good for settling stomachs. So she picked a good deal of the leathery leaves, stashed them in her rag pouch with her soap and other necessities, and wandered on.

Hawthorns grew in profusion along a craggy slope. Even from her vantage point, Rachel could see sparse clusters of crimson berries sprinkled throughout the white-flowered foliage. Crushed and dried, the berries would make a fine infusion, she thought, and climbed up the slope to reach them.

But once there, she realized that even the lowest cluster was above her head. Glancing about, she searched for another means of reaching it.

"Allow me," someone said.

Turning abruptly, Rachel nearly bumped into Rory's chest. He smiled his gypsy smile into her face.

"I didn't mean to frighten you."

"Nay." She exhaled softly, calming her breathing. Maybe this man was perfectly harmless, but if the truth be known she had always been cautious of men. Unlike Cousin Shona, who reveled in their attention, Rachel had never felt completely comfortable with them, even in her homeland where she was well-protected. "You didn't frighten me," she lied.

"Tis good," he said, and reached up, brushing against her shoulder to pull a cluster of berries from its mooring. "Twas not my intent." He handed it to her. "What are they for?"

"They aid in strengthening the heart," she said, and nervously stashed them in her pouch.

"Truly? Then we'd best fetch more."

He brushed past her and reached for another cluster, but it was too high. Turning back, he motioned to her. "Come. I'll lift you."

"Nay." How far was it back to camp? "I'm certain I have enough."

"But what if my heart fails from the shock of your beauty?" He grinned at her. "Come. Tis not like you to be afraid of a mere man."

Actually, it was just like her. But she supposed

she was being silly. Stepping forward, she reached nervously up. He settled his hands on her waist and lifted her easily from the ground.

Rachel snatched the berries quickly from the limb, but instead of putting her down, Rory turned to the right and lifted her a bit higher.

"You might as well gather those," he said, indicating a few berries that grew close to the truck.

Seeing the cluster, she grabbed them too. "'Tis enough," she insisted, eager to have her feet on the ground.

"As you wish," he said and set her down. "Might there be something else you need?"

"Nay. I'd best get back to camp."

He watched her, his dark eyes unreadable. "'Tis a strange lass, you are, Flora. Sometimes you seem bold beyond words, yet sometimes you seem most shy."

She shrugged as she turned away and strode for camp. Though she didn't trust him, she couldn't deny that it was exhilarating to bask in his interest. "Is it not a woman's right to be fickle?"

He laughed as he caught up with her. "Aye, I suppose it is. Your boldness added a certain charm to your performance."

She said nothing. They walked on, side by side.

"It seems to me you could do more," he said. "You are a natural performer."

She laughed, for nothing could be further from the truth. Unless twas a desirable thing to feel sick to one's stomach and weak in the knees when a crowd turned its attention on her, she was a truly lousy performer.

"You have a gift," he said, arguing with her inner thoughts. "It seems a pity to stifle it."

"Stifle it?"

"Aye. You should be more than Hugh's assistant."

"Indeed?" They were nearing the camp now. Nearing safety. Through the last few leaves, she could see the men fishing. Just the sight of Liam made her stomach knot up and anger well in her again. For a time yesterday, she had thought that he felt something for her, something more than the need to protect her because she was her mother's daughter. Something more than the fractious union of brother and sister. But at the last moment he had turned away, had probably spent the night with Catriona or maybe some village lass.

Her gut twisted harder.

"Indeed," Rory said. "I see no reason you could not perform the same feats as Catriona. You are as light as a swallow. I could lift you with one finger."

Liam turned toward her. Rachel jerked her attention to the ground in front of her.

"Hardly that," she said.

"Are you insulting me or challenging me?" Rory asked.

"Neither," she said quickly.

He laughed aloud, his teeth bright in the afternoon sun. "You are so serious, Flora. Methinks you are not very happy."

"I am happy," she insisted.

"I know your husband did not return to your wagon last night."

She felt a blush burn her cheeks, though she told herself she had nothing to be embarrassed about. "Tis none of your affair where he spends his nights," she said.

But in that moment he touched her arm and drew her to a halt. "I don't like to see such a bonny lass unhappy."

"I am not unhappy," she repeated.

"But you could be happier," he argued. "If your husband paid you more attention." He slid his fingers up her sleeve. "If he were a wee bit jealous?"

She sucked air through her teeth. "I've no wish to make me husband jealous."

"You lie," he whispered, leaning closer.

She met his gaze straight on. But she had always been a hideously poor liar, and suddenly there seemed little point to it. "Aye, I do," she murmured.

He chuckled, and she could do nothing but join in, for the honesty felt good, natural.

"But twould be wrong," she said finally.

"Maybe," he agreed, "but tis too late now."

"What?"

"They are already looking at us," he said.

She moved to turn toward camp, but he touched his fingers to her jaw, holding her head in place.

"Methinks it would work better if you would pretend you do not notice."

She should pull away, she knew. She should tell him to stop this foolishness. But his fingers were gentle against her skin, and his smile was alluring. In truth, it was far past time a handsome man treated her as if she were more than a living dowry. What could it hurt if she flirted with him for a spell? She was quite certain he was in love with Catriona. Who would not be?

"Maybe you have designs of your own," she said.

He raised his brows. "Such as?"

"Maybe you would not mind if Catriona too were a bit jealous."

"I hadn't thought of that."

Rachel laughed. "And I'm a monk."

"I hope not," he whispered, and leaning close, he offered his arm. "Twould certainly foil me plans."

Less than an hour later, they were traveling again. But the dynamics had changed. Liam still walked, and Catriona drove her own wagon, but now Rory sat beside Rachel. He had explained to the others that he hoped to teach her a few of the tricks of the trade. Not a single person had raised an eyebrow. Even Liam said nothing, but strode along beside the wagon as if deep in thought.

They stopped not far from the village of Darlington that night. A fire was lit and the chores seen to. But soon afterward, Rory sat down on the log beside Rachel.

"Are you ready to begin?"

Her thoughts had been far away. She turned to him with a start. "Begin what?"

"Your training, lass," he said, and leaning closer, grinned. "What did you think?"

She gave him a reprimanding scowl. "I think tis foolishness."

"You would not turn me down," he argued, looking abashed. "Not when you have such talent."

"I truly do not—"

"Not when your husband is watching us."

She couldn't help herself, but twisted toward Liam, and in the instant when her gaze struck his, her breath caught in her throat.

"You have his attention," Rory whispered. "Twould be good to use it wisely. Come, lass, practice with me."

Rachel hesitated, and in that moment, Liam rose to his feet, and turned away.

She wrenched her gaze from his back. "I'll do it," she murmured.

They moved to a clearing not far from a wee lochan. The sunlight was fast fading from the sky, but it seemed they did not need the light, for Rory worked by feel.

Maybe Rachel would have changed her mind but now and then she would hear Liam laugh, and her gut would knot. Aye, she knew he was teaching Lachlan a bit of sleight of hand, knew that he was well occupied with his beloved tricks, but still it irked her that he could so easily ignore her.

How many years had he been tormenting her? she wondered. Ever since she'd first met him, he'd either harassed her or ignored her. And all the while he'd acted as if her two cousins were nothing short of angels. It shouldn't have bothered her, of course, but it did. She'd always known she possessed neither Shona's charm nor Sara's alluring femininity. She was too forthright and too opinionated. It made her a desirable wife but not a desirable lover. And Liam it seemed, had little use of a wife.

Rory's attention made her feel, perhaps for the first time in her life, sensual and alluring and wanted. Thus, she did as he asked.

Twas a simple feat he taught her first—how to balance on one foot in the cradle of his two hands. From there they progressed to him scooting her up to sit on his shoulder. It was not a difficult maneuver, and yet there was an intimacy to it that Rachel was not accustomed to. An intimacy that made her laugh with nervousness when she made a mistake—which was quite often to her own way of thinking, though Rory insisted that she was doing well.

Finally fatigued from exertion and nerves, Rachel's foot slipped from his hands. She rocked back on her heel and nearly fell before Rory grabbed her and snatched her close to him.

They stared at each other from inches apart, breathing hard.

"I don't think I am made for this," Rachel murmured nervously, but Rory shook his head.

"'Tis not true, lass," he said, his hands still firm about her waist. "If the crowds but saw you perched upon me shoulder, they would come running simply to stare at your beauty. Truly, lass, you make me want nothing more than to—"

But suddenly there was the sound of galloping feet. The world tilted and Rachel was tossed to the ground while Rory flew in the opposite direction.

She lay on her back, stunned and speechless. But Rory was not so silent.

"Let go of me, you bloody bastard!" he yelled. It took a moment for Rachel to realize the Rom had been snatched away from her by Bear. "Get off me!" he roared, swinging at the beast with his elbow.

The bear dropped his hold on Rory's tunic and backed away, looking offended, just as Liam and Lachlan ran up.

"Tis sorry I am." Liam panted to a halt and pulled the bear off Rory. But at the same time he seemed to be stroking the beast. "Lachlan here was teaching me Bear's tricks, and I fear I made a mistake."

"A mistake!" Rory growled, his fists tight as he stepped toward Liam. "I do not think twas a mistake atall."

Rachel watched Liam as she lurched to her feet. His eyes were unreadable in the failing light and his smile tight and tilted. "What be you saying, Rory, that you think I might take umbrage to you malling me wife?"

Rory stumbled to a halt. "I was not malling her. Indeed, I believe she enjoys my company."

"Truly?" Liam snarled. "And how would she enjoy you if you were missing your—"

"Liam!" Rachel rasped. Flying between them, she grasped the Irishman's arms. Their gazes fused. "You've no right," she hissed.

He stared at her in seething silence.

"Nay," he whispered finally. "I've no right. But I swear to God it doesn't matter. If you don't come with me now, the Rom will pay in blood."

Rachel stared at him. She was tempted to tell him to go ahead and try it. Liam was no warrior, and Rory looked the type to defend himself. But despite everything, the thought of him wounded made her stomach turn.

"I'll retire to the wagon now," she said finally, though the word sounded stiff to her own ears. "I am tired."

She turned away. Liam held Rory's gaze for a moment longer, then pivoting about, caught up to her in a few quick strides.

The first few paces were in silence, then, "Could it be you thought you hadn't made enough of a spectacle of yourself yet?" Liam snarled.

"A spectacle?" She fought down the anger, the tears, the fatigue. "Whatever do you mean, Husband? I was merely endeavoring to improve me own skills."

"What skills be those? Luring a man into your bed?"

She forced a laugh. "Nay, Love," she said, making certain her voice was quite loud and obnoxiously cheerful. "I am quite adept at that already."

She thought she could hear him grind his teeth and turned just before their wagon to gaze into his eyes. "Do not you agree?" she asked, and reaching out, skimmed her fingers up the bare skin of his neck and onto his hard jaw. She felt the small muscles there twitch.

"Get in the wagon," he ordered, his voice low.

She slanted her face down for the express purpose of looking up at him through her lashes. "Shall I take that as an agreement, Hughie?"

"God damn it, Rachel, get out of sight!"

She laughed low in her throat and taking his collar, pulled it tight as she leaned toward him. "I like a forceful man," she said, and turning, did her best to make certain he didn't see her shake as she pulled the door open and entered the wagon.

Her heart was pounding, her gut tight, and though she told herself she hoped he would not follow her, she wouldn't have bet her life on it.

The door closed with a bang.

She turned breathlessly, trying to swallow her disappointment, but found instead that he was inches behind her.

"Nay, I'm not about to leave you alone," he growled. "Not with the Rom rutting after you like a bloody cur."

Her heart hammered against her ribs. "I like the Rom," she said, lifting her chin slightly. "He's been naught but kind to me."

"Kind!" he said, and slammed his fist against the wall of the wagon. The kettles shook with the force of his punch. "Is that what you call it now?"

"Aye." Anger and frustration made it difficult to breathe. "He's done naught but help me out and pay me compliments."

"Compliments!" he sneered. "And why would he do that, do you think?"

"I cannot guess, Liam," she countered, leaning toward him. "Maybe you can tell me. Maybe you have even—"

But her words snapped to a halt as he snatched her against him. His chest felt hard as iron beneath her hands, and his fingers on her arms were unyielding. "What do you want from me?" he snarled.

"Me?" She could feel his heart beating against her fingertips, could feel her own body tremble. "I don't want anything."

His fingers tightened. "I wish to hell I could say the same," he rasped, and jerked her toward him.

She should pull away, resist him, she told herself, but she had no strength, no will. His lips crashed against hers. She answered his kiss because she had no choice. He dropped her wrist and clasped his arms about her squeezing hard, and then his hands curved down her back, pressing her closer still, until he grasped her buttocks, grinding their hips together.

"Do you want something now?" he rasped.

"Nay!"

He kissed her again, hard, breathlessly, slipping his tongue into her mouth and shocking her with the invasion.

She shivered at the impact even as she pulled him closer.

"Now?" he asked.

"Nay," she denied, but she was panting when she said it.

"You lie," he growled. "You've wanted something since the moment I met you."

Aye, she wanted him so much she ached, but her

pride ached more. Curling her arm up between their bodies, she pushed him away, but he was far stronger than she. "I fear your vanity exceeds your good sense," she said.

"Nay, it does not," he said. "I know you well, Rachel Forbes. I know that from the first you have wanted me to want you. Even when you were little more than a child, you gloried in that."

She shook her head, befuddled and frustrated. "Gloried in what?"

He squeezed her harder against him. "In the fact that I could not bear to be around you knowing that you would never be—"

He stopped abruptly, breathing hard.

"That I would never be what?"

He stared at her as if shocked to find her there.

"That I would never be what?" she whispered again, but he pushed himself abruptly away. "Liam?"

"Do you need to hear me say it again? Didn't you understand the first time. Jesus, Rachel, you all but threw yerself at me a decade ago. I told you then you were not for a bastard like . . ." He paused, breathing hard. "I told you you were not what I wanted."

She was a fool Rachel told herself. A fool to still let it hurt. Surely the wound had scarred by now. And yet the pain ripped through her like the jagged cut of a dull knife. But she had cheated pain before.

Hardening everything in her, she laughed. "Poor Liam," she said. "Adoring me from afar for all these years, and never able to admit it."

"Adoring you!" he spat. "You were a spoiled brat then, and you are a spoiled brat now."

"Aye, and you've wanted me since the moment

we met. Only you fear the consequences too much to do anything about it." She forced a laugh. "Maybe you are wiser than I know, for my father might very well kill you if he knew your ilk dared touch me." She turned away. "You'd best run along now, Liam. I need sleep, and I've no wish to tempt you beyond your restraint."

"You think I am tempted by you?"

Her stomach knotted, but she forced herself to smile. "Liam," she said, "you would be tempted by a potato if you spent enough time in its company, and I . . ." It was the hardest thing she'd ever done to lean forward, to slip her hand behind his neck, to press her mouth against his. Closing her eyes, she swiped the tip of her tongue across his lips. Someone trembled violently at the caress, but whether it was him or herself, she would never be certain. Still, she forced herself to pull back and glance up through her lashes at him. "I am no potato," she finished.

She could see his chest rise and fall with each inhalation, could see that his fists were clenched and his jaw tight.

"Run along now, Liam," she said. "I wish to disrobe, and I do not wish to see you fail."

Silence filled the space. "You think I cannot resist you?"

"Don't feel badly, Liam," she said, settling down on her blankets. "Most men cannot."

"I am not most men."

"Nay." She turned toward him, and for a moment she weakened. "You are Liam the Irishman."

Their gazes clashed.

"And because I have no family name, you think me less a man."

Weakness flooded her, and she nearly reached

out, nearly touched his cheek, told him the hateful, foolish truth. But he had hurt her enough without offering more opportunity.

"Go away, Liam," she whispered. "I am hot and I am tired."

"Then disrobe." He shrugged. "But I stay here."

Chapter 16

Rachel stared at Liam. Anger and exhilaration and frustration battled inside her. A thousand emotions burned her. For a moment she'd been certain Liam had wanted her. Had thought of her like a woman instead of like an irritating little sister, but she'd been deluded before. Deluded enough, as a young girl, to think herself in love with him. But she knew far better than that now, and she wasn't about to let him win this hand.

She'd take her clothes off. Just see if she wouldn't. Reaching up, she set her fingers to the laces that bound the front of her gown.

Liam's gaze followed her hands, she noticed, and worried that he might see them tremble. But it was dark and she knew better than to think he might stay and watch. Nay, if there was one thing she knew about Liam, it was that he protected his own skin, and his skin might very well be forfeit if he displeased her father, the laird of the Forbes. He knew that as well as anyone.

True, he'd seen her naked before, but that was when they were soaked and freezing and she'd had a medical reason to undress. The same could not be said now, and thus he would surely leave.

Still, he remained where he was. Rachel licked her lips and froze. He would leave. Of course he'd leave, she told herself and tugged the lace loose. It sighed open, but that was no hardship, for indeed, she again wore her tunic underneath. Still, with his gaze riveted to her as it was, the action felt strangely erotic.

"Go now, Liam." She tried to make her tone light, as if his actions were of little concern to her. But she feared she only managed to sound breathless.

"I'm not leaving." His words were low. "Not with the Rom sniffing about as he is."

"Go," she said, and slipped the sleeves of the gown down her shoulders. The tunic slid sideways with the movement. "Or you shall surely regret it."

His nostrils were flared, his eyes intense. "I fear ye know precious little of me if ye think I would regret watching a woman disrobe."

She remained in stunned silence for a while. But a thousand memories of Liam trounced her. He was not the type to risk his well-being. Not for her. Nay. She was not worth the trouble to him. "And what of my father?" she asked.

He laughed. The sound was low and quiet as it forced from deep within his chest. "Twas you who said you have already lain with a host of men. So surely me watching you undress will seem no great sin to your sire."

"He didn't think of the others like a son." The words came out of their own accord. She knew better than to say them, for surely the last thing she wished to do was compliment this rogue. But it was true. Though her father had often jested about Liam's sleight of hand and Irish heritage, the Forbes of the Forbes would never have allowed any man access to his daughter and his nieces, had he not trusted him. Still, she regretted her admittance—until she saw Liam blanch, saw him pale in the dim light, saw him draw back as if struck.

How very interesting.

"I am no laird's son," he murmured.

She forced a laugh. "Hardly do you have to remind *me*, Liam. I but said he thinks of you as kin."

He tightened his fists and for a moment she thought he would surely turn away, but she'd misjudged him before.

"He loves *you* like a daughter. Yet you betray his trust," he said finally.

"I *am* his daughter," she snapped, frustrated and tired. "He would forgive me anything."

"And you said I am like a son." Tension snapped between them. "Maybe he would forgive me all, too, if I said you tempted me beyond me own control."

"And who do you think he would believe, Liam, if I told him you ravaged me? You? Or his own flesh and blood?"

The muscle ticked in his jaw again. "Ravage you! You think too highly of yourself, Rachel."

"Hardly that. Indeed, I do not believe I think highly enough of myself. But I tire of this talk. Get thee gone now."

"I told you nay."

"And I told you, I am going to disrobe."

He laughed, the sound low in the darkness. "The warning is beginning to lose its edge, Rachel. Rather like threatening a hound with mutton chops." His gaze was absolutely steady in the darkness, his voice the same.

She almost cried, almost dropped to her blankets and hid her head. Never had she wanted to be alone more than now, to lick her wounds. But she would not lick while he watched. So she pulled the sleeves of the gown lower. They slipped over her hands. The bodice drooped away from her breasts, down to her waist. The oversized tunic guarded her modesty, but suddenly it felt as insubstantial as air.

Liam watched her with unreadable eyes. "Are you finished with your wee exhibition?" he asked.

Rachel stared at him in silence, knowing he had won and hating him for it. Obviously, he was far from being tempted beyond control, and she could not go further. She nodded shallowly.

He grinned, the expression tight. "A modest wanton," he murmured. Silence echoed in the narrow confines of the wagon. "Admit the truth, Rachel. There have been no men in your bed."

Logic told her that she shouldn't be insulted by such words, but logic was as rare as hen's teeth where Liam was concerned, and she could not help but feel the sting of his deduction. Mother of God, her friends were preparing for grandchildren, and she had not yet felt passion's flame even once. Surely there was something wrong with her.

"Admit it," Liam ordered. "There has not been a single man." The words sliced through her like a well-sharpened dirk sliding between her ribs to her heart. But she bore the pain and raised her chin.

"Just because you will never share my bed doesn't mean that others have not," she said, and exerting every ounce of control on her muscles, she pulled her tunic upward.

It was stuck beneath her knees. She was forced to shimmy from side to side in order to tug it free, but she managed to do that before she stopped, unable to go on.

He stared at her. A mocking grin tilted his full lips, and his eyes sparked with laughter.

Rachel drew a deep shuddering breath and tugged again. The linen slid along her thighs. She shivered, pulling it a few scant inches higher, then stopping to breathe, as if she were exerting some heroic effort.

She dared not look at him, for if she did every ounce of her determination would surely be snatched away. Instead, she closed her eyes and pulled the tunic higher.

It slipped over her hips. She felt the air touch her private parts, her hips, her waist.

Sweet Mary save her from her own stupidity, she thought, but she didn't quit. The tunic rasped over her peaked breasts and upward. She drew the garment away like one in a trance, opening her eyes as it cleared her head.

Liam remained perfectly still, breathing hard and staring at her unblinking. She licked her lips, swiping her tongue over them in one quick motion. He watched the movement, and then, as though his hand was controlled by someone other than himself, he reached for her.

His hand felt feather soft against her flesh. She closed her eyes and exhaled softly. He skimmed his fingertips along the outside curve of her breast, so that his palm brushed her nipple and his thumb touched Dragonheart.

Fire spurred through her.

His hand slipped under her arm and down to her waist. And suddenly he was closer, so close she could feel his breath on her throat, but still she didn't open her eyes. Instead, she gave herself up to the feelings, to the slide of his hand down her back, to the skim of his fingers against her buttocks.

She trembled beneath his touch, and then he kissed her. Not with the harsh force she 'd felt before, but with midnight-soft tenderness, first her lips, then her cheek.

His other hand joined in the play, and he tugged her closer. They were chest to chest now, their bodies pressed against each other with painful intimacy. He caressed her bottom, slid his hands around her thighs, then skimmed slowly up her waist.

They trembled in unison. His hands were like magic on her skin and his lips hot against her shoulder. She moaned as his kisses slipped lower. She was a fool not to stop this, she knew. But she couldn't.

In a haze of heated desire, she reached for the laces that held his tunic. But suddenly he grabbed her hands and squeezed them with trembling strength between them. "Nay," he rasped.

"Why?" She couldn't stop the words, though she knew she was a weak-hearted fool for their escape. "Why not me, Liam?"

Tense as a bow-string, his body quivered against her. For a moment she thought he would continue. But instead he pushed himself away.

"Nay," he said again, and turning away, scrambled out the door.

Rachel remained in naked dismay, staring at the portal, her heart thudding hard and steady against her ribs and her stomach turning over.

Never, she vowed. Never, for as long as she lived, would she be such a fool again.

They reached the village of Gateshead well before noon, found a likely spot close to the marketplace, and prepared for their acts. All except

Rachel, who hid in her wagon and hoped for death.

Death, however, is rarely considerate. Instead, it was Rory at the door.

"Flora," he called, and since she was not lucky enough to be dead yet, she could do nothing but answer him.

"Are you ready?" he asked when she opened the door.

"Nay." She pushed her hair back. "I don't feel well today." And that was the truth.

"Maybe you but need some fresh air."

No. She needed to either kill Liam or die herself. "Nay tis—"

"Please," he begged and gave her a boyish look. Lachlan moved past, walking on his hands. "We've already practiced. I will not ask anything difficult of you. You'll simply ride on me shoulder and help me call a crowd."

"Really, I couldn't."

"Well, not in that," he said, indicating her garments. "But if you remove the tunic."

"Nay," she said, and tried to pull the door shut.

He held it steady. "He left you again last night, didn't he?"

She didn't want to talk about it. Didn't want to think about it.

"Shall I kill him for you?"

"What?" she asked, freezing.

He laughed, the sound throaty. "I but wished to startle you back to life, lass. You look as pale as a spirit. Take off the tunic and come out, we shall make him wish he were a real man."

"Nay . . ." she began, but he grasped her hand in his own and pulled it to his lips.

"You are a real woman, Flora," he whispered against her skin. "Let us show him."

She knew she should say no, but in that moment she remembered Liam's tilted grin. "Admit it," he'd said. "There has not been a single man."

And suddenly she had to go.

Minutes later she stepped outside. But now, instead of the harlot with the red gown and the red-slashed sleeves, she was the harlot with the red gown and the bare arms.

Rachel swallowed. It had been a simple enough task to remove the laces at her shoulders, simpler still to tug off the sleeves. It was walking out into the world this way that was nearly impossible.

She felt someone's gaze and turned to find Rory staring at her. But in that instant, she felt Liam's attention too. Glancing sideways, she saw him jerk to his feet and take a step forward.

"You dull the very sunshine," Rory breathed, already clasping her hand in his. "Come."

She turned resolutely away from Liam. Rory led her to the sleek, white mare. Rachel swung easily onto the bare back. In an instant, he was behind her, nestled against her backside.

Liam watched her.

For a moment their gazes met, and then, with painful effort, she turned the mare away.

"You'll not regret this," Rory breathed in her ear.

She would not let herself. It was well past time she moved on with her life. Liam was not for her. How many times did he have to prove that?

The market was filling with people.

"Up on my shoulder," Rory said, his whisper close to her ear.

She turned toward him. "I thought you said—"

"I but said you'd ride on me shoulder," he said. "I did not say where I'd be."

She considered refusing, but one thought of the

night before changed her mind. Move on. Move on, she told herself.

Holding tightly to the mare's mane, she rose shakily to her feet. Rory's hand was firm against her waist, then her hip, then her leg as she straightened. It took her several seconds to get the nerve to perch on his shoulder, though he felt solid and steady beneath her.

"Call them in," he said quietly.

"What?" She turned partway toward him, nearly lost her balance, wobbled a bit and steadied. "What?"

"Tell them of the show."

But she couldn't. It was bad enough that she was half naked and perched on his shoulder like a flightless bird. Bad enough that she'd thrown herself at Liam the night before. What was she thinking? There was little wonder he despised her.

But no. He loved aggressive women. Other aggressive women.

Good Lord, she was going insane, she thought. So why not go all the way? Straightening to her full, precarious height, she yelled, "Come experience the magic of the Roms." Her voice quaked, but she went on. "Never have you seen the like. You will be dazzled and amazed."

Already a crowd was gathering.

"Will you be there?" one man yelled.

She looked down at him from her great height, gathered all her nerve and said, "I will if you will, love."

The crowd hooted.

Excitement rushed through her. Maybe Liam found her lacking. But not every man did. Making a few more announcements, she dropped onto the mare's back and suddenly they were running, galloping through the village to find others.

By the time they reached their wagons, she was breathless and flushed, pumped with a rush of blood and her own wild freedom. Within minutes Catriona and Rory were performing, and seconds after that Liam began his juggling.

The tension that had been steaming between them all week was boiling now. The scarf Liam draped over her shoulders was like a physical extension of his anger, and when it bound her wrists, iron-hot shards of emotions sparked off each time he touched her arm or caught her gaze. The crowd was awed either by Liam's talent or their smoldering reactions to each other, but when the final trick was performed, Liam turned away, and suddenly Rory was there.

"Each time I see you, you become more alluring," he crooned, running his hand down her bare arm, and sparking off a million feelings that had been set aflame by Liam.

Rachel lifted her eyes to Liam's. Their gazes caught, anger against anger.

"Come with me, Flora," Rory whispered.

Liam stood unmoving, his ebony eyes moody, his body tense.

"I will give you what you desire," Rory murmured.

Liam wore the vest again, baring his arms and part of his chest.

"I will be the man he is not," Rory whispered.

The muscles stood hard and taut beneath Liam's leather. A thousand past memories flared between them.

"He cannot satisfy you."

"What?" Rachel rasped, realizing suddenly that Rory was leaning close to talk to her.

"Come with me," he urged, tightening his grip on her fingers. "I will show you heaven."

"Heaven?" She blinked at him.

"Aye. In me arms."

Realization came a bit slowly. "Nay," she murmured, shocked as much by the intensity of her own desires as by the Rom's boldness. "I cannot."

"But you can," Rory countered, closer still, his words a warm breath on her face. "As can I."

"Nay."

He laughed, the sound low and throaty. "Has it been so long for you that you need proof of me abilities?" he asked, and pressed up against her hip. Through the fabric of their garments she could feel the hard evidence of his arousal.

"Come."

"Nay." She drew back cautiously. Catriona appeared in the corner of her vision. She knew by Rory's sudden tension, that he too was aware of her presence.

"Later," he promised, drawing his hand from hers. "I shall meet you by the river, just beyond the bend."

Rachel opened her mouth to object, but he was already striding away. Stunned and tense, Rachel glanced toward Liam. His dark gaze bore into hers. But in a moment, he turned away and strode off. Rachel shifted her eyes to Catriona. The gypsy met her gaze dead on.

Turning quickly, Rachel fled to the privacy of her wagon. Inside, it was dark and cool. She curled up on her blankets and wished for the first time in her life that there *was* a Laird Dunlock, that she was promised to be married, that somewhere there was a man who wanted her, who cherished her, not for what she could bring him, but for what she was.

But that was hardly the case. She had nothing. No husband, no children, no future, just a royal mission that was growing dimmer every day.

She covered her face with her hand and let the minutes tick away. What was wrong with her? She was not the sniveling type. She was Rachel of the Forbes.

And she had been called to Blackburn to tend the king. But somehow the mission no longer seemed urgent. Why?

Had she allowed her own petty problems to become more important than the future of all of Scotland?

The door opened quickly. Rachel sat up, braced to see Liam, but instead Catriona stepped inside. The portal closed just as quickly behind her.

"So tis not enough that you have your own husband fawning over you?" she asked.

Rachel's breath left her lungs in a hard whoosh. "What?"

"You have to have Rory after you too?"

Rachel shook her head. "Nay. I've no wish—"

"No wish?" Catriona's voice was level. Her hand dipped inside her full skirt. When it reappeared, she held a knife. "If you have no wish, you should not seduce him."

Rachel watched the blade with frantic shock. "I did not seduce him."

"I have heard that from others," she said, calmly fingering the blade's edge as if testing for sharpness.

"From . . . from whom?" Rachel asked. What man would be fool enough to stray from a woman like Catriona? She scooted to her feet, prepared to flee, but there was too little space.

"He is Rom, with a Rom's allure for women."

Catriona tossed back her hair. "Still, I grow tired of his roaming eye."

Rachel swallowed. "I didn't mean to cause trouble."

"Trouble? What did you think would happen?" She scowled as if mildly disappointed by the other's naivete. "Have you not heard that we Rom's are a hot-blooded lot?"

"I didn't mean to—"

"'Tis my duty to be jealous of my man's attentions." She shrugged. "Although it is getting a mite tiresome."

"Maybe it would be no great crime if you neglected your duties this once," Rachel suggested, glancing at the knife.

Catriona canted her head. "I don't know. If I let one slide . . ." She shrugged. "Nay. I think . . ." she began, but a wail of agony shattered her words.

"Nay!" Marta shrieked. "Not my Lachlan!"

Catriona's eyes went wide. Dropping the knife heedlessly to the floor, she spun toward the door and leapt outside.

Chapter 17

The camp was silent. Rory stood beside the fire, Lachlan's flaccid body draped across his arms.

Catriona ran to them. "Nay!" she shrieked.

A crowd of strangers gathered about, their eyes bright in the firelight.

"What happened?" Rachel rasped, running from the wagon. It was then that she saw the stick protruding from the child's chest. "Dear God!" Her stomach lurched. She wanted to turn away, but everything she was held her there. "When did this happen?"

"He fell from the mare." Rory's face was pale. "I thought he was only stunned, but when I picked him up . . ." He shuddered. The boy's body shook in his arms.

"Put him down!" Rachel snapped. "By the fire."

Rory did as he was told.

Catriona dropped to her knees beside the lad.

"Move," Rachel said, pushing the girl aside.

"What are you doing?"

"God willing, I'm saving his life!" Rachel snapped, and wrapped her hand over the stick. For a moment she gave herself up to prayer. But there

was so little time. Tightening her grip, she drew a
deep shuddering breath and pulled. The stick came
away with a sickening slurp. Blood, bright
red and hot, pumped out in its wake.

"You're killing him!" wailed Catriona, and
clawed at Rachel's arm.

"Liam!" Rachel screamed.

He was there in an instant, running into camp.
"What has happened? God's breath!"

"She's killing him!" Catriona whispered.

"Help me," Rachel pleaded. Covering the gaping
wound with both hands, she turned her gaze im-
ploringly to Liam. "We've no time to spare."

"What do you need?"

"Lachlan!" Catriona whimpered again, stroking
the hair back from his pale forehead.

"I need her gone," Rachel said.

Liam grasped Catriona's arm, but she jerked out
of his grip. "Who is she?" she rasped.

Liam crouched down beside the Gypsy, catching
her gaze with his own. "She's the answer to
prayers not yet prayed," he whispered. "Let her
work her magic."

Catriona was silent as she stared first at Liam,
then at Rachel. "Please." Her voice was low. "He's
my brother. Let me help."

Rachel delayed only a moment, then, "Fetch
bandages," she ordered.

Rising shakily to her feet, Catriona nodded once
and ran into the darkness.

"Blankets!" Rachel ordered, whipping her skirt
up to cover the pumping wound with its fabric.
Liam lurched off toward the wagon and was back
in an instant with an armful of woolens.

Lifting her gown away, Rachel shoved a blanket
against Lachlan's wound. "Stoke the fire," she or-

dered. "Put an iron in the midst of the flame. I need boiling water. My herbs. More blankets. A clean tunic."

Liam rattled off orders to the others. The Roms hurried in every direction. Still pressing the blanket to the wound, Rachel tore Lachlan's shirt away.

Liam returned in a heartbeat with her rag pouch.

"The long leafy plant," she said, not glancing up. "Crumble it into a half-mug of warm water. Catriona." She knew the girl had returned. "Cover him with all the blankets you can find."

"Tis hot—"

"Cover him!" she snapped. "Liam, I've no time to waste."

He handed over the mug. Rachel paused for an instant, then whipped the blanket aside and poured the liquid into the gaping hole in the boy's chest. Beneath her hand, the lad jerked and moaned.

"Lachlan," Catriona whimpered, but Rachel ignored her.

"Fetch me the iron."

"Please—"

"Now!"

Liam snapped it from the fire.

"Hold his arms," she demanded. "Rory, you too."

The men positioned themselves on each side of the boy's body and leaned on his arms.

"Be ready," she ordered, then, "Please Lord," she whispered, and thrust the hot iron against the wound.

Lachlan screamed. Catriona sobbed. Rachel's hands shook as she pulled the metal away, thrust it into the fire and applied it again.

The boy was still now, silent, limp, and sweating.

His brow glistened in the firelight. But the blood had slowed to a dribble, seeping between his ribs in meandering, scarlet rivulets.

"Soak a cloth in boiling water, then bring it to me," she ordered.

They did so. She washed away the gore with the steaming cloth and reached out for the bandages. Quickly, she folded one and pressed it to the wound, then ordered blankets to be placed over and under him.

Rachel pulled them to his chin and tucked them under his sides. Finally she rose to her feet.

"Will he live?" Catriona's question was no more than a whisper, her eyes unblinking as she stared at her brother's small body, hidden as it was beneath a layer of woolen blankets.

"Tis in God's hands."

"What do I do?"

"Pray," Rachel said. "And if he wakes . . . even for a moment, give him water. I will be in the woods."

"I'll come with you," Rory said, but Liam straightened beside her, every wild instinct in him humming to life.

"Twould be a bad night for you to lose your wick," he said.

"What?" The Rom straightened and thrust out his chest.

Liam smiled and reaching down, lifted Rachel's rag pouch from the ground. "Tis dark. Twould be a bad night for you to lose your way," he said, then nodded toward the woods. "I'll accompany me wife."

Pulling a torch from the earth, he followed Rachel into the woods. Twas like her to forget she would need a light, he thought—at least at times like this. True, at other times she was clever and careful, but twas not her way when she was tending the wounded. Then she became this woman possessed.

"Bring the torch," she said, motioning behind her.

Liam raised the flame and approached. "What did you find?"

"Myrrh." She said the word most reverently, and bending, broke it off carefully at ground level.

Liam handed her the pouch. She shoved the plant inside without seeming to notice his presence. Then she was off again, striding through the woods, unconcerned for the darkness or any evils that might be lurking there.

Finally, her pouch filled with her precious finds, she hurried back to camp.

"How does he fare?" she asked, her tone taut as she swung her pouch to the ground and approached the child.

"He has not awakened," Catriona said.

Rachel pressed a palm to his forehead. "Has he spoken? Any movement?"

"Sometimes he moans."

Rachel nodded, stroked the child's cheek, then moved toward the fire, where she dropped yarrow leaves into the kettle there. Next, she busied herself with a hundred small details, ripping the roots from the witch hazel plant, hanging comfrey up to dry.

Finally she settled down on a log not far from the wounded lad.

Liam glanced up from where he sat on the ground, his back braced against the trunk of an elm. "You should sleep," he said.

Rachel shook her head distractedly, clasped her

hands together and stared into the flame. "The tincture will be ready soon. I'll use it immediately." Lifting her eerie gaze from the fire, she turned it on Catriona. "But you should sleep. He may well need you on the morrow."

"Where did you learn these skills?" asked the Gypsy girl.

"Lady Fiona..." Rachel began, but Liam stopped her, realizing suddenly that even he hadn't noticed her lack of peasant brogue.

"Me wife was a maid to a healer for a spell," he said, meeting her gaze with his own. "She learned much."

Rachel nodded distractedly. "Sleep, Catriona," she said, but the other turned silently away and remained where she was.

Two stubborn women and a wounded lad, Liam thought, and sighing, he closed his eyes and prepared for a long and difficult night.

Some time later a tortured wail woke him, jerking him from his dreams.

"Liam," Rachel cried.

He stumbled groggily to his feet and lurched toward them.

"Hold him down," she ordered.

He did so. She finished pouring the tincture onto the wound as Lachlan writhed in agony, his eyes wide and his arms held by his sister and Liam.

"Tis finished," Rachel gasped, but the boy continued his keeling moan.

"Please," Catriona begged, "do something."

Rachel bit her lip, then lurched to her feet and fetched a kettle from near the fire. Pouring a bit into a mug, she motioned them to lift the boy to a sitting position, then raised the cup toward him.

Lachlan mewled piteously and writhed in pain. She pressed the mug closer, but he turned his face away.

"Lachlan!" Rachel said sharply. "Are you Rom or are you not?"

He stopped his movement, but whimpered in misery and squeezed his eyes closed.

"Are you Rom?" she asked again, her voice low.

"Aye." The word was barely a moan of assent.

"Then you've a duty to your family," she said. "A duty to stay alive. Do you hear me?"

He opened his eyes. His nod was shallow. Rachel caught him in her gaze.

"You will drink this," she said. "And you will live. Do you understand?"

He nodded again. She pressed the mug to his lips.

He did his best to drink, but even that small effort seemed too much for him. The warm liquid dribbled down the side of his mouth. He moaned again, but his gaze never left Rachel's.

"You will drink it," she repeated.

He slurped at the cup, seeming to take forever, until his eyes were falling closed and his body was limp in his sister's arms.

"A Rom does not give up," Rachel murmured.

His throat convulsed one last time, and then he went absolutely still.

"Lachlan?" Catriona's voice shook.

"He's resting," Rachel assured her. Lifting a bandage from a nearby blanket, she wrapped it about the lad's narrow chest, and the vigil began again.

Liam slept and awoke and slept and awoke, and each time Rachel was there, sitting beside the lad, her hand on his brow or her fingers worrying at a potion. Night turned to morning. The familia awoke, but little changed. Rachel and Catriona remained, speaking in low voices, stroking the child's forehead.

The day passed slowly. Fatigue lay on Rachel like a millstone. Doubt gnawed at her. Maybe she shouldn't have given him the tonic. True, he was without pain now. But pain was not always her enemy. It could well be that he would not wake from his slumber but fall from it straight into the hereafter.

Restless yet fatigued, she wandered back into the forest, searching yet again for herbs. Liam shadowed her, saying nothing, simply following.

That night was no better. Marta found her bed, and Rory lay beneath the wagon. Bear sat on his haunches near the boy and alternated between haunted moans and weepy sniffling.

Finally, able to stay awake no longer, Rachel fell into an exhausted sleep. Sometime far into the night, she awoke to a small, creaky voice.

"Get away, Bear."

She sat up straight, pushing the blanket away as she launched toward the boy.

"Go away," he said again, turning his face from the bear's happy tongue.

"Lachlan!" Catriona's voice broke as she spoke. Crawling to him on her hands and knees, she pushed the bear away with some effort. "Lachlan, are you awake?"

"Aye." His voice cracked as he spoke. "But I'm thinking I may not ride the mare standing up again."

Catriona laughed and collapsed atop him amidst sobs and caresses. Rachel clasped his hand in her own and cried.

"God's breath," Lachlan rasped, his face showing his embarrassment. "First the bear and then women."

Liam squatted beside him. "Life is hell, lad," he said, wryly watching the women stroke him. "Still, I'm glad to see you amongst the living."

Chapter 18

"**Y**ou love him."

"What?" Rachel's hand faltered on Lachlan's brow as she jerked her attention to Catriona's face.

The Gypsy shrugged, her expression impassive. "You love him."

Rachel swiped the lad's hair back from his sleeping face and tried to look casual. "You needn't worry. Even if I did have feeling for your Rory, he's got eyes for you and none other."

"Tis not true." Catriona didn't bother to turn to where the Rom slept beneath the wagon some thirty yards away. "Rory has an eye for any bonny lass. And you well know it. But you must think me a fool, indeed, if you believe I speak of him."

Rachel tensed. "I've no idea what you're talking about then?"

"I've spent some time wondering why you flirt with Rory when tis your own man who holds your attention."

"Hugh?" Rachel rose to her feet and tossed back her hair, trying to imitate the fiery Gypsy she was not and deeply grateful that Liam had chosen this night to sleep in the wagon. "Hugh and I . . ." She paused. The truth was complicated enough, lies were like water-soaked knots that would never be unbound. "Our marriage was a matter of convenience, nothing more. You're young and romantic. Maybe you don't understand—"

"You love him," Catriona repeated, stepping forward. "And thus I wonder, why do you not sleep together."

Rachel opened her mouth, but no words came for a moment, and by then Catriona was speaking again.

"Has he been unfaithful? Is that the reason for your anger?"

"'Tis a matter between me husband and myself," Rachel said, busying herself with her herbs.

"I can say from experience that men are like that. I don't think me father was faithful to me own mother. And Rory . . ." She shrugged. "But he says that once we wed, he will be different."

Rachel knew she should keep quiet, but it was not quite in her nature to do so. "And do you believe that?"

Their gazes met. "He cares for me. Yet I wonder, why would fidelity become easier with the passage of time. Women age and men's eyes start to rove. In truth, Flora, I would give much to own what Hugh gives to you."

"Whatever do you mean?"

She shook her head as if surprised by Rachel's naivete. "I know what I am, Flora. None knows better."

Rachel turned toward her.

"I am young, I am beautiful, and I am Rom. Most men believe that to be an open invitation for their advances. More than once I have considered wedding Rory for naught more than his protection."

"You're not in love with him?"

"I am fond of him."

"But in the wagon..." She remembered the knife in Catriona's hand quite vividly. "You... ah ... seemed enamored."

The girl laughed, her teeth flashing white in the firelight. "Tis the Rom way to protect what is hers," she said, and shrugged. "I thought I would sharpen my skills."

"On me?"

Catriona laughed again, but sobered in a moment. "You'll never have a need to keep others from your Hugh." Rachel turned nervously back to her potions, trying to ignore Catriona's words and avid attention. "In truth, I am one to usually draw a man's attention, but I am not certain he has noticed yet that I am a woman."

Rachel snorted, anger and frustration rising in her. "Take heart, lass. He has noticed."

Catriona remained silent for a moment, then shook her head. "He has no time to think of another. You are all he sees."

"Believe me. Tis the furthest thing from the truth!" Rachel snapped, then wished she could draw back the impassioned words.

"Could it be that you don't know the hold you have on him?" she mused.

"Tis late," Rachel said. "You'd best find your bed. I'll see to Lachlan."

"You don't know."

"If you don't sleep, I will."

Catriona laughed in astonishment. "Tis the truth. You've no idea how your Hugh adores you."

"He does not adore me! He would rather be alone till the end of his days than to spend a moment in my company!"

Absolute silence filled the camp. Catriona looked as if she'd been slapped, then she grinned that scampish, sensuous expression that lighted her from the inside out.

"You are amazing."

"And you are daft," Rachel said, feeling irritated and fatigued.

Catriona ignored her. "So you turn him away. But in truth, I don't know how you can resist him. He is not an unhandsome man. In fact—"

"I don't care to hear your assessment."

"You're jealous," Catriona proclaimed mildly.

"He is my husband. And I am not jealous."

"You are jealous," she countered. "And you are trying to make him jealous."

The air left Rachel's lungs in a rush and her shoulders sagged. "I fear I am pathetically poor at it."

Catriona laughed. "Dear Flora, if you had the man wound any tighter about your finger, he would spin in circles when you let loose."

"Then why does he not . . ." Rachel began, but she could not finish the sentence.

"What?"

Rachel turned abruptly away.

"Why does he not what?"

"Why does he not sleep with me?" It was easier to say it to the darkness.

"Never?"

"Never."

"Not even on the night you were wed?"

It would be nice to share the truth, but part truths were hard enough and certainly more than she should admit. "Never."

She felt the girl's hand on her arm and turned

reluctantly at her urging. "There is much I don't know about. But driving men insane with longing . . . that happens to be my greatest talent."

"I've no idea what you're talking about."

"And I am a mole. Where did you learn to dance?"

"I don't dance."

"My point exactly," Catriona said, and hurrying to a nearby wagon, reached inside for a slim flute of sorts. Bringing it out to the fire, she practiced a few notes, then began a slow tune.

Rachel stared at her.

"Dance," she said.

"I don't dance."

Catriona scowled, drawing her brows sharply over snapping eyes. "We have taken you in out of the goodness of our hearts. You will dance and help pay for the funds you have cost us." The corner of a grin snuck through. "And you will make your Hugh mad for you. Dance."

The music began again.

She shouldn't do this, Rachel thought. She should concentrate on her mission and hurry on her way. But her soul disagreed. Dragonheart was burning warm and heavy between her breasts, and her feet suddenly itched to move. They began of their own accord. The tempo increased. Rachel stumbled.

"Lift your skirts, lass, before you break your neck," Marta scolded.

Rachel turned quickly to find the ancient matron watching her from beside the fire.

"You'd not be so alluring with missing teeth. Mark me words," she lisped. "Lift your skirts."

"But . . ."

"They're only ankles."

Rachel complied, lifting her gown a scant few inches, but she'd lost the rhythm and stumbled again.

"Here," Marta said, taking the flute from Catriona. "Let me play." She set the flute to her lips, then lowered it for a moment to squint at them. "Now you dance, the two of you."

Catriona nodded, then raised one arm above her head and lifted her skirt with the other.

Rachel haltingly did the same.

The music drifted softly into the night air. Catriona began to tap lightly to the tune, and then she began to dance. The beat rushed along. Cat's movements kept pace as she swayed and turned and tapped.

Rachel tried to keep up, but she was nervous and stiff.

"Nay," Catriona said, and grabbing her arm, pulled her to a halt. "Don't tell your body what to do. Let the music tell it. Let the music take you where it will. And when you are there, then dance."

Rachel stared at her in confusion. The music started again.

"Close your eyes," Cat whispered.

Rachel let her lids drift closed. The sweet melody lifted to her, through her. Images came to her. She was at her favorite lochan in her homeland. The sun shone. The grass was mossy-soft beneath her bare toes. She was young, a child. Her feet began to move, slow at first, then faster as the music sped along. She lifted her arms, letting them undulate to the magic, spinning and twirling until she was breathless and high and happy and the song came to a throbbing halt.

Rachel stopped, her heart pounding, her cheeks warm with the rush of spent emotion.

Catriona glanced at her and smiled. "He hasn't a chance," she murmured.

"Were I you," Marta rasped, "I'd begin making the babe's clothes immediately."

They were wrong, of course, Rachel told herself as she curled onto her blankets in the wagon. She didn't mean to make Liam jealous. She'd never hoped to do that. After all, she had no more interest in him than he did in her. Her objective was only to reach the king before it was too late. And yet, her dreams had changed. No longer did she see the boy king thrashing about on his bed. Nay, when she dreamed of him, they were dreams of contentment. Instead, she now dreamed of a lochan, of a broad, verdant glen and water as clear as the sky. But sometimes . . . sometimes a face would appear in the water. Fear would grasp her then and she would awaken.

What it meant, she didn't know, but she had no choice but to continue her journey to Blackburn, for she had vowed on her life to do so and to tell no one of her mission.

Maybe she should break off from the gypsy band, but that didn't seem right. Here she felt safe, or as safe as she could be. Here she was fed and protected. It would do her little good to leave the band for a faster course only to be killed before she reached the king's side.

Nay, she would stay with the Roms for a while longer at least, and while she was there she might just as well obtain some money to ensure her well-being. Surely there was no sin in dancing.

She slept most of the days as they traveled, and

stayed up at night, watching over Lachlan, who recuperated slowly but steadily. Sometimes Marta would play the flute and she and Catriona would dance in the shimmering light of the fire.

The village they arrived at late one evening was built on the side of a hill. Low on supplies and coin, they ventured straight into the city. Less than an hour later, they prepared to perform. Lachlan, bandaged and slow, sat atop his pony with Bear dancing along beside to announce the approaching entertainment.

Finally, the show began. Maybe Rachel should have become accustomed to the rush of nervous energy that spilled through her when Liam began his magic and all eyes turned to her, but instead, she was only becoming familiar with the feeling of nausea.

She glanced through the slit in the wagon's door and saw the Irishman preparing for his act. Her nerve wavered. Her heart pounded. What in God's name was she thinking? She was a healer. A lady, not a common dancer. But just at that instant, Catriona called her name.

Rachel shrank against the wall of the wagon, holding her stomach and wishing she were a million miles away, but the door burst open and there was nothing to do but follow the girl's orders. Nothing to do but draw the shimmery scarf over her face and step into the flickering firelight.

Marta's music welled up. She saw Liam turn toward her. But she shifted her eyes away, refusing to look at him. The crowd welled up before her. Faces turned expectantly—crofters, merchants, a well-dressed nobleman with a balding head and eyes that shone bright in the firelight. She froze, paralyzed at the sight of them.

Had she been able to move, she would have flown back to the safety of the wagon, but she stood immobilized. She couldn't do this, couldn't make a spectacle of herself just to prove Liam wrong. But at that moment she heard Cat's whisper as if it came from somewhere inside her.

"Close your eyes."

She did so gladly, not to concentrate, but to shut out the sight of the faces around her. The chandler's open-mouthed perusal, the nobleman's unblinking stare. But the music was still playing, pulsing in the very earth beneath her, thrumming from her feet to Dragonheart and from there to her very soul.

Her feet picked up the rhythm of their own accord, softly at first, slowly. But the music was building. She lifted an arm in supplication to its magic, and now her feet were moving faster. Her body bent and swayed like a willow bowing to the wind, her skirt whirled about her bare legs. The music throbbed faster still. The crowd was a blur and no longer mattered. Only the music mattered, the emotion, the dance, the movement.

Her hair, burnished as bright as the firelight, twirled about her. Her heart pounded and soared in rhythm with her feet, until the music dashed high and dropped low. She dropped with it, breathing hard and wild as she fell to the earth, her skirt like a crimson tide around her.

Noise erupted from the crowd. It took her a moment to realize it was cheering. Gathering her nerve, she looked up at the faces before her. Aye, they were cheering her, but there was more than happiness in their voices. There was desire, as hot and savage as a well-stoked flame.

Rachel rose shakily to her feet, bowed once, and

turned toward Liam. For a moment, he stood just as entranced as the crowd. Finally he forced himself to move, to perform, but there was a slow sensuality to their performance now as if the magic was nothing more than an extension of her dance. Electricity snapped between them like summer lightning, flowing from one to the other, drawing them close on every poor excuse, making them touch a moment longer, their fingers lingering, their gazes smoldering, until finally the act came to a halt.

They bowed side by side. Lachlan rode up on Bear. The crowd turned away.

Breathless and exhilarated, it took Rachel a moment to realize Liam was holding her hand. Their gazes caught and melted like molten steel.

It seemed as if he tried to pull his hand from hers but was not quite able to do so. Instead, he stood in silent immobility. "What are you trying to do, Rachel?" His words were whispered, a broken accusation.

He desired her. For this one moment she was certain of that. And yet still he did not want her. Twas that realization that made her pull from his grasp, made her turn and walk, stiff and proud toward her wagon.

But once there, beside the narrow vehicle, she found she couldn't bear the thought of its confinement. Snatching up her tunic, she raked it over her head, picked up her pouch, and glancing about once to make certain she was undetected, she disappeared into the woods that bordered the village.

The forest was dark and quiet. She walked for a long while, seeking solace, and finally, weary and spent, she found a peace of sorts.

Soon she would leave this life behind and return

to the one she knew. And the next time her father found her a match, she would take it. She would become a wife, a mother. She would become content. She swore it.

Eventually she came to a bog. Mist rose from the water, muffling the world in a blanket of silver. Still, she could make out a cluster of white blossoms in the darkness. She bent to smell them and recognized them instantly as elder.

Brewed into a tea, the flowers would be a potent fever tonic.

"I think we've come far enough."

With a gasp, Rachel spun toward the voice.

A man stood before her in the darkness. Not a tall man, but broad and squat. Moonlight gleamed off his bald pate and his rich garb.

He took a step toward her. "I hope I didn't keep you waiting."

"Waiting? Nay! Whatever do you mean?" She retreated cautiously backward, her mind spinning. Twas the nobleman from the village, the nobleman who had watched her with such avid interest. Of that she was certain. Why was he here? she wondered, but she didn't allow herself to answer that, for she knew his reasons, could read it in the hot recesses of his mind. "In truth I am meeting someone here," she said, struggling to keep her tone calm.

The sound of his chuckle rippled through the night. "Aye. You are meeting me."

Rachel forced a smile. She had been in such situations before. This was not the first time a man thought himself irresistible. But it *was* the first she'd been thought of as a Gypsy instead of as a laird's daughter who would be jealously guarded and fiercely protected. "Indeed, good sir, I don't even know you."

"You may call me Lord Pitney."

"Lord Pitney." She bobbed her head, trying to stay calm. "My Hugh is to meet me here in a short while."

"Hugh?" He chuckled again. "The lad what tosses the potatoes? He was occupied with the other girl when I left." He stepped closer still. "This Hugh is a lucky man to have two lovely wenches about him. But I see he is not enough to keep the likes of you satisfied, aye?"

She shifted her gaze sideways, planning her retreat and forcing herself to continue a banter. "You are much mistaken," she countered. "I am all together satisfied."

He smiled. "If such was true, you would not have ventured from the fold. So here is my question. . . ." He paused and crossed his arms against his chest. "Did you lead me out here for naught but pleasure, or are you hoping for some coin."

"Coin?" Her heart was beating faster.

"'Tis not that I am adverse to paying for the privilege of your company. I only wish to know beforehand."

"Pay! I fear you've got the wrong idea, gentle lord."

"Nay, I do not. But come now. I've already wasted enough time pursuing you. Let us find a likely spot," he said, and reached for her arm.

She jerked away.

Even in the darkness, she could feel his displeasure. "Come now, lass. 'Tis not nice to tease and run. We both know how this will end."

"You've misjudged the situation."

"And you misjudge me," he said, his voice dark.

She tried to spin away, but her foot had sunk in the bog behind her and she fell.

"Tis not quite the sort of place I would have picked. But if you insist," he said and bending, reached for her.

It was at that moment that Rachel kicked. Drawing her free leg back, she snapped her heel directly into his crotch.

He fell with a rasping croak, clutching his groin and swearing.

Rachel lurched to her feet, but her ankle ached, and her movement was too slow, and in that instant, he grabbed her arm in cruel fingers.

Rachel shrieked and kicked him in the face. His head snapped back, but in the same moment, he wrenched a dirk from beneath his tunic.

"You little vixen!" he snarled.

She scrambled away, but he was already after her.

In three strides, he had snatched her by the back of her tunic. She was yanked from her feet and tossed to the earth.

"I was prepared to be generous!" he snarled, standing over her. "But no more, I think. It seems your beauty has made you haughty." He dropped to the ground, his knees straddling her, his knife held in one hand. "I do not like haughty peasants. Tis not right. But you'll not be so proud without your pretty face," he snarled, and leaned close.

"Hello," someone called from the fog.

Pitney jerked to his feet. "Who's there?"

"Tis me," Liam said from nowhere. "And I rather like her face the way it is."

Chapter 19

"**W**here are you?" Pitney growled, taking a cautious step forward. Nothing but the muffling fog answered him. "Show yourself!" he hissed.

"Gladly," Liam answered.

Pitney pivoted about, knife extended, and in that moment, the Irishman stepped into view, his hands empty and arms stretched peaceably to the sides.

"It seems only sporting that you lose the blade," Liam said. "Twould put us on equal footing."

Pitney studied him for a moment, then threw his head back and laughed. "Equal! You think yourself my equal Gypsy boy?"

Liam's smile was slow, mocking. Even in the darkness, Rachel could see the satyr's slant of his mouth, the slash of white teeth against dark skin.

It was that expression that launched Pitney forward like a charging bull.

But in that instant Liam bent, curled his fingers about a felled branch, and swung all in one swift motion.

It cracked with resounding force against the side of Pitney's head. He staggered to a halt. The blade slipped from his fingers, and then, like a felled pine, he crumbled to the earth.

"Nay. We are not equal," Liam said. "I have a longer weapon."

Rachel stumbled through the fog toward him.

He caught her in his arms, squeezing her to him, drinking in the feel of her, the knowledge that she was safe, that all was well. "What were you thinking? What the hell were you thinking?" he asked, but he could manage no anger, only heart crushing relief.

"I just—"

He pressed her to arm's length. "You could have been killed! You could have—Jesus!" Snatching her to him, he squeezed his eyes closed and kissed her hair, her brow.

She was safe. She was well, he told himself. But he needed to see her, so he pushed her away a few scant inches and cupped his hand across her cheek.

"Liam," she whispered, but he kissed her to silence, one smoldering, aching kiss because he could not stop himself.

"I'll take you back to camp," he said finally, and took her hand in his.

She stumbled on her injured ankle and nearly fell. Turning with desperate speed, he lifted her into his arms, hugging her to his heart, savoring the burn of emotion that smoked through him. She smelled of life itself. He filled his lungs with her scent, filled his heart with her presence.

She was safe. And he would keep her that way, he swore as he strode rapidly on. Twas his duty to care for Laird Leith's little girl, he told himself. But her breast was pressed against his chest, wreaking havoc with the little girl image. That image he needed so desperately, that image he'd held on to with fierce tenacity for more than a decade. It had not been so hard. For she was an innocent, always had been an innocent. No matter how she had matured, she had kept a careful, pristine veneer between herself and the world. The sainted child had become the sainted lady. And yet that lady had drawn him with a nagging persistence. No matter how he'd tried to deny it. No matter how he'd tried to lose himself in more worldly women. But now—now the sainted lady had changed. Her skin was dark and smooth like sweet pecans, her hair was loose, flowing long and crimson black against the bright hue of her scandalous gown. But more than that—more than the physical, it was her demeanor that had changed. Where she had been cool and predictable, she was now wild and erotic. And yet, even now those qualities did nothing to negate her goodness, but only made her seem more real, more alluring, more touchable.

Her arms were tight about his neck. Her hair, long and dark and burnished, brushed his arm. He couldn't help but remember how it swirled when she danced. How it had hidden her face, making him long for a glimpse of her otherworldly eyes, her less than saintly mouth.

Those eyes turned up to his now. Her devilish lips parted.

He was mesmerized, trapped with no savior in sight.

"Liam." His name was like a prayer on her lips.

He tried to answer, tried to pull from her gaze, tried to find his voice, but no sound came.

"I knew you would come."

The words were sweet torture. What right did she have to trust him? None. He tried to tell her that, to lash her with the truth of who he was. But her lips were so close, and suddenly they touched his.

Lightning sparked through him, and she was the kindling. One moment he was carrying her to safety, and the next they were on the ground, his cape flared beneath them like a satin sheet.

Her eyes looked through him, but there was no incrimination, no distance. She lifted her hand to his cheek and ran her shivery-soft fingers across the stubble of his jaw. Her kisses followed, soft, vulnerable, so sweet it made him tremble with yearning.

He should not. He must not! he told himself, but now her hand was under his vest. His muscles coiled at her touch and he moaned. Twas a strange thing, one minute his vest was firmly laced in place and the next it was gone, magically displaced by her feather soft fingers, so that there was nothing between her touch and his heart. She ran her palm slowly down his chest, over his nipple, across the jumping expanse of his belly.

There was really nothing he could do. He was a weak man, always had been, and now he needed to feel her skin against his. It seemed unreasonably right to slip his fingers slowly over the cap of her shoulder and down her arm.

She closed her eyes, shivering beneath him. He could do nothing but kiss her where his hand ventured, on the sweet muscle of her upper arm, at the delicate crease of her elbow, over the tight tendons of her wrist, and then each finger, slowly, capturing every precious moment, every breath of life.

Her skin was dark, and if he tried, he might be able to pretend she were someone else, that he wasn't defiling the most perfect thing in his life.

But he couldn't bear to pretend, for she was Rachel, the woman he had wanted since the first moment. The woman he'd want for all time.

He kissed her lips with trembling passion, feeling the soft burn of desire clean down to his soul. The gown's laces sighed open, revealing the graceful swell of her breasts. He kissed her there, where the laces parted, and she arched against his cape and moaned. Suddenly there was little use for the gown. It slipped magically from her shoulders until she wore nothing but her own ethereal beauty and the dragon. She lay beneath him, unspeaking, unmoving, as natural as the earth itself, as beautiful as the stars.

Reaching up, she caressed his chest, then skimmed her hand along his side to pull him closer. Their lips met. Her hands slid lower, touching, feeling, lighting a fire that would not be quenched, not for as long as he lived. She was Rachel, the Lady Saint, yet she was more. He no longer had any hope of saving his soul by denying his heart.

Her fingers touched the laces of his hose. The garment slipped away, until they were flesh against flesh, naked in the misty moors. Lying beside her, he wrapped them in his cape and kissed her throat. Light as thistledown, she skimmed her fingertips along the center of his back. He pressed the hard shaft of his desire against her hip, and she turned and kissed him.

Passion flared like white lightning between them. He could wait no longer. Damn his bastard father, and damn his own worthless character. For this once, just this one sterling moment of time, he would allow himself a glimpse of heaven—where the Lady Saint resided.

He eased between her legs, and she opened for him. He kissed her throat, her shoulder, the high, proud swell of her breasts, just brushing her nipples, just allowing himself one tiny sip of that sweet nectar.

"Liam!" Her voice was raspy, her fingers tight on his hips, but she said no more. Instead, she pulled him into her.

She was soft and warm, as welcoming as a crackling fire, as sweet as summer dew. Her legs gripped him, her lips grazed his ear, whispering his name. He pressed in deeper, longing to push in hard and fast, to fly up the rise to the summit, but there was an impediment, her virginity. He had known it would be there, had known in his heart if not in his jealous soured mind. So he stopped his movement, letting her body relax around him, letting her adjust. But Rachel squirmed beneath him.

Liam squeezed his eyes closed and tried to remain still.

"Please, Rachel," he hissed, "I'm trying to wait till you're ready."

"Sweet Mary. I've been waiting for more than a decade, if I were anymore ready I'd already be done," she rasped, and with amazing strength, pulled him in deeper.

He pressed into her with a groan of unstoppable need. She pressed back, her legs wrapped tight around him. Together they found a rhythm as old as the seas, as predictable as the seasons. Yet each movement, each breath, each sensation was the first until they were swept into the heavens, soaring for a moment together before falling gently back into reality.

Euphoria faded slowly, leaving Liam with the bitter residue of guilt. Beside him, Rachel seemed small and defenseless, like a crushed wildflower, so fresh and untrammeled a moment ago. But now her eyes were closed, her body covered by his and his cape.

"We'd best get back to camp." He managed the words, though they sounded hoarse and rusty.

She opened her eyes. In the glimmering mist he found that they had not changed. Even the sassy curve of her lips looked the same.

"Liam." She reached out with one hand and touched his cheek, but he pulled quickly out of her reach and turned away.

He could feel her gaze on his back but refused to look at her, for he knew what he would see—a wee lass in a white night rail with a smile that stunned and eyes that mesmerized, Laird Leith's adored daughter, the Forbes's precious healer.

"Liam," she said again, but he reached out and jerked his hose on, and finally she turned away.

They dressed in silence. He wanted to let her wander back alone to camp, wanted to put as much space as possible between them, but when she took her first step, she faltered. There was nothing he could do but lift her into his arms. Nothing but carry her against his heart back to their wagon. Once there, he laid her down upon her blankets, and though he tried to draw away, he could not. Instead, he pulled her shakily into his arms and held her.

"Liam." Her voice was as soft as the dawn. "We must—"

"Shhh." He covered her temptress lips with his fingers and squeezed his eyes closed. "Please," he whispered, letting the pain wash over him like a cold tide. "Don't talk."

* * *

Rachel woke slowly. There was a niggling of discomfort in places heretofore undisturbed. Memories of the previous night rushed in. Memories of Liam's chest, smooth and hard as glass. Of his hands, slow and warm as he skimmed her body. She flushed at her thoughts, but she couldn't forget his expression afterward. Neither could she decipher it. It had been almost like pain or guilt. But surely not. Liam was not the type to be weighed down by his transgressions, while she had always been too responsible for her own good.

And yet, God forgive her, she felt no guilt. Instead, she felt free and joyous. Against her breast, Dragonheart seemed to purr with shared satisfaction. Even her ankle felt quite healed.

Brushing back her hair, she captured it in a sloppy swirl at the back of her head, slipped into her tunic and gown, and stepped outside. But as the faces before the fire turned to her, her confidence fluttered.

Catriona's gaze sparkled, Marta's bore a sly glint of satisfaction. Rory's held a fierce expression that looked almost like anger. Only the children seemed oblivious to the night just past. Fane had made stilts out of oak branches and Lachlan was testing his skill. Bear snoozed in the elongated shade of a mulberry bush, and Liam was nowhere to be seen.

"Break the fast," Marta said, her ancient voice creaky as she nodded toward the pot that simmered over the fire. "You look weak."

Rachel tried to convince herself that Marta's words had nothing whatsoever to do with the night just past, but there was little hope of that, or of stopping the blush that warmed her cheeks.

Lifting a wooden bowl from the back of a wagon, she stepped toward the fire. Everyone was quiet.

She scooped a bit of sowens into her dish and cleared her throat as the porridge steamed in the early morning air. "Have you, maybe, seen..." She almost said Liam, but caught herself just in time. "Hugh?"

"Let the lad rest," Marta said with a chuckle, but Hertha, always kindly, stepped up with a wooden spoon.

"He but went to water the horses."

"Oh." There was nothing to say to that, for truly it would be unwise to let them know she couldn't wait to see him, to touch him, to decipher his emotions and tell him all would be well. He was, after all, supposed to be her husband of some years. Surely that sort of impatient need would wear off eventually. Wouldn't it?

She felt her blush deepen. In truth, she didn't know how she could grow tired of touching Liam. Not after last night. And maybe, just maybe, there had been a sliver of truth to his words at the falls. Maybe he truly did care for her a little, she thought.

But just at that moment a stranger hustled into their camp. John rose abruptly to his feet. Rory widened his stance and reached beneath his tunic.

The man was dressed in common attire, his face partly hidden by a drooping leather hat. "I saw your performance last night," he preempted, coming to an abrupt halt.

The words fell into silence.

He cleared his throat and glanced nervously behind him. "It seems to me you be decent folk doing naught but making a living and protecting your own."

"Why have you come?" John asked.

"Lord Pitney has just returned to the village. He

says he was attacked in the woods during the night."

"We had naught to do with it!" Rory pronounced, taking a single step forward.

"In truth, it could have been any number of folk who might have wished him ill." For a moment the stranger's lip curled, suggesting that he himself was not exempt from the group. "He is a coward and a pig. But he is also lazy. If you are out of easy reach, I think, maybe, you will be safe," he said simply, and glancing quickly about, hurried back in the direction from which he had come.

The Rom's packed up quickly. Rachel could do naught but assist them. She would have a chance to talk to Liam soon enough, she assured herself, for they could spend all day in the wagon together. The thought sent a blush of quicksilver emotion through her, but just then she glanced up to see Liam mounted on the white palfrey with Lachlan riding behind him.

She scowled, wondering if she should approach him, but John's wagon lurched into motion, and there seemed nothing she could do but wait. Carefully avoiding Rory, she hurried up beside Catriona.

The horses' hooves echoed louder as they moved from the grassy campground onto the road.

"Well?" Catriona asked.

Rachel didn't turn toward her. "Well what?"

The gypsy girl laughed. Her eyes had taken on the color of the sky this morning, as blue as a harebell and as mischievous as a child's. "Was it wonderful?"

"I have no idea what you're talking about."

"And I am a capon," Catriona said, and laughing again, turned her attention to the road.

*   *   *

Rachel waited breathlessly for nightfall. True, Liam had opted to sleep outside their wagon before. But surely he would not do so tonight, not after what they had shared. She was certain of it. Thus, with just a few sparse glances in his direction, she ate her supper quickly, then retired to her bed and waited.

Time ticked along. From outside, she heard John and Hertha's soft good-nights as they herded their daughters off to sleep. The fire crackled. Catriona coaxed and threatened until Lachlan finally agreed to abandon his juggling lessons and find his bed.

It wouldn't be long now, Rachel thought, but still time marched on. Finally, fatigued and uncertain, she fell into her dreams.

Again she woke alone. By the silvery light that seeped into the wagon, she knew it was still early, the first glimmer of dawn. Somewhere far off a nightjar chirped its rapid call. The sound was lonely and haunting. Where was Liam? Rachel wondered. Catriona's mesmerizing face flashed into her mind, but she shook it out.

Today she would not be debilitated, not by uncertainty nor embarrassment. Today she would find out what Liam was thinking, learn why he was avoiding her. She was outside the wagon in a matter of moments. The fog was thick again, soft and silvery and silent. Peering about, she made out the forms of the other wagons.

From the direction of the river, a horse nickered, the sound low and muffled in the heavy fog. Lifting her skirts, Rachel strode in that direction.

Liam rested with his back to a rowen. Gone was the grin so characteristic of him. Instead, he sat in

silent retrospection, staring over the narrow band
of river that rolled away.

Gathering her nerve, Rachel stepped toward
him.

His reactions were as quick as a cat's. One moment he was resting and the next he was on his
feet, his eyes narrowed and his right hand curled
around the hilt of a blade that had appeared from
nowhere.

It occurred to her suddenly that he could have
used that same knife on Lord Pitney. That he could
have left the man dead in the woods and no one
would have been the wiser. But despite his distaste
for the nobility, he hadn't done that.

"Did I startle you?" She smiled as she said it,
nervousness like a wound coil inside her.

"What be you doing out here?" he asked. The
knife disappeared, though she had no idea where.

"I wished to talk to you."

He glanced sideways as if wondering which way
to run. "I must see to the horses," he said.

She noticed now that the white mare was grazing
only a short distance away, her rope trailing in the
heavy dew of the grass. "She looks content
enough," Rachel said, trying to keep her tone light.

"Aye, but the others be thirsty. I'd best see to—"

"Liam," she interrupted before he could turn
away. "I need to talk to you."

He pulled his brows low over his eyes. A muscle
jumped in his jaw, and though she had known him
most of her life, he looked formidable suddenly,
and unapproachable.

She cleared her throat. "About us," she began.
She'd spent most of the night planning what she
would say, hoping he'd come to her, waiting to
draw him into her arms and tell him how she felt.

But suddenly emotions clogged in her throat, making it impossible to speak.

She noticed without trying to that he looked no more relaxed than she. In fact, his hands were formed to fists and his lips pursed in a hard line.

"What of us?" he asked, his voice dusky.

She nearly winced at his tone. What little confidence she had disappeared like dew in the bright light of day, but she refused to drop her gaze. Instead, she stiffened her back and raised her chin slightly. Aloofness was a weapon that had rarely failed her.

"We cannot pretend that nothing happened," she said.

"Why?"

Because the touch of his hand, the sound of his voice, the throbbing feel of him inside her had made her so much more than she'd ever been.

"Because something did happen," she managed.

"Aye, but it will never happen again. That I vow," he said, and turning rapidly away, disappeared into the fog.

Chapter 20

The gown was yellow. Not the bleached yellow of straw, but the bright, radiant yellow of a celandine blossom.

Catriona, kneeling inside the wagon, held it up to Rachel's shoulders. "It will look good on you," she said.

"Nay," Rachel responded. "'Tis not that I am ungrateful to you, for you have done much for me already. But I will not be dancing again."

Catriona pulled the garment down in front of her. The wagon was silent, her gaze as steady as an arrow sent straight and true.

Rachel cleared her throat. "In truth, I must soon be leaving you."

"And Hugh."

"What?" Rachel said.

"You will be leaving with your husband, of course."

No. She would be going alone, for Liam did nothing but confuse her, and she could not afford to be confused. "Of course," she said.

"You'll need some coin, then," Cat deduced. "You would be a vision in this gown. Twould surely earn you a few extra coppers."

Rachel scowled down at the garment. It was a bonny piece, bold and bright and lovely. She touched the satin-soft sleeve, and in that moment her mind danced back to Liam. Why would he not talk to her? Why had he spent the past several days avoiding her? Had he felt nothing that night in the woods?

"He'd not be able to take his eyes from you," Catriona murmured.

Rachel jerked her gaze hopefully to the girl, but caught herself before she spoke. "I don't know what you mean."

"I begin to think he is not your husband atall."

"Whyever would you say that?"

Catriona shrugged. "You are obviously a lady, well-born and well-educated. What is he but a juggler and a magician?"

Flashes of the panic that had seized her at the falls returned to her. She could not afford to lose her disguise. "You're wrong. What would make you think that?"

Their gazes fused. "'Tis not what I think," Cat said. "But what Hugh thinks."

"Is that what he said?" Rachel whispered.

Catriona shook her head as if disgusted. "Grandmother thinks you have the gift. I am not even certain you have a brain. Wear the gown. Make him crazy."

"He is crazy enough," Rachel countered. "You can take my word on that."

"Nay. He is not," Catriona disagreed. "Not for you. You want him so slavering drunk on your beauty, so enamored with your goodness, that he can do naught but sing your praises from the highest roof."

Rachel tried to fight back the words but there

was little hope of that, for emotion was as heavy as sin inside her. "Do you think he cares for me a bit?" she whispered.

"Wear the gown," Cat urged. "And don't be shy about flirting with others."

From inside the wagon, Rachel heard Catriona's performance come to an end. She thought Liam might insist that she not dance again, but he didn't care enough even for that. She closed her eyes, tried to settle her stomach, gave up, and waited for the music to start.

It began as it always did, with that haunting rhythm that spoke of the sea and lovers and a thousand forgotten yearnings.

Her skirt hiked up as she stepped out. She felt, more than saw, dozens of faces turn toward her, but she pushed them out of her mind and let the music lead her feet. Slowly she lifted her arms above her head. They undulated to the music. Dragonheart thrummed the rhythm against her heart, and her body now took up the chant, swaying and turning in time to the beat, and suddenly the music became everything. Off to her right, she was aware of Liam watching her. To the left was the crowd. She danced toward it, her arms rising and falling with the notes.

The crowd parted before her. She danced down the center. Behind her, she felt Liam's gaze, and suddenly it didn't feel so cold, but almost as a ray of sunlight. It was not so hard to believe he coveted her. She was beautiful, she was alluring, she was woman.

The men turned toward her. Through the slash of the hair that whirled with her movement, she could see their wide eyes, their greedy faces. A fat merchant in a green doublet smiled at her. She spun around him, her feet beating like a drum upon the grass.

He reached for her. But she danced out of his grasp, on to the next man and the next.

She was a siren, a . . .

But suddenly evil struck her. She felt it like a blow to her stomach, taking her breath.

Her heart jolted to a halt. Her feet faltered as she skimmed the crowd. And there, not more than a yard away, stood Davin. He stared at her, his icy eyes narrowed, his huge body tense. Confusion consumed her. He'd been sent to protect her, to see her safely to Blackburn. She should be happy to see him, but instead she felt only fear. A vision flashed across her mind, a vision of Liam in pain.

She jerked as if the pain were her own. But it was all foolishness. Davin was her guard. Yet fear, cold and prickly, sliced through her. She jerked her feet back into the rhythm with a horrid effort. Her body swayed again, but her mind was torn, shattered by dark images of pain, of torture. Her mind said she should reveal herself. Her soul insisted that she hide.

But why would Davin wish her ill? It made no sense, and yet the feelings plagued her, gnawed at her, begging her to slink away, to find cover.

So she must do the opposite. The solution seemed so clear. She pressed down the fear, forced herself to move toward Davin. Her arms raised toward the sky, stretching her body upward. She felt his hard gaze on her, intense as a hunting beast's. Pivoting around him, she swayed to the beat, and suddenly the music was moving faster. She twirled again. Her hair swept outward, swiping across his chest. She heard the hiss of it against his blue doublet.

Faster and faster she went, nearly in his reach, nearly within his recognition. But she was no longer Rachel. Gone was the Lady Saint, replaced by this wild wanton.

The music came to a crashing halt.

Rachel dropped to the ground at his feet, the high portions of her breasts pressed well into view, her eyes averted, her burnished locks sprayed around her like a sea of sable.

For a moment all the world seemed to stand still as Davin stared at her, then, "Come along," he said to the men beside him. "'Tis a lady that we seek. Not a dancer."

Rachel's legs shook as she rose to her feet. Her head felt light and the world seemed to swim before her. Liam reached for her from nowhere and turned her toward the wagon. In a moment, they were inside. The door closed behind them.

They froze like rabbits in a warren. Fear lay as heavy as a woolen on them, but finally it dissipated, dissolving softly into the still air.

"Had I known you so wished to end your life, I'd not have been so determined to save it."

Rachel closed her eyes and released her breath. "Why would he wish me harm?"

"Why would you show yourself to him?"

She shook her head, worn and frazzled "I convinced him beyond a doubt that I am not Rachel of the Forbes. And a good thing, too, or your life would surely be forfeit."

"What are you talking about?" he snarled, his expression impassioned, his grip still hard on her arm.

"How do you think it looks to Davin, Liam? He

was commissioned to protect me. Indeed, he was doing just that when some ragged Irishman knocked him in the water and cut the rope, spilling his ward down the waterfall and away. Never did he find a body. Not a word of explanation did he receive. Were you him, Liam, who would you think was the villain?"

"So you say, you only danced to protect me from your guard?"

Nay, she had danced because she had been terrified of being discovered. Terrified that Liam had been right all along, and that her life was endangered by the very man paid to keep her safe. "Aye," she said, "just to keep you safe."

"Then why did you not tell him your identity? He's your guard. Surely if you wished you could have kept me safe from him."

She forced herself to shrug, pushing aside her terror, her confusion, Liam's haunting hatred of her. "Though he seems a stoic fellow, I fear Davin's feelings for me run quite deep. It may be his need for revenge would have been beyond my control. He is a very powerful man. While you . . ." Anger and hurt made her reach out to press her palm against Liam's chest. "Well, just now you amuse me."

"I am flattered." He gritted the words.

"As you should be."

"So you say you keep me around for naught but your entertainment?"

"Until I can find a better replacement."

He grabbed her arm in a hard grip. "You were a virgin," he growled, shoving his face close to hers.

She forced a laugh. "As, I assume, you were at some point, Liam."

"You were untried only two days ago. Don't deny it."

"Believe what you will, Liam, if it makes you feel better. But believe this also, I've no reason to think Davin is my enemy."

"No reason! Do you not remember twas he that meant to kill you on the ferry?"

"So you say. But I've no reason to believe so. He did me no harm before you tossed him in the drink."

Liam stared at her, his eyes narrow. "Then why do you not tell him who you are? Indeed, you could maybe still catch him."

"Maybe I shall," she said, anger burning through her, and reached for the door.

He jerked her back to him. "Over me own dead body!" he growled.

"As you wish," Rachel retorted, and yanked her arm from his grasp.

But suddenly she was flat on her back, Liam's face inches above hers.

"Twould be your body that would be forfeit, if you went to Davin," he growled, "and you well know it. Why do you torment me so?"

"Torment you?" She forced out the words. "Whyever would my actions do that, Liam? Oh, but I forget, tis most likely because of your undying love for me."

His hands tightened like talons, then loosened abruptly. He jerked away to scrape his fingers through his hair.

"You are making me insane!"

She sat up, feeling shaky and tense. "Me? I am all but a saint, Liam. Everyone knows tis true. So surely you can forgive me a wee bit of dancing—unless tis that you are jealous."

He said nothing, but stared at her with narrowed eyes.

Heart pounding, she crawled toward him. The taut laces of the bodice barely concealed her bosom. Hidden between her up-pressed breasts, Dragonheart purred, seeming to press her on. "You are not jealous, are you, Liam?"

His gaze, hot as a licking flame, sparked down to her exposed chest, then snapped to her face. "Don't be ridiculous," he said, but his tone was rusty.

"So you say you do not care what I do with other men?"

A muscle jumped in his jaw. His dark eyes blazed. "Why would I care?"

Maybe his words should have hurt, but the air snapped with tension, calling him a liar.

"You do not covet me for your own?" she asked, and sitting back on her haunches, skimmed her fingers over the bulging curve of her chest. "Not at all?"

"Nay!"

She shrugged, but the movement was difficult. She must be insane. "What a relief it is to know I am perfectly safe with you. I thought maybe after we . . ." She paused, her mind spinning for a word for what they had shared. "After we made love." She swallowed, knowing she should have chosen words that were more crass, but finding herself unable to do so. "I thought afterward, you would be inclined to think I should be yours alone."

His teeth were gritted. She could tell by the taut muscles that showed through the dark skin of his jaw.

"But since you are unconcerned, I see no reason

we cannot do it again." Leaning closer, she brushed her lips across his.

"You have no idea what you're dealing with," Liam growled, and grabbed her wrist.

She speared him with her gaze. "Don't I?"

"Nay."

"I thought I was dealing with a man." She meant to say the words caustically, but they didn't come out as intended, for he was too close, his eyes too entrancing. "A man, alone since childhood, yet able to survive by his wits alone. A man of goodness—"

"Nay!" he snapped, and leapt for the door.

In an instant, he was outside.

"We will be gone in minutes." Marta's voice was just audible from beside the wagon. "Twould be safest if you stayed inside, laddie."

"Nay," Liam said, his tone rusty. "Twould not."

True to Marta's words, they left the village in collected haste. Though no explanations were made, Liam wondered if old Marta too had felt the crushing evil, for they didn't stop for many hours, and when they did, it was only to eat, rest the horses for a bit, and move on again.

The afternoon wore slowly away. Liam stopped the mare's restless movement some distance ahead of the wagons. Atop a bouldered hillock, he stared over Lachlan's head at the world beyond. What was he to do? Maybe it was no longer safe to keep Rachel with the gypsy band. But surely it was no safer for them alone.

The questions nagged him, burning his mind, until finally, restive and frustrated, he slipped off the mare's back, leaving Lachlan to ride alone. The road dipped into a wide, sheltered glen and back up. Miles slipped beneath Liam's feet. The shadows grew longer.

From the wagon, came the women's hushed voices. Off in the distance a pipet called. The cart horses trudged along. Liam trudged with them, his mind gnawing at his thoughts. Had Davin recognized something familiar about Rachel? Would he follow them? And what of Warwick? Where was he? How long would they have before they were found? The worry turned to a weight, crushing him like a ponderous sack of feed, seeming to slow his feet, to muddle his thinking.

"Where's Lachlan?" Catriona's voice broke through his sweaty haze, and suddenly his heart was pounding.

Where *was* Lachlan?

But now he heard the mare's hoofbeats from up ahead. She turned the bend, trotting toward them. But her back was bare.

Panic broke over Liam like a wild wave.

"Rachel!" He yelled her name, but it was too late, for a man stood in the road ahead, a man who held a knife to the boy's throat. And beside him, not thirty yards away, a dark-robed figure watched.

Chapter 21

❦❦

"**L**iam." The voice reached for him, raspy and harsh, spoken from the depths of a nightmare too hideous to contemplate. "I wondered if you would be here."

"Warwick!" Panic squeezed Liam's throat like a tight fist. It couldn't be. He couldn't have survived the fire.

"Nay. I am not a ghost." Warwick chuckled, but the sound held no humor and issued from beneath the dark hood that shadowed his face. "Did you not know, lad? I am immortal, or soon will be, once I have the dragon."

The words chilled Liam like a damp wind, but he couldn't fail, not now. "What dragon?" He forced the words from between frozen lips, but there was little purpose, for Warwick only laughed.

"The dragon worn by the woman of the Forbes."

"There is no Forbes here."

"Your mother should have taught you better than to lie, lad. I am disappointed. But tis not yer fault, I suspect. A boy needs a father to teach him right from wrong."

Sweat dampened Liam's palms, though he felt strangely cold. "There is no Forbes here," he repeated, and speared his gaze on the sorcerer. He would not glance at Rachel. He would not. But in his mind, he willed her to slip from the wagon and into the woods. If she possessed a wee bit of the gift twas said she had, maybe she could read his thoughts.

"I could almost believe you, lad," Warwick said, his tone patient as he turned his head toward the wagons. "For she does not appear to be the lady my spies described. Indeed, she is quite clever, for her own guards did not recognize her." He chuckled. "I have been following the hulking northerner for some time, for I knew he would find her eventually."

"So Davin is your man," Liam whispered.

"You underestimate me. I do not need to own the man to use him. Indeed, it was quite a simple task to make you think the fellow on the ferry was her guard. But you felt my presence too soon. Yer powers are strong, lad, untrained, but strong. Twas me you felt on the river and me in the village, and I felt the dragon. I knew she had it even before—."

"Let the lad go." Marta's words echoed through the gathering darkness. She had stepped down from the wagon and leaned heavily upon her staff.

Warwick turned his attention to her, his face almost visible for an instant beneath his cowl. "Who are you, old woman?"

"They call me Marta." She stepped forward. "And I say to let me grandson free before tis too late for you."

"Marta." He raised his head. "I have heard of you."

"Aye!" barked the old woman. "And all you

have heard is true. You do not wish to tangle with me, Dark One."

"You know me?"

"I know you by your stench. Loose the child!"

"Send out the Forbes."

Liam streaked his gaze to Rachel, praying she would flee, but she remained as she was, frozen on the wagon seat.

"There is no Forbes here," Marta said. "Only me own granddaughters, and I will not see them with the devil."

"You are far out of your depth, old woman," Warwick hissed. "Not only do I know the Forbes, I have caused her to be here."

Liam caught his breath. Warwick stabbed him with his eyes. "So you did not suspect?"

Liam felt hot, probing fingers in his mind, and then Warwick laughed. "She did not tell you. All this time you risked your life to protect her, and she did not deign to tell you that she goes to tend Scotland's young king?"

"The king!" Marta snapped.

"It seems his mind was failing." Liam could hear the twisted smile in the old man's voice. "He was deranged, seeing things that were not there, as if someone was tampering with his mind. Indeed, some thought him quite mad. Thus, they sent for the woman to heal him."

Terror spurred through Liam. Warwick had toyed with King James's mind, knowing Rachel would be called forth to see to him. Warwick had known all along she would come. He had only to await an opportunity to waylay her.

There was no hope.

"So I have more power than you knew. Aye,

lad," the wizard hissed. "More power than you can imagine."

It was exactly what Liam had been thinking.

"I have had a long while to learn of the dragon," Warwick said. "Aye, I have learned." He nodded, one shallow movement of his cowl. "I knew it would come to her. There is some bond there, some unearthly bond between the amulet and the Highland women. Aye, I learned that some years ago when it was bound to the others. This dark-haired wench is the only one of the three who had not yet worn it, not yet felt its protection. Twas a simple task to threaten the king. I knew she would come, and once she was beyond her father's protection . . ." He shrugged, the movement almost casual. "There is nothing that can stop me now."

There was no hope, Liam thought frantically.

"True," Warwick intoned. "Unless you join me. Send the woman to me."

"Nay," Liam said, but the word was as insignificant as a sigh.

"I can take her," Warwick said. "I could kill you all, but I have always felt sentimental toward you, lad. And as for you, old woman." He flitted his gaze to Marta. "The Forbes is not your own. Give her to me and I will let your lad go. Refuse, and . . ." He nodded toward the man that held Lachlan.

The knife sliced across the boy's throat.

Catriona screamed. Lachlan's knees buckled, but he remained standing. A droplet of blood slicked along the blade and onto the boy's tunic. But only a scratch showed across his neck.

"The next slice—"

"I am here!" Rachel said.

"Nay!" Liam gasped, but she was already beside

the cart horse, her hand clenched in the animal's mane. "Nay." He turned his panicked gaze back to the wizard. "She doesn't have the dragon."

"Indeed?" Warwick did not turn his attention from Rachel. "Then where is it, Liam?"

"I have it."

The laughter was ugly, echoing through the woods like a banshee's wail. "It seems I believed that once before. It cost me dearly," he said, and threw back his hood.

Rachel gasped. Liam felt his heart clench in his chest.

The old man had no face. Instead, he had a patchwork of parchment scars stretched tight over angular bones. His hair grew in patches between the deserts of his scars, and from two hollow graves, his opaque eyes glared.

"Dear God," Rachel whispered, her knuckles white in the horse's mane.

"So I even revolt the renowned healer," Warwick rasped. "Or shall I call you the lady saint?"

"I can help you," Rachel murmured.

The laughter was hollow. "Aye, you can. Give me the dragon."

She lifted her hand to her chest, clutching the amulet. "Will you let my friends go?" Her voice was a whisper.

"Of course. I will let you all go."

Rachel shook her head. "You lie," she said softly. "Dragonheart is bound to me. You will not allow that to continue."

Silence ruled the woods.

Warwick watched her for a moment, then nodded shallowly "So you have your mother's gift. I wondered. Still, I fear it will do you no good, for my own skills are far beyond yours. And so you have a choice to make. Tis your life or the lad's, and you are a healer."

Rachel stepped forward.

"Nay!" Liam shrieked, and lunged for her. But in that instant Rory grabbed his arms from behind.

"So she is not your wife," the Rom growled. "But the boy *is* Catriona's kin."

"Rachel!" Liam yelled, fighting to get free. She turned toward him, her face pale in the darkness, but in a moment she stepped forward again. "Nay!" he screamed, but she was nearly there, nearly within the wizard's reach.

"Bear!" Catriona yelled.

The beast rose from the shadows with a roar, snatched Lachlan's captor in his powerful jaws, and flung him aside. Others leapt forward, but the bear turned with the agility of a cat. The closest one fell like a fly beneath his gigantic paw.

Lachlan spurted toward the wagons.

"Run Rachel!" Liam yelled.

She turned toward him and in that moment he knew the truth. She would not leave without him.

"Balls!" he rasped, and jerking his head backward, slammed it into Rory's face.

Bone crunched against his skull, but he only cared that he was free. Scrambling out of the Rom's reach, he flew toward Rachel, grabbed her hand, and yanked her into the woods.

Bear roared.

A man screamed, but the sound was truncated, chopped off in the middle.

"Leave them!" Warwick shrieked.

Branches slapped against Liam's face. Nettles tore at his clothes. His own panicked breathing blurred his concentration, but still, from behind him, he heard the tromp of a half dozen running feet.

"Faster!" His voice was no more than a hiss in the darkness.

Rachel tripped, nearly falling. He jerked her back up, and they were running again, streaking hand in hand through the darkness.

Forever flew behind them. They raced through the woods, gasping for breath, praying for life. Turning and running and turning again until finally Liam slowed to a walk.

"Have we lost them?"

She didn't answer, and when he glanced back, her eyes looked too large to be real, great amethyst pools of fear. Dirt streaked her face, and hollows of fatigue showed beneath her eyes.

"We'll rest for—"

The snap of a twig froze him to silence, and suddenly Liam felt Warwick's evil like a tangible force. Despair washed over him. They could not outrun their enemies' horses. But neither could they give up. Desperation speared through him like a hot lance.

"Come!" They stumbled back into a run, but they would not go far. There! The hollow of a tree, hidden by dried bracken and craggy boulders. "Get in."

"Nay!"

"Get in!" he snapped, planning frantically. He still had the black powder Marta had given him. If he were clever, she could yet survive. "I can escape better without you. I will lead them away."

"Tis suicide for you," she whispered.

"I will lead them away, and when they are gone, you will find safety."

"Hide with me." She clawed at his sleeve, but he grabbed her arms.

"You will not die! Do you hear me, Rachel! You will not die!" he rasped, and pushed her inside. The bracken closed firmly behind her. Even from a few inches away, he couldn't see her.

He stumbled away, praying as he ran.

Their pursuers were riding single file and stopped dead in their tracks when they saw him standing in their path.

"Look what we've found?" said the closest man, and lifted his bow.

"Nay!" Warwick commanded. "Don't kill him."

"Nay indeed," Liam agreed. He dredged up a cocky smile and stepped forward, prayers running through his soul like weary chants. "For I have something you may want."

"You have the dragon?" Warwick rasped, his tone reverent.

"Aye, I have it."

"Show me."

"Certainly," Liam agreed, and putting his hand to his neck, acted as if he were pulling a chain from beneath his tunic as he stepped forward.

The closest man exchanged his bow for a sword.

Liam increased his grin. "A strapping lad like you afraid of a simple juggler," he said. "And I am not even armed." He lifted his other hand to prove his point, but as he did so, he tripped a tiny string. Black powder poured from the bottom of his hose. Heart pounding, he took one more step, but as he did so, he scratched the steel of his shoe against a rock. He leapt just as the powder exploded.

The nearest horse screamed and reared. His rider yanked the reins, and the steed, pulled off balance, careened over backward, pinning his master beneath him.

Liam rushed forward. The horse thrashed, struggling to get up, and Liam leapt aboard.

They were running in a heartbeat, dashing through the woods. Behind him, he heard the screams and hoofbeats of the others. They were following him. Rachel would be safe. All would be—

Pain sliced through him like the blade of an ax, swallowing his senses. Blackness raced toward him. He fought for lucidness, for control. He must not fall, but he couldn't stop the earth. It flew toward him. His body struck it, but it didn't hurt, only seeming to echo through him like a haunting dream. Hooves thundered momentarily against his ears. Voices hummed around him, and then all went silent.

Not eighty rods away, Rachel cowered in her hiding place.

Where was Liam? What was happening?

Men yelled. Hoofbeats drummed, but the noise subsided in a minute. Even the sound of the horses' nervous tramping grew still, and then, after an eternity of terror, Warwick's voice came, rasping through the woods like the hiss of an evil adder.

"We have your love, Lady. He is unconscious and badly wounded, but I think you can yet save him."

Rachel lurched sideways, ready to leave her sanctuary, to run to Liam, but a flash of evil struck her mind. She trembled at its onslaught, grabbing Dragonheart as she crouched back into hiding.

Perhaps Liam was already dead. Perhaps she was already too late. Perhaps she could do nothing but save herself and the amulet. Terror and duty warred inside her. But the truth came to her slowly, stealing through the horror, through the fear; even if Liam had survived thus far, Warwick would not allow him to live, not if she showed herself. For then she would no longer have even a smattering of bargaining power.

Silence spurred through the woods, accented by nothing more than Rachel's own labored breathing.

"He's bleeding badly," Warwick called.

Nausea shook her. Gripping the amulet harder, she squeezed her eyes closed, but the tears still escaped, eking between her lids. Her throat tightened in agony.

"'Twill be on your soul if he dies!"

She must go to him. She must! she thought, and reached for the opening in the tree. But just then a vision of Liam's dead body flashed across her mind. She mewled like a wounded animal and hunched deeper into the tree's hollow.

If she revealed herself now, all would be lost. She could do nothing for Liam now. Nothing. But when darkness came she might have a chance. There might be some hope.

She must wait. Wait and pray that Liam would regain consciousness in time to aid their escape. Twas her only hope, she thought, but just then she felt a sharp stab of evil in her mind.

Warwick! She recognized him immediately. He was searching for her, trying to find her hiding place.

She tried to turn her consciousness aside. But he was already in her mind, wearing at her nerves, gnawing at her thoughts. Terror sliced through her. Sweat beaded her brow. She tightened her grip on Dragonheart and wrestled the powers of hell.

Home! She saw it in her mind. Her cousins! They

were there, their faces hazy at first. But in a moment they were clearer, and then clearer still, as if they stood before her in the flesh. Their laughter swelled around her, their hands took her own, and they led her down from Glen Creag to the quiet stream where they often played.

The song of the water here was sweet and melodious. A goldfinch tittered. The sound mingled with her cousins' silvery laughter. The smell of sun-warmed grass filled her nostrils. Contentment took her soul.

Twas there that Rachel fell asleep, lying on the grass with the sunlight warm against her face and the water chanting stories of love and happiness.

A scream ripped through the woods.

Rachel woke with a jolt. Her head thumped against something solid. Darkness. Everywhere. Where was the meadow, the singing water, the . . .

A scream again! And suddenly she remembered all. She was alone in the woods. Liam had been wounded and taken. And there was no one to save him. No one but herself.

The next scream was like that of a wounded beast, filled with the agony of endless centuries.

Her stomach twisted.

"Did you hear that, Lady Forbes?" Warwick's voice echoed in the woods.

She didn't answer, didn't move. Indeed, she could not, for her own roiling fear held in a grip as tight as death.

"But of course, you heard. For you are near. I am certain of that. You would not leave him. Not you, the Lady Saint."

The lady saint! The name mocked her. She was a coward. A traitor. Liam had risked his life to save hers, and how did she repay him? By letting him suffer while she hid like a whipped cur.

"You can yet save him, my lady. Tis not too late."

Hope soared through her. She squeezed toward the opening, but suddenly Dragonheart snagged on an unseen obstacle. She yanked at it, frantically trying to pull free, but it was caught fast

"He is asking for you."

She pulled at the chain again.

"Pleading for you to come." Warwick's tone was insidious, and suddenly, even through her haze of unearthly sleep and hopeless terror, Rachel realized his ploy. She leaned her head back in her narrow lair. He was merely trying to draw her out. Cause her to make a mistake. He was *not* certain she was near. He only hoped.

She had that one small advantage.

But perhaps Liam was already dead. Perhaps it was someone else who had screamed. Perhaps Warwick had killed Liam and would kill her too.

Icy claws of fear and hopelessness slivered through her. But with that hopelessness came a relief of sorts. She tightened her fist and found that Dragonheart was no longer caught. Instead, he lay in the warmth of her palm. His ruby heart glowed even in the dimness of the hollowed tree, mesmerizing her.

Yes, she would probably die, but she would not die foolishly.

Chapter 22

L iam was alive.

He sat not far from the fire, his back braced against a blackened tree trunk, his head slumped to his chest. Warwick stood slightly behind him, his face once again shadowed by his cowl. Some yards away, two men gazed off in opposite directions, but if there were others, Rachel couldn't see them.

Warwick spoke. Though she felt the dark hiss of his voice, she couldn't hear the words. But in a moment he reached toward Liam.

The Irishman's head jerked up. His gritted teeth flashed in the light of the fire, and perspiration shone on his face, but he didn't scream.

"So brave!" Warwick hissed, and reached to twist the arrow again.

A keeling moan of agony issued from between Liam's teeth.

"You may as well scream. Your lady love has left you to die. And with an arrow through your back. How dreadful," Warwick rasped, and reached forward again.

The moan turned into a low-pitched wail.

The sound tore through Rachel's soul. Her legs felt stiff. She forced them to move, one first and then the other. And yet it was as if they belonged to someone else.

"She could have saved you," Warwick said, "but she chose to flee. You might as well—"

"I am here." The words came from her own lips, but they seemed distant and remote. She felt numb and heavy, as if her own body were asleep and she only watched the scene from somewhere far above.

Yet as Warwick jerked in her direction, she felt the blow of his attention. Not directly, but as if she were buffered by a gray, muffling cloud.

"Lady," he sighed.

Liam's head jerked up. Dark and vague, his eyes held the dull horror of a hunted beast's. "Nay!" He groaned the denial, but the word was cut short in a moan of agony when Warwick reached forward again.

In a second the sorcerer stepped toward her, one hand outstretched as if to ward off her worries. "So you have come."

"Aye." She didn't retreat, maybe because she could not, maybe because she had lost all sense, had fallen into another dimension, where nothing was real, where horror and pain and misery could not quite touch her. "Aye, I have come."

"Tis good. You are just in time. Our Liam is fast fading."

"He is not *our* Liam."

"Oh, aye, he is." Warwick's voice registered surprise. "Surely he has told you."

She said nothing.

"He is my son."

No. It couldn't be true. Twas a lie. Her mind roiled with the horror of his words. She stumbled back a step, but her heart was already steadying her. It didn't matter. Parentage did not change the man. Her mind cleared gradually.

Warwick's two warriors had turned toward her, she realized, and behind her someone moved. She didn't know how far away, nor did she know who it was. Yet she sensed an evil presence.

"Twill do you no good for your men to take me, Warwick." Her words echoed dully through the forest, as if they came from someone else, someone who didn't taste the bitter gall of terror. "For I am alone."

"Alone?" The wizard canted his head, and it seemed, even from this distance, that he held his breath.

"I don't have the dragon," she intoned.

"Run." Liam's command was no more than a whispered plea, but she heard it none the less, felt it curl through her soul like the pungent scent of wood smoke. "Please, Rachel."

She tightened her fist around nothing and braced her knees, lest they spill her to the earth.

"You do not have the dragon," Warwick said, his voice taut as he nodded. "But you know where it is."

"Aye. I know."

"Then I think, maybe we can convince you to share that knowledge," he said, stepping toward her again.

Laughter echoed through the stillness suddenly. The sound was eerie. Eerier still when Rachel realized it had come from her.

"Could it be that after all this time you know so little of the dragon that you would believe that?" she asked.

The woods were as still as a tomb. Not a soul

seemed to breath, until the sorcerer spoke. "What do you mean?"

"You could never force the truth from me, Warwick." She said his name out loud, disdainfully, though the effort made her ache in some deep indefinable way. "Never."

"I think you overestimate yourself, my lady."

"Nay, I do not." She felt, abruptly, very old. As ancient as the sky, as stoic as the sea. "And if you do not tell your minions to stop where they stand, you shall regret it."

His laughter was raspy. "And what would you do?"

She was filled with coldness, as if the warmth of the sun had never touched her. "I will kill myself."

The dark cowl shook spasmodically, as if he denied her words, but she continued.

"The dragon hones what gifts the wearer already holds. Surely you know that much about this thing you covet so," she said, and nodded once, for she could feel his thoughts and knew that he believed her. Perhaps stranger still was the fact that she believed her own words. "Aye," she added, raising her chin slightly. "It hones one's God-given gifts."

"Then your threat has no sting, Lady, for you are a healer," he rasped.

She smiled, the grim expression of one who expects to die. "Healing and death are but a heartbeat apart. Surely you know that, Warwick. Stop your men or I shall do what I say."

"Halt." His command was low and quiet, but she knew it was obeyed. He spread his hands peaceably before him. "Tell me where the dragon is." His voice was wheedling, and maybe in another world it might have been bewitching, but not now, for she was far beyond sanity's gates.

"Put the Irishman on a horse."

"What say you?"

"Tell the man behind me to put the Irishman on a horse."

A chuckle issued from beneath the cowl. "You may have powers, my lady, but so have I. Surely you do not think our Liam can yet save you."

"Nay, I do not," she admitted, but the words sounded like someone else's, spoken from a thousand leagues away. "When he is safe, I will bring you the Dragonheart."

"Nay." Liam's denial was little more than a whimper of agony, yet she heard it, rasped in pain as he tugged at his bonds. "Nay, Rachel."

"Aye." She didn't dare look at him, didn't dare risk the trance that held her. "Set him free and you shall have what you covet."

She felt the wizard's thoughts on her, and did not try to hold him out. Instead, she let him pillage her mind, and there he saw her blank, dark hopelessness.

"Cut him loose," Warwick rasped.

A man hurried from the darkness to her right, bent, slashed Liam's bonds, and pulled him to his feet.

"Nay, Rachel! Nay!" Liam pleaded.

She tried to block out the desperation of his voice, to hold up the insulation that had buffered her thus far, but the trance was fading. Her knees shook, and for a moment weakness washed her like a deadly tide, almost drowning her.

"You shall live," she whispered.

"Nay," he repeated, but he was already being dragged to a horse.

The firelight gleamed off the broken shaft that protruded from his back.

Rachel swallowed the bile and fought back reality. "Please, Liam," she whispered. "For me. Tis all I ask."

She opened her eyes. Their gazes met in the firelight's glare, and for a fragmented instant, their thoughts clashed. Not the thoughts of Dragonheart superimposed over her own. But the raw thoughts of her tortured heart—thoughts of hope and togetherness.

"Nay," she whispered, but it was not verbalized, only moaned by her soul, and before she could say it aloud, he was being pressed onto a horse.

With a grinding effort, she pulled her attention back to Warwick. "Promise you will let him live," she whispered. "You will take him to the road and set him free. Promise on the dragon."

"On the dragon," Warwick rasped, and nodded to his man.

But in that instant, Liam screamed. His mount lunged forward.

Rachel's trance exploded like a puff of black powder. The haze was ripped from her eyes. Reality leapt at her—Liam on a horse, racing toward her, one rein flapping!

Warwick yowled like a wounded beast, but suddenly there was nothing but the racing horse, the swallowed distance, the hope.

It took no thought, no meditation. Rachel reached up. The stallion's mane brushed her hands, and suddenly she was snapped from her feet. For a moment she floundered. The air was crushed from her lungs as her chest crashed against Liam's leg, but suddenly her heel found purchase, and she was aboard, clinging to Liam's waist.

They were flying. Branches flashed past like

a ghost's bony fingers. Behind them, men swore and hooves thundered.

From over her shoulder, Rachel caught a flash of movement in the darkness.

"They come!" she gasped, but there was nothing more they could do but flee blindly, not knowing where they headed.

A branch slapped their steed's face. He lunged to the left, nearly unseating them. They grappled for a hold, but already the stallion was running at an angle to their pursuer's course.

Liam tried to pull him to the right, but an owl swooped at them from nowhere. Panicked, the steed lunged left again, and suddenly, as through a haze, Rachel saw Dragonheart. It hung just where she had left it, winking magically from the darkness. It swept toward them. She could do nothing but reach up, open her hand, feel it slap warm and glowing into her palm.

Warwick's shriek pierced the woods, as if he was everywhere and nowhere, as if he were already feeling the fires of hell.

Beneath them, the stallion stumbled. Liam jerked forward. Rachel snatched him back against her as the steed struggled to his feet. They were running again, but their pursuers were closer now, nearly upon them. She could hear their mounts' pounding hooves, could feel Warwick's evil like a gigantic vise squeezing the hope from her lungs.

"Fly," she whimpered to Liam. "Fly." But he was slipping, drooping sideways.

She tried to hold him on, to stay aboard, but suddenly the ground dropped out from beneath them. The horse jolted downward. Water sprayed up, and Liam was snatched out of her arms.

There was nothing she could do but go with him.

Nothing, but let herself fall. Their horse struggled to his feet, his hooves thrashing wildly as he scrambled for the opposite shore. Water roiled over them in great waves of icy blackness, dragging them under.

Noise crashed against Rachel's ears. She neither knew nor care what caused it. She could only struggle for the surface. But it was nowhere. Panic gripped her, squeezing hard. She kicked wildly and suddenly air rasped into her lungs. She pulled it greedily inside, aching with the sweet pain of it.

Something brushed her arm. She jerked at the contact, and realized with rending panic, that it was Liam. She'd lost him. He drifted sideways, his face half-hidden in the waves. She lurched through the water, snagged his tunic and dragged him back against her.

Something scratched her face. She gasped at the contact, but it was only a half-submerged log, thrust loose by the thrashing horses and set adrift. Reaching out, she grabbed it. It was slick and wet, but she managed to drag it closer and push Liam toward it.

"Hold on!" she rasped, fighting for breath and strength and the slim reed of hope.

Liam jerked spasmodically, his fingers clinging to the wood as they slid sideways down the river.

"The water!" Warwick shrieked. "Back to the water."

"Which way?" someone yelled.

"Shh," Rachel breathed, praying for silence. "Shh." Noises clattered behind them. She closed her eyes, one arm clasping Liam in a frozen grip, the other clinging to the log.

The river scooted on. Caught by an eddy, their vessel listed. Liam's head dipped beneath the waves. Rachel whimpered in terror and dragged him back up. His face gleamed pale and wet in the fickle moonlight, the log turned, nearly escaping.

The river rolled and tumbled, fighting to lose her. But she fought back with ferocity. Every minute was a new battle, every second a waking nightmare.

She had no idea how far they had gone. Time ceased to be in this living hell, but she dare not exit the river, for beside the twisting banks there were no longer any trees to hide them. Worries plagued her. Where was Warwick? Was Liam alive? But no, she wouldn't let herself think of that. She was a healer. God had given her that gift, and why but to heal the man she loved.

She closed her eyes. Fatigue dragged at her like the cold, heavy waves threatening to spill her into darkness.

"She is near," Warwick rasped from the shore above. "Find her."

Rachel jerked awake. Warwick! Within hearing, and worse, within thought. He had followed her by some sense other than sight. Even now she could feel him groping for her mind. Like a clawed, evil beast he grappled for her thoughts.

"Nay," Liam whimpered, only half lucid.

"Shh." Rachel moved closer to him, one arm still wrapped about his shoulders as she dragged them into the reeds along the shore. Her feet struck the mucky bottom, anchoring her there. But still it was difficult to keep them hidden in the swaying grasses.

"Nay!" Liam's voice was louder now and he thrashed in the water. "You'll not have her."

"Liam," she rasped, her lips numb against his ear. "Shh, all is well."

"He is near!" Liam moaned. His eyes, dark and haunted, gleamed in the moonlight.

"Nay," she soothed. "The wizard is not here. You were dreaming. You are safe."

Surreal pain sliced through her. Warwick's scarred face loomed up. She almost screamed, but choked it down. Games! He was but playing games with her mind.

"Cold," Liam chattered.

"Nay, tis warm," she whispered. "'Tis lovely here in Lochan Creag. My favored place to swim."

Images of evil pressed in on her, swallowing her will. She shoved them back, battling to remember serenity, to remember the peace she had once known with her cousins beside the lochan.

"Naked?" Liam murmured.

"What?" She breathed the word and jerked her gaze to him, but his eyes were closed, his forehead pressed against the slick curve of the log.

"Are you naked when you swim?"

Death! Torture! The images sliced across her mind. She slammed them back, grappling for serenity. "Aye, I am naked," she rasped. "The moon is bright. But none will see me here."

"None but me."

She choked a laugh. It was sharp with hysteria, heavy with terror. "Except you. Hidden behind the . . ."

"Boulders," he murmured.

"Rocks!" Warwick screamed. "They are near rocks."

Liam jerked. Rachel closed her eyes and squeezed closer still.

"You are hiding there," she whispered. "Between the boulders."

"Watching you," he chanted.

She didn't know if he understood her ploy. She only knew that he complied.

"The birch leaves are whispering above you. The moon shines on their silvery leaves."

"And limns your bonny face."

She swallowed hard. "You lie very still, only inches from me. You can hear the water lapping the shore."

"I can." His voice was singsong.

"You are close enough to touch me, but you do not."

"How I want to," he whispered. "Always. Since the first moment I saw you. You were laughing. Never, not for an instant, have I forgot the sound of it. Like the song of sunshine it was, and when you turned to me . . ." He paused. "How long I have tried to put you behind me."

"Find her!" Warwick screamed.

She whimpered at the sound, but in that moment, Liam drew closer of his own accord, so close that she could feel his breath on her cheek.

"But I could not, for the slightest thought entrances me—your eyes, your voice, the curve of a smile." Reaching up, he ran a finger slowly over her lower lip. "But I dared not touch, dared not stand too close lest I lose me shallow control and dishonor you."

"Twould not have been a dishonor, Liam," she whispered.

"I should never have told you I love you. Should not have bared the truth." His fingers slipped to her chin. "They were the words of a fool, for there is no hope for me now—no way of drawing them back. No hope," he said, and slid an inch deeper into the water.

"There is hope," she rasped, wrestling him back

up. "Every hope. Even as I linger in this magical place, I think of you, Liam."

"Don't toy with me feelings, lass," he said and slipped again.

"Nay, Liam, never." And it was true. So painfully true that she could no longer deny it. "'Tis why I have never wed, because each man I compare to you. Each smile I compare to your roguish grin. Each conversation to your clever wit. Each step to your easy grace. Each moment, each word ..." She paused, letting her heart ache with the regret of opportunities lost, letting her mind drift with the cold and the fatigue to a place that was warm and lovely. "Even here in this magical place when I see the moon through the branches, it reminds me of you. Like a mischievous satyr's, it grins down at me. I know I should resist you. But I cannot, and so I smile back and pretend we are lovers."

His forehead tilted weakly against hers.

"I think of you as I traipse back through the woods," she whispered.

"With no clothes?" His eyes fell closed.

"Up ahead there's the road. It seems to shine in the moonlight."

"It shines on your breasts." He sighed. His fingers loosened on the log.

Rachel tightened her grip, squeezing him against her body. "I step onto the path. The mud is soft between my toes."

"Such wee bonny toes."

"Then I hear something." She gasped as she felt the emotions of her story in her chest where her heart throbbed against the dragon. "I pause, holding my breath and praying I will not be found."

"But you will be," he whispered, neither lifting

his head nor opening his eyes. "For I have followed you."

"Aye." His head slumped against her shoulder. She pressed a kiss against his wet hair. "Aye. Tis you. We hold hands as we run down the road."

"Then we make love?"

She concentrated on the road far behind them, the road down which they had taken the wagons, the road far behind the Rom family that had befriended them.

"We run as fast as ever we can. Our hearts pound, our feet stumble for fear that we will be caught and separated."

Silence. Evil slipped farther and farther behind them.

"Then we make love?" His words were barely audible.

"Aye," she whispered. "Then we make love."

Chapter 23

Liam awoke slowly. Pain stabbed through him like a fiery lance. It began in a red hot flame at his shoulder then dulled to a throbbing burn that encompassed the entirety of his being. He lifted his lids with some difficulty. Even that tiny movement hurt, setting up an ache that pulsed relentlessly inside his head.

But the effort gave him no satisfaction, for even with his eyes open, he could see nothing. And yet it was not dark, but rather a nondescript, endless gray. He tried to scowl, but found it was too much effort. Pain pounded through him like the insistent beat of a drum. So this was Hell. He wasn't surprised. Nay, he deserved to be here, for he had failed her, had left her alone and undefended.

He let his eyelids fall closed and wished for forgetfulness, but it would not come of course, for this was hell. Instead, he remembered her eyes, bright with hope, with life. Dear God, he could not suffer enough for having abandoned her.

"You're awake."

Her voice!

A flash of hope cut through him like the edge of a knife. He tried to turn. Agony burned him but he ignored it, forcing his muscles to do his bidding.

She was there, cushioned by the gray nothingness that surrounded him. "Rachel?" He tried to reach out, to touch her, to prove that she was real, but his hand refused to move.

"You're awake," she repeated, and her voice trembled with fear.

The sound sliced through him, and now he noticed that her eyes were unusually bright. How clever Satan was, for who could think of such a subtle torture as her tears.

"Don't cry, lass. Please." He tried again to touch her, but he should have known that would not be allowed. Hell would not be hell if he could touch her. Hell would not be Hell if she were here. And so she was merely a misty image sent to haunt him, to burn his soul, to remind him for an eternity that he had failed her.

He didn't try to move again, but lay still, absorbing everything about the apparition before him. She was dressed in naught but rags. Her tunic was gone, leaving her arms bare. Such bonny arms. But there was a scratch on one, and the back of her opposite hand was scathed.

Such subtle torture to see her wounded, to know that it was his fault, and to never be afforded a chance to redeem himself.

"I was afraid . . ." The words lay there in the misty silence for a moment, burning him. "I was afraid I had killed you," she whispered, and a single, diamond tear slipped down her cheek.

His heart knotted in his tattered chest. "Tis not your fault, lass. Tis mine. I . . . failed."

"Never," she murmured, and reaching out, laid her fingertips against his cheek. "The arrow. I could not pull it out. I . . ."

But he couldn't hear the rest of her words, for nothing reached his senses but the feel of her flesh against his.

His heart lurched, his breathing stopped, and he stared, eyes wide, watching her, the bright amethyst of her eyes, the tangled mass of her hair.

Could it be that she was real? Could it be?

Forcing his muscles to obey, he reached up. Agony ripped through him, but it registered as nothing more than a dull ache as his fingertips touched her cheek. Her eyes fell closed and she tilted her head against his touch.

"You're real."

His breathy words lay in the silence, whispered like a revered prayer.

"What?"

"You're real," he said again, and hiccuped a painful laugh. "Tis not Hell."

She shook her head. "Nay, Liam, I am sorry. The pain . . ." Her face scrunched as if she herself had felt the agony. "There was nothing I could do but push the arrow through."

"Dear Jesus!" He smoothed his palm across her cheek, then down the length of her neck, letting his fingers tremble against her throat. "Dear Jesus, you're still alive."

"Of course I'm alive!" She pressed a hand atop his. "Tis you who has been near death. Tis you who has been wounded."

He shook his head, for he could, quite suddenly, feel no pain, but only the soaring euphoria that came with her presence.

"I feared I may have hit your heart." Her voice broke. "The arrow became stuck between your ribs. I couldn't get it out. Dear God, I had to twist it through the . . ."

"You are real," he said again, and though his arm shook with weakness, he didn't draw his hand from her face.

"Aye, Liam, I am real."

"But I thought . . . I feared . . ." He ran out of breath, out of words, and in that moment she gently took his fingers in hers.

"I am real, Liam," she whispered and turning his hand, pressed it against her chest. It took only a moment before he felt the thrum of her heart against his palm.

He closed his eyes, feeling her life in his soul, filling himself with her presence, with her being.

"I am sorry," she whispered. "Forever we were in the burn. I feared . . ." She swallowed. "I feared you were dead, but I did not dare leave the water, lest they spot us. Not until morning did I find a place to take you out." She shivered beneath his hand, remembering. "Twas a horrid nightmare."

"Nay," he murmured. "Not a nightmare, but the sweetest of dreams."

"Dreams—"

"Aye. I dreamed," he whispered. "Of a wee maid in the water. Her ebony hair was swept up atop her head, and her neck was as long and slim as a swan's. She had the delicate grace of a doe." He paused. "And she was naked. Twas maybe the most cherished moments of me life."

She did not return his smile. Indeed, her eyes were haunted, and her fingers tight against his as she pulled them into her hand.

"He was in my mind," she whispered.

Liam wished with all his soul that he could wonder who she meant, but there was no question. Twas Warwick she spoke of.

"He was searching for us in my mind."

Dear God, he wanted nothing more than to hold her, to drive the fear from her heart, to make her smile. "You fooled him, lass," he said. "And you brought us to safety."

"But for how long?"

He longed to tell her all was well, that she was safe, but he knew far too much of the wizard for that.

"We must leave this place," he said, and tried to draw his hand from hers. Pain slashed through him with the effort, but she would not release his fingers.

Instead, she clenched them more tightly. "You cannot move. Not now. Twould surely be your death."

There was terror in her expression, terror for him. The bittersweet agony that coursed through his heart made the pain in his chest dull by comparison. He considered telling her that it didn't matter if it killed him. He *had* to try to save her. But it sounded ridiculously melodramatic, even in his own mind, and she would not listen. "We must go," he said instead.

"Nay." She touched his cheek with her free hand. "Think on it Liam. We have no food, no horses." Silence ebbed around them. "No hope."

"Nay." He breathed the word, for he could not bear to hear her say it, even if it were true. "Nay, tis not so, Rachel. We have every hope, for we are alive."

"But—"

"There are no buts. We are alive and safe." He glanced about himself, noticing their surroundings for the first time—the towering height of the elms, the silvery gray moss beneath his back. "Twould be an unforgivable sin to give up."

"But—"

"Please," he whispered. "Hell seems in no hurry to have me. Surely heaven can wait for *you*."

"Liam, I fear—"

"Nay. Please . . . don't fear. I could not bear it. God has saved you. You've only to travel north. You will come out of the woods. You will find help."

"Without you?" She breathed the words as realization of his meaning dawned on her.

He tightened his grip on her hand. "You said I cannot move. Hence, tis the only way."

"But . . ."

No buts. None! She must live. "You can do this. For me."

She stared at him, her eyes as purple and intense as a gathering storm. "I don't know where we are, Liam. How would I find my way back once—"

"Nay!" he snapped. She jumped at the harshness of his voice. Liam closed his eyes and forced himself to loosen his grip on her hand. "Nay, Rachel, you must not return yourself. You can send someone for me once you reach the king."

"Send someone! But it would take me days to reach—" She stopped abruptly and pursed her lips. Her eyes narrowed. "Damn you," she whispered. "You plan to die."

"Nay. I—"

"You plan to send me away and die like a martyr."

"Rachel, please . . ." His voice broke.

"How selfish you are!"

"You will not die!" he rasped.

"You think I could live knowing I left you here alone?"

"Please!" It was the only word he could manage,

but she was already shaking her head.

"We stay here," she said. "And here is where you mend."

"Nay! Warwick—"

Her gaze speared him. "Do not say his name to me," she said.

"He must not find you."

"And what of you?" she asked.

Fear roiled in him, but he fought it down. "It doesn't matter. He will not hurt me."

For a moment she did nothing but stare at him, but then she choked a laugh. "Will not hurt you? I fear I am the wrong person to believe that lie, Liam."

He stared at her, hating himself. "I am his son, Rachel." He paused, waiting for her to recoil, but she did not. "'Tis true," he said, certain she didn't believe him. "Some years ago, he told me. I called him a liar, but I knew the truth even then. I am—" He could find no words to continue.

"What?" she asked. "What are you?"

"I am in no real danger from him, Rachel."

"You jest."

"Nay. I do not." He fought to keep the desperation from his voice, for convincing her was everything. "Think on it. He could have killed me many times over. But he did not. He wants me alive."

She stared at him, her eyes absolutely level. "Why?"

Liam tried to hold her gaze, but he couldn't. "How am I to know? Long he has sought me."

"And you think, maybe he wishes to give you your inheritance?"

"Maybe."

"He is evil." She said the words slowly, her voice deep. "He hopes you will assist him in that evil."

Liam forced himself to raise his eyes. Their gazes caught.

"Even if he did not kill you outright, what would happen when you refuse?" she asked softly.

"What makes you think I would refuse?"

He tried to stare her down, but not for a moment did her gaze waver.

"I know you well, Liam."

"And so you think me too noble to join forces with Warwick?"

"Aye."

He forced a laugh. "I would not have thought you the sort to overestimate me."

The woods were silent.

"I do not."

Her words sliced with a bittersweet pain through his soul, but long he had been fighting this battle. He was not about to lose now. Not when the stakes were so high.

"For many years I thought myself a bastard, Rachel, belonging to no one, wanted by no one. But that was much preferred to knowing the truth." He hissed the words, barely able to force them out, for here in the midst of nowhere, there were no barriers from her.

"And what is the truth?"

"I am his son! Do you not ken what that means?"

"Aye, I know," she said. "It means you are evil!"

The air exploded in Liam's lungs. He could not even manage a nod, but watched her, breathless, hopeless.

"Aye, you are evil because your sire is. Just as my hair is red because my mother's is." She lifted a fistful of sable hair from her shoulder.

It was tangled, he noticed, and that knowledge alone nearly made him weep. "Rachel . . ." he began, but she interrupted him, slicing her palm through the misty air between them.

"Do not use your sad tales on me, Liam," she said. "For I know just what you are."

"Please go." They were the only words he could force out.

"So you do not have to see me die?"

He clenched his fist tight as anger boiled inside him. "You will not die. Not because of me!" he shouted.

"Nay. Not because of you, Liam. But *with* you, if I must."

He shook his head. "Please, Rachel, I cannot bear—"

"And I cannot bear to be parted from you," she whispered. "Don't you see, Liam? Long ago I knew my mind well. Twas not a child's foolish whim that brought me to you on that night. Twas fate's command. I was meant to be with you."

• He shook his head again, but she refused to move away.

"Here we stay," she said. "And here you mend."

Rachel's herbs had been ruined during her wild escape down the river. But even before removing the arrow from Liam's back, she had begun to search for more. Luck and tenacity had been kind; she had found enough to pack into his wound.

Gathering fallen boughs from deep in the forest, she dragged them to the place where Liam watched her from his mossy bed. Once there, it was simple enough to prop them into the crooks and crannies of the ancient oak. Using Liam's knife which had survived their escape, she cut vines from nearby trees and entwined them in the opposite direction. Above that, she placed large sheaves of decaying bark or whatever she could find that might hold out the rain, until finally a small area was sheltered from the elements.

"Did you ever wonder why the duke of Tunnicliffe decided against wedding you?" Liam asked, his gaze steady on her face.

Rachel turned from her handiwork toward him. "You should sleep."

"Twas Erna," he said.

She scowled at him as aged memories seeped back to her. "Erna? The potter's daughter?"

"Aye."

"What has she to do with the duke?" she asked, approaching to sit beside him on the moss.

Liam sighed as she touched his forehead. "Do you remember when he came to meet you?"

Leaning her back against the kindly tree behind her, Rachel turned her gaze up to her makeshift shelter. "I was five and ten, I think. Twas Midsummer's Day."

"Aye."

"I wore my best gown and plaited my hair with scarlet ribbons. I felt quite important—until he failed to appear."

"Erna met him in Craegsmore."

She lowered her gaze to his face and studied him in silence for a moment, then, "Whatever for?"

"It seems she took it into her head to pretend she was you."

"Erna? She was . . ."

"Ugly?" he supplied readily.

"Nay. I was about to say—"

"Fat? Pockmarked?"

"Rather rude."

"The duke seemed to agree with your assessment," Liam said.

Rachel stared at him, waiting for an explanation that was sure to come eventually.

"He was quite revolted."

"And why, may I ask..." she began, but stopped abruptly. "Twas your idea."

"Aye." He sighed softly. "More than a decade ago, it was; and in all that time I've not felt a twinge of remorse. But I am sorry now." His face, always so filled with life and laughter, was somber, and she wished with all her heart that it was not so, that she could see him smile, even if it were she who endured the consequences of his mischief. "You should have been a duchess."

"And why is that, Liam?"

"Because you deserve all that is good."

Tears filled her eyes. How many years had she longed to hear him say just that? "And do I not deserve love, Liam?"

He said nothing, but still she could feel his gaze on her face. "Do I not deserve to cherish and be cherished?"

"Aye. You do."

"Then I deserve you."

"Rachel..." he whispered.

"Would you deny that you love me, Liam?" she murmured. "Would you deny it again? Even now?"

He stared at her a moment, and finally shook his head.

She smoothed her palm over the dark stubble of cheek, then leaned forward and pressed her lips tenderly to his. He returned the caress, but when she moved to draw away, he pulled her back, his eyes pleading.

"Stay with me," he said.

"I must search for herbs."

"To heal me?"

"Aye."

"You think some plant could be more healing than the feel of you beside me?" he asked. "Than knowing that you have chosen to love me?"

There was nothing she could do but lie down beside him. Nothing, but nestle into the strength of his shoulder and fall asleep with his breath soft and warm against her cheek.

Chapter 24

Rachel woke to the soft sound of rain on the bark above their heads. Drowsiness lay on her like a warm, heavy blanket. Beside her, Liam still slept, his arm lay over her waist, his ungodly long lashes a downy slash of darkness against his skin.

The rain pattered on. There was nowhere to go, nothing to do but fall back into the folds of sleep.

The world was dim and pink when next she awoke. Hunger gnawed at her stomach. Beside her, Liam slept on. His stillness worried her, but when she placed a hand to his brow, his flesh felt cool and normal.

Careful not to disturb him, she slipped from under his cape. A bit of her impromptu roof had washed away, causing a puddle to form near Liam's feet, so she mended that.

Her stomach roiled again. She had no idea how long she had slept, but it didn't matter. Not here. All that mattered was that she keep this man safe. Hence, the first thing she must do was find food. Placing a bit more bark upon their roof, she noticed that some of the vines had worked loose. She wove them more securely together, then wondered if the same concept might work for a net.

Excited by the thought, she retrieved Liam's knife, severed pieces of vines, and wove them quickly together. The river was not far away, and though it was not simple, she discovered a means of securing her net near the shore.

Wandering farther into the water, she gathered plants from the depths and dragged them onto the bank. Aunt Flanna had long insisted that twas a diet of aquatic vegetation that kept her steeds so strong and fat through the winter months. So surely the same plants would do her and Liam no harm.

Breaking off a bit of the seaweed, she tasted it. It was not likely to replace bread and honey as a daily staple, she decided, but starvation was an unwelcome alternative, so she ate some more, then draped handfuls of it over the nearby rocks to dry.

Not far away, she spied a glimmer of something that shone in the evening light. Hurrying to it, she bent to pick up a half shell from the silt. There in a small cove, the water lapped softly against the rocks. Beneath her bare feet, the stone felt smooth and soft. Following the flow of the water, she came to a tiny cave of sorts, barely large enough to crouch inside. She crept in, hoping to find some crustacean to make her supper, but there was nothing.

It was damp inside, with water condensed on the stone roof that dripped slowly down onto the rocky basin below. Thousands of years had worn a deep, smooth depression into the stone. Cupping her hands, she dipped them into the water and took a sip. It was then she noticed the rock was loose.

*   *   *

She knew the moment Liam awoke, sensed it in some untouchable part of her. Still crouched, she lifted a half-filled shell from the ground.

"How do you feel?"

"I don't feel anything."

"What?" Fear swamped her. She hadn't allowed him to move from the spot where she had originally dragged him, but maybe her precautions had been unnecessary, for maybe he *couldn't* move.

But at that moment, he shifted ever so slightly and added, "I don't hurt nearly as much as I should."

"Oh." She tried to hide her relief. There was no need to let him realize her worry. No reason to remind him how close the arrow had come to ending his life or at least to ending all movement. In truth, experience and anatomy told her that he should not have survived at all. She could only thank God that he had. "I'm an excellent healer," she said, and lifted the shell toward his lips. "Drink this."

He eyed it dubiously. "What is it?"

"Eye of newt."

He made a face and she laughed, for he was alive, and with him lived hope. "I jest," she said. "I fear I've been unable to find the proper newt thus far. Drink it. Tis something to aid in the mending."

Their gazes caught, his somber and dark.

"How do I know you're not trying to drug me in an attempt to take advantage of me person?"

A shiver stole up her spine, stealing her breath. "Perhaps I am."

"Then I'll drink it."

She lifted the shell to his lips, and he drank, though not without a grimace for the bitter taste.

"I've never had to take such noxious stuff to be seduced before," he said.

"But you've never been seduced by the likes of me."

"Nay," he breathed, "I haven't."

Reaching out, she touched his hand. "Tell me you are mending."

"I am," he said. "Don't worry."

"Can you move your arm atall?"

"What's that aroma?"

He was trying to distract her, and she well knew it, but she let him, for doing otherwise might spoil their careful pretenses that all was well. "Soup," she said.

He raised his brows. "So you have finally moved me to the king's palace. I wondered when you would."

She smiled. There was a silent agreement between them. An unspoken pact that said that for now they would speak of no evil. Instead, they would take what they had and be grateful for it.

"Nay," she said. "I brought the palace to us."

"Truly?"

"Aye." Rising to her feet, she stepped over him. It had not been a simple task to transport the weathered cave rock to their tiny shelter. Neither had it been easy to start a fire around it. But she had managed both, and now, in the worn depression of the rock, seaweed simmered with snails and sorrel. "I've prepared a feast."

Kneeling by the fire, she retrieved the dried gourd she'd found. Dipping it into the soup, she scooped a bit of broth into the shell and turned back toward him.

But when she did so, she saw his grimace of pain as he tried to turn over.

"Let me help you," she insisted, and rushed forward, but he didn't wait. Instead, gritting his teeth, he levered himself into a seated position.

It took him a moment to catch his breath, then, "Twill be a poor seduction if I cannot even sit up."

She felt like weeping for his pain, but sympathy rubbed against their careful game of make-believe. "Maybe I want you helpless," she said.

He leaned back, breathing hard from the exertion, and waiting a moment before he spoke again. "And why would that be, lass?"

"My seductions haven't worked terribly well in the past. Maybe if you are helpless—"

"I have always been helpless where you're concerned."

She waited for the Liam of old to laugh, but he did not. The new Liam made her nervous. "Tis not true," she murmured, lowering her gaze.

He watched her in silence. "For one so wise, you know me little, Rachel," he said, and reaching up with his hale hand, touched her cheek.

A thousand errant emotions sprang up in her. She closed her eyes and pressed her fingers to his, but in a moment she felt his hand tremble and carefully lowered it to his lap.

"Drink this," she urged and lifted the shell to his lips again.

He took a sip, raised his expressive brows at her, and sipped again, easily draining the shell. "And here I thought all your greatest talent was tormenting me. I never guessed you could cook."

"I didn't make it." She hurried back to the fire and refilled the shell. "Cook prepared it. The servants set out the crookery . . ." She lifted the shell as she approached again. "And of course our royal cupbearer shall pour the wine." Reaching to her right, she lifted a hollowed chunk of wood from the earth. A few droplets of water lapped over the side.

"Ahhh." He sipped at the broth she offered again. "The privileges of traveling with the royal entourage. But what shall we do for entertainment?"

"I shall think of something," she said flippantly.

Liam's lips quirked slightly. "May I make a suggestion?" His tone was low and quiet.

Her heart thrummed heavily in her chest. "Suggestions are always welcome."

"There is that dance you performed in the village."

She felt suddenly warm and shy and lowered her eyes as she offered him more soup. "I have no music."

"You need no music."

The poetic silence of the woods surrounded them. She shifted her gaze to his, and wondered in poignant panic what would happen if they survived this place. Would he retreat into the irritating tormentor he had always been with her, or would his gaze still burn her when it touched on her face?

"Liam—"

"Nay," he interrupted. "Don't say it, Rachel. Please. All we have is now. Let us use it wisely."

She retreated into silence. They finished the soup together, and though it seemed inexplicable, it was both filling and satisfying.

"Twas a fine meal," Liam said, still leaning back against the slanted oak. "And now I be ready for me constitutional."

"You cannot even stand up," she reminded him.

"Then twill make what I have to do quite difficult."

She scowled at his words, but in a moment realization dawned. He had a call of nature. "Oh."

"Oh indeed."

"I shall . . . fetch a . . . vessel of sorts."

He quirked a brow at her. "A vessel?"

"To . . . you know."

"You jest." There was dry humor in his voice. It did nothing to staunch her embarrassment. "You cannot move."

"Watch me," he said, and drew his feet up under him.

"Liam, you can't," she cried, rushing to his side.

"You're wrong," he argued, and easing carefully out from under his shelter, pushed himself to his feet. For a moment, he thought his legs would fail him, but he gritted his teeth, pressed his back to the tree trunk, and stood his ground. "See?" Even that single word was hard fought to produce. "'Tis no great feat."

"Liam, sit down. Please." Rachel was grasping his arm as if he were no more substantial than a new born calf.

"I fear you don't understand, my lady," he said, trying to sound cavalier. Swooning would put a definite damper on that act. "I have need of a privy."

"Let me assist you."

"I am shocked," he exclaimed, but the words were horribly weak and the world seemed to be going black. He leaned his head back against the trunk of the oak, and in a moment the dimness passed. "Maybe you could help me a wee bit."

"Liam . . ."

"I cannot sit here forever. Saddle my royal steed. I am off to the hunt."

"Your steed is weary," she said, tugging at his arm, "and needs more time."

"More time?" Despite his efforts, he couldn't contain his seriousness. "You think me so foolish as to waste these moments with you, Rachel? Nay. I will have full use of my faculties."

Surprisingly, when he stepped forward, his legs actually moved. He lurched slightly as he did so, and Rachel clutched one arm as if he were as venerable as the trees about him. But still, he was moving, albeit at a snail's pace.

His foot caught on a root. He struggled to catch himself, and in that second, pain ripped through his chest. He gasped for breath and stability as colors swarmed in his head. But eventually the colors faded and he found himself still on his feet.

"Well . . ." His voice sounded as strained and raspy as an old man's. "Isn't this pleasant." He found that he had somehow grasped her hand where it held his arm. He loosened his claw-fingered hold and prayed for some semblance of pride. Had she not done enough to save his worthless hide? Lifting his hand, he patted her fingers. "How lovely to be out for a stroll with a bonny maid like you."

"Are you well?" she murmured, her gaze searing his face.

"Well?" With every bit of self-control at his disposal, he forced himself to take another step. It jarred his ribs and ripped at his lungs. "Well, is a relative term, my dear." Another step, creaked out of his limited resources." Why, in my younger days I could—" His foot caught again, jarring his insides like so many sacks of loose grain. But he was getting accustomed to the pain. "I could stand up all by myself, I could."

"Could you now?" She was trying to pitch her voice up higher, to play along, but her grip on his arm spoke of her tension.

"Aye. I was quite the stallion." He took a few more hard-won steps, then leaned warily against a towering elm as he tried to slow the crashing beat of his heart. "Still am, in fact." If he didn't fall right off his feet it would be a splintering miracle. "But for just now, I think I may have . . . ventured far enough." And his bladder was about to explode. He managed to bring his hands to his laces.

"Let me help you with that," she said, still gripping one of his arms.

"Jesus, Rachel!" he rasped. "Give me some pride, will you!"

"I only—"

"Go stand . . ." He motioned behind him with short jerks of his head, being careful lest he rip something loose in his chest. "Over there."

"Truly, Liam, I have seen your—"

"Then you know how astounding it is," he said irritably. "And since I've no wish to see you faint just now, you'd best move aside."

She released his arm slowly and finally strode away.

Liam's hands shook as he untied his laces. They were bound tight from being soaked and stretched, and for one panicked moment he thought he would disgrace himself, but finally his fingers did his bidding, and he gratefully emptied his bladder.

Tying his laces proved to be no simpler, but he managed. Turning about was nearly impossible. Nevertheless, he did so without losing consciousness. Even a few tottering, independent steps were accomplished.

"You might consider assisting me now before I

fall on me face," he said, barely daring to glance toward where Rachel waited.

"I had no wish to rush you," she said, striding back to his side.

"I am quite finished. But twas no mean task." He shuffled along a few careful steps. "Most men don't have such troubles, you know."

"I am surprised you can walk atall, what with the gargantuan weight of the thing."

He jolted to a halt. "God's balls, Rachel, what has come over you?" he rasped.

"I think it may be the Roms," she said, taking his arm.

He sighed, but despite everything, his martyred act included, he could not stop the rise of his desire. "Your father will have me drawn and quartered if he hears you talk like that."

"I had not planned to proposition him."

"Is that what you're doing to me?" he asked, his ribs feeling, quite suddenly, too small for his heart.

"I thought I'd give you a bit of time to heal first." Her hand was warm against his arm, but she didn't turn to look at him.

"Holy Christmas," he said, straightening with painful effort to place his hand dramatically over his heart. "I am healed."

Her laughter was silvery sweet. It tugged at his soul, and for a moment, as he stared into her angel eyes, he could not speak, for they had not changed since the first moment he had seen her. They were just as brilliant, just as mesmerizing, and the sight of them brought back a thousand vintage memories. Rachel with her cousins, with the sick, with him . . . quietly tormenting him with her distance.

He could not let her die. He could not.

"Rachel . . ."

"Shh," she said and raising a finger to his lips, refused to let him speak. "It has all been said already, Liam," she murmured. "This is where I stay."

Warwick was not mentioned, nor pain, nor the possibility of never seeing their loved ones again. Instead, they settled in beside the fire. Night was coming on and its warm crackle felt kind and homey. Rachel covered him with his cape.

"I must go check my nets," Rachel said, straightening on her knees.

"And leave me here alone when I am in such pain?" Liam asked.

"I thought you were healed."

"That was when I thought it advantageous to be so," he said. "Now I see that you were only toying with me, and have no intention of propositioning me atall."

Their gazes met. Silence as warm as the fire stretched between them.

"Come lie with me," he urged.

She did, and although that fact still seemed the most miraculous of events, it also seemed so right. Her weight against his hale arm should have sent spasms of pain through his tattered chest, but instead it only thrummed a soft blur of pleasure through him. Never before had anything felt so perfect. They fell asleep together, their bodies close together, their minds in synch.

Sometime during the night it began to rain again. The occasional hiss of a droplet striking the glowing embers woke them. They lay together in companionable silence for a while, her head cushioned against his arm.

"I've dreamt of this," he said softly. The truth seemed so easy now, so simple, undeniable almost, which should have scared him, for the truth had never been his particular friend. A good lie had always suited him better. "More times than I can count."

"You've dreamt of being pierced and lost?" she asked.

He chuckled. It hurt, but the pain was almost pleasant, for she was there. "Nay. Of being here with you."

"Methinks you are too easy to please," she said.

He laughed again and their conversation moved on. They talked of a thousand things, old memories, people they had known, food and feasts and hopes and dreams, until the rain stopped and they fell once again into the soft folds of slumber.

When next they awoke it was daylight. The sun had won the battle for the sky and smiled down on their tiny haven in the woods. Rachel shifted in their mossy bed.

"I'll go hunt up some breakfast."

"By yourself?"

"Cook is busy."

"I'll accompany you."

She gave him a dubious look. "I fear you'll only slow me down."

"Were you planning to run down a stag?"

"Stay and rest."

"I've been resting. Help me up."

She did so, though grudgingly.

He managed to walk by himself into the woods to relieve himself as she did the same in the opposite direction.

Not much later they were arm in arm, making their way to the river.

Liam squatted carefully on the shore. Dipping his hands in the gentle waves, he scooped up some of the water and washed it over his face. It had been some days since he'd shaved, and the water felt wondrous against his skin.

"I fear twill be a hungry morning," Rachel said, glancing downstream.

"Cook is out of sowens?"

"My net broke."

"Oh?" Liam pushed himself to his feet. Despite his expectations, his eyeballs remained in his head, and no unsuspecting body parts abandoned him because of the movement. The world only spun crazily for a second or so. "You made a net?"

"Just over there." She pointed to a place where snagged branches and a couple of boulders made a natural trap.

"Clever lass." He stepped forward.

"Not so very. I fear I can see its tattered remains even now," she said, and indeed, when they reached it, they found that the net had been dragged apart by the waves. Still, a bit of her hand-iwork remained in place, and miraculously, in that net, two small trout were caught by their gills.

"Clever, *beloved* lass," Liam said. "If you'll fetch me my knife we'll dine well this morn."

She did as requested, and as Liam filleted the fishes, she improved her net and replaced it in the crystal waters.

They wrapped the fishes in oak leaves and buried them in the embers. Then Rachel rose to search for medicinal herbs and whatever staples the woods may have to offer.

The minutes before she returned seemed lonely and long, but finally she appeared, carrying an array of goodies in her pouch that had somehow survived their misfortunes.

"Look what I've found," she said, seeming as

happy as a child as she spread out her treasures for him to see.

It didn't take her long to see to her herbs, hanging some to dry, boiling a few, then pouring the extract into a hollow gourd. Nor did she delay in starting to brew another batch of soup, or roasting the newly found chestnuts in the ashes.

Their meal seemed sumptuous beyond explanation. The morning wound on, the sun growing brighter, the day warmer. In the shade of their makeshift home they ate some of the soup, then talked of old times until sleep found them.

Finally, as the sun settled over the western branches of the woods, they wound their way back toward the river, gathering anything that caught their fancy, feathers, unfurling fronds of bracken, bonny bits of broken rocks, all which they dropped into Rachel's pouch.

The water in the tiny cove was glassy smooth and shone like amber as the sun struck it in a western slant.

They held hands as they stared out upon the beauty of the world. And though Liam was vaguely certain there was a reason he should not kiss her, he couldn't remember what it was.

Her lips felt like magic against his.

She drew back finally, breathing shallowly through her devilish lips, her eyes just a shade brighter than the water that lapped across their feet.

Clearing her throat, she dropped her gaze to his chest. "Twould be a likely time for me to change your bandage."

Liam winced. "I admit that I hoped my kiss would put you in mind of more pleasant things than torturing me."

"If we soak the cloth it won't be so difficult to remove. I've made a soap to cleanse your wound," she said, and lifted the gourd she'd brought along.

"You've been planning this torture all the while?" he asked irritably.

"Twill not be so bad."

He harrumphed. "I've borne your ministrations before, Rachel. I'm certain the bandage is fine as is. In fact . . ." He lifted his arm, prepared to spew forth some likely lie about his amazing recovery, but her next words stopped him.

"I will bathe you."

His breath caught in his throat. "What say you?"

"I will bathe you," she repeated.

He tried to think of some clever rejoinder, but he was far past that hopeful event. Every aching muscle in his body was tense, and his lower regions were already tightening painfully. "As you said," he managed, barely able to press out the words, "tis certainly time to be rid of this bandage."

Chapter 25

Rachel's lips tilted ever so slightly—the devil in the saint, and then she reached up, soft as gosling down and touched his cheek. Her fingers rasped through the bristle of his whiskers.

Still he couldn't breathe, and when she kissed his lips, there was no hope. He reached for her, unconcerned for the pain in his chest, but she pressed his arm gently down with her opposite hand and skimmed her nail pads across his bristly chin and onto his chest. For a moment he felt the heavenly sweetness of her flesh against his, and then the soft grate of her touch against his bandage.

He almost protested, for he feared she planned to begin her ministrations immediately, but her fingers did not stop. Instead, they slid, slow as summer over the rigid, waiting muscles of his abdomen and down to the laces of his trousers.

Liam sucked a draft of air between his teeth and squeezed his eyes closed as he waited. His breeches eased open. He felt the air against the heat of his skin and tightened his fists.

She moved a scant step closer. He could hear her breathing, could feel the smoothness of her fingers against his abdomen, his sides, his hips as she eased the fabric down over his buttocks.

His erection, hard as need, was pulled sideways, but it could only bend so far before it popped back up. For a moment she went still. He heard the soft intake of her breath, and then she was moving again, easing the garment downward, over his thighs, down his calves.

He stepped out of his hose and glanced breathlessly down at her. At that very moment, she turned her face up.

Their gazes fused. He reached down and drew her to her feet. Between the ragged laces of her battered gown, her breasts rose and fell. Brushing his nails along her jaw, he skimmed past her ear and smoothed his palm beneath the weight of her burnished hair.

Their kiss was magic, as pure as the flowing water, as clean as the air they breathed. But he could wait no longer for foolish poetry. Beneath his impatient fingers, her laces eased loose. In a moment, her shoulders were bare. Such bonny shoulders. He kissed one.

A tiny moan escaped her. He had not thought his desire could harden any more. But seeing her thus, with her head thrown back and the light of the waning sun falling on her hazelnut skin, was more than he could bear. Her clothing slipped away. She stepped out of the circle of fabric. Liam skimmed his gaze over her, the taut swell of her breasts, the curve of her waist, the sweet, gentle flare of her hips and the smooth endless length of her legs.

Dear God, she was beautiful beyond words, and when she reached for his hand, he followed her without question into the sun-warmed water. It rose to his knees, and there, in the shelter of two boulders, she pulled him down into the lapping waves.

The soft fingers of the water smoothed over his buttocks, licked his scrotum, eased up his abdomen, and touched the lower portions of his bandage. It wasn't until it seeped through the fabric to his wound that he jerked at the impact.

"Nay." She breathed the word as she pressed a gentle hand to his chest. "Nay, all is well," she promised and slipping her body over his, she kissed him.

Suddenly it didn't matter if his chest was seared in two, if his heart burst asunder, if he were drowned here in these quiet waters.

He kissed her mouth, her cheek, the elegant length of her neck. She arched away like an enchanting sea nymph, her legs as slick as silk against his own. Her waist, when he touched it, was as tight and tiny as a willow, and her breasts . . . They gleamed, wet and ruby-tipped in the sun's last rays. Reaching up, Liam curved his palm over one. Dragonheart brushed his hand. He kneaded the soft flesh gently, and she moaned. Letting her head fall back, she braced her hands against him.

Pain stabbed through his chest as she brushed his wound. He jerked at the impact.

"Liam?" She pulled her hand away as if burned. "I'm sorry." She leaned over him, her breast pressed warm and heavy against his arm, her eyes full of worry.

He tried to catch his breath, but couldn't quite manage it.

"Are you badly hurt?"

Dragonheart's chain had been hooked over her right nipple. The image was strangely, almost painfully erotic.

"Liam?"

"Aye," he rasped, and managed with some effort to pull his gaze from her breast. "Aye, I am in great pain, but I think you can mend me."

"What can I . . ." she began, but in that instant he skimmed his hand down her back and over her buttocks, gently sweeping her atop him.

She settled over him like a soft wet dream.

"Oh," she said, her tone breathy.

Reaching up, he kissed her lips and rocked his hips into her.

"Oh," she said again, her voice throaty this time and her hips rocking on their own. Bending forward, she kissed his lips. Her ruby nipples brushed his chest, her sweet bottom brushed his penis.

And somehow, with no apparent effort at all, she glided around him. The blessed agony nearly overwhelmed him. He closed his eyes. The moan escaped on its own.

"Liam?" she murmured, her tone worried as she ceased her rocking. "Shall I quit?"

"I'd rather you drown me."

It took her a moment for his words to sink in, but when they did, she moved again, a fraction of an inch, pressing onto him like a beloved scabbard. A slow, painfully slow scabbard. But he would not rush her, would not take that slow torture from her.

Besides, there was nothing he could do. He lay in the water, the sand cradling him, the waves caressing him and her body clutching him like a precious jewel.

She eased farther on, then farther. He inadvertently allowed a groan to escape, but either she was past caring for his comfort, or she no longer expected to kill him with this sweet torture. And now he could wait no longer. Pressing his hands into the silt of the river bottom, he ground his hips upward.

Their groans melded. He moved again. Her body answered, arching slowly into the movement. Utopia swallowed him. Water lapped higher about their straining bodies. Muscles flexed and tensed and strove. Breathing escalated, hearts hammered. Passion gripped them hard and fast, not caring about the consequences. Only caring for their escape from reality into this hot, torrid bliss.

Tension built like a storm inside Liam, bubbling and bulging and straining to be set free. He pumped harder, and she answered, riding him like a mermaid on a wild sea steed, her head thrown back in frantic ecstasy. It was that vision that pushed him over the edge, that made him crash past the barrier of need.

He pulsed desperately into her. She rasped a high-pitched shriek of anguish, stiffened above him, and then softened, shoulders rounding.

Their heavy breathing mingled as she slumped forward, but before she dropped onto his chest, she slipped off his hips and onto the welcoming sand. There, cradled in the V created between his arm and his body, she let herself relax.

He shuddered once and tried to breathe more normally.

"Are you . . ." She took a few deep breaths. "Are you quite well?"

Ecstasy smiled on him. Nothing mattered now. Nothing but that she was his for this moment. He hugged her closer. "I think I shall survive."

"Liam?" She raised up on her arm, hovering over him, her worry warm on his face.

"Rachel." It took more strength than seemed

practical for him to stroke her arm. "Saint Rachel."

"Hardly that." Her gaze slipped from his face to his chest. "I made you bleed again."

"Small price," he rasped. "If you want me head on a platter, you've but to ask."

"I got what I wanted," she sighed.

He raised his brows at her. This new Rachel might be enough to kill him, but death had never looked so appealing. "Did you?" he breathed.

"Aye." Her hair draped like a curtain of glimmering silk past her face. "For now," she said, and smoothed her hand up his arm.

Liam blew out a slow breath. "I may need a few minutes before a repeat performance."

She laughed low in her throat. "Then I might as well see to your bandage."

"So you were just trying to distract me. I knew it was too good to last."

"Nay, not too good," she sighed. "Not for you."

Miraculously, the process gave him little pain. Her hands were like magic against his skin, touching, smoothing, her brow puckered as she stared at his chest.

"How does it look?" he asked, glancing down, but she stopped him with a hand beneath his chin.

"Tis healing well," she said, and leaning forward, kissed the muscle just above the wound. "You shall soon be the scourge of the Highlands again."

"Umm," he said nonsensically. They lay against the sand a bit longer, lounging in the sun-warmed waves. Gentle currents washed by, causing their thighs to brush, or their fingers to touch until they could no longer bear to be separated by even the shallowest droplet.

Reaching up to the boulder, Rachel retrieved her

gourd of soap. "Tilt your head back." She leaned over him. One satin-slick breast crushed against his chest, and with that contact there was little chance he would refuse her.

He leaned back, letting his hair drag in the water. Rachel scooped her palm over the crown of his head, swept back any stray hairs, then poured a bit of her extract onto his scalp.

Feelings as warm as sunlight caressed him, but there was more to come. Her fingers circulated gently against his scalp, and with each movement, her breasts slipped against his naked skin. He groaned hopelessly at the contact.

"Am I hurting you?" she asked, her eyes finding his.

"Aye. Hurt me some more."

She smiled that smile that would have made any saint pay penance each day of his life and joined her other hand with her first. Now she was leaning over him, seeming intent on washing every hair and granting him a view that all but stopped his heart.

Her breasts were round and kissed by the sun, capped with rosy puckered dollops of heaven as they bobbled and bounced so close to his face.

"Dunk."

"What?" he managed.

"Dunk your head."

He did so, though twas no mean task to take his gaze from her breasts. She smoothed her fingers through his hair again, skimming his scalp with her magical fingers.

Maybe he had been wrong all along. Maybe Hell did not await him. Maybe, in fact, his simple association with the Lady Saint had given him free admittance into heaven. Maybe, in fact, he had already passed through those hallowed gates and was even now in the hereafter. It seemed the only logical solution as her hands slid down his neck to his shoulders.

She had to reach wide to accomplish this, and thus rose to her knees to do so. Such a position granted him an even more astounding view. He made no objection when she straddled him again.

The crisp feel of her hair against his nether parts only stimulated him further. Already he was throbbing, but such a fact hardly stopped her. Instead, she leaned forward so that the tips of her nipples teased his chest.

Liam gritted his teeth and refused to move lest he awaken and find that it had all been another dream of longing. But the feel of her hands as they encircled his arm seemed too real. She washed him studiously, as if they had nothing in the world but time, as if all her life she had waited to touch him so, running her fingers, soft as a dream down his biceps, washing each finger, drawing his scathed knuckles to her mouth to kiss them gently. And with each movement her sweet bottom rasped against him. Twas almost too much to bear. Almost, but he managed.

His belly tightened as she ran her hands down its tense expanse, and when she slipped her hips off his and her hands skimmed lower still, he couldn't help but watch with breathless anticipation. Her fingertips slipped onto the scar-smooth head of his penis. Liam rasped breath through his teeth as the sensations seared him.

She lifted her eyes to his. Their gazes met. Hot, rash desire joined and melded. He reached for her, but she pulled easily out of his grip and straightened. Reaching for her gourd again, she poured a bit into her palm, then slipped her hand over his erection.

Painful ecstasy gripped him. He arched backward, pulling air through his clenched teeth in a hiss of aching need. But her hands didn't stop. Instead, they slipped up and down, caressing, washing, enlarging. It felt suddenly like his skin was too small for his body, as if there was too much need in him to be contained. But just when he felt he could bare no more, her hand slipped lower. New agony coursed through him. His legs jerked. His hips strained of their own accord, needing.

Her unsaintly hands skimmed lower still, encircling his thigh, but this new movement was only a more subtle form of the same torture, for her wrist still brushed his testicles.

His breathing escalated by the moment. True, he had loved her only minutes before, but that had done nothing to dull his need for her. Indeed, he ached now with it.

Rachel leaned forward. Her hair floated in the water, tangling over his erection. A spasm of need jerked through him. He could wait no longer. Pressing her onto the sand, he crushed his lips to hers.

She answered his kiss with a passion of her own. Her breasts, soft as a sigh, pressed against his chest, and she groaned as he entered her.

Passion that seemed to have been spent was renewed. He strained against her, absorbing everything, every inch of flesh, every raspy breath. His knees sunk into the silt beneath them, but he didn't care, for now her legs encircled his hips, drawing him closer, pulling him deeper. She gripped his arms in fingers too strong for her fragile form and pulled him inside. He sheathed himself to the hilt, groaning at the agonizing ecstasy as they strove once again for release.

He knew the moment she reached climax, felt it in the tautness of her muscles. They gripped him like velvet steel. He gritted his teeth and held on a few more seconds. But there was no hope of prolonging it. No hope whatsoever, and in a moment he spilled forth and finally fell forward, letting his elbows sink into the river's sandy bottom.

They breathed in aching unison, their hearts pumping like running steeds, their bodies finally lax.

"Sorry." She barely breathed the word, but he heard her and managed to draw back a scant fraction of an inch. She panted softly, her breasts like love against his tattered chest. "I should not have . . . pressed you. Your wound—"

"What wound?"

She smiled and touched his cheek. He covered her hand with his own and pulled it to his lips. Then, reaching past her, he lifted the gourd and poured a bit of the extract into his hand.

"My turn," he whispered.

She shook her head, but he only smiled.

"Surely we cannot have you running about paradise all dirty."

"Is this paradise?" she murmured.

"Aye, lass. Tis," he said, skimming his hand up her arm. "Tis where dreams come to play."

"Dreams?" She sighed as he skimmed his fingers into her hair.

Now that the urgency of coupling was over, pain pulled at his wound, but he didn't care. Her expression was soft, her eyes closed. Night was falling softly about them, darkening the water, but she only seemed more beautiful, her bedtime hair flowing on the waves.

Pressing his fingers up her scalp, he pushed them through the seal-slick tresses. She was naught but magic, every inch of her, every breath of her, every thought, movement, moment.

"You had best return to the shelter before you get cold," she said.

"Could not happen, lass. Not when you look as you do."

It seemed unlikely that she would blush after what they had just done, but even in the darkness, he thought it was so.

"Come." She rose like a sea nymph from the water. "I'll take you to the fire, then return to wash our clothes."

"You'll be naked?"

"What?"

"You'll be naked when you wash our clothes?"

The blush again, maybe. "Nay. I'll . . . fetch my tunic."

He released a sigh, but all was not lost.

"I'll stay," he murmured.

"Liam—"

"A hundred fires could not warm me as much as the sight of you does."

He was certain he remembered her writhing wildly beneath him, but now she seemed strangely shy. Still, she finally rose to her feet and snatched her gown from the shore. He had a momentary glimpse of the golden moon of her buttocks and then she was gone.

The world had slipped by for only a few moments before she returned. She'd dressed in her tunic just as she had threatened. It seemed a shame, perhaps a crime to hide such loveliness, but all was not lost, for the tunic had not been intended to be worn alone.

Dropping his retrieved cape onto the shore, Rachel picked up her gown and diminished soap and approached the water. When she crouched beside the burn, Liam was afforded a brief glimpse of paradise, for she had not tied the neck of the tunic which had always been too large for her. One bonny, kitten-smooth shoulder peaked out as she bent to scrub the much-abused garment.

Never had laundry been so fascinating. Every movement of her hand was poetry, every dip of her body spoke of a magic that was all her own. Even her feet were perfect. Narrow and delicate, they seemed the epitome of who she was, the Lady Saint.

It didn't take her nearly long enough to finish the job. She wrung out the garments, draped them over her arm, then rose to fetch his cape. In a moment she was stepping back into the water to assist him.

The air felt deliciously cool against his bare skin, but when she offered his cape, he realized the sacrifice he had just made. Not only could he no longer watch her from his watery utopia, but with the tunic and the cape between them, he would not be able to touch her either.

Life was too short for such dire punishments. And he'd been hideously wounded.

It was no great feat of acting for him to shiver.

"Here." She lifted his cape, but he shook his head.

"I'd best dry off first, lest I soak me cloak."

She scowled. "I have nothing—"

"The tunic."

The darkness was soft with silence and seduction.

"I could use your tunic," he expounded.

Her sinfully red lips parted, but he was so close to her now he could feel her weakness.

"You wouldn't deny a wounded man a towel would you?" he asked.

"Methinks you have things other than warmth in mind."

"Nay," he murmured, stepping closer still. "I swear I shall share me own body's warmth with you."

He reached for her hem and she didn't stop him. It came easily away, slipping over her wet hair until he held it in his hands.

Bathed in pearlescent moonlight, her beauty snared him, and for a moment he forgot to breathe.

"Liam."

"Aye," he murmured.

"I thought you were cold."

"Oh, aye." He dried himself perfunctorily, but the ruby bright tips of her breasts were peaked. Maybe she was cold. Maybe not. But all the options made him hurry through his toweling.

In a moment he eased his cape over his shoulders, then brushed it about hers. Her arm felt as warm as midday against his. He knew he should hurry her back to their camp before she became chilled, but instead he turned inside the warmth of his cape, shivered at the feel of her breasts against him, and kissed her. The caress was slow and sweet and filled with a thousand emotions he could neither identify nor condone. But neither could he quell them.

Maybe the journey back to their temporary home should have been painful, but it was difficult to concentrate on such things, for she was beside him.

They snuggled together inside his cape as they ate their evening meal, but their utensils were neither sturdy nor dependable and soup is a tricky thing to eat without a spoon. The seaweed kept slipping off her impromptu ladle onto interesting body parts. There was nothing Liam could do but retrieve them, licking them from her belly or her hand or . . . wherever.

Twas the wherever that intrigued him the most, but Rachel gasped as his tongue lapped the crinkled hair between her thighs.

"Liam . . ." Her voice was raspy as she pulled him back up. "We mustn't. You need your rest."

"Tis not rest that I need," he assured her.

"You must be good," she reprimanded, her voice soft but firm like all her other attributes—her limbs, her breasts, the alluring curve of her buttocks. The warm, ripe thoughts enticed his fingers to stray over her shoulder and down. His kisses followed.

"Liam." She arched away, breathing hard. "I must see to your wound."

"And I must see to you."

"Nay." She pressed a hand to his chest. "I will not have you bleed to death for me own . . ." She paused, seeming breathless.

He watched her, fascinated. "What?"

"For me own pleasure."

It was the throaty way she said *pleasure* that left him mindless and immobilized. So that by the time he was able to move again, she'd already fled to fetch her herbs and bandages.

But even the process of tending his wound was nothing but pleasurable, for he was afforded the heavenly feel of her hands against his flesh as she smoothed on her ointments, the breath-stopping sight of her beauty as she bent or flexed or breathed.

Finally, she bandaged him with strips of her underskirt that she had washed days before, and then, cuddled in the security of their tiny enclosure, they talked of dreams and memories and happiness.

"Why did we not realize long ago that we belonged together?" Rachel asked, sleepily snuggled against his chest.

"Tis hard to know the fit if you cannot try the garment," Liam said, and kissed the top of her head. His hand played a sleepy rhythm against her arm.

The world was silent but for the crackle of the fire.

"You are happy with the fit, Liam?" she asked quietly.

"Aye. Tis like a sword in a sheath."

She sighed as she turned her face into his chest. "Tis more the size of a claymore," she murmured, and fell asleep.

Chapter 26

The days passed in a silvery mist of make-believe, a delirium of laughter and baths and lovemaking. And with each hour Liam found his wounds improving and his strength increased.

Not for a moment did they discuss the hopelessness of their situation. Not for an instant did they think of Warwick or evil or pain. Those things were far away, lost in another world. A world they had abandoned.

Each day there were fish in Rachel's homespun net, as if they were sent from heaven to sustain them. Herbs were dried and crushed and used. Utensils were designed and laughed over.

Another evening flowed in. Supper was consumed, then Rachel saw to Liam's bandage. Later, he watched her as she hummed to herself and buried fresh fish in the embers to be smoked.

With his back to the venerable oak, Liam was afforded the luxury of appreciating her every movement.

She was not a saint, he realized, but an angel, a narrow, fleeting slice of perfection that he neither deserved nor had ever hoped to know. Indeed, these past days with her were more than he should have ever had, for she was all goodness, all hope.

And he would not let her die!

The thought crashed abruptly through him. He tried to push it back—to find the sweet oblivion they had built here, but he knew suddenly that it was gone. He could pretend no longer. Not even for the blessed feel of her flesh against his. Twas nothing short of a miracle that they had survived this long. He had known they would die, that Warwick would find them, and maybe, somehow, that knowledge had set them free. Free to revel in their last days. But the wizard had not come. Miraculous as it was, they remained alive, and now his wounds were mended enough to see him from this paradise.

He could delay no longer.

"When is Shona's babe to be born?"

Rachel stopped her humming to glance up at him, and for a moment he forgot everything but the fire-bright beauty of her eyes.

"In a few months' time," she said, straightened slightly. "As you well know."

"You will tend to the birthing?"

"Why do you ask?"

"I simply ask," he said, but pain nagged at his soul as he wrapped his cloak more firmly about him.

"I will tend her."

"Then I needn't worry for her welfare."

"Nay." She sat down next to him and swept a lock of hair from his forehead. "You needn't worry. Shona is strong. The strongest of the three of us cousins."

He knew he should draw away from her, for even her slightest touch made him weak. But he couldn't quite muster that much discipline. "'Tis you that is the strong one," he countered softly. "Tis you who will keep them safe."

She canted her head at him, her expression concerned. "Liam, is something amiss?"

"You will escape."

"What?"

He tried to ignore the emotion in her eyes. For her he could be strong. "When they come, you shall escape, no matter what happens to me."

"What are you saying?" she asked, and reached for his hand.

"You know very well what I speak of, Rachel."

She shook her head, but he gripped her arm hard, pulling her closer to him.

"When Warwick comes, you must not fail. You must not! You shall return to your family."

"Don't say his name."

"There will be a riderless horse, Rachel. That much I can do. You will take that horse and flee."

"So even now, after everything we have been through together, you expect to die, to sacrifice yourself for me."

The woods were silent.

"How many lives have you saved?" he asked.

She yanked her arm from his grasp. "I've no idea what you speak of."

"How many?"

"It does not matter," she whispered. "Not if I cannot save you."

"Rachel—" he began, and snatched up her arm again.

"Nay!" she snapped. "You do not—" she began, but she stopped abruptly. Her eyes went wide. "He's coming."

Terror, as cold as hell sliced through him. So it was a premonition of his approaching evil that he'd felt. He jerked to his feet, pulling her up with him. Too soon! Dear God, it was still too soon, Liam thought. He didn't have his full strength. What if his plan didn't work? What if . . . But he must not fail. He would not.

"Give me the dragon!" he rasped.

"Why?"

"Tis what he wants. Give it to me and flee." Please, God, make her see the sense in this.

"We've discussed this before, Irishman," she said, her words barely audible. "If you choose to die, I choose to die with you."

Frustration and terror roared up inside him. "Give me the dragon!" he demanded, but she leapt back, out of his reach.

"You want to save me, Liam?"

"Please, Rachel." He lurched after her. "Don't do this."

"Then come and get me."

He lunged. Desperation made him quick. Premonition made her quicker. She jumped back. His fingers grazed her arm.

"Rachel—"

"Nay!" she rasped, and spun away.

Pain ripped through his chest. Branches slapped at his face, but he wouldn't stop, wouldn't lose her. He could hear her frantic breath, could hear her racing footfalls. But the terror was running them down, looming over them.

From somewhere behind he heard a man yell. Rachel turned back momentarily and stumbled.

Liam was upon her in a moment, clutching her arms.

"They found our camp." Her words were no more than a whimper.

"Aye." He pulled her against his chest, breathing

in her presence. "Please, Rachel, give me the dragon."

"I cannot—"

"Then I will take it from you."

"And let me die alone?"

"You will not die," he snarled through gritted teeth. "You will not."

But she nodded jerkily. "I cannot survive without you Liam. I swear it."

He snarled something, then snatched her to his chest.

The sound of hoofbeats tore them apart.

"Hurry!" Liam gasped, and spinning away, pulled her after him.

Terror pursued them like rabid hounds. Distance rushed past on dark wings, but whether they went miles or yards, he couldn't tell.

"There!" The cry came from behind, spearing through him.

"Liam!" Rachel gasped.

"Run!" he ordered, and pulled her on, though there was no hope. They'd been spotted like wild hare, and like wild hare they fled, blindly racing through the woods.

But in a moment the trees thinned.

They burst into the full light of day. Ahead of them, the land disappeared as if sliced off by a giant knife.

"Halt!" a voice shrieked, but hope flared through Liam. The river must lay just ahead. It had saved them before. They lurched forward. Just a little farther. A wee bit.

"Jump!" he yelled. But in that instant, he realized there was no water below them, only a long drop to death. He stumbled to a halt, dragging her with him. She staggered, dropping to her knees at the edge of the cliff.

Stones, disturbed by their frantic pace, hurled into space and down to the dry gulch an eternity below them.

They stared in mindless defeat, all hope blown away like dust in a wild gale.

"Liam." She whispered his name. Her hand trembled in his.

"I'm sorry. So sorry." He turned slowly to face their pursuers. There was no longer any point in running. Open land rolled away from them on three sides. Their only escape lay straight below them. Rachel glanced down the hopeless precipice one more time then rose slowly to her feet beside him.

A half dozen men rode toward them.

"Stay back," Liam warned.

A chuckle escaped from Warwick. His cowl had fallen off during his wild ride through the woods, and his head looked grotesque, terrifying, his eyes like glass orbs in his scarred face. "Of course not," he said. "I have only been following you so that we might talk."

"Don't come closer," Liam repeated, and reaching toward Rachel, grasped Dragonheart's chain.

She stiffened, prepared to have it yanked from her neck, but the amulet slid easily from her into his hand.

"I'll toss it! I swear I will."

Silence echoed around them.

"Liam." Warwick's tone had changed to wheedling care, though his men kept advancing. "Would you do such a thing just to wound me?"

"Tell them to stop."

He did so abruptly with a simple movement of his hand. "What now, my son."

"Don't call me that."

"Why not? You know tis the truth. You are mine. Spilled from mine loins."

"Maybe from your loins, old man, but not from your soul."

The wizard laughed again. "So you still wish to believe you are different from me?" He opened a hand and swept it in a slow arc before him. Suddenly there seemed to be nothing but the wizard, nothing but the power he wielded like a spiked mace. "But why, Liam? Why? Do I not have the power you desire?"

"Nay, you don't," Liam said, but twas all he could do to force the words past his terror, for the entire universe seemed filled with Warwick's presence. "You have nothing I desire."

Again the old man laughed. "Tis not true." His hellish eyes turned toward Rachel and he smiled. "You wish for power. You wish for wealth."

"Nay," Liam countered.

"Aye. You wish for her—the daughter of a laird."

"You're wrong."

His steed took a few steps forward. "I am right. But you know you are not worthy of her, for you have nothing."

"You are wrong," Liam repeated, his voice rising.

"You have nothing. No riches, no home, no power."

Dear God, it was all true. She'd been raised to wealth and privilege, the treasured daughter of a powerful laird. Liam had nothing to offer her. Nothing.

"Join me." Warwick's voice was as deep as the cliff behind him. "Together we shall take what we will."

The wizard's power reached out like a powerful hand, drawing Liam in.

"She shall be yours, my son. Her and all that is her father's."

They had been happy in their simple haven. How much happier would she be in opulence? Glen Creag could be theirs. Servants. Comfort.

"No longer the bastard from Firthport." Warwick was approaching slowly, his voice a soothing murmur. "But a prince among men. You have the gifts, lad. You've but to use them."

Liam still held the dragon, but no longer was it clenched to his chest. Instead, he held it before him, palm up, his fingers open.

"Come to me," Warwick entreated. "And all shall be yours."

Liam took a step forward.

"Nay!" Rachel gasped.

Her fingers closed over Liam's arm. Reality jolted through him like forked lightning. He jerked toward her. Her gaze struck him, bright as the promise of hope.

"Please, Liam. Don't do this."

His soul shook.

"Join me!" Warwick hissed.

The command pulled at Liam, drawing him in. He turned.

Rachel's hand tightened on his arm. "If he has the dragon, all will be lost."

The truth of her words seared him like a hot lance. Liam clasped a desperate hand over hers, filling his soul with her strength.

"All will be yours!" shrieked the wizard.

Liam's heart seemed to burst in two, his mind torn asunder, dragged apart by the force of the wills that battled for him. But where Rachel was a glowing flame, Warwick was a roaring inferno.

"It shall be yours," he repeated, his voice like thunder.

Without volition, Liam's legs moved, pulling him away from her. Her tiny flame of goodness flickered.

"I love you," she whispered. "I'll love you for all time."

The breath was dragged from Liam's lungs. He turned stiffly toward her. Their gazes met and melded. Peace flowed from her touch like a river of sweet wine, filling his soul, his mind. He was lost in her eyes, in her truth, in her goodness, drawn toward her like a saint to heaven.

"For all time," he whispered, and lifting the amulet, slipped the chain over her neck.

"Nay!" screamed Warwick. "Take him!"

Hell exploded around them. The warriors spurred forward. The very earth trembled beneath their horses' pounding hooves, but Liam's gaze was caught on her face.

"Forever and always," she whispered.

Death thundered nearer, opening its slavering jaws.

Liam glanced at the riders, then down the endless precipice. Twas no hope that way. None at all. But there would be no torture. Only death. "I am sorry," he whispered.

"Nay." She touched his cheek with fingers that trembled. "We shall be together," she said, and clutching each other, they turned toward the cliff and jumped.

Chapter 27

The air was sucked from Rachel's lungs as they plunged toward the earth. Fear wrapped about her, pulling her down toward the jagged jaws of death. She clung to Liam, waiting for the pain, the ripping agony.

But time had stood still. Death was in no hurry. And now, instead of falling to their doom, it seemed almost as if they were floating.

She heard something billow above her. What was it? Angels' wings? She could see nothing, nothing but the flaring bloom of Liam's cloak, and then it came—the landing.

She shrieked as she felt the impact. Liam was ripped from her arms. But the solid crash of earth didn't meet her. Instead, she streaked through something semi-solid. Claws scratched at her face. Demons snagged her clothing, and suddenly she was snatched to a halt.

She gasped for air, for reason, but there was none. Where was death, where was pain?

Where was Liam? She glanced about. Branches scraped her cheek, but there, not more than a few inches away, Liam hung by his cape upon the gnarled limbs of an ancient sycamore.

She tried to reach him, and in that moment, realized that she too was suspended—with his cape
stretched tight over the branches between them.
Glancing down, she realized she couldn't see past
her own feet. Still, her movement shook her precarious balance. Beside her, a branch creaked. She
caught her struggling breath and grappled for a
hold. Already it was too late. She was falling again.

But even before the thought registered in her
scrambled mind, the drop had ended. She struck
the earth with her rear and stayed where she was.
Liam dropped beside her like a bad apple.

They were both gasping for breath and reason.

"God's mercy!" she cried. But their relief was
snatched away as arrows rained down from the
cliff above.

Lurching onto their hands and knees, they
scrambled toward the center of the tree that had
saved them and ducked there beneath the dense
leaves. The arrows sputtered to a halt, but in an
instant they heard the thunder of galloping hooves.

Warwick could not descend as quickly as they
had, but neither would he give up.

"Hurry." Liam gained his feet first.

Rachel felt the tremble of his hand as he closed
his fist over her fingers. Or was it, perhaps, her
own hand that shook so?

She managed to stand, though her knees threatened, for a moment, to spill her back to the earth.

"Can you walk?"

"Aye."

"Good. Could you . . ." His voice shook, and he
paused for a moment, glancing up the cliff from
which they'd just jumped. "Could you carry me?"

Her giggle was wild, and suddenly they were

laughing together, howling like deranged banshees as they limped along the ravine.

Water ran the length of its bottom, but it was no more than a few inches deep and would do them little good, for once Warwick found a way to descend he'd be upon them. They hustled across the stream. The land here was as smooth as a road, but seemed like little more than a trail of death. The hills loomed above them, promising exhaustion and pain, but there was little else they could do but climb upward and hope for cover at its crest.

The ascent was as difficult as it seemed. Rocks and holes tripped them up. The snaggled branches of heather tore at Rachel's skirt, but they dragged on.

They were nearly to the top, nearly hidden away, when they heard the cry from below them. Gripping Liam's hand with ferocious fear, Rachel glanced down.

Even now Warwick's men were lifting their bows.

"Run!" Liam rasped.

She tried, but exhaustion smothered her. An arrow hissed past on the wings of death, singing into the earth not three feet away.

"Hurry!" Liam cried, and pulling her upward, drew her onto the hill's crest.

They dared not delay an instant, but galloped across the hill toward the distant trees.

Exhaustion held them in a tight fist when finally they reached the woods. Gasping like broken billows, they stumbled into its welcoming arms. Shadows wrapped about them.

"Rest," Rachel gasped.

"Aye." Liam's voice was almost indistinguishable as he dragged her deeper into the forest. "Soon."

In actuality, it was not soon. But finally, finally, they found a tiny spot beneath a decaying , slanted beech tree and a trio of boulders. There they fell onto a pillow of leaves, and there they stayed, exhausted and spent, falling into the grasping arms of sleep.

The evening was peaceful. Nothing stirred. The sky was a deep, midnight blue. The world was at peace. Rachel lay on the sand, staring into the stars that winked overhead. Her mission had been completed, that much she knew, though in truth she was too lazy to recall the circumstances, too drowsy to think of the trials past.

Here there was peace and contentment. Here there were no troubles. The king was well. Somewhere, perhaps a thousand miles away, it seemed she heard his laughter. And in all the world there was no Warwick. She knew that too, felt it in her soul.

Overhead a hawk swooped lazily. A cool breeze blew across her skin. Happiness soared through her. The hawk circled nearer, its wings spread wide, its long neck curved toward her. She smiled at it. And it seemed almost to smile back as it swooped, circling yet again.

Nearer and nearer it came. The air swirled around her. The sand beneath her shifted. A huge bird, it was, blocking out the stars, blocking out the sky, filling her senses, and yet she was not afraid, for she was home, she was safe.

She turned toward the soaring bird, and suddenly she realized it was not a bird at all.

Rachel awoke with a start. Her breath rattled in her throat and her hands were shaking.

"What is it?" Liam sat bolt upright beside her,

his words gasped and his hand already clutching hers as he peered into the surrounding darkness.

"Twas not a bird."

For a moment he still didn't turn toward her. But finally the hand that clutched hers relaxed a mite. "What?"

"Twas not a bird." She barely dared to press out those tiny words, for in her mind, she was still there, still gazing into the midnight blue sky that was not sky. Watching the bird that was not a bird.

"You were dreaming," Liam said. "Tis past. Lie down."

"Nay." Something akin to desperation speared through her, though she knew not why, and she realized suddenly that in one hand she was grasping Dragonheart. "Twas not a dream."

Liam leaned a scant inch closer. His gaze fell to her closed fist, then focused on her face in the darkness. "What was it?"

"Twas a . . ." She ran out of words, out of breath. "The wizard must not have him."

He shook his head.

"Dragonheart. He must not have the dragon."

"We shall yet escape, Rachel. All will be well once we—"

"Nay." She shook off his hand. "All will not be well, Liam. Not until the dragon goes home."

Liam watched her in silence for a moment. When he finally spoke, his voice was deep and cautious as if he did not truly wish to hear her answer. "Home?"

"Loch Ness." She breathed the words and heard his corresponding rasp of understanding.

"I was there, Liam. Or rather, Dragonheart was there. But I thought it was me, looking up at the sky, but it wasn't sky at all. Twas water, as cold and clear as eternity. And there was something else." She whispered the words, then shivered a little, though she was neither cold nor afraid just now. "Something it loves."

"Something the dragon loves?"

"Aye. We must go to Inverness."

"You jest."

"There is no other way."

"Rachel, you are tired, you are stunned. The dragon . . . the dragon boggles one's mind. This I know, but you mustn't take it too seriously."

"Too seriously! Tis you that told me it has come to protect me."

"I—"

"And you were right, Liam. But only partly so. It has come for me to protect it."

"This is madness."

"Aye, madness," she said. "But think on it, Liam. Never will we be safe so long as there is a chance that the wizard might find it."

"We can hide it away."

"Away where? He will never give up. That much you know. How much have our loved ones suffered already because of him?"

Her words hung in the darkness like evil birds of prey.

"Then I shall kill him," Liam intoned.

"Nay!" She grasped his hand in desperate fear. "You cannot, Liam. He has powers you cannot understand."

"He is mine sire. I think I can understand."

"His powers do not come of the earth."

"Then I shall draw upon the same powers to undo him," he said. "To save you."

Leaning forward, she pressed her fingers gently to his lips. "Don't say such things, Liam. Tis not true. Tis not in you to follow his path."

"You don't know what I am capable of."

She smiled through the darkness. "Aye, I know. You are capable of all that is good. For that is what's in you."

"You don't know that."

"You're wrong."

"Rachel—"

"Shh," she said, pressing his lips again. "Dragonheart wants to go home."

They didn't wait for morning before continuing their journey. Though fatigue rode them like cruel horseman, they crept from their hiding place.

Warwick expected them to travel north to reach the king. Thus, they headed east, hoping against hope that the wizard wouldn't see their tracks, wouldn't be able to follow them, would indeed finally head for Blackburn in an attempt to intercept their course.

At the first light of dawn, they found a patch of wild berries. The fruit was sweet and bountiful. They ate as much as they could shove into their mouths, drank from the nearby stream, then slept through the daylight hours.

That night they began again. Sometime before dawn, they guessed they passed Blackburn Castle many miles to the west.

Liam ached to take Rachel there, ached to deliver her into comfort and peace. But he knew there was no hope of that. She would not go, for she was committed to this course. She forged on, barely looking back, rarely stopping except when she could go no farther and would drop like a rock into sleep.

But it was not long before their sleep was interrupted. They awoke together, snapping to wakefulness and staring with mute terror into each other's eyes.

"He's near."

Liam was never certain if she spoke the words or merely thought them. But it didn't matter, for he knew her mind, felt her fear tremble through their entwined fingers to his soul.

Near, so near. It was the only thought he could find, consuming, aching, eating out his soul until his heart could barely beat with the pressure of his agony.

"We shall know happiness again." Her words were whispered, disjointed.

"Rachel."

"Believe." She touched his cheek. Her fingers trembled against his face, but her eyes were steady. "Believe with me."

He tightened his grip on her fingers, forced his eyes closed, and his mind from the terror. "We shall lie together in peace, knowing we are safe."

"Aye." The single word trembled. "We are safe. Nothing can touch us. Tis dark all around us."

"I feel your skin against mine."

"Aye. I hear the soft murmur of your breath. Beneath us the pallet is soft, filled with sweet herbs."

"I—"

"Gone!" Warwick's voice snarled through Liam's mind like a rabid dog's.

Liam snapped his eyes open. Had he heard the word or was it merely in his mind? But when he looked to Rachel, he saw that her eyes too were wide with paralyzing fear.

"We are found," she whimpered.

"Nay." He breathed the denial, though his soul was certain he was wrong. Still, as they cowered in their hiding place, no warriors stormed down on them, no all-powerful hand reached down to snatch them from life. "Nay," he said, finding his breath, forcing his lips to move. "We are gone. Lost to him. Away in our own place of safety and peace."

She did not speak, did not draw her gaze from his. Instead, she stared at him in wide-eyed terror. Sweat beaded her brow. Evil marched closer. Like an army on the move, it threatened to consume them. And in that moment, he leaned forward and kissed her.

She answered back with savage need. Lost in their sheltered copse, they lay back on the spongy moss. His fingers trembled on the laces that confined her bosom and managed to free them. Her flesh felt like sunlight and hope against his fingertips. He kissed her throat, her ear, the high rise of her breasts.

"I love you," he whispered.

Her hands skimmed his abdomen. In moments, his laces were freed. Terror and adrenaline and hopelessness combined in one heady rush. They joined like wild animals, taut with a burning need to live each second to the fullest, until finally they fell, exhausted and spent, into a deep, unnatural sleep.

They awoke slowly, groggily. The sun was still up, they thought, but in a while, they realized that they were wrong. The sun was up *again.* They'd slept through the day and the night.

And in that time where had Warwick gone? They had no idea, but neither could they afford to contemplate it, for they dared not open their minds.

Instead, they found what food they could and pressed on.

The nights were haunted and endless, but there was not much farther to go. Neither was there any longer a need to guess in which direction lay Loch Ness. Somehow, though she was too exhausted to guess how, Rachel knew.

Dragonheart hung warm and soft against her skin, but behind them, evil gained on them until every step was torture, every thought painful.

"I have failed." Liam's voice was barely audible, though they stood so close their arms brushed.

"Nay," she countered, too weary to turn toward him.

"He has come."

Rachel's heart squeezed tight.

"Nay," she whimpered. "You have got us this far."

"Tis not me."

"Aye." The word trembled. "Tis your cunning, your wisdom, your goodness that has brought us safely here."

"He calls to me." Liam's voice was deep. "Even now he calls. Were I good I would go to him. Go to him and destroy him, but I cannot."

"Because you are evil?"

He didn't answer. His eyes were as dark as terror, but it was far too late for him to hide his thoughts from her.

Instinctively, her hand touched the amulet. Beneath her cold fingers the metal felt smooth and warm.

"The dragon wants you."

He reared back, his body immediately stiff, his eyes intense. "Nay."

"Aye. For it knows tis you who can save us—can save *him*."

"Nay," he said again, but she slipped it from her neck and onto his.

"Save us," she whispered.

"Rachel." His voice was agonized, but she pressed her fingers to his lips. They trembled against his flesh.

"I love you," she whispered.

The thunder of hooves rose from the bottom of the hill, and yet, for a moment, he could do nothing but stare at her. Then he turned away, the cords in his neck taut as he gazed into the valley below them.

"Back down!" he commanded.

"Nay!" Rachel gasped, her heart pounding in her throat. But in that moment he grabbed her hand and pulled her down the hill they had just ascended.

Hoofbeats thundered around them, echoing in her ears, growing like a giant heartbeat. But still they continued down the hill slipping and sliding, barely about to keep their feet in their harried flight.

Off to her right, a man shouted.

Rachel jerked toward the sound, terror overwhelming her, and in that moment she fell.

Chapter 28

Evil reached for Rachel like an iron gauntlet. She jerked, trying to catch herself, to gain her feet. But Liam fell upon her. His cape swooped over her like a falcon, covering her with its giant wings.

Horses thundered past, nearly trampling them, spurring up great divots of grass and mud that spattered on the cloak above them.

Evil smothered Rachel, tore at her, ripped at her lungs. She tried to scream, but Liam's hand covered her mouth. His own face was pressed to her shoulder, his shudders like the trembles of a child.

But finally the evil backed off a quarter of an inch, enough for her to breathe. Liam's hand slipped from her mouth. She pulled in a desperate draught of air, recovering slowly. But Liam was already on his feet. He pulled her with him, not wasting an instant, not a breath.

They slid the rest of the way down, hit the bottom and ran, hand in hand, blindly, hopelessly, going seemingly nowhere.

They had only minutes before Warwick realized he'd been tricked.

She knew the moment it happened, felt it in her

soul, sensed the wizard's evil intent turned toward them again.

Liam ran all the harder, pulling her along behind him. Her lungs ached with their flight. Her legs trembled. Sweat rolled between her shoulder blades. Her skin steamed in the cooling air, mingling with the fog that rolled up from the valley. In a moment she could see nothing but silvery mist.

Still, she could feel Warwick closing in, could hear his horses coming on, though in truth, she couldn't tell if the hoofbeats were reality or nothing more than an echo of her own blinding terror. Her knees trembled. She spilled forward, but Liam caught her, managing to pull her back to her feet.

There was no longer any hope of running. Instead they walked, not knowing which direction they headed, only following the fog that blanketed them like silver magic.

But they couldn't stay there, couldn't risk immobility, for Warwick was just behind them.

They began an ascent.

"If we leave the fog we are surely lost," Rachel whispered.

He didn't turn toward her. "Just over the hill."

Rachel glanced behind her. Evil! So close she could smell it, taste it on her tongue. She could no longer speak, and when Liam continued up the hill, she had no strength to resist.

But the fog didn't diminish. Instead, it boiled softly around them, climbing the hill, higher and higher, and then finally, when Rachel was certain she could go no farther, the mist drew reluctantly back.

They stood at the crest of nowhere.

"Urquhart Castle," Liam whispered.

Rachel glanced at him, but he was not turned

toward her. She followed his gaze, and there, off to her left, she saw the misty image of a fortress upon a distant hill.

"If we could reach it they might take us in," she rasped.

But Liam shook his head. Already he was moving, nearly running down the hill toward the billowing fog.

It swirled about them again, welcoming them. And now all was a haze, the world, her mind, eternity. Evil dulled every other element, until she couldn't tell if she were awake or sleeping.

It almost seemed she heard the slap of water on shore, but it was drowned in the sound of her own mental screaming.

"Nearly there. Nearly," Liam rasped.

She had no idea of what he spoke, but neither did she have any choice but to follow, to hope the evil would be left behind.

Another step, another eternity, but suddenly something leapt up from her feet.

She rasped a shriek and jumped back. Liam circled her with one arm, jerking his dirk free with the other. But the demon at her feet was nothing more than water.

"You will survive. You will," Liam chanted, and though Rachel could not tell who he spoke to, she stumbled along when he tugged her hand.

They followed the river forever, searching for a way across. But the fog that had saved them thus far was now their enemy, for they couldn't see the opposite shore. There was no way to determine its width, so they traveled on, knowing that anyone who followed would know exactly which direction they were headed.

Evil was as smothering as a blanket now, surrounding them, killing them.

She heard the hiss of death before she saw it. It flew past her. She screamed. An arrow quivered in the sand ahead of her.

"Run!" Liam shouted, and grabbing her hand, pulled her along in his wake. But in a moment, he fell.

She screamed his name, certain he'd been shot, but in that instant, she saw the boat. Liam was sprawled half inside it.

"In! Get in!" he yelled.

A shriek of rage pierced the fog behind them. Another arrow hissed through the air and shuddered into the boat's hull.

Rachel turned toward their pursuers, her legs no longer working. But in that instant, Liam pushed her inside and shoved the boat into the water. Waves lapped about them. Liam grabbed the oars, pulling fiercely. They slipped onto the lake.

Horses appeared like dark specters on the shore.

Warwick screamed and raised his arm, pointing toward them.

The closest rider spurred into the water. The horse leapt toward them, throwing up geysers that splashed over Rachel's cowering form. Liam pulled harder. Another arrow sang past, nailing her skirt to the floor as it hummed into the wood. Yards away, the horse plunged again. The rider loomed nearer, sword raised, nearly upon them.

"Toward me!" Liam rasped, plowing the oars through the water.

Yanking her skirt from the arrow, Rachel twisted about and scrambled away. Her free hand fell on something. Yanking it up, she turned in a panic and threw. It was only a net, but the force of her movement tossed her off balance. She toppled sideways, grabbing hold of the gunwale to save herself.

The boat reverberated beneath her hand. A sword was imbedded in the wood between her fingers. She jerked her attention to the warrior's face. He yanked his weapon free and raised it again. Rachel screamed and threw herself sideways, but in that moment the warrior toppled from his mount.

Half-crouched in the prow, Rachel watched him sink below the waves, his head caught in the net she had thrown, his body yanked under by his mount's powerful strokes.

The water boiled around them, the horse plowed on. But in a moment of panic, the steed turned back and disappeared into the mist. The water calmed.

She glanced toward Liam. Their gazes met, but neither spoke. Weak with relief and exhaustion, Rachel crawled forward to press herself against Liam's thigh.

The world lapsed into unearthly silence. She could hear nothing but her own harsh breathing and the rasp of the oars against the water.

Stunned and exhausted, she did nothing but sit, nothing but stare into the silver mists that enveloped them.

"It could have made me worthy of you."

Rachel turned at the sound of Liam's voice. He lowered his eyes, catching her gaze, one hand clasped over the amulet on his chest.

She shook her head in bewilderment, then glanced behind her. "We've no time to waste, Liam. They will not quit."

"Warwick was right." His tone was melancholy. "I could have been your equal."

She stared at him in silent question. Beneath them, the boat, rudderless now, spun in a lazy circle, reminding her of their hopeless flight.

"Liam," she said, and dropped to her knees to face him. "We must go."

"Nay," he intoned softly. "We are here."

She glanced to her left. Nothing but silver grayness filled her vision.

"Dragonheart is home," Liam said.

Understanding seeped into her soul. "He led us here?"

"Aye. From whence he came."

Reaching out, Rachel covered his hand with her own. Even through his closed fist, she could feel the dragon's emotion. Not excitement, not happiness. But something infinitely more intense.

"I could be wealthy," Liam murmured. "I could be lordly."

She stared into his enraptured face, feeling his struggle as if it tormented her own soul. "Or I could love you," she whispered.

He lowered his eyes to hers. Their souls met. And Liam smiled.

Loosing his fingers, she reached up and smoothed her fingers across his cheek. "Let him go," she murmured.

Liam lifted his hand.

But in that instant the boat lurched. Rachel twisted about. The kindly fog was ripped away. Warwick loomed over her!

She screamed.

Liam had an instant's image of Warwick's twisted face, but in that second a dark figure leapt over the prows of their boats and plowed into him. He careened backward, crashing against the side. Darkness slammed up to meet him. He fell toward it, but in that instant, he heard Rachel's shriek of terror.

His fingers curled around something and he swung. The brigand dropped sideways. Liam scrambled to his feet, blindly searching for Rachel.

Not in the boat! He snapped his gaze to the water. She was there, her dark hair spread upon the waves. A ribbon of blood seeped across the surface.

"Nay!" he screamed, and leapt toward the water.

Pain struck his skull. He staggered sideways. An arm closed over his throat, holding him captive.

Panic consumed him

"Rachel!" he rasped.

"So the game ends."

Liam turned his bulging eyes to the side. Warwick stood only inches away, his dark cowl thrown back.

"It ends and I win." The wizard reached forward. His fingers closed over Dragonheart. Past him, Rachel sank below the surface.

"Nay! God!" Liam shrieked, and wrenched to get free, but the arm tightened, cutting off his air.

"God!" Warwick rasped, stepping close. "You speak to God?" He laughed, the sound low and horrible. "There will be no help from that front. Not for you."

Liam turned his eyes toward the wizard, and suddenly he was entranced, enraptured.

"You know that you are my son."

The words fell like poison on Liam's ears.

"Aye. I know."

A twisted smile. Warwick's presence seemed to burn through Liam's chest where he held the amulet in a gnarled grip. "Then you know better than to appeal to God," he rasped.

"I am not evil." They were the only words Liam could manage.

"On the contrary," Warwick said. "You are mine."

"I am not evil," he whimpered, but he could no longer pull his gaze from Warwick's, not even for Rachel.

"Not evil?" the wizard asked, his voice as dark as the night. "Then I give you a choice, Liam. Stay and work with me. See the strength of the dragon put to the test. Or die with the woman."

Liam opened his mouth to speak, to tell him he preferred death. But the words would not come. Time stood still.

Beneath them, the boat bucked. Warwick tottered sideways, thrown off balance.

Dragonheart dropped against Liam's chest.

Hope burst within him.

"Rachel!" he screamed and lifting his feet, crashed them against the wooden seat.

Caught off guard, his captor stumbled backward. The back of his knees struck wood. He loosened his grip, trying to find his balance. Liam twisted away, but in that second Warwick reached and yanked Dragonheart from his neck.

The wizard screamed his victory, but it didn't matter. Nothing mattered.

Jumping to the seat, Liam scanned the lake. A stream of dark hair flicked the surface of the water. Please God, please, he prayed, and leapt, but fingers snagged in his tunic. He was dragged back in, his arm twisted behind him.

Warwick rose to his feet, his hand clasped about the amulet. Past him, the last sign of Rachel disappeared.

A shriek of animal terror howled from Liam's lips.

But suddenly the world was shifting radically.

Beneath them, the boat heaved upward. Warwick screamed. Men yelled, grabbing for safety. But the boats tipped more. Behind him, the guard fell away. Liam twisted about, prayed once and dove.

Dark waves settled over his head. Around him, water bubbled and cracked as a boat overturned. Bodies thrashed past him. He dove deeper, trying to see, to think.

Where was she?

There! A dark shape. He pulled himself toward it, grabbing at the hair, turning her toward him.

A man's face appeared in the murky water.

Nay!

He pushed it away, lungs bursting, searching for air. He broke the surface with a gasp, dragging in breath after breath.

From the single boat still remaining above the water, he heard Warwick's wail. But he didn't care. Gasping in one last agonizing breath, he dove again, plunging through the turbulent waters.

Another body floated past him. Not her. Where? Where?

A huge, dark form slashed through the water. Thrashing waves pushed Liam backward like a howling wind. His arm brushed something. He turned, and there she was. Rachel!

She floated lifelessly, her wild hair her only moving feature.

"Nay," he moaned. Water streamed into his lungs as he grasped her gown and hauled her toward the surface.

But he had lost his sense of direction. Panic burned him. Blackness threatened. But he could not fail!

His fingers felt the end of the water. Air streamed over him. He broke the surface choking and coughing. Rachel did nothing. Nothing but float in the water, her neck flaccidly draped over his arm, her lips as pale as her face.

"Rachel!" he croaked. "Rachel!"

She said nothing. Did not even move.

Horror burst over him. Despair ravaged him. "Nay, I will not let you go." He shook her, coughing and gasping, but she did nothing.

"Back!" a voice shrieked.

Liam raised his gaze to the source of the noise. Warwick crouched in the boat, gripping its sides with white-knuckled hands.

"Get away!" he screamed, and now Liam saw that the boat was tilting dramatically, falling sideways, being dragged away as if down a huge, spinning funnel.

He felt the pull of it on his legs, saw the boat slip into the whirlpool, heard Warwick scream as he was dragged into the deep. But none of it mattered. Nay, none of it, for Rachel was gone.

There was nothing for him now. Thus he would go with her, go with her and hope the God who loved her would understand his need to be with her for all eternity.

The wild currents of the whirlpool tugged harder at him, and he let himself go, dragged soundlessly down into the depths, letting the waters fill his lungs, letting death take him as he pressed a final kiss to Rachel's brow.

Chapter 29

"**W**elcome back," said a soft voice.

Liam opened his eyes. Perceptions seeped slowly into his consciousness, a beamed ceiling, stone walls, bunches of dried herbs festooned upon them. Carefully, he turned his head.

An elder version of the woman he would love forever, sat beside his bed. Fiona Forbes, healer of Glen Creag.

"I feared you wouldn't return to us," she said.

"You brought me back." It was a statement not a question, croaked in painful reason from Liam's parched lips.

"Nay, twas not me," she countered.

"Nay?" For one agonizing, heart-twisting moment Liam held his breath, praying against all reason that she would say it had been Rachel, that somehow she had not died, that God Himself had decided He couldn't bear to take her from him.

"Twas Hawk who found you," Fiona said. He realized now that her voice was thin with fatigue and her eyes red with sorrow. But he couldn't pity her, for though she had lost a daughter, *he* had lost everything.

"Hawk," Liam intoned, and squeezed his eyes

closed against the pain that crushed him. He knew better than to hope for miracles, for indeed, he had seen his beloved breathe her last breath. Had held her flaccid body in his arms. He should be grateful that for a while, for a few fleeting, crystalline days, she had loved him. But he was not grateful. "Hawk," he said again. "How could he be so cruel?" Liam raised an arm to cover his eyes, to wish against all logic that he was not alive, that he had been allowed to accompany Rachel into death.

"Cruel?" The voice of Haydan the Hawk interrupted his misery. "Twas not to be cruel that I brought you back, lad," he said.

Liam glanced up at him. Never would he be able to look at the huge warrior without thinking of Rachel. Never would he be able to see any Forbes without longing for her. Pain ripped through his heart. He curled his hand over his chest, but there was not even an amulet there to comfort him. There was nothing.

He closed his eyes in misery.

Hawk approached slowly to take a seat only inches away.

"The wound is deep, but the pain will fade, lad," he said quietly.

"You are wrong," Liam whispered.

"I know something of pain," Hawk said.

"And do you know how it feels to have your heart torn from your chest?"

Hawk scowled at him. The ultimate warrior could brook no whining. But what did he know of loss? He had never loved.

"The injury is grievous, aye," he said. "But the Lady Fiona said naught of you missing your heart. What say you, Lady, has the Irishman lost that precious organ?"

Fiona managed a wan smile. "Surely I would have noticed."

"How can you joke?" Liam asked, his voice choked. "How can you bear it?"

Fiona reached out, her expression mournful as she touched his hand. "All will be well. You will see. The pain will pass."

"All will not be well!" He jerked away. Unable to bear her compassion. Tears burned his eyes. "She is . . ."—he could barely manage the word—"gone," he whispered.

The room was silent. Nay! All the earth was silent with the crushing weight of his loss.

"Gone?" Hawk asked, but Liam was beyond answering.

"Liam," Fiona whispered.

"I could not save her!" he rasped, turning toward her, seeking forgiveness though he could not grant it himself. "I am sorry. I . . ." His voice broke. "I failed."

"Save . . ."

"Liam." The voice was small and raspy and seemed to come from inside his very heart.

The breath stopped in his throat. Every muscle, every nerve, every hopeless, aching part of him quaked as he turned away from Fiona to the opposite side of the bed.

Rachel was there, her small face still sleepy as she straightened from the chair where she rested.

"Rachel." He breathed her name, not daring to believe, not daring to blink.

"Liam," she said, and reaching out, touched her palm to his cheek.

The sweet impact soared through his soul, jangling his senses. "I thought . . ." He pressed his fingers over hers and still she didn't disappear, didn't disintegrate into nothing more substantial than his fevered dreams. "I thought you were dead."

"Nay. Nay you did not, Liam," she whispered. "Surely you knew I was here. Surely you remember."

"Remember?"

"The dragon," she whispered. She was so close, so sweetly close. "The dragon of the deep."

Memories as slippery as eel skimmed through his mind, images only half real. Endless water, hopeless sinking, then the feel of sleek reptilian skin, clawed limbs, nightmares too frightening to ponder, and yet not frightening at all.

"It saved you?" he whispered.

"Aye."

"Why?" he asked, then answered himself. "For Dragonheart."

"Nay. For you," she murmured, and kissed him.

Feelings as raw as an open wound squeezed his heart. She was alive! She was well! There was a God! He reached up to touch her face, to draw her closer, to kiss her lips.

"So you are awake," a voice rumbled.

Liam jerked away from her, waiting for the dream to shatter like a hundred others. But still she was there beside his bed. Her father, however, was there too.

"M-my laird!" Liam stammered. Laird Leith, the Forbes of the Forbes, looked as stern as ever, his bearing noble, his presence undiminished with the passing of the years—the epitome of everything Liam was not. "Aye, me laird. Thanks to your lady's ministrations, I am indeed awake."

"And which lady might that be, Liam?"

Laird Leith's eyes were as steely steady as they had always been in Liam's dreams. Steady, unblinking, and all-knowing, as if he could read every lurid thought Liam had ever entertained about his precious daughter. He knew, Liam thought. He knew all they had done together. Everything that had transpired between them. True, at the time they had been certain that naught but death awaited them. But still, she was a laird's daughter, and Liam, well . . . he would be lucky to still think himself a bastard.

Was it too late for a good lie? Even a bad lie might suffice. But no glib untruths came to mind.

"I am told that Warwick is dead," Leith said.

Liam scowled, but reprimanding the laird for speaking the name aloud seemed foolhardy at best. If he were wise, he would be grateful now for each moment the laird allowed him to share his daughter's company. For now, surely all knew his feelings for her, and none would accept that.

"I believe he is dead, me laird. But in truth," Liam said, "I have thought that before."

"He is dead." Rachel's voice was soft with quiet assurance.

The laird nodded, but his gaze never left Liam's face. "Me ladies, if you would leave us for a time, I would have a word with the Irishman."

Twas a bad idea, Liam thought, and when Rachel's fingers slipped from his, that opinion was only magnified. Lady Fiona rose to her feet and wrapped an arm about her daughter's shoulders as they met and exited.

Haydan the Hawk rose slowly, exchanged one prolonged glance with the laird of the Forbes and followed the women, closing the door behind him.

Tension crawled with chilly fingers up Liam's spine. The silence grew.

Leith paced slowly to the nearby window. "I know the truth," he said quietly.

"The truth, my laird?" Liam questioned, hoping his voice didn't quake like his insides did. But suddenly he could remember every touch of Rachel's fingers against his skin, every word, every breathless joining. And he was certain each scandalous thought showed on his face.

"Warwick was your sire."

Liam's jaw dropped, but whether this knowledge was more or less dangerous was questionable. "Aye." He found his voice with some difficulty. "Aye, I fear tis true."

"Fear?" Leith's gaze, sharp as a hunting falcon's, held him. "Why?"

The man, Liam was certain, had never known fear, had never felt its burn and never would.

"He was . . ." Liam searched hopelessly for his voice for a moment. "He was evil."

The eyes, still hard as an eagle's. "And you? Are you evil too?"

"I . . . hope I am not, but—"

"You saved me daughter." The words lay flat in the silence. "Is such the deed of an evil man?"

"Nay, me laird, but—"

"So Dragonwynd will be yours."

Liam shook his head, trying to find some reason in the other man's words. "Dragonwynd, me laird?"

"Warwick's estate."

"Estate?" Liam echoed.

"He was not always the personification of evil," Forbes said. "He was once the right hand of kings. Valued by kings and thus granted gifts by kings. Dragonwynd was given to him by James II. It was once a great fortress. But twas not enough for him.

He was greedy, and he was cruel, and when the full measure of his cruelty became known, Dragonwynd was attacked in an attempt to take him. But even before the gates were torn asunder, the wizard had fled."

"Dragonwynd?" It was the only word Liam could manage.

"Twas not enough for Warwick," Leith repeated. "Will it be enough for you?"

Liam tried to speak, to digest the words, to realize his good fortune. Never had he hoped to be given anything, much less a fortress. He should take this offering and be eternally grateful. After all, it was unlikely that even *he* could steal himself a fortress. Much easier to be given one. A home, he told himself. A place to belong. No more wandering. No more namelessness. He would be Liam of Dragonwynd.

And he would not have Rachel.

The truth struck him with the force of an arrow to the heart.

"Is it enough?" Leith asked again, his tone gruff.

"Nay." Liam could barely force out the word. "Tis not."

The silence felt like molten lead against his ears.

"What else, then?"

"Your daughter."

The great laird's eyes glinted. "What?"

"I would have your daughter's hand."

The laird of the Forbes towered over Liam's bed, his scowl dark as thunderclouds.

"Tis a bit late for her hand, isn't it?"

God's balls! He knew what they had done in the woods. Liam's heart rattled a rapid beat against his ribs. "My . . . laird?" he asked breathlessly.

"After all these years of mooning over her. After

she has held your heart for half your lifetime, tis about time you asked for her."

He couldn't quite breathe or focus or think. Could it be? Could it possibly be? "I would be good to her," Liam whispered, the words rusty in the stillness. "I swear I would."

"Aye," Leith said with a shallow nod. "Aye. You shall, or I'll use your guts for my bowstrings."

Today was the day he would wed Rachel Forbes.

Liam clenched his fists and paced once more. Twas not possible, he thought, and yet, if the hubbub of the last two weeks was any indication, it was entirely possible. Still, since becoming betrothed, he had seen far less of her than he had in the month prior.

Laird Leith and his brother Roderic had insisted they escort him to Dragonwynd, his inheritance. The estate was a towering expanse of crumbling stone on the edge of the sea. The nearby village was prosperous, the people thrifty, the land not devoid of its share of fertile valleys.

Liam had looked it over much as he looked over the assemblage now gathered at Glen Creag, with a sense of mind-numbing disbelief. Things had happened too fast. Things he neither deserved nor indeed had ever dared to hope for. Things that scared the living devil out of him.

He skimmed the crowd. Guests had been arriving for some days now, guests like the Duke of Rosenhurst, every Highland laird within three days' riding distance, and the king of Scotland!

Liam wiped his hands on his ceremonial plaid and tried to be diverted by the entertainers. Catriona spun into the air like a launched missile and landed, smiling and unwinded on her bare feet.

It was a sad day when the sight of her bonny form didn't even strike his interest.

It seems it was Catriona who had summoned help. Knowing Rachel was bound for the king, she had raced to Blackburn Castle after Warwick attacked her band of rovers.

Hawk, already alerted to the fact that there was trouble, had immediately set out with the gypsy girl at his side. They'd reached the spot where Warwick had attacked the troupe of entertainers, then followed and lost the trail a dozen times before, some days later, he had spied a mounted party on the road.

It had been none other than Shona and Sara. Panicked over the disappearance of their cousin, they had set out to find her. They, their scolding husbands, and a large company of warriors.

It had been Sara who had realized Liam and Rachel were headed toward their way to Loch Ness. And thus their rescue.

Catriona bowed to the assemblage at large, then to the king, then to Haydan the Hawk, who sat just to the young monarch's left. Royalty was spread through the crowd like the pox.

Where the devil was Rachel? She hadn't changed her mind had she? Twas possible of course. After all, she'd broken betrothals before, and if the truth be known his abilities as a magician and juggler may not stack up well against titles such as duke or earl, which she had already turned down.

Liam worried at his silver brooch. Twas a gift from his bride's mother. The sporran, big as a horse and ostentatious as a crown, was a gift from Rachel.

"Nervous?" The voice came from his right.

He turned his gaze to Shona, Rachel's auburn-haired cousin.

"Tis more the kind of crowd I'd pick pocket than I'd marry into," Liam complained.

"I'd suggest that you keep your hands busy elsewhere," Sara said, joining them.

"Aye. Where is our cousin to busy his hands?" Shona asked.

"Shona!" Sara reprimanded.

But the auburn beauty only laughed. "I'm but trying to make certain that our Liam gets bestowed instead of beheaded. You know how King James likes his baubles."

"I think his attentions are fully engaged elsewhere," Sara said, glancing toward where Catriona gave the king a single rose.

"He's only eight years old."

Stepping sideways with the grace of a fawn, the Gypsy gave the second rose to the hulking guard that sat beside him.

"Aye. And Haydan the Hawk is four times that. Neither would notice if the entire assemblage were sucked into hell with Warwick."

"Don't mention his name," Liam said, although as hard as he searched, he could feel no sensations of evil. Warwick was gone.

"So you are to be wed?" asked a deep male voice.

Liam turned as Sara's husband joined them. Sir Boden Blackblade was a huge man, dark and solemn, with a devilish dry wit and enough of a past with Liam to make the gleam in his eye a worry.

"Aye," Liam said. There was a time he had resented Boden's hold on Sara, but that was before he had possessed any hope of winning her cousin's love.

Even now it seemed impossible. Where was she anyway?

"So where is the bride?" Roderic the Rogue shouldered his way through the crowd. As Rachel's irascible uncle he had a right to cause trouble where he would. And now seemed to be the time. "You don't suppose she has changed her mind, do you, Liam?"

Shona widened her eyes, her penchant for a joke nearly as great as her father's. "Maybe she's realized her mistake and fled Glen Creag altogether. Mother . . ." Glancing past her sire, she caught her mother's gaze. "Are any of the horses missing? Maybe Rachel has run off with her lover."

"And maybe tis your Dugald who has seen the light and left with someone likely to cause less trouble," suggested the Rogue's wife, who was, if the truth be told, not the sort of pot who should call the kettle black.

"You've not yet left Father," Shona rejoined.

"That's because I'm charming beyond words," said the Rogue, curling his arm about his wife's waist.

"Tis because you are a hopeless flirt and she dare not toss your affections to the populace at large," Fiona said, entering the fray.

"Tis because she adores me," Roderic countered.

A round of differing opinions yipped up, boisterous dissension amongst a family that had forged a bond that death itself would not break.

But why was he here, Liam wondered, searching the crowd again. He was not a laird. He was not even Liam the bastard. Warwick had taken even that. He was . . .

But suddenly he saw her. The crowd parted in awed silence, drawing back to cleave a path to him.

Dear God, she was an angel. An ebon-haired celestial being dressed in gold. The gown caressed her body like a lover's hands. She looked as regal as a princess, as untouchable as a saint.

He couldn't breathe, couldn't think, couldn't speak as she drew near. Her otherworldly gaze lifted to his, her sinner's mouth quirked in the slight suggestion of a tremulous smile.

She stopped only inches from him, but still he couldn't move.

"Well hell, lad, say something," Roderic urged, nudging his arm.

Liam swallowed, his heart like a wild steed in his chest.

"Liam . . . speechless!" Shona said in awe. "Do you think you can save him, Lady Fiona?"

Liam heard the voices, but in that instant Rachel's hand brushed his.

"Rachel." He breathed her name like a parched prayer. "I have nothing to give you. No family, no name. Not even Liam the Bastard any longer."

She smiled that smile that spoke of kindness and chaos. "Nay," she whispered. "No longer a bastard. From hence forth I will call you Liam my love," she said, and slipping her hand behind his neck, she kissed him to the wild applause of their family.